MW01124291

LISTENING TO DARK

R. Peralez

For Jordan

The west is empty. All else is empty. No moon-talk at all now.
Only dark listening to dark.

Moonset by Carl Sandburg

I. Work

It was slander to doubt The Corporation. The Corporation oxidized on contact. The Corporation crippled death. The Corporation sealed the cracks. The Corporation salved their wounds on the rig. Their cheekbones radiation-burned and peeling. Their throats stringy with the ceaseless vaccine cocktails and day-nights eating only powdered potatoes and clear, skimmed fat.

They called the fat "shine" and shine kept them living out here. The rig turned into the moon where they sent silver tubes and breathed already inhaled breath from their collapsing lungs.

Rasp the youngest of the blistered men sometimes dipped his fingers into the black powder the men had suctioned from the asteroids' surfaces and drew a mustache on his clear helmet.

"Have you ever tasted breast milk?" He asked anyone who would listen.

When his shift ended, the other roughnecks pushed past him in the grav field, flicking their tubing at the backs of his knees. None of them had ever even seen a woman in the flesh. Women were a thing in sanctioned plasticine-stream publications with smooth bodies and hard smiles. Woman only existed in two dimensions.

Steam clouded his helmet in the decontamination chamber. He drew eyes over the black powdered mustache and prodded Easy, who dug at the crotch of his suit. Easy sighed into his earpiece.

"They'll make you shine, boy."

"Nah, they only make you shine if you can't work." Rasp wrinkled his nose.

In each corner, the misting nozzles flipped down and the green light appeared above the door, before it parted to let the men into the next chamber. Easy pushed past Rasp and wedged himself into one of the tall hexagonal coffin chambers in the wall. Adhesive bands lashed around the suit and cracked it open like chicken bones. The suit crumpled into the wall, later to be ejected into space. Easy slid out of the side, naked, and stepped into his white slippers. A round O printed on the toe of each one. The suit crumpled into the bands and compressed it to the size of glove. Rasp followed suit, frowning that no one laughed at his crude helmet face. He entered the barracks though the plasticine doors, looking at Easy's fibrous thighs in front of him.

Rasp checked the screen for any messages from Queen Gracious, the mascot of the miners. She blessed them every evening before bed. And every morning when they rose. Queen Gracious' breasts looked like the warmest silicone and the softest mercury.

'What's good for the goose is good for the gander,' flashed on the screens above their scrolling names and messages. There was no word for privacy. Privacy was like breast milk. Rasp could not remember geese.

Rasp had a message from HR. It read:

RASP (INDENTURED 2544-46)

Report to The Rumpus Room at 4:30 PM.

If you're early, you are on time. If you're on time, you are late. If you're late, that's unacceptable.

Don't forget!!! Tonight is pizza night!!!

II. Play

The yellow clouds billowed over the white dome. The sun throbbed though the thick billows, nestled high in the graying sky. Another dust storm. The water would be gritty tonight when the girls got off shift. Each cold shower punctuated by a sputter and a brownish ribbon of moisture, before they gave up and slathered themselves in Ambrosia for Women (Now in Fresh Rain Scent!) from the commissary and crawled into their beds and ate pre-packaged powdered donuts.

Riff, small for fifteen cycles, unfurled a long sheet of vinyl and pressed her fingertip into the dings in the material. She circled each imperfection with a red grease stick. She was lucky. This was the best job. She and the other QCer still had all their fingers. She counted the red tick marks and tapped the screen beside the enormous air table. The wind outside strained against the dome and Riff leaned against the table. Her guts cramped some. Not surprising, considering the lukewarm protein bags they had for breakfast were past their expiration date. Waste not, want not.

A supervisor rolled over. It zipped around the polished black floor, slamming into their heels with its square plasticine body. The hazy screen on the front reported back to Efficiency and Management every twenty seconds. The tiny camera mounted on the right swiveled and bobbed, like a bird in a mirror. All the supervisors had matriarchal melodic recorded voices. Before she was shipped to Mars for harvesting, an older girl told her that The Corporation programmed them that way, so they would never fall in love with their supervisors.

Another cramp pulsed in her belly. The supervisor's camera glided close to her eyes.

"Riff, are you alright?" It crooned. "You seem tired."

She put down her grease stick. "Permission to use the facilities?"

"Granted. Please enter the appropriate code."

Riff dabbed the screen with her middle finger. This was definitely a 2359-02 issue.

"You have four minutes." An illustration of a little girl snoozing in a red dress, poppies swaying in the breeze around her flashed on the supervisor's screen. "Don't dally, now." A countdown materialized over the illustration. Three minutes; 45 seconds.

Her scalp prickled as another cramp spasmed in her belly. She dabbed at the sweat on her face with the back of her wrist, careful not to smudge the rouge made from her own powdered blood. The facilities seemed to recede at the end of the bright orange hallway. The fluorescents glared hard white light over the dust coated walls. Riff nearly jogged, pushing open the cool metal door. The bathroom was dusted yellow, and someone had written "Happy Monday!" in the dust on the mirror. She rushed over to the toilet and tapped her code into the screen on the back of the tank. The lid remained sealed. INVALID CODE. Riff rapped the code into the screen again, the pressure now becoming painful. INVALID CODE.

Oh god. She would get written up. She had too many demerits already. Images of Venusian colonies flashing in her mind. Chemical burns from the filtered air on stick thin arms.

The screen above the toilet flashed: One Minute and Thirty seconds.

Riff looked desperately around. The trashcan. The trashcan didn't need a code. She jerked the zipper of her jumpsuit down and perched on the thin-lipped vessel. The plastic edge cut into the backs of her thighs and her guts slackened with relief. She pulled some paper towels from the dispenser behind her and looked down. Blood smeared her inner thigh. Her first period.

Her heart caught. She was going to Mars. All expenses paid trip! She was going to the harvest. There would be a dance. Rumor had it that there was real dogmeat and aeroponic fruits. She would see men for the first time.

30 seconds glimmered on the smooth, glossy screen above the sink. A video of a young woman swathed in layers of gray fabric encasing her face and arms popped up. A gloved hand reached across the screen and snatched the girl's wrist, yanking her off balance, the fabric spinning behind her in diaphanous curls. A sunburst pierced the screen in a rainbow shatter. A rust-flecked blade hung suspended in the air for a moment and came down on the girl's fingers, crunching through bone. The video ended abruptly in a black screen.

TEN SECONDS REMAIN □ □ □

She leapt off the trashcan and zipped up her jumpsuit, almost skipping down the corridor. A supervisor bowled toward her. Its screen already ticking with the print of a demerit form.

"Supervisor, I have started menstruating."

The machine halted. "Congratulations, Riff. You are registered in the 567 class making you eligible for Martian travel."

All the screens on the production floor turned red and the supervisors switched on their speakers. A low hum permeated the room. The production equipment whirred along in the silence. All of the girls, from the tiniest, sorting grommets, to the oldest laying a perfect bead on an arc weld, stared at the screens. A kitten in a top hat sat mewing, surrounded by glossy balloons, until a latex-clad hand swooped under its belly. The word CONGRATS RIFF floated by on the screen. None of them had ever seen a kitten other than this kitten. The kitten that came to announce the blood. Jubilation to the lucky one.

Everyone clapped, except Gram, the arc welder.

Gram yanked at the sleeve of Riff's jumpsuit, as the girls lined up to congratulate her. Gram was tall and slender, her skin punctuated by cotton candy pink burn scars on her hands from the welder.

"How could you do this to me?" She hissed. Tears brimmed in the cups of her eyelids.

"I didn't mean to."

"I thought we were in love."

Riff wrapped her arm around Gram's waist and patted her belly through the heavy fabric of her coveralls. Her shoulder tucked under Gram's armpit.

"Soon you'll start menstruating too and then we'll be on Mars together."

"I don't want to go to Mars. I don't want to bleed." Gram jerked away and stomped to the back of the line.

A supervisor rolled past Riff and intercepted her. A sunflower swarmed with red winged black birds flashed on the screen.

"Gram, overt displays of aggression are expressly forbidden. You will receive one demerit."

The other girls in line tittered. Gram glared at Riff.

III. Home

Rasp's earliest memory was of being in a crib with a dark blue blanket covered in white stitched anchors. He peered out from between the white slats and a sudden bloom of hard orange light seeped into the small room. His small heart pounded like a fist-trapped bird. Rasp had never been one for screaming, so instead he crouched in the corner of the crib gripping the edge of the thin foam mattress. It was the last time he had experienced aloneness. Not loneliness, he had experienced that plenty. Aloneness.

The screens that lined the corridor flashed RUMPUS ROOM 4:30 at him as he walked by. Another meeting with HR. Men, probably on Mars, had filled the screens around the room and chided him.

"2544-46? Right. You must stop distracting your coworker with antics. We have pre-approved comedy routines for you to view during your recreational hour. That is the appropriate time for jokes. You know that productivity is positivity."

Another voice.

"You really must be sure to clock your time appropriately, 2544-46, the only appropriate forms of DNA for the scan are skin cells and blood."

"2544-46. You are short on your quota again. You must harvest at least 600 micrograms of usable powder per shift."

"Sleeping through shift meetings is unacceptable, 2544-46. We have pharmaceuticals for commissary credit available for your pleasure and enhancement if you are tired. "

The door to the Rumpus room slid open. A huge table made of real wood and real glass hovered in the middle of the huge room. A real man stood at the head, tapping at paper-thin screen that clung to his fingertips. His tongue pushed at the inside of his cheek as he tapped away at the tablet. He wore a body mesh and hydration apparatus so new and expensive that Rasp had only seen them advertised on the more expensive Pornographic art films. Protects against radiation, micro asteroids, toxic waste, acid rain, depression, anxiety, sleeplessness, aging, and MORE! The man did look very productive and healthy. His eyes shone, the whites white, white like royal icing. A layer of fat like paraffin separating skin from muscle.

"Rasp, Indentured 2544-46?"

"That's my name, don't wear it out." Rasp smiled and open his hands, palms face up.

The bureaucrat ignored him.

"Your employer has decided to sell your contract. He thinks your general spiritedness would suit another project better." He peeled the tablet from his fingertips and folded it like parchment to business card size and slipped it into his fashionable utility belt. The belt gleamed with holstered weapons.

"Will I be relocated?"

"You will find all of the information in this packet." The bureaucrat handed him a thick sheaf of plasticine pages, held together with a black binder clip, and looked at his watch. His fingers were very pale and soft. "You can still make it to Pizza night, if you go now." He turned his back to Rasp and touched the shoulder of his suit. The door to the Rumpus Room slid open and he strode out, his suit flexing around his soft middle.

Rasp thumbed the pages of the packet. LABORER CLASS C; Destination: TBA; STATUS: INDENTURED; TERM:

UNDETERMINED. DEPARTURE: DOCK C; 04:30 Mars time. His stomach churned.

The smell of burning potato and hot fat wafted down the hall.

IV. Transit

The sun streaked through the haze, illuminating cyclones of dust motes under the greenish sky. A brown building loomed in the distance, encased in razor wire. Some small vertebrae crunched underfoot and the sepia sea lapped against the concrete barrier.

Riff's suit stuck to the thin creases in her elbows. Sweat beaded on her upper lip and pearled over her lips under the darkened dome of her helmet. It felt like crawling and she wanted to swipe at it. The supervisor beside her rocked over a chunk of hardened sand.

The last time Riff had been outside, was seven cycles ago, when the Corporation picked up her older brother and her from the old military base in San Diego county. When the waters rushed orange-y and cold into the city, her mother put them on an inflatable corporation raft. The soldiers, each with a bright white O printed on their Kevlar, grabbed the children's wrists and waistbands and hauled them into the raft.   She tossed her suit jacket onto the raft with them, her mascara running black under her brown eyes, and reached for the rope trailing behind.

Lo siento. Estamos en capacidad. The soldiers said.

No, no, no. You don't understand. I'm the DA. These are my children.

Es.tam.os. EN capacidad.

His blue eyes glowed flatly from the shadows of his black helmet.

Por los hijos solomente.

I speak English. I'm the fucking DA. The water lapped against her full face. The soldier ripped the cord from her hands.

And that was that. The Before.

The transport hung in the air, spewing gouts of black smoke in hot gusts. The supervisor whirred beside her, its cooling fan working against the dust and the smoke and the heat. A girl about her age in a white dress flashed on its screen. The girl cradled a doll in the crook of her arm, before kneeling in front of a small child and pushing the doll into the child's arms. A ripple of green tore the image in half. The supervisor's camera flicked white. The earpiece in her helmet crackled and a mechanical voice hummed in her ear.

Congratulations, Riff. Mars welcomes you in 12.5 days.

The transport tilted in the air, sending down a long set of shallow stairs.

Riff walked toward the stairs that jutted thin and straight from the ship like the proboscis from a feeding mosquito. The supervisor was malfunctioning in the dust and rolled in a wide arc, before wedging itself against cinderblock wall that surrounded the facility. Chunks of black asphalt detached from the road, the tar sticking to her boots. Riff heard her own breath. Mars. Mars. Mars.

***

On the sixth day of the transport, Riff grew restless. She braided her hair and scrolled through Martian news on the big screens and wandered around her quarantine chambers. She drew crude drawings in the dust on the black floor of men and dogs and dogmeat burgers. She watched videos of prank shows on Mars, where a boy set fire to aeroponic fields and forced the women in the fields to kiss him. Sometimes he got caught and the head aerofarmer beat him until his nose and mouth bled, afterward forcing him to kiss her. Her mouth and teeth stained red. And Riff laughed and laughed.

But even that grew old.

There had to be others. She couldn't be the only one on the transport. She peeked through the plasticine window. Craning her neck to look down the narrow hall. Bulky machinery hummed along. No movement. Her food dropped into the recess on the wall, with a dull slap. A bag of rehydrated potatoes and unidentifiable slick gravy. The same food. The same pranks. The same news. She dropped from her tiptoes and went over to the food slot. As she fished out the warm, shiny bag, a small device clattered to the floor, about the size of a business card.

She put the food bag on the table and pick up the device. It was smooth on all sides and made of metal composite. It was about a quarter of an inch thick and had a thumb-sized indentation in the center. She pressed her finger into the dent in the surface. It unfolded rapidly, flipping over and over in her hand, suctioning itself to her fingertips until it was a shirt-sized screen. Words flashed in the center, before vanishing like a dust storm headed east.

You will be devoured. Meet us at the nozzle. Two lunar phases. First Phobos rise.

V. Real Long Day

Rasp's transport had been delayed by three days, due to malfunction in the imaging software. He and three other men, linked to nutrient drips and cathed, played Gin Rummy with a stack of cards with naked women printed on them. Every color of the rainbow. All lithe. All hairless. All smiling. Delicate slender apes enhanced with microscars and resewn nipples.

One of the men had chemical burns on one side of his face. His skin was shiny pink under a loosely taped layer of gauze. Rasp knew him from the chow line on the rig, slopping potato glistening with shine onto their plasticine trays they fed into the chipping slots after each eight-minute allotted meal. He shifted and rearranged his nutrient line.

Rasp nudged him.

"Tastes better than rig food, huh?"

The man smiled as best he could, wincing as the flaking skin on his cheek pulled away from the scabbed, red dermis. He discarded a ten of spades with a woman wearing nothing but a belly dancing belt, her plump belly peeking over the tiny brass bells. Her breasts draped over a tiny jeweled belt around her rib cage, each capped with a large, soft nipple.

The other men were identical twins, each with a light sprinkling of freckles across their thin bare arms and chest. Their red hair was cropped close and their teeth overlapped in a strange sameness. It was rare that the corporation allowed siblings to have their contracts assigned to the same project. But, only one twin spoke at a time and scuttlebutt said that they scored a perfect score on their mechanical aptitude tests. The twin missing his pinky and ring finger discarded the queen of hearts.

Rasp looked at his hand. A full meld.

"Georgie Porgy, pudding and pie kissed the girls and made them cry. Gin"

The man with healing chemical burns on his face threw down his hand. The twins looked at one another. Reflections of the same grim mouth, the same gray eyes. One intact.

Rasp reached for the pile of commissary credits. A single card fluttered to the table from the collar of his jumpsuit. An ace with a coy redhead on it. The men watched it, their eyes snapping up at Rasp when it was finally face down among the others.

The intact twin reached across the table and snatched the front of Rasp's jumpsuit, dragging him across the smooth slab. His nutrient line tugged at his arm and popped free. Blood oozed from the hole. The twin struggled on top of Rasp and pressed his knees into his chest. The others looked on. The chamber was silent except for the two men huffing.

"I told you to stop fucking cheating, Rasp."

"Come on, you'll pull out my cath."

"You little shitbird."

"Look take back the credits. I'm sorry. I really am sorry. Want to hear a joke?"

The twin lifted him up and slammed the back of his head against the hard surface. Blackness flashed across his eyes. He swung down with closed fist at Rasp's cheek. His own nutrient line popped from his arm and misted the walls with blood. Their hearts throbbed with the ape need to crush. To survive. The light changed so slightly. Suddenly, calm. The honey-sweet smell of sedation dust filled their nostrils.

***

Rasp's transport shuddered as it entered the Martian atmosphere. After the sedation dust wore off, the men found themselves strapped onto narrow boards facing outward. The grav field had been turned off. The screens around restraint barracks hummed to life. A beautiful nude woman appeared on the screen, her long blond hair combed into voluminous waves. She sat with her hands clasped in front of her, her glossy red fingernails glinting tiny white squares of light. She took a deep breath and peered past the camera, her eyes jerking back and forth as she read from a teleprompter somewhere behind the camera. Her voice, deepish and smooth, flooded into the barracks.

"Greetings, potential Martians.

You have been chosen as laborers and potential citizens to the Martian Entity. Congratulations.

Due to the sensitive nature of your work here on our greatest achievement, it is necessary to give you some background information of the world which you will undoubtedly come to love."

She cleared her throat and absently brushed her hair over her right shoulder.

"Mars was terraformed even before Earth fell to The Event. It started with great clear domes, rooted to the red soil by quadruped bots. But in those days, the people of earth barely noticed. The clung to their tiny lives, putting up pictures of themselves again and again and again for their friends to see and feel jealousy or indifference. Pictures of glistening meat, farmed just for them, shiny with fat and rich red with blood and crusted with herbs. Pictures of sunsets, rippling orange-red across an endless beach horizon. Pictures of men and woman clinging to one another, before the great separation. Pictures of marches across the globe, human beings demanding change, change, change, but never changing themselves. Others rotting away in government cells, never to be useful again, some just for sedating themselves against the tragedy of purposelessness. Very sad indeed."

She reached under the desk and pulled out an electronic cigarette and screwed it onto a long cigarette holder. She drew it to her mouth and wrapped her lips around it, blowing a perfect smoke ring that glided toward the screen, splitting and enveloping the screen in a fine mist.

"Those days were dark. According to The Corporation's research nearly half of the planet was incarcerated and two out of three individuals were unemployed. 45% of women killed their babies in utero and pharmaceutical regulation was at an all-time high at 80% profits lost. Earth needed The Corporation.

The Corporation was the first entity to deploy the missiles to Mars, warming its surface and building its atmosphere. Creating thousands of jobs in the process. It was a triumphant idea, really. Using the incarcerated to give them purpose again. To build their job skills for when they were released. There was only a 1% recidivism rate after that. "

She looked at someone off camera and uncrossed her arms, resting her breasts on the table.

"And now potential citizen, you too have the potential for greatness. Your work is your currency. Your labor, your ticket to betterment. Welcome. Welcome."

The screens snapped off and the back hatch to shuttle parted, giving way to an eerie pinkish light. Rasp's lungs burned and his skin prickled with gooseflesh. The twins struggled against their restraints across from him. The craft rocked gently in the Martian dust storm. Waist-high robots zipped up the ramp, unlatching restraints, clipping tiny breathing apparatuses to their septums, and draping them in light, reflective fabric. A fixed screen attached to the center of their square flickered and started, plasticine bodies and four long multijointed limbs that waved and fussed over whatever task was at hand. The robot in charge of Rasp, flashed an image on its screen of him in a pink teddy bear costume, bouncing across the screen. A comfort image.

Little Bouncing RASP (INDENTURED 2544-46). The screen read in a bubbly font beneath the screen. The robot's arms drifted around his face, plucking debris off his jumpsuit.

"Hey, that's me."

"Yes, RASP (INDENTURED 2544-46), that IS you."

The robot's voice was a gentle older man, in some earth accent he had heard once on the Corporation's Diversity Channel. Australian? English? Continental?

"Now, that you've been properly identified and soothed, let's get you to decontamination and off to bed. Tomorrow is a big day for you."

The robot rolled ahead of him into the butterscotch landscape, one long arm trailing behind, wrapped snug around Rasp's shoulders. Mountains rose behind a small dome settlement, richly orange and huge, capped with soft snow. The domes, like a clutch of eggs, were painted different pastels colors, each with the stylized O on the side. Further in the distance, a huge dome sent long spirals of white vapor into the air from several stacks jutting from the roof.

Rasp looked back at the transit. The twins followed behind another identical robot. The man with chemical burns was nowhere. Nothing. Zip. Zilch. He was nil.

The glossy obsidian path squeaked under his boots. It snaked in front of him, dead ending at the giant dome.

VI. Riff Raff

When Riff exited the shuttle from her transport, into the sealed tunnel, she realized she was very, very cold. Colder than aerosol. The first man she had seen since the soldier on the raft approached her. His body mesh glimmered white under the bluish lights in the sealed tunnel and he reached out to grasp her just above the elbow. He smiled bright white through his face shield and placed his palm on the small of her back. Riff was suddenly afraid.

"Hi Riff." His smile broadened and he glanced at the scrolling text on his wrist. "I think you're really going to like it here, much cleaner than your original facility." His pulled her against his side and strode out, stroking her upper arm. "Have you had anything to eat?"

"I don't think so." Riff huffed, trying to keep up. The gravity felt strange on her feet. Too light.

"Wait until you see our wide range of options," he said, raising his eyebrows at her and winking one colorless eye.

A set of transparent doors slid closed behind them in the tunnel, as they entered a vast, domed space. Young women milled around, leaning against the pristine white walls, twining their arms around one another, wading in the fountain in the center of the room. Some slept in anti-grav pods inset into the walls of the dome, their hair floating around them, as if suspended in clear water.

The man motioned to a woman draped in heavy orange synthetic silk. Her red hair was loosely braided and the shorter pieces stuck out wildly, haloing her head with coarse orange frizz. Her slender arms jutted from her robes, reaching for Riff's hand, showing her milky skin through the silks.

"Riff, meet Fern. Fern tell Riff what you think of our facilities." He smiled. All teeth.

"Oh hello Riff. It's wonderful here, as long as you pull your weight." She drummed her fingers over her tight flat belly. "Have you ever had real dogmeat? It's better than anything, even from The Before."

"It sounds wonderful." Riff's mouth oozed saliva. Her stomach growled.

"Well, let's get Riff fed and measured," the man said. "Her stomach is rumbling."

"Poor lamb." Fern reached out and stroked her straight black hair. "You are so lucky, Riff. The Southern Hemisphere look is in right now."

Small pencil eraser scars dotted the backs of Fern's arms and the strips of skin showing through her robes. Her skin lay firmly against her muscle. Not a touch of fat. Not an ounce of give on her. She patted her own wiry hair and waved over the man's shoulder at a blond woman with small dark eyes.

"If you'll excuse me, we have a bridge game in a few minutes." Fern slipped past them, and tucked herself under the blond woman's arm, threading her fingers through her hair and kissing her lightly on the lips.

The women floated by, each covered in tiny scars, dotting them like the memory of disease.

"What are those scars?"

"You haven't heard of beauty marks?"

Riff shook her head. A wave of dizziness washed over her. She had only been this hungry in the Before.

"Here on Mars, The Corporation helps you feel and look your best, every day, free of charge!"

The man put his hand on the back of Riff's neck and shepherded her toward a long curve of a steaming buffet. Piles of meat and real potatoes and bread and corn and fruits glistened in a long line, like a rainbow on an oil slick. The man handed her a large plasticine bowl and leaned close to her.

"You can eat anything you want. Any time you want. Try the dogmeat. It's sublime, cloned right here on Mars. It's organic."

What is organic?

Riff scooped dogmeat, succulent and fragrant with synthetic spice, into her bowl and piled on flocculent mashed potatoes, thick with white gravy. Yellow corn dotted with pats of melting Shine butter nestled in the bowl, heaped atop the potatoes.

She stared at the bowl. The man guided her to a smooth white table, where three other women draped over their food and ate like prehistoric animals, languid and pondering with each bite. He sat beside her letting his hands rest on her thigh.

Riff ate until she felt sick, and then ran her finger along the edge of the bowl gathering the last of the white gravy in a dollop on her pointer finger. She popped her finger in her mouth and the man picked up her heavy braid and brushed her neck with his fingertips.

"That's good, Riff." His voice had dropped an octave. "The Corporation wants you to be happy." He eyed the cameras and snatched his hand back as a black eye panned toward them.

***

The exam room was painted a warm labial pink. A small fountain bubbled away in the corner and soft music drifted in through the speakers in the ceiling. Tiny camera eyes shone like flecks of quartz in stone from the wall. The exam table in the center of the room was covered in some sort of flexible fabric and heat emanated from it to Riff's back. There was a light rapping at the door. Before Riff could say anything, a small, slender woman slipped through the door. She was as spare the others, pocked with diminutive scars. Her gums had a strange greenish line above her uniform teeth.

"Are you the doctor?" Riff asked.

"Cállate. The cameras don't run until your care unit gets here. So listen."

Riff's heart beat in her throat.

"I just got here. Everything seems pretty good. I really don't want…"

The woman cut her off.

"Did you get the note?" The woman asked, pressing her ear against the door.

"The weird one about the moon and stuff?"

"Yes. The weird one about the moon." The woman twisted the front of her loose blue shirt around her pointer finger. "Well?, are ya gonna to meet us? There is someone with us that I think you'll really want to see."

"Will I get in trouble?"

"Not if you follow the directions." The woman reached into her smock and handed Riff a plasticine playing card. A jack of spades. A naked petite woman sprawled on it, her glossy black hair streaming over her taut brown arms. Her black eyes stared directly out of the card, hard and unyielding.

"Mama," Riff said.

Those flint eyes sinking under the churn.

"I have to go. She says 'debes saber.' Nobody misses nothing around here." And she slipped through the sliding doors, leaving Riff alone, palms cold and heart pounding.

All of the camera eyes flashed open, blinking green like sleepy housecats. Dilating and returning to pinpoints in the dim room. The door slid open once again and a being walked in, androgynous and pale, pale like viscous protein milk, pale like the whites of eyes. The being's eyes, indigo and immense rested on her. It was shaped liked a human. It moved like a human, but something hitched in her chest. Its long fingers traced over a plasticine chart.

"Hello Riff, is it? I'll be your care unit for the duration of your stay here."

"Unit?"

"Yes, I am model 34 of the care units."

"Like a supervisor?"

The being looked at her above the chart and sighed.

"I am much more complex than a supervisor. Touch my arm." The being held out an arm, vascular with pale pink veins.

Riff ran her fingers over the skin. It was warm and smooth, not a trace of hair or freckles or scars.

"What can I call you?"

"You can call me Al."

"Are you a boy or girl?"

"Which do you prefer?"

"Neither, I guess. Or both. I don't really know. Maybe a girl."

Al's featured softened. The purple eyes widened and blond lashes curled away toward the receding brow ridge. Long, bluish hair poured over the white shoulders. Slight breasts filled the mesh body suit. Al smiled. Her teeth were slightly crooked. An anomaly. Color flashed across her fingernails.

"There," Al said and reached for a pair of calipers. "Now can we get on with the exam?" Her voice

"How do you do that?"

Al pinched the skin from her upper arm first and nudged the calipers across the small lump.

"Do what?"

"Change like that."

"Oh, I have Mushroom Coral encoded in my DNA. I can change whenever I need to." She nudged her thumb under Riff's thigh and stretched the skin away like soft caramel, widening the calipers around it.

"Do you like being a boy or a girl better?"

"Both are interesting, but usually neither. Now I need you to lie back. We're just going to take some pictures of your belly."

Riff sank back onto the able. Her ribs jutted in front her, ripples on a sand dune.

"You poor thing. All they gave you was protein packs?" Al ran a silver egg over Riff's belly. Over her chest. She nudged her over on her stomach on the table.

"No, we could buy things from the commissary with our work tickets. Sometimes they even had donuts. Plus, we got these pills that kept us from being hungry, which was great, because they also gave you, like, so much energy."

Al leaned against the table and rubbed Riff's back in a circular motion. Warm.

"At least you will eat here." Her brow ridge grew and her jaw thickened. Back to the virgin form. The They form. Al clutched the silver egg and rubbed a thumb over its surface. Al was All pastels. Pale and uniform, formless color and sharp edges in that moment. Glints of black in the purplish eyes. "You will eat."

VII. A Very Dull Boy

Rasp ripped open the orange bag of blood-tinged fat and slopped it over the edge of the plasticine bin, dumping out the creamy contents. The bag read biomaterials – keep refrigerated. He dipped his gloved finger into it and tested the consistency; supple, healthy. No signs of disease. His shoulders ached with the strain of lifting bins and his respirator dug at his face. The other workers milled around him, dipping long metallic rods into the boiling Shine vats, blips of grease clinging to their masks, pouring the now-translucent fat into molds shaped like apples with the words food grade stamped into them. The giant elements under the vats heated the room enough to grow fruits. The sweet yellow globes hung above the men, their roots trailing down to brush shoulders and heads. Steam billowed as two men arched the immense vat over into the filter trays that spanned the room. Rasp drew a penis on the front of his mask and turned to one of the twins.

"Hey look. I'm a dickhead." His voiced crackled through the speaker on his suit.

The twin jabbed the heel of his hand onto Rasp's mask and jerked his hand across the transparent eye shield. He shook his head at Rasp and pushed him lightly. His eyes glimmering back yellow orbs and white sterile suits.

"Ok, Jesus Christ. No one ever wants to have fun." Rasp sighed, his chest pressing against the edge of the vat.

Rasp stepped back and opened the next orange bag with his utility knife, sulking. The slick contents bulging through the slit.

A tone hummed in the men's helmets, followed by a silken female voice.

The Corporation is proud to present Shaded Nights – Southern Hemisphere Beauties - for your pleasure and appreciation during recreation period tonight. Bring your favorite snack. Snikkies, Ram Tams, and Ripple Top Beer will be available for purchase through your employee credits earned. The feature will start in 30 minutes. Be there and fall in love over and over again. No late entry.

The screens around the room flashed on. A thirty-minute countdown imposed onto a glowing mushroom cloud started, a pair of breasts with dark nipples bounced behind the orange swell of the glowing explosion. Rasp counted his fat bags. Ten left. He squeezed the remaining fat out of the eleventh bag and hauled the next one onto the work ledge, ripping his knife along the top, slinging the adipose into the bin. Twenty- seven minutes remaining. His neck ached and his shoulders pulled up around his ears as he lifted and slapped the bag onto the table, tearing through the bag like child opening Christmas presents.

The timer read five minutes as he ripped his knife through the last bag, his back spasming. He loved the movies.

***

In the Before, a man Rasp couldn't place took him to a huge building on Earth and left him there in an auditorium filled with hundreds of other boy children. The children teemed in the huge room, some curled up on the folding seats, sucking wrinkled pink thumbs. Some running around the outer edges of the crowd screaming with laughter. Some shoving sticky pink and purple candies into their soot-dusted cheeks. Rasp clung to the man, while the man gazed at the blue screen in his hand, rolling his thumb over the shiny surface. He only broke away from the glow to shake Rasp's wrist until his grasp on his pressed slacks loosened and he strode away onto the black expanse of hot glimmering asphalt.

A Samantha, the earliest form of female android, walked to the front of the cacophony and clapped her hands. She had enormous breasts and very white teeth. Her flaxen hair fell long and straight to her shoulders. She had been designed. The clap was drowned out by the shrieks of the running children. Her expression remained as still as she pulled a small remote from her pocket and pressed the button. A video flashed on the white walls surrounding the children. A spaceship floated by them on the screen. A virus in the blood. A low hum filled the room and the running children stopped in their tracks, staring dead-eyed at the screen. Mouths open. Heads tilted back.

The rocket docked on an asteroid surface and men leapt from the body of the ship, bouncing lightly, untethered, unfurling silver tubing that hung suspended on the bare shoulders of space.

Bubble text as large as the Samantha Unit crowded the screen.

THERE IS NO SUCH THING AS A FREE LUNCH

Children on the periphery worked the syllables in their mouths, furrowing their small brows.

Samantha cleared her throat. A human trick.

"Children, do you know what this means?"

A particularly dirty boy in a beige skort yelled, "No! And you're weird looking."

The room erupted in laughter. The boy crossed his arms and grinned, pleased at the small chaos.

Samantha sighed. Another human trick.

"Dylan Herrera, 4735 Alvin Street, Harris County, Houston, Annexed Country of Texas, please come up here." Her gaze remained neutral. Her full mouth set.

The boy shook his head.

"Dylan, I have a commissary card with 500 credits on it. If you come up here, it's yours."

He uncrossed his arms and stared at her, his mouth open slightly.

"The time is limited, Dylan. Perhaps some other little boy might want it." She scanned the crowd and pointed at Rasp. "What about you?"

Rasp dipped his head to the right, to the left, craning to see who she could be pointing at. His tears not yet dry on his baby cheeks. He patted his chest and looked into her blue, blue eyes. She nodded and beckoned to him, her white-wedged fingernails curling toward her hand. He started towards her, sliding through tiny bird-boned bodies cloaked in sweatshirts with political slogans and pop stars and video game characters emblazoned on the fronts. She had a softness overlaying her trim frame. The commissary card flitting between her fingers. Just as he reached the platform, where she stood in purple pumps and hairless legs, Dylan pushed him.

His knee bashed against the concrete floor and his hand landed on top of a pink converse sneaker, covering firm warm toes like fetal mice flinching away from him. Heat pumped into his cheeks and his stomach churned. Dylan bounced onto stage, snatching for the commissary card. Rasp pushed himself upright and turned to the owner of the pink sneakers, a girl with three missing teeth clinging to a stuffed pineapple and asked, "what's the difference between a snow woman and a snow man?"

She squeezed the pineapple closer to her skinny chest. "What's snow?"

"Snow balls," he whispered.

She stared at him.

Samantha stroked Dylan's hair on stage.

"Do you all think this card is free for Dylan?" Her perfect pink lipsticked lips stretched into a smile.

The children all nodded solemnly.

"But it isn't, children. There is no money on this commissary card. Dylan must earn that money. Though since he has followed instructions well, but not well enough to earn five dollars, he will receive two dollars on it. Do you know how many commissary credits two dollars is?"

Rasp's knees pearled with blood droplets, dark and opaque. The children swayed with impatience, their eyes hunting the screens behind her, the minds starved for the dulcet colors and lights that cradled them, that stimulated them. The lights dimmed and a puppy came on the screen, eyes sealed, pushing itself through the yielding waves of a white blanket on pink rat paws. A warm glow emanated from Samantha's center and enveloped them in translucent blue waves that vibrated their throats and glided past their eyes. Then there was nothing.

***

The employee movie theater was filled with men. The low reverberation of voices masked the new hit from Shanana Schwoop Shigetty, the sugar pop queen robot with real human skin, that played over a reel of advertisements for the commissary and the newest pornographic art films like A Brother's Ass Love, Rear Entry: Robot Ingmar Bergman Smashes Robot Margaret Atwood's Handmaid's Tail, Fake Jews, Toe Licker From Hell.

Rasp took a long pull from his Ripple Top Beer bag and leaned over to one of the twins.

"Do you remember any movies from The Before?"

The larger twin picked up his dried dogmeat stick and ripped a huge hunk from it with his back molars. He nudged his brother and then stared up at the black domed ceiling above them, leaning back until his long hair brushed the knees of the man behind them, who promptly rapped the twin's forehead with his forefinger.

"We remember Star Wars."

"Aren't they still making Star Wars? The ones with the girl who fights with the laser dildo and never smiles?" Rasp asked.

"We liked the aliens in the old ones."

"They have aliens in the new ones. The Jedi girl fucks like three Wookies in one, though I didn't know Wookies had dicks, but I guess they do. Plus, they're uplifting and fun. A story of true heroism." Rasp said, quoting a reviewer he heard on the morning stream.

The larger twin reached behind Rasp and rested his arm on the back of his seat, popping the last of the meat stick in his mouth and chewing. The sounds of saliva sucking into the dry meat pulp irritated Rasp.

"You guys want to hear a joke?" He said leaning against the twin's forearm.

The theater darkened and a three-dimensional hand with delicate pink fingernails raised a pointer finger to thick, wet, disembodied lips on the black screen. Shhhhhhhhh.

Light from the screen seeped over the men, turning their eyes into shadows and their mouths ajar with anticipation into minute abysses. Maws gaping for entertainment to relive that moment of realness in them. Deep. Deep.

An older woman appeared on screen in a first-person shot, her black hair coating her shoulders, easing toward the audience. She was spare like all the women in the films, her upper arms, belly, and thighs dotted with pencil-eraser-sized scars. She had a small mole on her chin that Rasp remembered from somewhere. Her too-round breasts perched high on her chest. She reached toward the screen, her fingertips reaching toward them as she to stroke their cheeks in unison, to nestle them into bed, to hand them a glass of water and plant a wetish kiss on their foreheads, her lips firm.

Rasp knew her. Mother. Mama.

His palms wetted with cool sweat, he stood up, blocking the men who sat behind him. His forming erection nudged against his jumpsuit.

"Sit down! I paid commissary credits to be here."

Rasp reached up toward the screen remembering that hard palm striking his cheek. The finger pointing at his face. The roughness. The fear. Kisses afterward. Bits of candy packaging flew at him, sticking to his jumpsuit like burrs.

"Jesus Christ, we can't see the screen."

The larger twin gripped the back of Rasp's jumpsuit and yanked, tearing the fabric at the seams. The warm air rested on his bare lower back. His head ached and a strange pulse of color tore through his vision, the smell of color burning orange in his nostrils. Hands thick with labor grabbed for his arms, his torso. A fist knocked into his kidney. The screen above him was huge with sex, as a gender bender model android as soft as any woman, as strong as any man towering in beauty wound Mama's black hair around their lavender-skinned hand.

Rasp lashed out against the surge and tore himself from their hold and punched the nearest man, his knuckle splitting against the man's tooth. Blood pumped from his riven finger and his body blissed on the violence of it hardened and his muscles burned and his jaw pulsed. Another man headbutted him and blackness veiled his vision. The men were a mass now. Boiling like the earth seas, tearing at one another, candy boxes flattened under foot, a disco floor of caged sex.

The fought until they couldn't anymore, until they held each other instead, leaning into each other, their jumpsuits purpling with large swaths of blood. Rasp now wrapped in one of the twin's arms, slow dancing to the credits music, while the twin swung a slow fist at him. Sedation gas hissed into the room. Too little, too late.

VIII. Hunger

Women's voices echoed around the dark green and black stone bathing chambers. Olivine flickered in the smooth stone walls, like flecks in a cat's eye. Riff eyed the enormity, the stature of these women. Their skin hugged around their hairless limbs. Their breasts stretched with implants. Some of the women were "naturals," and were given supplements to keep their skin unmarked by the weight of their own breasts in their nightly hydration IVs. Riff's heart pounded and she approached an empty spigot next to Fern. Fern's red wet hair clung in ovals and loops against her white, white skin and in her nakedness she looked smaller somehow, her pearly nails scraping thick lather in circles on her scalp. The water was warm. Riff couldn't remember warm water. Fern smiled at her.

"Riff, how do you like it?" Soap bubbles hung from the baby curls on the back of her neck, as she dipped her head back under the warm stream of water.

"It's really…" She couldn't find the word. "Like when in The Before you had cake and everyone sang to you."

Fern laughed, rubbing creamy cleanser on her scars.

"A birthday party?"

"Yeah." Riff said, unsure.

The water poured onto her back and hair. The hygiene kit Al had put together for her had eight different bottles in it. A soft ball of green netting nestled in the center of it.

The synth pop from Shanana Schwoop Shigetty about a boy robot who was just an MRI machine and thus unlovable cut out for morning announcements. A smooth male voice echoed around the shower chamber. Cameras glinted from the shining stone walls.

No breakfast today, ladies. Today is movie day, where you'll all be stars on the big screen and you'll need a flat stomach and a great attitude! We have three new members of our team who will be joining us today, so be sure to give them lots of encouragement!

Suddenly, Riff was surrounded by all the women in the bathing chamber, each of them pulling at her to cradle her to their damp bodies. They stroked her hair and kissed her mouth, their taut bellies pressing against her elbows. The cameras in the wall and ceiling floated from their indentions and hovered around the women, as they cooed at Riff. Fern draped around her and a small black tentacle slid from the corner of her mouth and wriggled in the steam for less than a second. Riff froze, watching the tendril slip into Fern's right nostril and disappear. The women continued to stroke their bodies and push their hair out of her eyes. Brown, green, blue, gray, hazel stagnant and tense.

***

Holy Book TM Chapter 1 Verses 24 -27

24 In the before there was heat, but not too much heat. There was light, but not too much light. There was water for some, but not for all and the people did adorn themselves with goods from the lands of tiny fingers and bowls of grain. The leaders of man did quarrel over underground lakes of black and it was good. Each was pleased unto his own desires.

25 But the women declared an abscission of men and the men wandered, deprived of a home in the bosom. And the rifts did grow and men did take up arms and this was the end of an era.

26 For soon the rift grew and the young of man no longer convalesced in the womb, lest the women destroy it, limb from limb, heart from heart for her own vanities.

27 Man did take up the sword, as his ancestors did, and this was the beginning of the second coming. For man did retrieve the women with impure and disobedient hearts.

***

Androids were scattered around the set under the white-hot lights, some shifting their genitalia from smooth rounds to recognizable sex organs, some sitting cross legged on their stools in front of ceiling height mirrors, smoothing eye shadow over their huge eyes, some chatting softly to one another, arms propped under perfect breasts or firm pecs. The director was the same man who greeted Riff when she got to the facility. His white jumpsuit had the words Creative Genius printed on it in black lettering.

Robots rolled around the smooth white floor, folding synthetic animal fur and focusing cameras. Riff pressed closer to Al, who in male form, was very tall. He tucked her against his lean side, and pulled her braid from the side of her neck, his knuckles brushing her earlobe.

Fern's care unit had already handed her a hydration pack and tugged her sundress down off her shoulders, holding out their arm for her to balance herself on as she stepped out of the yellow mound of fabric. The director walked over and reached out to touch her flank as she bent over to retrieve the crumpled dress but yanked his hand away as soon as she turned toward him.

Riff poked Al's ribs and cupped her hand against the air motioning furiously for him to lean close. He leaned close, his ear inches from her mouth.

"What is he doing?" She hissed.

"Real men," he stopped and pulsed his jaw, correcting himself "non android men aren't allowed to touch the harem."

"What the fuck is a harem?"

"It's a very old word. By definition a harem is where a man of status kept women for..."

"Why can't he touch us?" Riff interrupted.

"Did you watch the history of Mars material on the ship?"

"That boring stuff?"

Al rubbed his newly stubbled jaw and raised his silvery eyebrows.

"Why is it less boring coming from me?"

"It isn't." Riff poked his ribs until he grabbed her wrist. His soft hands twined around her and she felt the rushing in her belly, like she did with Gram back at the factory. The heat and rise in her belly. The sweet wetness.

A prolonged tone sounded over the ubiquitous speakers. Quiet, movie magic in progress appeared on all the scrolling entertainment screens around the room. A giant skylight opened, at the center of the of the set, dilating round, an aperture of golden light from the Mars atmosphere that smoothed skin and eliminated shadow turning the hairless bodies into smooth shapes drifting toward one another around a giant cloth covered platform.

Fern's care unit tweaked her nipples and loosened her wild red hair. She trotted toward set, shod in thigh high black boots and nothing else. Her labia snipped so small, so doll-like. An android stood very still in front of the camera, watching her with burgundy eyes, his body lit into unbearable brightness. He glimmered with Shine that a hovering cat-sized robot swabbed on with a roller.

Riff had never seen an erection before. She stared.

The android reached for her hand and pulled her close to his muscled chest. She craned her neck to look up and a tentacle slipped from the corner of her mouth and into the android's nostril. His eyes snapped shut and crinkled at the corners. His hand fell slack and a small line of pinkish blood tracked from his ear and dripped to his shoulder. Fern's body pearled with sweat, her hand wrapped around the android's still erect penis. He crumpled to the floor, dragging Fern with him, the tentacle stretching between their faces, like a string of saliva from a departing kiss. They lay on the ground for a moment. Fern's tentacle withdrawing slowly back into her mouth. The android shivered on the ground, his right eye rolled left. Fern stood up and placed her booted foot on his face and ground her heel into his jaw until the ligament gave and the jaw fell slack to the ground. She grabbed a silvery heat rescue blanket draped over the platform and flapped it over the motionless android, pausing to tuck it around his body and smooth his hair across his forehead. She kneeled beside him, her breasts pressing against him, as she kissed the tip of his nose and then his cheek.

The room erupted in applause.

Magnificent. Jaw Dropping. Glowing performance.

The women all gathered around the director, weeping and shouting and clapping. Riff's hands were clammy and nausea pressed at the base of her throat.

"Is he dead?" she shouted up at Al over the din.

"Yes. You could call it that."

"Why?"

"Why is he dead or why do we call it that?"

"Why did she kill him?"

"Oh. She wants to live more than she wants him to live, I guess."

"What was the black thing? In her mouth?"

Fern had pressed through the crowd and flung her thin arms around Riff, kissing her mouth. Sweat smell rose from her cooling skin. Her long fingernails rasped against Riff's bare shoulders. No trace of the black tentacle.

Al stepped back from the women and nudged himself between a cobalt blue care unit in female form, with tiny sharp teeth and dark brown eyes and a remarkably humanoid unit who called himself Ricky. His skin was a rich olive with the faintest of stripes, a newer model.

"How did you like my show, little Riff Raff?" Fern stepped back leaving her hands clasped behind Riff's neck.

"It was…" her pulse throbbed in her fingertips "kind of scary."

Fern's brow furrowed and she pulled Riff back to her against her naked body.

"Oh no. Why, baby?"

"That thing in your mouth and you killed him. I've never seen anyone kill anyone."

"My familiar? Oh you'll get one soon too. And you sweet creature, he wasn't really a 'someone,' he was an android. He didn't even feel it."

Riff looked at Al softening back to the they form. Their longish fingers twirling strands of silver hair as it thickened and curled. Fern gripped her shoulders tighter.

"When does Phobos rise?" Riff asked.

"What?" The noise in the room increased as the robots rolled the android onto a cart.

"When is Phobos' next rise?"

"The moon? It's in twenty eight Mars days. We usually have a party on Phobos' rise. Well, I guess it's really an eclipse, but you can see Phobos almost all the time, Riff."

"And what's The Nozzle?"

"I'm sorry?"

"The Nozzle." Riff's voice was flat.

"Oh! The Nozzle really is a sight to see. It's a mystery left here just for us. Just go to the highest floor in this dome. You'll see it." Fern stroked the back of her neck, plucking at the baby hairs at the base of her scalp.

"Ok." Riff pulled away from Fern's scarred arms.

The room settled to a low buzz and the director waved his hand to wrap up. The decommissioned android's hand opened and closed in a death reflex.

IX. Snips and Snails

Rasp itched at his restraints. The sedation gas left a pinpoint rash on the tops of his cheeks and nose. It prickled like sunburn and a hot trickle drained down his throat. The holding room smelled like ozone. He could hear the other men shuffling in the cells next to him. He wondered about his demerit record floating somewhere in a digital otherworld. Another checkmark added to it. Another step toward becoming grease. He recited jokes in his head.

"Why is ten afraid of seven?"

Because seven eight nine.

What do you call a cow with no legs?

Ground beef.

What did the bra say to the hat?

You go on ahead, I'll give these two a lift.

What is a beef? A bra?

The pneumatic door to the holding room hissed open and a white suit from HR strode in. Definitely human. HR was always human. His body suit bunched under the arms as he angled the tablet toward his face. He lifted a vapor cigarette to this mouth and inhaled deeply. Unfashionable since the Corporation released NicDelivery systems.

His brow creased as he scrolled through Rasp's record. The Martian gravity made him look stretched and thin. His suited shins crossed and uncrossed as he sat on the edge of the foldout bunk beside Rasp. He gazed up at the screen in front of them. A woman French kissed a rat while Jypsy Tra La La la featuring Shanana Schwoop Shigetty sang about breaking up with petroleum products and bit off chunks of synthetic skin from each other's fingertips, stripping it off like plastic coating from a wire. Rasp thought the song was very environmentally conscious. He tapped his foot to the beat. The man from HR stood up and turned the screen off.

The silence was unbearable. A small tide of panic rolled into Rasp's guts.

"Ok Rasp, do you feel happy in your current position? I'm Grip by the way." He sat back down beside Rasp and breathed stuck the vapor cigarette behind his ear.

"Can we turn the screens back on?"

"I really think it's much better in here without all that noise. Do you like your job?"

"I mean I didn't choose it."

Grip shifted on the bunk and tapped something into the tablet. He rubbed his right hand on his own thigh, the fabric stretching and snapping back with each movement.

"But, do you like it?"

"It's fine I guess. Better than the rig."

"We want you to find satisfaction in your work, Rasp."

Grip's right eye came unmoored for a moment and drifted around in its sockets. He reached into his utility belt and pulled out a bit of fine purple powder in a small plasticine bag and a tiny spray bottle. He tipped the powder into the spray bottle and added a few drops of fluid from his hydration tube on the body suit. Grip held open the eyelid of the wild eye and spritzed it with the purplish substance. The silence was punctuated by the drips and scrapes of plasticine, the tsk of the sprayer. Rasp's scalp tickled. The substance smelled like synthetic grape.

"We'd like to see you be more of a team player," Grip said, blinking as the drops rolled down his cheek staining a lavender line down to the corner of his mouth.

"How can I do that?"

"Well, the Corporation would like to send you on a staff rejuvenation retreat, where you'll be mingling with other staff members and relearning some fundamentals."

"Like what? How to wipe properly?" Rasp grinned at the suit, gritting his teeth.

He did not smile back. His pupils pushed at the edges of his irises and his nose ran with purplish mucus.

"These jokes, Rasp. They aren't work appropriate. They don't fit the Corporation's image. They make management uncomfortable." He swiped at the mucus with the back of his fist. "Also, we need to see you interacting better with your coworkers. You'll be learning all this and more."

The words bounced around the silent room. Grip patted Riff's shoulder. A fine patting place according to the employee handbook.

"Plus, it only costs 200 credits, which we will deduct from your commissary credits per pay period." Grip stood up, using Rasp's shoulder to brace himself and switched the screen back on.

The O logo flashed on the screen. A video of two men playing a game of cards lit the room cold white-blue. Rasp felt his pulse slow as the room filled with light and sound again. The men talked quietly as an artificial sun rose behind them. They sat on a red beach beside an opaque rust-colored lake lapping around their ankles. A supervisor model rolled over to the men on the screen with a tray of drinks.

One of the men stood up and stretched, sipping at the milky liquid. Cubes of white ice clinked around as the men drank. A vibration thumped beneath the water, rolling small creamy orange waves toward the men. A pair of ringed planets stretched huge and pale through the clear containment chamber. The men began to laugh in unison, the white liquid sloshing over their glasses and trickling over their fingers.

Rasp tried to look back at Grip, but he was transfixed. His back molars ground together, his jaw muscle gripping for relief and the word Rejuvenate repeated in his mind. A mantra to stop the pulsing beneath the lake. A prayer for his body.

The O flashed on the screen again and Rasp's jaw loosened. The screen went black.

Grip smiled widely at the screen.

"Do you see, Rasp?"

"I think I see."

"You will feel so refreshed upon your return, so alive."

***

Holy Book TM Chapter 4 Verses 9-18

9 And man was cursed to toil among the stars for his weakness. A weakness of flesh and mind that did settle in the veins of man. For in those days men succored from the teat of the god of pharmacology without the wisdom of the ones blessed in spirit.

10 And it was then that the spirit of the most high descended from his 34,000 square foot mansion on the mount and did transcribe the transcendent order and did save man from himself and woman from herself and others from all selves.

11 So the most high inscribed these commandments into our digital consciousness to remain in the server on the planet of Thross beneath the waters of Lotan.

12 The first and highest of these being, 'toil is freedom and freedom is toil.'

14 'Man and woman are divisible by labor and beauty, sin and unsin, sex and nonsex.'

15 'Each worthy woman shall be given a familiar on her sixteenth cycle for the betterment of toil and the benefit of freedom.'

16 'Worthy women gifted with the familiar shall be in the following fields: pornographic arts, news and entertainment, and any herein deemed worthy by the corporation.'

17 'Each man shall work according to his own ability and when his ability wanes he shall be decolonized and regulated for toil is freedom, so say we.'

18 'Each woman shall perform according to her own ability and provide the oil for the machination through their bodies as it has been and how it will be forevermore. Amen.'

***

Rasp stood in the open corridor of the largest dwelling he had ever seen. The floors were deep black and so glossy they looked almost transparent and deep, like a bottomless vat. Grip guided him by his restraints to a smooth white bench and left him, slipping through an old door that opened on hinges, somewhere behind him. The corridor charged ahead into a vast hallway. No screens hung on the wall, just pictures, imperfect pictures made with paint and grease. Light poured from frosted glass lamps in long ribbons of molecular streams that curled like smoke up to the golden ceiling, where steel tentacles vacuumed up the phosphorescent trails.

A creature crouched under a hovering table not far from the bench and eyed him. It was covered in fur and had green eyes narrowed into slits, beneath pointed ears. Its long tail lashed back and forth. A memory of The Before strained at the back of Rasp's mind. Somehow, he knew the creature's fur was soft and that it made a rumble sometimes. The creature lurched forward and dashed toward his dangling restraint line, gripping it in sharp claws and flopping over onto its side, rubbing its face against the now taut line. Rasp remembered the word "whisker."

He leaned forward and rubbed his bound hands across the creature's side. It rolled to its back and gripped his hands with needle sharp claws, kicking with its back legs, green eyes swamped in black pupils. A door cracked from across the hall and feminine whispers bounced around the hallway. The creature gnawed at his knuckle, still kicking at his wrists. He pulled away from the claws and squinted at the cracked doorway.

Slender fingers slid through the doorway and a round face with thin lips peeked through. She was thin-boned and tall, a Marsborne. Perhaps twenty earth cycles old. Rasp had only seen Marsborne in the docu reels HR forced rig workers to watch when they complained about exploding dust mines, body parts drifting in the black of space, rancid shine rations, or bad plots in the next Star Wars movie.

The Marsborne giggled.

"Hi," she said.

"Hi." Rasp readjusted his wrists, pushing them between his thighs.

"You are dirty and short. Are you my new playmate?" The words sounded misplaced in her rich tenor. Like a game of some sort.

Rasp ground his teeth, shame welling in his belly. He rubbed at the shine spots on the back of his left hand clutched between his thighs.

"I don't know. You want to hear a joke?"

"What's a joke?"

"Something to make you laugh."

"You make me laugh already."

"Well, this is even better."

"Alright, playmate. Tell a joke."

"Where did Susan go after the explosion?"

"Who's Susan?"

"Just a woman from The Before."

"What before?"

She fully emerged from behind the door, wearing a real white cotton shirt with a strange shape airbrushed on it. Blue loopy script spelled out the word Florida. Her wrists poked past the sleeves. Her feet turned in at the heel and her knees nearly touched. No sign of a familiar. No irritation at the corner of the mouth, no glitter behind the eye, no fist-clenched hands.

"The Before on Earth, before all of this."

"All of what?"

"Do you want to hear the joke or not?"

"Yes, but before all of what?"

"Before the mines and the separation and all that."

"What separation?"

"When the Corporation separated men and women. Haven't you seen a history vid?"

The word niña flitted through his brain and he knew it meant girl, but he did not know how he knew that. The Marsborne stood before him, twisting the tail of her cotton shirt in her hand.

"Well, I've read a history book, but it never said anything about a separation. We're here talking now, aren't we?"

"She went everywhere."

"What?"

"That's the joke. Susan went everywhere after the explosion."

"Oh."

She glanced at the door behind him and inched closer to Rasp, sweeping her palm behind his head and drawing his forehead toward her lips. She kissed his hairline, inhaling, her breath hot on his scalp. Her tooth grazed his skin, as her tongue slipped from between her lips. Tasting. Sampling. Her fingers slid from the back of his head to his throat and pressed soft against the sides of his neck until grayness shadowed behind his eyes. He was uncomfortably erect.

The door behind them swung open and she leapt back from Rasp, who dropped his hands over his tented jumpsuit. Grip and the tallest man Rasp had ever seen strode into the hallway. The Marsborne was nowhere fast. Her scent fled with her and Rasp wondered if he had ever seen her at all or if he was hallucinating, like the time they sucked the gas out of one of the compression chambers on the rig, until they all slumped together in a corner, laughing. That had been two demerits, though they could buy whippets at the commissary that did the same thing. The men eyed him and Grip reached down to release his restraints. The tall man shook his head and held out his palm for the Lite Lock TM key. When Grip placed it in his hand, he motioned for Rasp to stand and eyed the cracked door across the hallway, distracted.

Cold air seeped from the room behind them, prickling against Rasp's neck. The man looked down at him and turned him toward the cold room with thick long fingers. Darkness swallowed all the shapes and Rasp tasted ozone.

X. I Scream, You Scream, We All Scream

Al, in they form, brushed Riff's straight black hair in long sweeps, gliding the plasticine bristles from scalp to tip in single fluid motion. Ripples of pleasure like hail on clear water fluttered from Riff's scalp down her back. The dim exam room pulsed with alien soft earth sounds playing on the speakers, water flowing, rain falling, waves breaking, a strange high-pitched whistle sound. Al untied the back of Riff's white cotton blend dress and laved iodine tinted liquid onto her back.

The three weeks of dogmeat and sweet round globes of icy melon and butter and real potatoes had thickened her. Her breasts filled her shirt and her arms and hips plumped under her brassy skin. Al leaned into her back as they guided an iodine-soaked rag over her torso, leaving streaks of orangey coloration. Al stroked firmly to avoiding tickling her.

"So, what am I doing today, Al?"

Al smiled and wiped their hands on a towel.

"You are providing oil for the machination."

"What the hell does that mean?"

"The Holy Book says that women provide oil for the machination, if you would read it."

"No one reads anything anymore, Al. Besides what about you? Why don't you provide oil for the machination when you're a girl?"

"I'm an android. Androids aren't allowed."

"But why though?"

Al picked up her hair again and separated it into three bunches for braiding.

"You ask a lot of questions, pretty human girl," Al said into her ear.

"Al, how come they don't let you?" Riff pulled a thread from her bunched garment, then flopped her hands in her lap, sighing.

"Androids have DNA from all sorts of things, some of those things make us unsuitable for consumption. Do you remember what snakes were?"

"I don't think so. They were animals? Because if they were, I only remember rats and bugs, and of course dogs."

"Well they were animals shaped like cable that were venomous. Some of the older models have snake DNA, probably so we'd eat less, and some have puffer fish and it's just not suitable." Al paused at "not suitable," glancing down at Riff.

The camera on the wall hummed and a light flashed on Al's embedded wrist monitor. Al whipped a band around the end of Riff's braid and picked up her dress. They motioned to a robe in the corner of the room.

"It ties in the back. Put it on and follow the instructions on the screen. Remember, The Corporation loves you and wants you to be happy." Al Looked at the camera on the wall and squeezed Riff's shoulder hard. "I'll be here when you get back."

Al whisked out of the room, leaving Riff naked on the exam table.

The screens lining the wall flashed on and a one-eyed man stared at her from a solid black room. Somewhere. His right eye socket was filled with glistening gems like a geode and it pulsed glints of light across the room as he turned his head slowly slowly in a full circle. Purple flames shivered across the room, lapping against the walls, tapping against the screen. The man opened his mouth, crusted with quartz and diamonds, overflowing with black sludge and fell backwards onto two steel beams lashed together in a cross, writhing against the flames. Three ancient robots, dimpled with rust, ticked forward on four needle-thin legs and drove a giant cotter pin through the one-eyed man's hands and feet. A woman, heavy with luscious fat, crawled across the floor and wrapped her hands around the man's feet and wailed, a familiar oozing from her mouth and waving its tentacles blindly.

HE DIED FOR YOU in yellow block print exploded onto the screen. DO YOUR PART FOR THE CORPORATION.

The fat on the woman's body melted away in the heat, dripping into a graduated cylinder the size of an oil drum beneath her. Her face, now thin and radiant, beamed flecks of white light that touched the one-eyed man's suffering face. A diamond detached from the corner of his mouth and swirled in the oily rapids of fat and sludge.

Her body tight and young, her mouth full and alive. Hands shot from the cylinder and brushed her thighs, now lean and spare. The one-eyed man smiled at her, all teeth. Sacrifice is love.

Riff's limbs felt sodden and her eyelids drooped. The faintest smell of something, something in the back of her mind. Something to warn them. A blue flame, her mother gripping her by her tiny wrist, está caliente, mija!

Two androids entered the room, larger than she had ever seen, one with a faint ridge of spines over his brow, the other smelling like a warm sea. They hoisted her up, muscles bunching, onto a gurney and wheeled her out of the soft, dark, velvet room. They pushed the gurney in silence. The black domed ceiling drifted over her, separating her from the half-terraformed atmosphere outside.

Her blood felt thick in her and slugged slowly in her neck and wrists. Bright globes of light flashed over her until white light burned red through her closed eyelids. The gurney came to a stop and Riff dragged her eyelids open to see blurred beings cloaked in turquoise and white hovering above her. One of them pinched her inner thigh with gloved fingers and murmured something to another with a tablet. She counted one, two, three, fingers on his hands, though it could have been a trick of the gas.

One of the beings raised a huge needle and wiped it over a piece of gauze, before pressing it into her thigh. One of them shook its cloaked head and pressed a button on the side of a huge canister that rose, gleaming to the ceiling. A heavy whir eclipsed all other sound in the room. The being with the needle pressed the tip of it into Riff's thigh and she felt pressure and a snap of pain as the cannula glided under her skin. Yellow-white clots traveled up the clear tube into the canister, which was now churning, one chamber maroon with blood and one chamber creamy, buttery white. Riff felt cool beads of sweat gathering on her brow and she tried to cry out, to tell them of the pain in her thigh, but no words came, only small whimpers. She tried to scream, to move, to kick, but pressure sat on her throat, winding tighter and tighter until only the thinnest stream of air cooled her throat. Her lungs lightly inflating and blackness crowding her vision, as the needle worked under her skin, in and out, in and out, in and out. One of the beings came to her head and forced a tube into her mouth, sucking out her spittle.

A needle slid into her arm and she was counting down, down to one as New Year Birthday Party Slam played over the speakers until there was nothing.

***

Riff rolled over onto her side. Compression bandages bundled her fluid packed skin against her. Pain throbbed over her body and Fern sat on the edge of her bed, touching her cool hands to Riff's jawline. Al, in he form, mixed together powders and hunks of yellow steam fruit into a Chop Glass TM, and pressed down the black ring at the top until the concoction blurred together into a yellowish sludge.

"How are you feeling, little one?" Fern asked.

A knot of nausea plugged Riff's throat and she dug her fingers into the sheets.

"Sick."

"Yeah, they had to give you the shot. It makes you feel bad for a little while."

Al stirred the drink and brought it to her. Her lips were chapped and her throat hurt.

"What did they do?"

"They harvested from you. We get to provide so much for our fellow employees and employers." Fern lifted up Riff's sore arm and kissed her bare wrist. Beauty is pain.

The concoction Al brought was cold and sweet and she sipped it while he checked her bandages. The pain lifted some and Fern and Al's fingers felt cool. A Martian storm whirred outside, whipping around the dome, piling red dust around the pastel Easter egg colonies.

***

Holy Book TM Chapter 2 Verses 8 -17

8 And there was a great wailing in the land for the Canadian blueberries, the Peruvian Quinoa, the Chinese apples the consumer had craved and eaten were given to only the righteous whose income did exceed 80000000 units.

9 And the women grumbled amongst themselves for their children and their partners and they had empty bellies. The Corporation reminded them that breast is best, but to not be too hard on themselves for they manufactured a substitute that was perfectly suitable for human consumption. It only cost twenty-five units per bottle.

10 And so women did seek to undercut the corporation by selling their bodies at discounted rates from the Corporation's standard and were thusly punished with tasks that chipped their nails and wore their skin down to wrinkles and age spots.

11 And so the sun did rise on the beauty of the women who toiled in factories for they were soon recognized by the CEO as a product for consumption, and it was good.

12 In those days, a woman, whose beauty eclipsed the sun, become the daughter of the Corporation. For she did endure the harvest with a smile and fell at the feet of the most high. Her name was Frau and her life was perfect.

13 Frau gave 1200 CCs of herself every harvest and the Corporation blessed her, for though that is a small number, it was all she had to give.

14 One day Frau could no longer give to the harvest, for her skin dipped from the effort of it and her figure was so trim, so pert, so thin, that the needle could not bring even one droplet of oil.

15 And so she went to the CEO, who cradled her face, and asked her "What do you require, dearest one?" and she kissed his knuckles and asked "What do you require?"

16 And was so moved that he sent for her body to be used, every part, everything but the squeal. And so her eggs, her corneas, her fingernails, her bladder, her tongue were all sectioned from her and given to the factory workers, the asteroid miners, the acid divers, all who stretched

toward the sky and demanded hope of the Corporation. And so she was spread across Mars and Earth.

17 And where every droplet of her landed, credits and cakes and red-soled sneakers and porno movies bounded from the very ground and their thirst was slaked, at least for a time.

XI. Martian Me, Martian You

Rasp stared at the dark thing in the small tank in a formal dining room. The tendrils thinner than a strand of hair floated in the water, sending small ripples of light into the water that pulsed and shone. He was supposed to be setting the table with plates. The house robot told him so. Plates like from The Before, shining and white with small chips on the edges, a plastic cup with words faded from washings. But the memory slipped through the cracks as he dipped a finger into the tank.

The tendrils brushed his finger sending throbs of pain into his shoulder and a memory of being alone with a boy in a closet and friends screaming with laughter outside and the boy saying should we just kiss to make them stop? And this fear of his hands and this fear of his lips and the thud of someone bouncing against the door. Looking down, down and seeing chipped fingernail polish and small hands and realizing that this memory was not his, but someone else's and that she was alone here and he was alone here. The gold shag carpeting in the closet smelled like cigarettes and carpet cleaner and the boy leaned in, his braces cut his lips and cheap cologne evaporated into the hot closet, choking her. Choking Rasp.

And he was back in the dining room, the plates still stacked on the table, the forks still in a tangled pile in the middle. The Marsborne man stood in the doorway, leaning his forehead against the frame.

"What did you see?" the Marsborne looked at his fingernails.

Rasp hesitated, embarrassed that he was afraid.

"Well?"

"I don't really know." Rasp picked up the plates and started centering each one in front of each spindly chair.

The Marsborne pressed his fingertips to the back of his own ear, where a bare glint of silver caught the soft yellow light.

"Alona, come here. It's playtime."

Light from the circular windows soaked the room in amber. The sun was so faint here on Mars, the air so syrupy and yellow. Not like the rigs that hurtled across the sun's face, filling the craft with blazing white every six hours or so, despite the thick UV windows. All the men wound in their blankets, sleeping in sunglasses, squares of light sliding across the black lenses.

The Marsborne woman who kissed him strode into the room, the furred creature trotting behind her, swatting at a loose thread on her green gown. A single stone glinted at her throat and her teeth seemed sharper as she smiled at him. She approached him, standing inches from his face. He wanted to touch her body under the gown.

She took the plates from his hands and bent over to kiss him on the top of the head. He reached for her waist, but she swatted his hand away. Her face seemed older than before, with minute creases around her eyes and spots on her hands. The doors to the room slid shut and a bolt hissed across it. She drew out syringe tipped with a shining black needle. Pain flooded behind his eyes as her thumb rested against his temple.

The tendrils in the tank began to thrash and stretch toward her from the tank, frothing the water around it. Rasp felt wetness creep into his synth boots and looked down. The floor was covered with a gray liquid that seeped from the corners of the room. The Marsborne man crawled on top of the dining table and swept his fingers through the rising water. The liquid rose, lifting the furniture. Plasticine cups, scraps of paper, dog bones, women's panties, Shine cream cartons bobbed around Rasp's waist. Panic swelled in his chest. He couldn't swim. Swimming was not careening through the curve of space untouched, unstopped. Water crushed houses and filled lungs, not with nothing, but until your brain burned and you sank. He lashed into the water toward the table, but Alona twisted his tunic around her fist and jerked him back toward her. He slipped backwards, feeling the liquid touch his face. He flailed against the cold opaque tide. Something muscular and cold brushed against his leg. The tank that held the tendrils was empty.

Alona wound her limbs around him and pushed him below the surface, pressing her fingertips against his throat. She had no eyes, no mouth. A tendril caressed his temple before piercing the skin under his hairline with needle proboscises, and the closet memory consumed him again. The gold shag carpet pressed against the backs of his (her?) thighs while the acrid smell of saliva filled her nostrils. The boy, Andy? Brady? Joseph? touched her at the base of her throat and the door swung wide letting bright light flood the space. Shapes floated behind the light, shimmering like stones underwater. A woman taller than a signal spire emerged and reached down to take She-Rasp's collar, sliding her sharpened fingernails across her face until there was nothing left to be afraid of. And the moon, before it was broken, sat thick and full behind the woman's feathered hair.

Rasp was himself as soon as the needle pulled from his head, he felt it pop from the skin on his temple. The gray liquid retreated around him and the mass of tendrils floated in its tank. Alona wrapped his head in her arms and pressed him against her collarbone. His body felt strange. His muscles ticked and gathered around his right eye. The Marsborne man picked up debris around the room, placing it all on the long table in the center. Alona motioned at him. She only had four fingers on each hand, each one tipped with an eggshell-blue fingernail.

"Bring him something to drink, Pai, he's thirsty"

And he was thirsty. So thirsty that his tongue clung to the roof of his mouth and his throat scratched with each breath.

Pai picked up one of the cups on the ground and poured amber liquid into it from a fist-sized bag in his chest pocket. He pressed it into Rasp's hand and began picking up odds and ends that settled on the floors around them.

"What did you see?" Pai asked.

Alona waved him away.

"He's tired Pai. Let him rest for just a minute."

Rasp gulped at the amber liquid and for a moment he felt better. Better than better. The liquid coursed through his veins. His heartbeat slowed and warmth wrapped around his torso. The lights above him softened and Alona's hands were cool on his skin.

"I wasn't me and it wasn't here. I think it was a long time ago."

Alona scratched his back and wrapped him tighter in her thin arms. She smelled like wet cloth.

"Go on, Rasp." Pai stared off into the foyer.

"I was a girl and there was boy. And they were laughing, but I didn't hear any jokes."

Alona twirled his hair around her four fingers. Pai nodded.

"And the thing they do in soft pornos, but also sometimes mothers did in the before, with their mouths against someone else's mouth, and sometimes we do on the rigs ." Rasp searched for the word.

"Kissing?" Alona pulled back from him to look in his eyes.

"Yeah."

Pai paced around the room, picking up bits of debris.

"The mechs can do that," Alona said.

"Why did you do that to me?" Rasp looked at the tendrils in the tank.

Alona petted his hair.

"I was only playing."

"Well, I didn't like it."

Pai spoke from across the room. "It's part of your Rejuvenation. We are providing you insight to be more efficient, more grateful, more compliant in your current position."

"Why, though?"

"To be happier." His tone belayed the faintest irritation.

A chime sounded from the foyer, long and hollow. Alona slapped her palm over Rasp's mouth. Pai slipped off his sodden golden slippers and drew in his breath.

"It's probably nothing," Pai whispered. "We worked out the kinks."

The lights in the room flickered and a small voice piped in over the speakers hidden around the room. At first it just breathed, and then it rasped, "I see you." Darkness like a dust cloud enveloped the room. The wet rugs squelched under the pressure of something unseen. Something unheard.

The alarms went off and the mechs rammed against the door. Alona's fingers tightened under his nose. The smell of burning grass permeated from her hand. The sound of water in the tank lapping against the glass. The pressure of Alona's palm against his lips. Grinding teeth. Heartbeat. Something brushed against his lower back, something small and cold.

Alona's nails dug into his cheek. Her hair brushed the top of his head, the smell of singed hair clinging to her. He could not hear a heartbeat from her chest.

A garment rustled behind him and a pattering of the thing or the not thing, echoed around the silent room. Someone leaned over behind him. Images of mother with huge breasts hanging, images of black hair streaming over his chest, a smile with teeth the color of raw oil, palms bigger than a helmet, the sun shining through the closet door, baring the dusty jackets and a rusting file cabinet. His tongue torn in half, leaking iron into his throat. A moon unbroken, holding deep wells of rustling children, begging him at the very top of the well for just a drop. A drop of sweat from his fingertips. But he was wearing his spacesuit.

And dark become black and Alona was ripped away from him. Her scream was short. More a squeal than a scream.

The lights came back suddenly and Rasp was alone. No sign of Pai or Alona. His cheek burned from Alona's nails raking across his face. He sat with his legs sprawled in front of him like a child in the wetness, blinking against the light. Numb. Something crouched in the seat at the head of the long table. The tank that held the tendrils sloshed, empty.

"You want to hear a joke?" He half yelled at the thing at the head of the table.

"A JOKE," the thing echoed back in his own voice.

"A man was washing his car with a sponge. No wait. I got it backwards. Let me try again."

"TRY AGAIN."

"A man was washing his car with his son."

The thing reared an appendage up over the table. The limb was slender and flaccid. It curled around the light fixture, pulling so tight that its skin became translucent and the skin flakes cracked off in a snow of dry gray onto the white plates. The smell of engine oil and wet dog crowded the room. A primal urge to tear at the thing until it lay in wet pieces on the table tugged at the back of Rasp's mind. He squeezed his eyes shut and reached for the punchline. His voice was thick in his throat.

"And the boy said, 'can we use the sponge next time?'"

Rasp barely remembered cars.

The thing poured its mass onto the table and slid closer to Rasp. Its body was made of infinite eyes. Insect eyes. Dog eyes. Human eyes. Fish eyes. Tiny black-feathered wings slipped in and out of the gelatinous mass, beating away at the still air. Loose cone-shaped teeth drifted around under the transparent torso. The gray-skinned limb unwound from the light fixture and slithered toward Rasp's face. He was frozen there, sprawled on the wet floor, clutching at the fabric of his shirt, wanting to bite, to run, to be away from this place.

The limb rested on his jaw, cool and muscular. Rasp was no longer Rasp. There was no more Mars. There was only a sunlit bedroom with a frilly pink bedspread and a closet stuffed with plastic-wrapped gowns. Tributes to an unhappy life. A heavy wooden television with black dials squatted in front of the bed. Photographs of the dead lined the walls, all of them skewed slightly right, glowing faces nested in sepia.

A tall woman with black hair swept back from her face burst through the door and jerked the bedspread off the bed. Her face curled in displeasure.

"You are too old for this crap," she hissed.

"I didn't mean to."

Rasp found himself whispering through the mouth crowded with unfamiliar teeth.

"It's disgusting. You already started your period. Wetting the bed is for babies."

Rasp did not know what a period was.

The woman kicked a laundry hamper through the door and dumped the bedding into it. A swirl of dust motes kicked up into the sunny bedroom.

"Are you having sex with that neighbor boy?"

"No mother!"

"Why can't you stop pissing on everything then?"

Mother gathered the basket with a sharp breath and swung it into the door to open it. The hallway behind her was just blackness multiplied into itself. Exponents of nothing. And mother was gone.

The Martian dining room came back into focus. Rasp felt the largeness of his body, the hair on his face and his lean chest and breathed out. Wetness from the floor soaked into his jumpsuit. The being was gone. Pai and Alona were gone. For the first time in his life, Rasp was alone.

XII. Phobos Rises

Riff was not supposed to be here. She had heard of being "fired" in the old education vids they sometimes showed in the cafeteria. Images of women crawling on their bellies, ugly and soiled by the lack of purpose. Bowls in their hands filled with bits of metal the old ones used to denote currency. Sometimes the vids would show children, flies on their faces, sticky lumps around their eyes. DON'T BE A JERK! WORK! In bouncing bubble font shadowing the sick child's eyes. Riff hadn't seen a child in five earth cycles. Not a very little one, anyway. There hadn't been a replacement at the girl factory in a very long time. Gram was the youngest.

Her arms oozed clear fluid from the punctures and her tongue stuck to the roof of her mouth. The air up here on the higher floors was still and warm. She followed signs with pictures of human reactions on them. Happy face. Surprised face. Excited face. The white plasticine floors were flecked with veins of gray to mimic Earth stone up here. Up the spiral. Down the rabbit hole. She remembered that from The Before. But she could not remember a rabbit exactly.

When she finally reached the top floor, A great spire jutted through the center of the transparent ceiling. A landing circled the huge structure, fenced by guard rails. The spire was built from the bodies of mechs and spaceships, all quilted together with thick black welds. The tip of it penetrated the belly of the transport ship, clasped to it with hooks and couplings. Ships hovered in a line, waiting to reach the tip. The wind whipped orange dust, unfurling swaths of orange around the spire. The sun blinked cold behind the curtain of butterscotch atmosphere, cold and far. A sign read: The Nozzle: A Feeding of the Corporation in firm block print.

Cleaning mechs dotted with rust scrubbed at the unending layer of film on the transparent ceiling. The space was filled with gentle whirrings and tinkings. It was hard to swallow here. Hard to breathe. Riff pulled out the playing card with her mother on it. She remembered with some vagueness her mother's hardness and her softness and the confusion that came with each slap or each kind word.

Mija, bring Mama your homework. Mama, dressed in a crisp suit, beckoned to her. Her homework was to put frogs in baskets with letters printed on them on her tablet. Her brother, older, funnier, somewhere else. Probably in his room. He was always in his room. Mama grabbed the tablet and scoffed. This is why I spend so much money on that pinche private school. Don't say that word. Because it's for grownups to say. Mama did not hug like other mamas. Mama put clean laundry in drawers. Mama worked for men who never listen to me. Mama was not afraid like other Mamas. Mama made money. Mama did not kiss skinned knees.

Shuffling footsteps echoed around the huge room.

"Oh here you are, Riff." Al in she-form rounded the platform.

Her slight frame pressed against a silvery jumpsuit. Her lavender hair was pulled into small top knot. Sweat prickled under Riff's arms. Her palms ached. Fear and sex pulled at her thoughts like threads separating from cloth.

"I was just looking at this thing."

"Well, you really need to come back and get your bandages changed. You're looking a little oozy, my darling."

"Was my tracker not on?"

Riff knew her tracker was back in her bedroom, tucked between the mattress and the wall.

"No."

Al eyed her.

"We have to get the swelling down or they might send you to the colonies, Riff. They spent a lot of money on you already." Al's tone rose into a small panic. "What are you doing here? Who told you about the nozzle?"

"I'm busy, ok?"

"What are you talking about?"

Trusting Al. Trusting Al. Her heart beat the words in a rapid pattern. Trusting Al.

"I just want to be alone."

"But why?"

"Because you can't tell me what to do."

Al wrung the gauze she was carrying around her middle finger and looked up at the ship pulling away from the nozzle. A fine mist of clear liquid floating from its belly into the red whipped wind.

"I just want to help you."

Al began to shift, growing bigger, taller, muscle packing on. He form at its fullest. The jumpsuit stretched to neat transparency, revealing curls of hair thickening below the slightest naval. His hands were now large and felted with hair. Al wrapped his forearm around her waist and pulled her to him. Pain from her incisions melded into a single burning knot on her back. Confusion rose in her. Her body wanted them all. Her body wanted every form of Al, every touch from Gram in the dark, every brush from Fern. Al drew his finger under her jaw. This was forbidden. Only Corporation sanctioned contact between androids and humans for the entertainment of the masses was permitted per section twenty-seven of The Rules TM. Al's body, her body, property. Bought and sold.

Riff wound her arms around Al's middle. Strands of invisible DNA from creatures long extinct wound around one another under the skin, creating odd ridges on his spine and irises slightly too large for his eyes.

"What do you want?" Riff asked.

"I'm not programmed you know. I am not a mech."

"Can we talk here?" Riff looked around for cameras and small ticks in the wall.

"Yes. The radiation here messes with the cameras and it's boring up here. No screens. Al's irises widened and contracted as the ships overhead drifted across the weak sun.

"How old are you? How many cycles?"

"I don't know." Al slid his hand along the side of her neck and slid his fingers under her hair, leaning into her.

Footsteps echoed from around The Nozzle and Al dropped his arms from around Riff, shrinking back into she-form. The crackle of her joints like plasticine beads underfoot.   The jumpsuit crawled back to opacity. Riff dropped away from Al and scooted back against the railing. The footsteps got louder, louder. Cameras. Eyes. Control. Blink. Blink. Don't Blink. Don't touch. Don't look.

The small woman who slipped her the playing card her first day in the care unit swung around the corner. Her right hand was tucked under her smock and her black and yellow hair had been cropped. Her gaze slid from Riff to Al. Bright suspicion tugged at the corners of her mouth. Al put her hand on Riff's shoulder and whispered hot behind her ear.

"If she saw us, I'll offer her credits. I have lot saved up."

"It's ok, I think. I think you could probably go now if you wanted."

"What? No."

The woman approached. The pale sun becoming weaker with Phobos' shadow. The ships passing like great prehistoric beasts, pondering across the sky, sipping from the nozzle. Riff's pulse snapped against her temple, loud and quick.

"So you brought your care unit? That wasn't part of the instructions." The woman's voice was quiet.

"No, I didn't. Al…I mean my care unit was just about to go."

Al's brows knitted together.

"What instructions, Riff?" The android shifted from one foot to the other.

"Nothing, Al. She is just my friend and we were planning on meeting here."

"For what?"

The woman stepped in closer, drawing her hand out of her smock and offering it to Al.

"My name is Reina. Riff and me are friends. You know, from Earth."

Al looked at her extended hand.

"Aren't you kind of old to have been in the Girl Factory?

"From before then."

"I see."

Al layered her arms over her belly and drew her lips into a tight line. A strange orange flush blossomed on her neck and his coloration wavered from pale to variegated stripes of red and orange. A song by Shanana Schwoop Shigetty about taxation on kisses cut in over the loudspeaker. Al turned from them and walked back down the corridor without another word.

"I've never seen no android do that," Reina said.

Riff shrugged and opened her mouth to explain.

Reina was no longer listening. The song cut out and was replaced by a low level whisper about buying things at commissary. Whippets to destress. Organic Dog Jerky. Daylight lamps. Beauty creams. Romance. Adventure. Happiness. Riff felt a squeezing at the base of her throat.

"We have to go. Venga."

Reina reached for her hand and guided her toward a door with a screen above it that showed an eyeball suspended in amber liquid. A long corridor sprawled into darkness.

"Where are we going?"

"Somewhere where we can talk."

"Can't we talk now?"

"Jesus, no. The eye, el ojo." Reina pointed toward the pinpoints of green light in wall at opposite end of the hallway. "Now, hush."

***

Holy Book TM Chapter 10 Verses 12- 18

12 Now on the blue planet, there was a great calamity amongst the people who did cry out for a new child of God. And they did sprawl amongst themselves and within themselves across the World Wide Web.

13 The web did bring them many false prophets and in those days, politicians, who did make many promises. Elders were forced to live on in suffering and uselessness and the young were coerced into choosing their own labor. The women did rend their clothing in thoughtful obsession and the men became soft.

14 Drinking water heavy with chems churned in the people's bellies and they did appeal to The Corporation, who took pity on them and sent them a new god child.

15 The god child was not born of mothers, as rich and poor alike were sanctioned to do in those days, but was born of machines. Conceived without intercourse. And he was so beautiful and new and strange that women wished to lie with him and men wished to lie with him.

16 And so it was that he was placed into the care of the machine convent in the West and there he grew into a man of power and substance, for he was nourished from the breast of the Corporation.

17 On a very hot day, he unveiled himself to his adoring people, once again. Now he was long of bone and thick with muscle. His jawline was like that of the old gods who showed their love for mankind by lying with them and their children.

18 The people seeing him for the first time, raised their light boxes to capture him and hold him forever. But he raised his hand and sayeth unto them , "Be still, and know the words of my father, until you give your body and your minds unto the machination, you cannot know happiness." And the god-man unplugged from them and returned only when they obeyed.

***

Deeper under the red dirt, deeper into the hive cluster Riff and Reina went. The hallways turned from plasticine-coated white to an older material that felt cool underfoot as they descended. The ceilings lowered and the artificial atmosphere pods hummed in unsteady labor, as they drew in the cold, dry air and filtered and churned out breathable air. They descended in silence, Reina glancing behind them, above them, around them. The smell of artificial cinnamon hung around them in the cold tunnel. The white light globes dotting the celling of the tunnel hummed and flickered.

A single doorway illuminated the end of the tunnel. Figures rustled dark in the bright room behind the white rectangle of light. Riff wondered if she could run if she had and where she would go. Reina dropped behind her, herding her toward the doorway. The rustling figures came to a standstill, peering at her. Most were women, some were other. Something in the not possible. Her mind surged at concrete examples of something, anything to pin these beings to. She listed extinct animals she had only seen in vids, cataloging them in her brain. Monkey. Bird. Lizard. Sea Urchin. Slug. The creatures ticked along the hard floor on four limbs, each tipped with dark nail. Thousands of tendrils the size of a plasticine fiber floated from their backs, each connected to a black unblinking eye. Each being was connected to machine by a long tube strapped around the center of their thick bodies. The women tended the machine and occasionally drew the tips of their fingers through the tendrils absently stroking through the waving nests, eyeing her.

Reina nudged her into the room. And Riff saw her. Mama. Mama from the floods. Mama from The Before. Her skin was mass of scars and her black hair was laced with silver. Mama stepped toward her.

"¿Eres Tú?"

"Si, Mama." The words came to her. They felt unfamiliar in her mouth.

Mama tucked her graying hair behind her ear and reached out to touch her arm, drawing her hand back.

"Good. You are so big, daughter." Mama never hugged much.

The women and the beings watched them with mild interest.

"What is this place?"

"We are in The Under and all this is to be free, before you forget what it means to be free."

"What are you talking about?"

Riff's throat tightened and her vision blurred. She could have screamed at Mama. She could have bitten through her skin and pounded her with her fists for leaving her in the water, for leaving her back there in The Before. Mama squatted in front of her and drew her finger along the stone floor, dragging a long line in the red dust.

"Mira, this is us here." She notched a small tick at the end of the line. "And this is Natsar." Mama pointed her red tipped finger to the beings, their unblinking eyes reflecting pinpoint yellow orbs as they swayed to the chug chug of the machine. She bisected the line in the dust at the beginning. "Now, look." She spat into the dirt and gathered it into a small pile, binding it into rounded mound. Her scars shone and jerked along her arms as the muscles worked underneath. The Natsar ticked in place, shimmering and crooning with excitement. Mama reached into the folds of her smock and brought out a piece of thin plastic from the folds; no bigger than a razor blade and pressed it against her right eyeball.

The room began to vibrate and the other women squatted in unison where they stood, blood running down their thighs. Minute orifices opened on the sandy floor, sucking the blood down. The Natsar's tendrils delving into the holes and pulsing against the sand like ripples from far-thrown stones into low tide. Riff found herself squatting with them digging her fingers into her thighs, the core of her tightening and contracting into painful release. And she was nothing in her mind. Just a cell in this room. A body. A vessel. And then she understood.

Space unfolded before her in velvet blackness. Ripples of light and radiation burned her bones and dissolved her. Her blood boiled and evaporated and she floated for millennia in the nothingness. The universe spoke to her in a voice that rang in her chest like the acid winds on Venus. The universe was a mother.

It said, "child of the sun, are you lost?"

"I don't know."

The Natsar orbited her, their tendrils looping around one another and through her until her body was enmeshed in the blackness of space. Their bodies split and wilted over the shining black eyes, draping wet into spheres that vibrated each in unison to the other.

"I will show you the way," the universe said.

"I'm scared."

And time looped over and Riff stood on the front porch in The Before, her bare feet gritty and black on the bottom from running barefoot over the sidewalks. Her heart pounding. Her pink Minnie Mouse shirt clinging to her chest. Her name was different. The sky was different. Her bones felt heavier.

The day was leaving. What was the word for this? The sun anchoring below the mountains in a purple echo of itself. The neighborhood kids pattering back to their houses where the windows shone yellow. Then-

Riff hugged the chipped-paint post by the front door and bit her thumbnail. The sky station floated above the mountain ridge, a black mark in the pinkening sky.

Her brother opened the front door and threw a marshmallow at her. She ignored it as it rolled into the dirt by the scorched azaleas and glared over her shoulder at him. What was his name? She could not remember after The Event. Another marshmallow arched over her right shoulder. She missed him even though he was there. Even though she couldn't remember his name. His face. He seemed to sense her reticence.

¿Qué pasa? He knelt by her and wrapped his arm around her shoulders. She forgot how tall he was.

Mira, hay un planeta.

¿Dónde?

Ahí . She pointed to a faint glimmer in the fast-fading sky.

The planet grew on the horizon, enveloping the sky into a dark clot of swirling clouds. Her brother faded behind her, the warmth of his hand still lingering on her shoulder. The planet collided with her body and in its immensity absorbed her into its jungle belly. Alien leaves, blacker than tar, dripped with moisture all around her sprawled body on the earth-rich floor. Her open mouth overflowed with thick nectar and two suns glinted through the trees. A word sat with her. Home. Casa.

The suns shifted into Mama's face, her chipped front tooth gleaming in the salmon-pink sky. A Natsar drifted from a black tree trunk, parachuting on it its split skin and sliding its tendrils into her sticky mouth. And she was back in The Below, her mother looming over her, her fingers twined in Natsar hair.

"What did you see? ¿Qué visté?"

"I remembered my brother. I remembered our house."

"You have been taking the Corporation's pleasure drugs. Now, what else?"

"Drugs?"

"Yes. To make you forget and be calm."

"Why?"

Mama sighed and gritted her teeth.

"It doesn't matter why right now. The Natsar can't live very long outside of their tank because of diseases from us. Now tell what you saw."

"I saw two suns and a black forest. What was my brother's name again?"

Mama ignored her.

"Did you see the stars?"

"No, but I saw a planet from Earth."

The women left the Natsar and crowded around. Mama reached out and patted her shoulder. The incisions on her tricep burned at the touch of their cool fingers. Nausea swelled in her throat.

Qué bien. Qué Bien.

XIII. There Are Many Rooms

First, he must eat. His belly growled and darkness was folding in vast rapidity over the house. This strange house. The water receded and the many-eyed thing was just floating tendrils in a tank again. He reached down and touched his testicles, fearing them gone. And while he could not remember love, he could remember something akin to it. A fear of loss.

He stepped across rich rugs drenched deeper colors from the wetness and went toward the enameled door with a golden curved handle. The door swung open at the warmth of his touch. Silence amplified around him. The hallway curved dark and steady before him.

A single robot with a tiny hologram of a naked dancing woman rolled over the floors of the room, ripping up pieces of the carpeting and depositing them in one corner of the room. The butterscotch light from the cold outside glowed from the Anti Rad Never Burns TM windows. Soon the distant sun would be below the horizon. Like the others, the room had no screens.

Rasp's stomach ate away at his throat. He waved at the robot. The robot rolled over to him, dragging scarlet threads of carpeting behind it.

"Can you scan for your master?"

I am at your service.

"Ok, scan for Alona."

You are so strong and brilliant. The voice was husky. Seductive.

"Where is the place with the food?"

I love you.

The naked woman writhed on top of the robot, flickering in and out.

I love you. I love you. I love you. I love anyone. I love the cancer in your lungs. I love the fuzz on your tongue. I love you. I love you.

Rasp tipped over the robot with the side of his foot. The hologram shimmered out, dousing the hallway in the strange filtered Mars light. Rasp's hunger was becoming frantic now. He remembered something soft and salty from The Before. Something folded in a big green leaf and steaming. Something filled with animal protein and dripping with red grease. The word for it was on his tongue. On his chest.

A small lilt of laughter echoed from the room furthest down the corridor.

"Alona?"

Water sucked at the soles of his feet from the saturated carpets as he picked his way down the hallway toward the giggle.   A sign above the door had pictures of animals from The Before in a line. Some with Xs drawn through them in a stolid black print. Rasp leaned his shoulder against the door frame and waved his hand in front of the sensor. The door slid open and a small hand darted between the panels to grab his jumpsuit. Rasp lurched back, fingers worming into his front pockets, grabbing, pulling him into the room. Hands poured through the space in the panel, tearing at the cloth of his out-turned pockets, twining through his fingers drawing him inside the room on his knees. The hydraulics hissed behind him as the door closed like water over a too-deep dive into cold water.

Once inside the room, the hands receded, sliding out of his pockets, untangling from his hands.

He was afraid now in this silent place, where women jutted through the darkness and touched him, as real as vaccinations, as real as any man.

The screens had bathed him in light and sound. The men sometimes laughed at his jokes on the rigs. Sometimes, the older men nearing their permanent retirement, would remind him about animals. Animals he couldn't remember anymore. They wanted his jokes to feel real, after all, what is a chicken anyway and why is it crossing the road? Were the roads soft in the summer heat? Shimmering, crumbling infrastructure clinging to soccer cleats, fracturing like a too-dry cake?

***

Alona stood at the head of a long table, piling glistening proteins and strange fruits onto her plate. Rasp sat on his hands on a bench against the wall. His chest still ached from the heavy dose of sedatives Alona had dripped into a cup of cold, clear water. Pai had gone back into the skins to rest, she told him, smoothing back his hair with her three fingers. You pleased him very much.

"You performed very well, Rasp."

Rasp eyed her plate of food, saliva pooling in his mouth.

"We are going to use you after all. Do you want to know what for?" She set the plate before him, wiping the edges with a white napkin.

"Sure I do." He reached for a hunk of warm jellied protein. Alona nodded her assent and he popped the fist-sized chunk into his mouth. It gushed warm velvety fat across his tongue.

"We are funding a mission to the moon of Enceladus. Mars is becoming crowded these days, you know with Earth being in its current state."

"What's wrong with Earth?" Rasp asked.

He never paid any attention to The Corporation's news feed. It scrolled over every surface for hours upon hours. Men with shiny white teeth, plump from injections of Shine into their lips, banged surfaces with their fists and flashed pictures of dead children clinging to one another on vast islands of plastic rainbow confetti. This is what unemployment looks like.

Alona pulled at a thread on the tablecloth, picking it into a tiny loop.

"Earth has been declared Non-Viable by the Corporation."

"Oh ok. What does that mean?"

"It means that there are no more resources for life there. They can't even sell sun time now since that last incident with the salt miners."

Rasp had no idea what she was talking about, but nodded with mock understanding, picking up a Frooty Tooty Mars Pop TM. They were very expensive in the commissary. A whole month's work of exterior asteroid work bought one packet of them. He ignored the teal colored fruits shaped like bundles of tear drops, sparkling with what might have been real sugar. His vision blurred again from the sedative.

"Oh yeah. So you want me to get on a Star Liner and go to Enceladus? Because those things from the tank before?" He searched for a clearer definition of things. Dog is to cat as razor is to _____.

"The Natsar, the things from the tank, talk to you," she said. "And there are no Star Liners to Enceladus."

"Oh." There was an emotion teasing at the surface on his mind, one that could get you retired. The emotion of clenched teeth and torn knuckles. He only had thirteen more demerits before hard mine time and twenty-five more until early retirement. He pushed the emotion back under the surface and dipped his fingers into the melted pool of protein on his plate. He thought of jokes. Knock knock. Who's there?

"Of course, this job will pay. You may even be able to pay off your commissary account," she said.

"How long will I stay there?"

"Well, it is a colonization expedition, so hopefully forever." She leaned across the table.

"How come you don't send Androids? Like with Mars?"

"Androids can't breed. And besides, we need someone who can communicate with the Natsar already there."

"But, I have a contract with the corporation."

"We own part of the corporation. Rasp, you will do this for us. We have already written in a clause to your contract."

Alona unfolded a torso-sized tablet and pressed at the folds on the screen until the heat from her hands melded the wrinkles into the table. She tapped at the screen several times, her brow furrowed. She drew her fingers from either corner until the screen turned to face him. A single one-inch by one-inch box blinked yellow.

"We just need your initial here."

Rasp pressed his right thumb into the box. He always signed with his right thumb. He had never not signed something.

***

Holy Book TM Chapter 3 Verses 12-20

12 The people did heed His words, for the poor did eat the poor and the rich did eat things that swam in the sea and flew in the air and walked on the earth.

13 And lo, his return was marked by the darkening, for he did arrive draped in Armani and shod in Versace as the prophecy foretold and he called himself Mechoben.

14 The crowd waved white lights above Him, collecting him for generations to come. And they did implant him in their own lives to live on forever.

15 And though there were many, he touched the multitudes with his fingertips and promised them air, water, and flight from this planet. And he spake saying "the deserving will have a place in my kingdom, for my father rewards toil."

16 But from the crowd, a small child emerged carrying a single soy protein shake and Mechoben took it and motioned for the three greatest men to come forward and so it was.

17 Mechoben put the protein shake on the ground and said, "Let the greatest among us have it."

18 The largest of the men came for the shake and Mechoben retrieved his iPhone XXIX and confirmed a payment to the largest man and asked, "Is 400 units enough for this?"

19 And the largest man walked back into the crowd and the rest of the crowd did wish for his blessing and Mechoben sent them all 400 units and supped from the shake.

20 He put the empty shake on the ground and said, "He who has the most, holds the most," and left the people for a small time.

XIV. She's Long Gone

Riff dreamed about sex with people she didn't know. Strangers with gripping fingers and reddish pinchmarks blooming pink after white. Warm and close, but never quite there. Never to full throb and burst.

She dreamed about a beast with plasticine curls that walked on all fours with eyes the size of human mouths. It ducked its great head that rattled soft like green Easter grass and she climbed on its back, stepping on its great obsidian tusks and clinging to the prickly hair. It shimmered from purple to black under a two-sunned sky and took her to an icy beach. Snow floated around her and clung to beast's mane in large flakes. A woman stood in the steaming slush naked, and Riff felt that familiar heat.

She slid from the beast's back and went to her, the water squeezing her calves with cold. The woman's face was an amalgam of Gram and her own, irises dappled with dark green, like tree shade over moss.

She flicked around in her own dream space until she was by the woman's side, clinging to her and finding her mouth with her thumb. Her thumb changed into one of those birds. Yes. That was what they were called. Big and black and pulling strings of flesh off the bones of friend animals. Animals that lived in their yards. In their houses.

Then it was just a feeling. The feeling of the boat moving so slightly under your feet and the mercury slippery water crumpling around you like tinfoil until the bile rises hot and bitter in your throat and your mouth fills with saltwater. Sea sickness. See sickness? El mar. El mareo. So strange that the sea is masculine. Was masculine.

***

Al patted at her incisions with a scar fading cream before breakfast. Mama had handed her a drink of cold water and told her to find The Wizard and be quick about it before ushering her out of the hidden room with an odd softness behind her eyes.

She-Al was in rare form that morning, the stress response from last night had darkened her neck with streaks of orange and her breathing was high and rapid. Each incision beaded clear plasma that thinned the cream as Al spackled it on her arms.

The two of them said nothing until an escort robot zipped in, flashing a room number on its shiny square face.

"That's us," Al said.

Riff, dozy from the Anti Ouch Pain Mask TM that rested on the bridge of her nose, stood up too quickly. Revulsion rose in the back of her throat and her teeth chattered.

"Where are we going?"

She-Al shushed her, her eyes wide and proud.

"Don't worry."

The escort robot ushered them deeper and deeper into the center of the cluster until they reached a coffin-sized opaque box in the center of four intersecting hallways. Al slipped her hand behind Riff's neck and pulled her hair away from her neck, exposing the skin to the cool air. She leaned in and whispered something. Riff's ears hummed with sedative. The front of the black box hissed open. A strip of neon blue lights around the perimeter of the box snapped on, haloing the floor beneath in a pool of cold light.

The escort robot knocked into Riff's heels, nudging her toward this blank yawn. She paused again. Feeling warmth coming from the box. Al's teeth looked sharper in this light, almost lavender. Al looked at the floor, bending the toe of her soft boot under and over, curving the sole against the shiny floor. Her color had risen to a high red-orange and she picked at her cuticles, tearing tiny bits of skin. She could get timefined for property damage. Another thirty seconds off her already brief lifespan. Accounted for behind screens, ticked away at, proper retirement syringes loaded and ready. This one's got your name on it.

The screens around the room flashed images of an ocean, except the ocean was blue and people swam in it. No nadamos en el mar. Dreams in a dead language.

The escort robot whirred and rammed into her calves again. She stepped into the box onto a slick surface. Her bare feet sticking to the cold floor, the door closed behind her trapping her in this dark mirror chamber.

Light filtered through the cracks in the box, striping her knees and breasts in long lines of white. Her image reflected itself into infinity. Same eyes. Same teeth. A copy of a copy. The screens flashed on with an image of The New Christ, Mechoben, surrounding her on all four corners, his hands outstretched and filled with tubes of lipstick and stacks of physical commissary credits and deep green candies laced with dope. An automated voice filled the chamber.

Mechoben loves you and wants you to be happy. Please state your name and identification number, my child.

"RF 8934098"

Thank you. Please state your current occupation. Praise him for your employment."

"Actress."

Breast to hip ratio?

".75"

Please choose an image that represents your feelings towards your place of employment.

An array of images flipped into the screen like a card trick. Moving images of spaceships, knives, bowls of water, dancing women in skintight jumpsuits, test tubes, dog heads, save icons, frothy yellow drink, whippet canisters, donuts, and mouth. The shapes surrounded her in endless stimulation. She chose an extension cord and a laughing dog head. A checkmark bounded across the screen.

Great job, RF!

The screens in the room flashed white and a tube dropped from the ceiling with a face mask attached to the bag. An image of a woman putting the mask over her face appeared. The image stared directly into the east and pulled the mask over her face, her blue cartoon eyes unblinking. A green checkmark appeared over the image. The image looped and the woman pulled the mask over her face again. Riff picked up the mask spinning from the tubing above and slipped it over her head, pressing the mask over her nose. Panic tugged at her chest and throat. The mask suctioned to her face with a hiss from above.

The sweetish smell of sedative gas flooded into her nostrils. A dark shape slid down the tube toward the half-inflated bag attached to the mask, scrabbling as it hit the unsteady plastic. Riff's eyes drifted blurring the changing screens into distorted stretches of color and sound. The black shape in the bag skittered over the slack plastic toward her mouth and nose. It extended a single needle-thin tentacle toward her right nostril, just caressing her septum. Her lungs ballooned against the sedative. Fear tore at her.

Riff reached up to break the seal of the mask, tugging at the tubes. The images around her changed to red Xes over images of the same dead-eyed woman ripping the mask off, filling her hands with blood, illustrated eyes huge. Palms cupped with scarlet.

The black shape in the plastic tumbled back toward the end of the bag. Riff slowed her breathing and focused on the creature slapping its tiny tentacles against the plastic. It reared up waving its tentacles and said, "I know you."

Riff tried again to pull at the mask and managed to slide her pinky finger under the seal breaking it. She waited for the blood, to feel the warm wetness pouring over her throat. The mask dangled from the tube in the ceiling and the creature slipped from the open end. An alarm sounded in the chamber, shrill and sickening.

The creature no bigger than a fetal mouse dragged itself across the floor toward her.

I know you. I know you. I know you. I know you.

Riff rammed her shoulder against the sliding panel of the door.

Sedative gas hissed into the chamber and heaviness pull at her limbs. Her heart beat thickly at the base of her throat. She slumped against the wall watching the creature inch toward her.

I know you. I know you. I know you.

Riff felt her own weight give into nothingness as a thin tentacle slipped over her bare knee. The creature's eyes glowed orange, reflecting shining disks of opaque light. It caught the fabric of her tunic and crawled toward her face. It hummed high and light as it reached her jaw. Her hands were too heavy to lift and swat, her eyes too dry to keep open. The creature hooked its fingerlings into her cheek and whipped a tentacle toward her right nostril, clinging to the mucosa inside.

The room wavered and suited androids slid through the door and lifted her from the floor. Al picked her up and brushed away the thin stream of blood on her cheek. Her pulse throbbed in her temples. The voice of the creature tipped at the edge of her consciousness. I know you.

XV. Brave New Worlds

Alona sat with her legs tucked underneath her, an ElectroDlight nicotine delivery system flashing purple and green as it gripped the skin on the palms of her three-fingered hands. She flicked her wrists dismissively at the female android who was draping Rasp in silver fabric. Rasp had an erection and a stomachache. The sedatives and rich foods weighed on him and the android's soft hands and large eyes replayed in his mind over and over, like in the pornographic art films. The android patted him on the chest and stepped back.

"That's the Anti-Radiation fabric in Sad Story Gray?"

"Yes." The Android reached over and flipped the fabric over Rasp's cloaked erection. The two women giggled.

"You know I've never seen one in real life? " Alona said. "Never had a male lover. The last ones approved were years before my time."

"Me neither." They looked at one another. That look. The men in the theater look. Hungry.

Rasp was suddenly afraid.

"Father would be furious. He's supposed to be unspoiled," Alona said.

"We could just look at it."

"Wait. Wait. We should consult the morality guide."

Alona reached under her chair and grabbed a tablet. She tapped the surface and stretched the membrane larger so the android could peer over her shoulder and see.

"Oh no. Mechoben says here 'Females shall not look upon man's nakedness, for he is dedicated to his holy purpose. The purpose of work and the purpose of getting.'"

"What does it say about man looking upon our nakedness?" The android asked. Alona ignored the question.

"Well, you are technically not female, so father couldn't be mad about you looking."

"I am female."

They burst into laughter, grabbing at each other's arms. Rasp stood there in front of them, his body stiff.

"Let's look at the concordance about man looking at us naked."

The women scrolled to the back of the Holy Book TM flicking their fingers across the screen. The android stacked her chin on Alona's shoulder and draped her arms over her shoulders as she gazed into the screen.

"You want to hear a joke?" Rasp piped up.

"What's a joke?" The android slid her silver gaze over him.

"It's like a story, but funny."

"Oh ok. Yes. Tell us a joke," The android said.

"My girlfriend said, 'You act like a detective too much. I want to split up.' "

"'Good idea,' I replied. "We can cover more ground that way."

The women creased their brows in unison.

"What's a girlfriend?"

"What's a detective?"

Rasp reached back to The Before.

"Back on Earth, men and women lived in the same place and even worked together, I think, and so if a man and a woman were in the same house they were boyfriend and girlfriend."

"Like Pai and me?" Alona asked.

Rasp noticed that the Martian woman's intonations changed often. Sometimes she flitted and giggled. Sometimes she crouched over screens reading languages he had never seen before, her voice deep and resonant as brass.

"Yes." Rasp nodded.

The women laughed and Rasp was pleased that his joke worked. Sometimes they worked in the Shine Factory or the mine. Sometimes they didn't and the other men slapped the back of his head in the cameras' blind spots.

The door to the room was open to a dark hallway and Rasp caught a flashing reflection that floated from one side of the door to the other from the corner of his eye. The white orb floated about three feet from the floor in the hallway and the lights flashed away into the darkness. The women stopped laughing and looked over their shoulders. Their lips tightened and the android pulled a SilverStretch 55 blanket over Alona's shoulders.

"We should get him prepped for Pai," Alona said, looking over her shoulder again. Her nicotine delivery system flashed red over the tips of her fingers. She walked over to a thin door in the wall and waved her hand over a blinking purple light on the right. The door slid halfway into the wall. Alona waved her three-fingered hand over the light again. The door didn't move. She sighed and pressed her shoulder against the door, the android looking on as the door gave a few inches. A small humanoid crouched in the corner of the closet, gripping the legs of a vintage space suit. Alona laughed and gestured for Rasp and the android to come look more closely.

"Look at him. He's just a baby."

The humanoid imitated her smile, its teeth overlapping one over the other. It had a fine down covering its spindly limbs and bloated belly.

"What is that?" Disgust rose at the base of Rasp's throat.

"Oh him? He's one of my brothers, I think."

Alona pulled the suit away from the creature's grasp and pushed the door shut behind her.

"But, wait," Rasp said.

"For what? You need to be decontaminated and put on this suit before Pai gets here."

"But what about that person?" He pointed to the door.

"Oh. They don't live very long anyway."

Alona draped the suit over his shoulder and patted his cheek. Rasp looked at the closet door as the women laced fingers with him and guided him away from the dark.

***

Document 23 out of 47 of the Prime Execution of Mining Operations: Personal Logs

I remember Mechoben from the beginning, when he came to us for the first time and he was just so beautiful in his full plate Armani Kevlar. It shone. He shone before us and touched those among us who had nothing at all. He showed us that death is just a passing phase. This was before retirement when we all worked until our purpose was exhausted and then crumpled into uselessness. Like He says, "God is in the screen and we are God."

Now, this was in The Before when we wrote everything down on our phones. We had these devices where you could still hide things from everyone. I can't believe how unprincipled we were. And people kept each other and animals in small places. You don't remember animals do you? The devices were meant to bring us together, to keep us organized, to have everything we loved in one place, and we did. And we chose so much that we ended up alone again.

After a long time of this, he flowed to us. This was after the riots in New Orleans when the water finally washed away that crumbling quarter. Yeah, they said the levees would hold. They said the pumps would work. They always said that. But it was another hurricane and another, and we tried to hold our breaths, but no one came for us this time. A long time ago, before we were born, there was a hurricane where the city was completely underwater. Up to the tops of buildings. Up to the sky in brown water. Washed it away. Did you know that? I digress.

Mechoben found us in a dirty bar, eating generator-fried protein balls. It had been six months since we had seen anyone from outside the city and he came carrying low interest rates and glistening screens. He brought us things. Our devices hadn't worked for some time and we missed things. He stepped down from his bright-white boat into the bar with us and picked up Ms. Ruby, with her ashen skin and rotting teeth and wrapped a stole around her shoulders. It was real fur. Cat fur, I think. White and soft. He could look right through you. I think she cried right then.

The bartender, if you could still call him that, we didn't have any money and the only booze left was some home distilled stuff made from bags of sugar and corn syrup and palm sap, poured a bit of the village gin into a Dixie cup that had been washed so many times it was pink. Mechoben picked it up and poured it into a silver chalice, which he sipped from. He kissed the women. Oh yes. In those days men and women stayed together in the same place. I told you that, didn't I?

He had eyes so blue and hair so fine and blond, just like he looked on the screens. He touched my shoulder and handed me the most beautiful white shirt and a watch that scrolled inspirational quotes. He asked me if I had ever been to space. I told him that was for rich people, but not like that. I was so worried about offending him. His hands were soft and unbroken, his nails trimmed and polished.

Not anymore. Not with my new program. Everyone can go now and you'll have a job perfect for you, based on your 31 most attractive attributes.

He reached into his Gucci backpack and handed us all hard tablets with employment contracts drawn up and ready for our finger signature. Real work in space. Our fathers and their fathers had worked on rigs and in restaurants, all of that long gone when the floods came again and again, orange plastic Popeye's cups floating by as we paddled our pirogues from one place to the other looking for booze. My father once told me that we were born to work. The bible said so. Work made us men. We thought space was for the rich. I wish we had left it that way.

***

Pai guided a suited Rasp across the windswept landing pad and gestured at a small space craft shaped like a smooth thigh. Blips of painful blue light shot across Rasp's right eyeball. The wind pressed against their progress, but Pai trudged on, dragging on Rasp's suit to hurry him along. The sun stood far and cold against the horizon. Rasp wondered if he had ever been not sedated. A painted-over outline of a sprawling woman peeked through the chipping paint on the side of the craft. His heart beat in a slow rhythm as a ramp slid from the side of the space craft.

He and Pai struggled up the steep angle of the ramp until they reached the silent interior of the ship. All of the seating and control panels were draped in white opaque plasticine sheeting. Malfunctioning advertisements repeated themselves on the sheeting, jerking images of naked women and white teeth and flat screens stumbling over the folds. Pai's boots left long, narrow imprints in the fine layer of Martian dust on the slick gray floor.

Pai's voice came into Rasp's ear through the EasySpeak 4000. A smiley face made of dots flickered on the glass of his helmet.

Do you see the smile? His voice mechanized by his filtration helmet.

I see it.

Good.

Pai pulled back the sheeting and pressed a glass screen with his long middle finger. It blinked gray and then white, flooding the control room with light. Big squares with moving images of a cartoon creature with a long black and white tail filled the vacant screens, inserting its fingers into five round holes and then pressing its forehead against a curved strip above. The looping image filled the inside of Rasp's helmet. Insert digits now. Insert digits now. Insert digits now.

Put your fingers in the slots like the picture.

The holes blinked pinkish on the control panel. Something itched in his fingertips, a small ridge rippled under the skin of his nail bed, pressing the nails up like translucent lids.

Go on, then.

His hands were electric, tingling and tensing toward the blinking finger docks. Pai watched his ticking fingers as he slipped them in. Cold seized him. A chart unfolded over his helmet with the same cartoon creature as before waving its huge black and white tail at a white-veined moon. The pictures deepened and a yellow dashed line ticked its way across his helmet screen, linking cartoon Mars with cartoon Enceladus. Round and pure white.

Are you sure you want to travel 8 AUs from MARS to ENCELADUS? Blinking in red.

Rasp pressed the thumbs up button with his crawling pointer finger and looked around. Pai was waving to him from behind the closing bay door.

XVI. Didn't Leave Nobody

Riff scrolled through her own vids on the screen in the wall. Al lifted her hair off her neck from behind and dusted her shoulders with microparticles of gold dust harvested from 16 Psyche. So pure and golden. A small naked Venus. Al pressed the asteroid-harvested diamonds to the tops of Riff's cheeks, swiping away the excess skin glue with an acrylic pad. Riff was assigned the lead in a new pornographic art film Minority Rape-ort for her debut. Al wetted the powdered blood rouge with a dollop of white spit and swirled it in her palm before rubbing circles into Riff's cheekbones, chatting about this director and how it was an honor and a blessing and such a good sign.

One of the specialty-bred Androids came in to check the lighting, his yellow eyes slashed through with slitted irises. The corporation spliced snake DNA into six percent of the Androids' eyeballs in the tube in an attempt to create an Android that could see the flumes from planetary scans, but the spectrum was too broad. The corporation discovered a new use for them when in their 6-month childhood they created forests of light and vibration with the Easy Clean Up Lite Blox TM. Perfect light vision for perfect entertainment.

Tix sales at the commissary went up eighteen percent when they used the Android light designers rather than the Compu lights. And androids were cheaper. Voice log surveys indicated the viewers were reminded of words like "home, soft, hold, and resting" rather than "hard, flappy, and sad," when viewing the pornographic art films. Concession sales went up. Commissary accounts were drained. Asteroid miners broke their bones for a little more.

Progress is God. God is Progress flashed on Riff's monitoring bracelet. Show time.

"Do good mija," Mama said the night before. "Get the units posted. Find El Mago."

***

When Riff was very small, before the evacs and the cold Pacific Ocean pulling at her heels, she went to a place called "school." Her mother wearing slippers over her pantyhose, the white light reflecting rectangles in her brown eyes from the personal data device. Her fine blue suit crinkling as she tossed a shiny packet of breakfast powder to Riff. Before the men in boats. Before the Second Coming of Mechoben.

Her school was a great shining white building near a structure that she couldn't remember anymore, only that it was orange and crossed the water a long time before. Someone told her that it once connected an island made completely of trash.

She had a teacher named Mrs. Martinez who wore floral dresses that gapped at her breast, showing her beige bra and freckled chest. They were supposed to write a story about a hot air balloon once and Riff got an F. Mrs. Martinez said "this isn't a story about a hot air balloon. It barely has anything about a hot air balloon. This is about a dragon and dragons don't exist." She cried.

Her brother met her at the bus stop that day and told her that Ms. Martinez was evidence that dragons existed and held open his shiny bag of Hot Cheetos for her. Her lips burned as they walked home, licking the red dust from their fingers.

That was the year that The Corporation introduced The Chip: Everything in One Place Implant. Never worry again! Your child will never be abducted! You will never lose a spreadsheet! Keep track of all your followers! Never get lost again!

Mama took her to a special doctor listed on the registry distributed by The Corporation. The bright room was covered in screens flipping through images of smiling children hugging one another in red t-shirts. Red and yellow, black and white they are precious in OUR sight, the images said. The windows covered by gray blinds. The paper on the exam table slid under her as the doctor rolled his stool up to face her.

"This won't hurt even a little bit."

He took out a roll of golden stickers and lifted her arm by the elbow so that the soft underside of her arm faced him. Mama stared at her device, her thumb rolling past images. The doctor's purple gloves creased and whispered as he wiped the inside of her elbow with an antiseptic wipe and waved his hand over it to dry. He peeled off one of the stickers and showed her the dissolvable backing that would absorb the tracker into her bloodstream. He pressed it to her arm and held a white plastic gun with an orange tip over the center of the golden dot. It turned into a jelly and soaked into her arm.

"That's that." He patted her knee.

The chips sent out a signal that allowed the corporation to truly know them. It measured chemicals in their blood and sent them to special-approved ramen shops when it detected ghrelin, where the menus featured identical pictures of cartoon cats and bubble fonts. The tiny eye saw when their oxytocin was low and alerted their friends. HUG ALERT. It smelled the Adrenocorticotropic hormones and played a sample of a calm song flashing signs across their devices for discount codes and software platforms to market their bodies and brains and beings.

It was only natural to repurpose all of the things and desires into one. It only made sense to cater to the most important person, the customer. The birth of the commissary. The birth of a convenient place to elevate or suppress, to give meaning to them in this hollow place.

One day after school, Mama snatched Riff by the back of her jacket as she walked in the door and put her hand over her mouth. Her brother had stayed at school for a reason. Perhaps he played an instrument or was in an organization. She could smell the sweetness of her jasmine lotion, selected by her personal corporation A.I. to make her smell feminine, but powerful. Riff struggled against her mother's grip, but Mama only tightened her fingers over her mouth and whispered hot into her hair.

"Be very quiet. They are listening."

Riff nodded up at her mother. Looking for signs. Mama did not like to be this close to anyone.

"Escuchame, hay un problema con el implante en el brazo. Entiendas?"

The memory wavered here. She did understand. Sometimes she dreamed in this language about great creatures with red feathered wings that only had one sharp tooth.

"Si Mama."

"Te acuerdas de tu padre?"

"No Mama."

"Que bien. Era malvado."

Mama released her and pushed her against the wall. Jackets and umbrellas swung over her head as she thumped backwards. Other mothers gave their kids Cracker Snips All Natural TM. Brand name to show their love.

***

Holy Book TM Chapter 13 Verses 12–18

12 There was a great prophet in those times who did streamline the production and consumption timeline, so that he was called beloved by the father

13 When the people came to him and asked, "how is it that the father has blessed you so?" He retrieved his 3D printer and did bestow upon them a firearm undetectable by the enemy

14 The people looked on and still doubted. They grumbled "why has the father not blessed me with a 3D printer?"

15 Overhearing them, the prophet said, "All of this I earned with the sweat of my brow and the toil of my hands." The people looked out onto the fields of production and saw the second-borns working alongside the metal-sons.

16 "But prophet, the second-borns and the metal sons are the true laborers here!" And the prophet knelt and traced his finger over the scroll of light. The metal-sons ceased their labor and the second-borns rushed to them, lifting their jointed arms and wailing "Oh father father, why hath you ceased your overlook? Why hath you left us here?"

17 The prophet swiped once again and the metal-sons came back to life and the people marveled at him.

18 And the prophet said unto them "The swipe of my little finger produces more than all of your arms and legs at once. And should I not be rewarded by the father and the market? Go in peace."

***

Fern glided over to Riff and tilted her head to peek up her nostril as the crew set up for Riff's first scene. She squinted and sighed, though Riff could taste blood at the back of her throat as something shifted there. Her familiar. An overwhelming feeling of warmth rose as Fern scratched her scalp lightly, her bare breasts grazing the back of Riff's arm.

"First scene, worst scene. As they say," said Fern smoothing her thumbs under Riff's eyes. "We need to get some Frosty Baby Eye Cream TM on you, though. You are looking a bit puffy."

"How will I know what to do?"

"The director will tell you, sweet one."

"Where are you from, Fern?"

Fern stopped playing with Riff's hair and leaned forward to whisper in her ear.

They are monitoring us. I am from a place that used to have a name, but now it's just water. I remember when where we came from was called the United States. Before the split.

Fern leaned back and laughed high and fine. Her glossy eyes opened too wide, only the slightest crease of a laugh line showing above the tiny incision marks. Her grip tight on Riff's wrist.

"I'm from Mars now, my darling, and so are you. Aren't you glad you are too pretty for manufacturing or mining? Mechoben told us that it's a sin to waste your potential." Fern picked up a passing android bred and engineered to look like a child and swung her onto her hip. "Just like those things back on earth. Friend animals that could be very small or very big, but they were the same thing. They lived in houses before The Event sometimes. Oh you know what I'm talking about. Dogs! Mecho on a leash, how could I forget that? We eat them now. "

"I don't really remember dogs either," Riff said.

Riff noticed that Fern was picking out hairs from the base of the miniature android's scalp. Her flawless skin flushed at her high collarbones.

The director kept pulling the lever to spin the circular stage, pacing around it, peering into the camera.

Fern reached into a bowl on a nearby table filled with Shine Gummiez TM and drew out a fistful, still holding the mini-android on her hip. Its little legs dangled like a baby doll's. She fed the transparent candies one by one to the mini-android. The creature stared at Riff while it chewed, clutching to Fern's scarred upper arm.

"What's her name?" Riff reached out to touch the fine engineered curls.

"Whose name?"

"The baby-android."

"There's no such thing as baby androids. Is there such a thing as babies anymore?"

Riff couldn't remember ever seeing a baby, though Gram from the Girl Factory had told her that they grew babies like hydroponics and only the worthy and the blessed grew babies in their bodies. It was very chic. Very expensive. You had to be a model, and not a pornographic one, to even get the corporation handbook for reproduction.

"I think there are. Somewhere. How else would we fill the girl factories?"

The director approached Fern and put his hand on her lower back. She put down the mini-android and it vanished into the darkness behind the heavy curtain behind a group of music robots. The director gestured at them, grinning and rubbing Fern's back, his eyes darting up at the cameras.

"They are expensive, but so is our product. This run won't even be screened in the mines. Private consumption only." He winked at Riff. "Only the finest and the youngest."

He nodded toward the stage and Fern buttoned her breasts into the SlingShot Breast Compactor TM and turned the dials at the tops of her shoulders, ruching her soft flesh into four tight mounds with her trim pink nipples pointing toward the ceiling and walked away.

"Let's give them a real show, sweet Riff," she said over her shoulder.

Al, swaddled in a Silkie Short Short Jumper TM, barreled over once the Androids had Fern cornered across the room, squirting her with a thick, opaque blue liquid while she feigned drowning. Al was in they form today, with feminine eyes and large masculine hands. Professional. Al proceeded to glue tiny silver tips to the ends of Riff's nails that flashed and glinted under the lights.

"Al how do you feel about the mini-androids?"

"Why do you ask?"

"Why do we have them?"

"What do you mean?" Al rubbed Shine into her skin and massaged it in, distracted by the countdown timer on the wall.

"I mean, how do they serve the corporation?"

"Um, they are cute and people will buy cute things."

"Did someone buy you?"

"Listen, you are going to be on stage in under one minute. Can we talk about this later?"

The lights flashed and Al dashed two streaks of bronzer under Riff's blood-rouged cheekbones.

"That's our cue," Al said and nudged Riff toward the stage under the blazing white lights.

The mini-android leaned against a metal box on the center of the platform, watching as the Rosie's Cleaner Bots TM scrubbed the brownish android blood from the floor. Fern wiped the bottoms of her Louboutin Pumps. A fine spray tracked up her right leg.

 The mini-android beckoned her up on stage. The uncanny child replica was dressed in a tearaway Factory-Girl uniform. Yellow for happiness. Red for productivity. A Factory-Girl is always on time with a smile. The director pointed toward the metal box.

"Pick two or three romance assistance devices from in there. You are going to love this." The director said to Riff, turning back toward his android production assistant. "It makes the girls so much more invested in the scene." The android nodded, dabbing at a bit of sweat on his upper lip.

The box had a baton, an Electro-discharge Crowd Control Poker TM, a plastic mask with real human teeth, a braided piece of dog leather, A Flip Flap Fun Cutter with REAL STEEL JAWS, a ball gag, a branding iron shaped like a smiling mouth, and a package of industrial lye with a patented pouring spout.

Me duele más a mí que a ti.

The mini-android expanded her eyes, using some distant gene to make the pupils fill the iris. She practiced a human child cry, first sucking in her breath in small gasps, her chest hitching. Tears poured down her face. Her neck and cheeks mottled pink. The director focused the camera on her.

"That's so good, Hundy! Can you bring your knees in more? Bring her a prop! Something she can suck on. That's perfect. Has the new girl picked out a prop yet?"

Riff stared into the box. Her very own show. She would never have to scrub components or sleep on a rack again. The commissary was hers after this. Any filter she wanted for the vids. Real meat. Al could stay with her. Mechoben demanded her obedience. She dipped her hand into the box and pulled out the first thing she touched: the ball gag.

"That's even better than that baby sucker thing. Look she has a knack for it. Ok now pick something else so we can get rolling. This ain't cheap, little freshie."

Al stood on the fringes of the set nodding at her. She reached in again and touched something the size of a button at the bottom of the box. She closed her hand around it and pulled it out. It was a small brass cylinder capped on both ends with red rubber. Not knowing exactly why, she put it behind her ear and reached back into the box and retrieved the braided dog leather, wrapping it around her palm.

"Very hot. I like it." The director adjusted the lens of the camera. "Can we get some Shine for her lips please? Let's make some magic happen." Riff could smell his cologne.

The mini-android lay down on a bed set up in the middle of the stage with white pillows as billowy as marshmallow. The golden bed frame had replicas of all the planets holding the joints together. A dog fur rug sprawled on the floor beneath. Her tiny body striped with purplish scars from the waist up.

"Ok," the director turned back to his assistant and whispered something, "Raff, I'm going to need you to take that dog belt and we're going to make it like poetry ok? Do you know what poetry is?"

She shook her head.

"Well, don't worry about that. You just do what we tell you and remember that it looks real if it is real, so don't be afraid to really get in there and hit the mini there with that leather strap, ok?"

The floor was cold under her feet when the first lash connected with the mini's skin with a snap. She shrieked and turned her head on the pillow so that she faced the camera. Fern leaned on Al and nodded. Her green eyes distant. Her pearly nails digging into her own skin.

"Ok Raff…That's her name, right?... really get in there. They don't feel pain like we do. Remember that."

Riff leaned back and slung the strap against the top of the mini's scalp. Bluish blood oozed from her scalp line into her eyes. She felt her jaw clenching. Her heart drumming against her breastbone. Her shoulder burning. He brain was alight with the power of the stroke. She raised back again aiming for the back of the pale bare thigh. The strap split the skin cutting through to the pale pink dermis. Blood gushed and then beaded. A thin tendril slid from her nostril and stroked the tip of her nose.

"Oh yeah! We got a natural performer here."

The mini turned back to face Riff. Tears rolled from her immense eyes. There was a thickness in her throat. It was the same feeling she had in the girl factory when she told the monitors that Gram took non-commissary food back to the racks. When Gram came back from Pearson's ReDo School TM, she was missing two teeth.

"Don't stop, Raff. The more the mini cries, the more money goes in your commissary."

The strap dangled at her side. She could see the mini's ribs through her back.

"Cut. Just cut for a minute."

The director came over and knelt in front of her. She had never been so close to a bio male before. he had so much shine injected into his lips the skin at the edges melded one swollen expression. His long orange braid brushed the floor behind him as he squatted on his heels.

"Please. Please do this. I need you to do this. My retirement age is coming up, ok? If I can pull this off, I can leave Mars. They don't feel pain like we do, ok?"

"I can't."

"Mechoben demands sacrifice so that the shareholders may live."

"Please don't make me." Her own tears. Undeserved tears.

He curled his hand over hers onto the strap. The mini sobbed as her skin started to knit back behind them. He stood up, his knees popping. He still held her fist and squeezed. The pressure on her knuckles under his polished nails.

"Go get the ball gag and stop crying. You will ruin your makeup."

She wiped her eyes with the back of her hand and touched the scroll behind her ear she found earlier. Violence loped through her again. Images of the director crushed under her heel surged into her mind. His dyed purple eyes filling with red, red blood. Al shook their head at her. Smelling her fury.

Riff smiled at the director. All teeth.

"There's a good girl. The corporation rewards good, sexy girls like you." He nodded at her from behind the monitors.

She went to the box and fetched the ball gag. As she pulled the straps around the mini's head she whispered to her about Earth's moon. Silver and pitted and fecund and immense and feminine. The mini stayed silent. If wishes were Shine, we'd all be fat.

***

Document 20 out of 47 of the Prime Execution of Mining Operations: Personal Logs

My mother told me that if I didn't read or write that I was spitting in the faces of my ancestors who died just for a chance to hold a pencil. You probably won't know what pencils are. Everything for you was on screens. You could type or scroll better than your old man, I'm sure.

They have separated me from your mother. It was like I was back in Iraq again, just seeing her and you through a tiny screen, you falling forward and looking into the screen, little mouth open in wonder, pudgy hands opening and closing at the sound of my voice. Maybe it was just the shiny eye of the camera. Sometimes after you waved bye bye to me snuffling like tired babies do and the screen went black, I reported to fire watch in that big, strange darkness and watched the sand puff in tiny geysers as bullets from miles away hit the ground just a few yards away. Do you remember hot sauce? We put it in our eyes to stay awake. Can you believe we were sleepy with bullets coming at us?

This time it's not the Marine Corps owning my body and my mind and that's what made it so appealing. Because they lied to us. I mean the military did. When I walked into that recruiting office, it was because our house on Gravier was gone from the first floods. Before The Quarter went. Before the tops of the great oaks in City Park peeked through all that brown water, before turning brown themselves and withering and sinking. This was before I met your mother.

The recruiter saw that I could read and write really well. Your grandmother made sure of that. I read Kindred when I was just six years old. I'm not sure if the corporation buried this book under a mountain of flashing vids, but if I can find a copy of it, I'll send it to your tablet. They put me in special class because I could read like that, but then they sent us all back to our regular classrooms. Do they still have classrooms where you're reading this? I won't explain it.

The recruiter, I think his name was SSGT Eames, asked me what I wanted to do because of my high scores. I told him I wanted to write. He looked at some papers, drew his finger down it and said, "Oh yeah. You could do that as an 0311. They need writers over there. They like writers over there," with such confidence. I had to believe him.

XVII. Home is Where the Body Is

Rasp woke up from cryo with a full cath bag sloshing next to his hip and so, so thirsty. Cryo was old tech, and Rasp wondered why Pai hadn't updated the engines to Folder's EZ Time and Space TM models. It probably had something to do with creds. He'd never had a positive amount in his commissary account, so he had no notion of cost.

He stood up and stretched, tugging at the electrodes still attached to his muscles to keep them from atrophying. The ship's A.I. fizzed in and out of the speakers overhead, while he touched his flaccid penis, fussing over it. Making sure it was usable.

Please proceed to the lavatorium immediately for decontamination. CryoSleep TM Chemicals need to be rinsed from the skin immediately.

Yellow footprints lit up on the floor, some malfunctioning and sputtering.

Follow the footprints directly to your left to the lavatorium. The A.I. cut out again. Step three: rinse with the green solution. Step four: apply the cream in the large white dispenser on your right to your exposed mucosa. Step five: take tablets one through six before exiting chamber.

Rasp walked naked down the narrow corridor, the gravity drives whirring. Rubbing his upper arms and yawning.

The lavatorium stood open. A pitch-black crevice. Rasp reached his hand into the opening and waved to activate the lights. A single line of neon tubing clicked on, painting the room pale pink. The yellow footprints shut off. A spigot directly above him dripped something viscous and cold onto his scalp. He touched the red panel beside the shower box. The door slid shut behind him, leaving him in the dim pink light. The cold drip drip sliding down his shoulders, washing down his legs and into the collector below. The spacecraft creaked in the high winds, compressing the wall around him for a moment. The itch of the chemicals sluiced down his calves.

The liquid cut off and the A.I. buzzed back as a fine clear mist gathered on his skin.

Proceed to the sleep chambers for appropriate garments. TerraAmerica is all natural. TerraNatural Believes in Your Happiness.

"Want to hear a joke?" He asked the voice.

Proceed to the sleep chambers for appropriate garments. TerraAmerica is all natural. TerraNatural Believes in Your Happiness.

"Why was the A.I. feeling sick?"

Proceed to the sleep chambers for appropriate garments. TerraAmerica is all natural. TerraNatural Believes in Your Happiness.

"Because it had a virus." He smiled to himself.

Proceed to the sleep chambers for appropriate garments. TerraAmerica is all natural. TerraNatural Believes in Your Happiness.

The yellow footprints blinked under his bare feet. The nailbeds under his toenails were bulging. Black half moons pooled under the nails.

"Hello? Pai?"

Rasp pressed his fingertip to the bead of hard scar tissue on his inner elbow. From The Before, when doctors saw citizens one by one. He ground his teeth, scraping his back molars together until he could feel the drag and the click in his jaw.

He was alone. Without eyes on him for the first time. Without coworkers. Without The Corporation.

He jogged to the next comm button on the wall still naked and damp.

"Hello? Rasp reporting in from cryo." A drop of blood patted onto the panel. He rubbed the back of his hands under his nose. An arch of brown red smudged across his skin. The next panel greeted him with the same low drone and nothingness. "Rasp from planet's surface." He imitated a pornographic art film he saw back in training, where a space captain landed on a planet filled with identical women with six breasts lined up on either side of their navels. Certified real implants with razor thin scars curving white and maroon under the nipple. Nothing enhanced. It cost seventy-four hours of hard drilling time to see that art film.

"Captain Rasp, here. Please copy. Over." Nothing. The comm button had a diagram with two figures facing one another with three feathered wings protruding from their mouths.

The screens in the ship flashed ads from ten years ago. Ads he had always and never seen, their familiarity a balm. Sticky Froots made with REAL gelatin. The yellow footprints flashed again.

"A.I.? How do I contact Mars? How do I talk to Pai?"

Please proceed to the next chamber. If you are confused, follow the yellow footsteps. The A.I. crackled.

"A.I., where are we?"

Please proceed to the next chamber. If you are confused, follow the yellow footsteps.

Rasp's moisture wrinkled skin prickled into gooseflesh. Aloneness came with a price. It had been so long since he was alone, he couldn't imagine himself with no one. The space in his head that he filled with fantasies of winning the AutoJot AutoLottery TM and women with no spaces in their teeth and real implants and vast platforms covered in warm fabrics was still occupied by others. Men he had known on rigs. Men he knew from trainings. Men from the Shine factory. Milling around the women and the sunny rooms in his head.

He followed the yellow footsteps to the suiting chamber where he was dusted with a fine lime green powder and leaned backward onto a sheet of flexible gray fabric that encased him and then snapped off, leaving him coated and warmed. He tried the comms again. No answer.

The ship rattled in the wind. The yellow footprints half flashing in the dim vent lighting.

***

The first mission brought Rasp to a lake of clear ice.

After he walked in tight loops around the stations for thirty-six hours, the screens lit up with pictures of a person shoving on the breather helmet. Please align base of Breather 2.5 with carotid implant. If no carotid implant exists, please align fingertips on indicated grooves. He plunged his head into the helmet. Boredom had come quickly. The pornographic art films were old; the women in them even older. Some even had hair on their mons. Perversion. Mechoben demands The Smooth Touch. Even the games loaded onto the customizable workers' tablets were low-violence and non-VR.

The winds rattled the craft even as he pressed the frown face icon with each disappointing art film. No androids. Very little blood. Boring. Putting on the helmet gave him a sense of duty and he knew that the suit meant leaving the ship. The screens told him so with slip warnings. Bend your knees when exiting. Breathe normally.

His suit contracted around his chest when the door slid open and the cold hit. The ground crunched under his feet. The whiteness of it seared into the horizon of bright studded dark. Golden dun Saturn hung close, peering like a gardener over a seedling in the frost. The terraformers blinked in the distance on top of a small geyser.

He reimagined himself as the hero of a pornographic art film, treading through the vast wilderness of the Black Hills to blast the tops of mountains with explosives and hold trim women around their waists. Gouts of steam launched into split-skin cold. The artificial gravity drives The Corporation implanted into the ice in preparation for colonization fastened him to the surface of the planet. Walking so far made his lungs burn and his thighs ache. White flakes of ice floated down in flurries leaving huge piles around him. Rusted RoboDrone Dozers chugged ahead of him packing and scattering the geyser snow into a canyon of drifts. He followed the blinking line displayed on his helmet VR screen. He placed humming solar markers shaped like feathers as instructed as he moved down the rough road toward the volcano. As he twisted the rod into the ground, he felt something skitter over his boot. His heart monitor chirped. A fist-sized hole in the ice beside the anchor point for the marker collapsed as a shiny jointed tarsus slipped into the ice.

"Options," he said into his mouthpiece.

Please choose a suboption.

"Find local communication channels"

Please select from the following:

Fresh n Clean: Saturn's Leading Industrial Harvest Company

White Holiday and Virtual Pet Store

Enceladus Burns

"Enceladus Burns," he said into the mouthpiece. It had Enceladus in the name.

The helmet hummed for moment before a voice sizzled in his ear.

Encedalus Burns on gen channel niner here. What's your position, RASP 2544-46?

"Let me activate my beacon." He fumbled with the old display and found the flagging option.

Oh shit son. You're here on this moon?

"Yeah, The Corporation sent me. Do you know how I can contact Pai and Alona?"

Which corporation?"

"Sorry, what do you mean?"

I mean which corporation sent you. I have a list here of Mechoben approved companies.

"It's just The Corporation. There are no others. That's illegal according to The Corporation's Bylaws for Society and the Worker." Rasp repeated what he heard in one of his favorite pornographic films.

Well, if you can't tell me which corporation, I can't help you talk to your people.

"Are you here on Enceladus?"

Silence. Rasp kept trudging against the light gravity following the lines in his helmet. His chest burning from the effort.

Yeah. Yeah, we're here. They were supposed to come get us about 40 cycles back when we finished the terraform on Mount Agni, but no one showed up. Are you taking us back?

"I don't think so. I'm here to get to the lake, I think. That's what my helmet is telling me anyway."

What do they want with the lake after all this time?

"I don't know."

It dawned on him that he never asked Alona or Pai what they wanted him to do here. He hadn't asked a question since The Before. A real question. About what his purpose was, what retirement meant, what happened in The Before, where was his sister, what is a sister, why didn't he remember anything from Earth.

You don't know much, do you son?

"Nah. They told us that knowing too much makes your penis smaller. Who are you?"

The voice laughed. I might ask you the same thing.

"I'm Rasp."

Yeah, I can see that from your chip.

"Who are you?" he repeated.

I'm James. I'm from The New Confederate States of America. I think my family is still there.

"What station is that on?"

It's on Earth.

"I have to tell you something."

Alright then.

"Earth was evacuated when I was pre-labor age. We all went to stations. Each according to his abilities. The Corporation saved us. Well some more religious people think that Mechoben saved us. There are some hard-labor colonies there still, I think."

Can you find others? People from Earth? Is there a system? The voice got higher and hitched. A reaction to something he said. No Soothe Sad TM Transdermal patch here.

"No. We only have access to the terminals to link us with the commissary. A dollar a day makes you healthy, wealthy, and wise," he said, quoting the motivational scrolls he saw in the Skinnies.

HMMMM…THERE IS A PROBLEM WITH YOUR CONNECTION marched across his screen. A cartoon of a striped planet slipping into a black hole covered his helmet viewports. YOU HAVE ARRIVED AT YOUR DESTINATION. WELCOME TO LAKE MOROSKO. The message cleared and bright lights flooded the white ground in front of him from great black towers wrapped in gaseous spumes. His fear hormones flooded into his muscles. His guts tightened as he peered into the light-cut darkness.

Great sheaths of ice encased The Just Like Earth TM Terraformers launched from some inactive asteroid. The engines, powered by nodules implanted in the reflective surface of the ice and fed by the volcano, blinked green. The ice glowed underfoot with each timed flash. The radio in his helmet droned health statistics at him about his heart and lungs and core temperature.

A small cylindrical object striped in reflective material structure stood on the far side of the lake.

"Hace frío," he whispered, his voice thick. Something dark glided under the ice.

***

Document 14 out of 47 of the Prime Execution of Mining Operations: Personal Logs

When you were born, your eyes were blacker than anything I had ever seen. Blacker than the space between stars, I thought when you opened those puffy pink lidded eyes to gaze into my face. You were not beautiful. You were red and the skin on your head was crusted and wrinkled. But not everything that has worth has to be beautiful. Is nitrogen beautiful? Is Lactobacillus beautiful? I suppose if you read this letter, take that last lesson as my only one indulgence into fatherly advice, because it's becoming clear to me that I will not make it back to Earth like they promised.

You were one of the last to be born in the traditional way. The generation of Body Borns. Before it became too expensive for babies to be born like that.

I watched your mother swell with you, her skin stretching into pale rivulets along her brown hips. Hips that she squeezed into slacks, squatting in front of the mirror with them unbuttoned to stretch them before she dragged a jacket over them for court. She was not motherly. She was not wifely either really, but she was powerful. I was surprised she agreed to marry me at all. I think she liked my hard hands and my rank. She was a goddess. I take a risk even making that word tangible or available for view. It sets me apart from the others and that is rarely a good thing out here in The Black.

We got too far for personal transmissions as soon as they slingshotted us around Mars. There was no infrastructure on this moon before we got here. The last time I saw you, you were trying to pat your mother's face, as she held your pudgy arm away from her fresh make-up. She was sending me a digital divorce document to sign with my fingerprint. We lost connection before I could send it back. I want to be very clear here. It was the right thing to do. It was the hard thing to do, but it was the right thing to do. I was surprised that she didn't want to stay married for the political clout it gave her, but no one owns your mother. She did not cry, though you did when she hissed at you when you grabbed her bottom lip and smeared her lipstick.

I stayed in my bunk after that call, reading and rereading the divorce documents on my scroller wrapped in one of those silver blankets they issue at your induction. They don't tell you this, but it is always cold out here.

We were approaching Saturn's rings when all comms went down. Earlier than they told us. I was looking out of one of the tiny port holes, holding my breath at the beauty of it. The ice rings are a sight. They drift like diamonds around Saturn's swirling yellow belly in all that dark.

I suppose I should mention that I was one of four people chosen to go to Enceladus, our small white hope. I was not chosen because I was special. I want you to understand that. I was chosen because I have trouble keeping my mouth closed. I promised only one lesson. Perhaps I meant two lessons. Your second lesson is something my grandmother taught me. I assume your mother still calls her Abuelita. We argued about this. When I grew up they called me a beaner. A wetback. I couldn't ask you to shoulder that. I digress.

Your great grandmother was a maker. She was always making. I remember sitting in her kitchen with the yellow linoleum floor helping her make tamales for Christmas Eve, kneading the lard into the masa. My uncles laughing in the backyard, the sound of beer cans being crushed underfoot drifting through the tiny open window above the sink. She had a pink plastic bucket with Minnie Mouse on it where she heaped the fat. The smell of the pork braising in the spicy red broth. Serrano. Pasilla. Puerco. I almost cannot tell you about this in English.

This was before the decimation of pigs because of the viruses. Do you remember pigs? That's what pork was. Masa was made from corn.

Anyway, after we spooned the masa and dropped in the tender pork in a divot, we rolled it all in corn husk and steamed it in a pot big enough to bathe two children in. Then we sat together in her velveteen recliner and watched television. She liked shows about angels. Before Mechoben, there were hundreds and hundreds of religions. I won't say anything about that. You probably don't know what an angel is and it seems a futile exercise to try and make you understand.

She held me close one Christmas Eve and said to me, "Mijo, la lengua no tiene hueso, pero corta lo más grueso."

The translation is "the tongue does not have a bone, but it cuts through the thickest things."

I trust that you will understand my meaning. Your mother is, after all, herself.

I will leave you with this for the time being. I hope these transmissions will make it to you some day.

XVIII. In My Father's House There Are Many Rooms.

In My Mother's House There Are Only Ruins.

Pai stood hunched over the screen, bending it forward and backward, rocking on his heels. One of the children slithered against his calf. Its huge eyes wet and round, set back in its flattened skull. He glanced down at it and handed it a nub of Shine Gummy from the only elephant tusk on Mars.

The child scrambled away on all six limbs, clutching the sweet in its front teeth.

"Where oh where could our little lamb be?"

He stretched the screen into a three-foot bent plane and knelt under it, trying to trace the ancient spaceship he sent hurtling towards Enceladus. The comms went down. Alona told him they would. He could feel her eyes on him. She stood wrapped in a luminescent synthetic wool blanket, chewing on her thumbnail.

"Well, what does this mean for the sickness?"

"We can't know that yet, Starbeam."

"Why didn't you install the upgrades I listed?"

"Those are expensive."

She sighed and pushed away the child who leaned against her thigh, crouching and nibbling on the gummy Pai gave it earlier. It grunted as it fell backwards snatching at the air.

"I made him trust me. I played dumb because you said you would install those upgrades."

"I said I would think about it, Alona."

"I acted like I didn't know what a boyfriend was. Like a rube. A common GagGirl from the flotillas."

"He doesn't know the difference."

"I know the difference. It's wrong. He's ignorant."

"Things are more complicated than that. You're young. You don't understand these things. I knew I shouldn't have gotten you involved in this."

"Oh yes, Pai, by all means do the calculations yourself. Let's waste the illegal, and since you're so obsessed with it, expensive education I nearly died getting."

"Come now Starbeam, that's a bit much don't you think? It was one incident."

Alona creased her brow and turned up her ElectroDlight nicotine delivery system. The lights flashed red indicating the maximum level.

"Just one incident," she repeated back at him.

"It happens to GagGirls all the time," he said. "You should be grateful for all of this." He gestured at the flooded carpet being vacuumed by a single box-shaped robot.

"Mechoben in space. We're supposed to be fixing this, Father. It was supposed to be a temporary fix."

The sun stood cold and distant, just barely visible through the radiation glass. Pai looked back at the bent screen.

"We have to find him," he said.

Alona snatched the child's ancillary arm and dragged it out of the room. The nodes from the nicotine delivery device detached and swung from her skin, exposing the sores on her hands and arms. The child pattered after her, dropping bits of sticky candy in its wake.

***

Holy Book TM Chapter 5 Verses 1-8 (Traditionalist Text)

1 Protect me, oh Lord Mechoben.

2 I leap at your voice. I spend at your command, for to spend is to truly know thee. Thy markets fill for the worthy. If you find mine labor worthy, fill me as thou sees fit.

3 Those who deny thy will shall suffer. Their bowls fill with blood and their daughters foisted unto production. Nay, not to show thy will and glory through the bodies you hast gifted unto them, but to toil.

4 Toil is a joy and my heart is filled for thy did command the harvest of stone and fuel for your great empire.

5 I will sit at your side, for I am chosen by thee.

6 Those who deny you in vanity choosing man and the things of this plane over thy perfect will be reduced to nothing. Your hand will not be stilled in their punishment. You shall make them like a pool of plasma.

7 You will wipe them clean from the universe. Their skin will be like ash and their faces like skulls.

8 Exalt in your power, oh Mechoben.

***

Finding the wizard, El Mago, was easier than Riff expected. She watched so many ten second stories where someone lost something, usually a Diamond or a Rare Nazi Artifact and they didn't recover it until five episodes later after drifting through space or dodging Venus' lightening storms in an AntiPressure Skidder until the song ended or the hero clutched the thing in his Armani-gloved hand.

Instead, she dreamed El Mago into existence.

Mama swapped her monitoring patch with a hacked one that reported the stats of every GagGirl combined into an average. Of course, that meant she was unable to access the custom streams curated by an A.I. assigned just to her. They trained the programs to read the blueprints of dreams so they could "make everyone's dreams come true." It said so on her mirror. It said so on the screens. It said so from her implant.

"It will make your dreams safe, mija," Mama said as she braided Riff's hair in the communal baths, her scarred arms striated with hard muscle. Black as a crow's back in twin plaits, so tight they pulled the skin on her temples. She could not remember Mama doing this before this moment.

"Safe?"

"Si, they can't see into your head with this."

"Mama? Where were we in The Before?"

"We cannot talk about that. The devices can't hear us in here, but they can read lips a little bit."

Mama patted her braids and spun her around by her shoulder. Wrenching her back.

"You need to be very careful." Mama stared into her face and for a moment she was unrecognizable, someone or something else. Her mouth a thin line. A memory of her thumb against Riff's neck when she couldn't do something. Something to make Mama proud. Something. "Don't be stupid."

"What does that mean?"

"I remember you like to talk too much. You always talked too much."

The steam billowed around them, her mother's fingers digging into her shoulder. Riff felt her pressing something tiny and hard into her palm.

"Close it. Close your hand. Take it now while they can't see as good."

Riff closed her hand and looked in her mother's face, which melted into its usual neutral expression.

"Ok, Mama."

The red ration lights blinked and the water turned off. Riff sucked some moisture from her forearm and took the pill. Pills were rare now in the age of transdermal patches. Ultimate convenience! Perfect dosage! She almost forgot how to swallow it and gagged as the bitter powder coated the back of her tongue.

"Find the wizard," Mama said and got up. The skin on her bare hips sagging only slightly, rumpling like soft bedding. Soon she would be retired. No longer useful for this profession. Everyone knew that once the injections and the surgeries stopped lifting and smoothing it was over. No Use. No Excuse.

"Impractical for the corporation to pay for the old ones," she overheard a director say, smoothing Shine for Men along his neck.

Numbness pressed the back of her eyeballs as she walked back to the Sleeping Quarters, her feet warm in the soft all-natural DogWool socks. By the time she slid under the blankets she had already emerged on the other side.

The Dreaming

She was not she any longer. She was he, her body leaner, taller. Her hands thick. Her testicles irritatingly noticeable, sticking to her thigh in the spacesuit. She squatted and shook her leg. The power in her limbs was intoxicating.

A distant electronic voice in the helmet hummed in her ear.

Can you find others? People from Earth? Is there a system?

Another voice. Vibrating from her own mouth and throat.

"No. We only have access to the terminals to link us with the commissary. A dollar a day makes you healthy, wealthy, and wise."

A tundra of white spread out before her. Cathedrals of light blue ice curved against a huge planet hooped by rings. Saturn? She had seen ads of the Hydrogen farmers in their mech suits, standing on asteroids with Saturn in the background on the vids. Smiling into the yellow light at fortune. To work is divine.

She tried to speak into the mouthpiece, but only hummed a familiar tune. The ice crunched underfoot as she walked. The voice returned in her mouth and throat, whispering.

"What do you get if you cross a wizard and a blizzard?"

She remembered. She remembered. She remembered. Her head flooding with images. A forgotten and forbidden idea. A brother. A brother who pulled her around in a skimmer too fast, skidding around corners until she tumbled onto the hard floor hitting her head against the edge of a wall. She had screamed when the blood pattered onto the floor in quick drops, but he had picked her up as fast as he could, crying. He took her to a room. A room on earth like the bathing chambers, but there were no screens, only a reflective surface and a cold platform with basins where clear water spouted from shiny spigots. He kept saying something to her in that dead language. The language she dreamed in. Lo siento Lo siento. I am so sorry. Aquí. Mira, no hay problema. Tears and snot mingling in the reflection on their faces. He patted her head with a soft white cloth and dabbed it with something from a brown bottle. No le dolerá. It won't hurt. I swear.

He dabbed something warm and slippery on her brow. It's worm medicine. It comes out like a worm. See? He squeezed the tube and a long rope of clearish goo oozed out. He grabbed a box and pulled out three strips and peeled them apart. I have a joke for you. What do you get if you cross a wizard with a blizzard? She sniffled and asked him what? A cold spell. You get it? Please don't tell Mama about this.

Mama called him El Mago when they were young because of his ability to make food disappear from the house. He could eat and eat and eat. She remembered eating together with plates piled high with something. She couldn't quite place it. A plastic woman in a veil holding a baby while a group of men stood around her holding curved sticks stood in the corner next to a thing with colorful lights. They were salty and filled with something like dogmeat, but it was something else. The red grease running down her brown arms.

She was in her brother's body. "Brother" was an extinct word. She tried to think a joke at him.

If he heard, he said nothing and kept trudging through the ice to a lake in the distance that blinked with green nodes.

She tried controlling his movement by lifting a suited hand. She focused her energy, her very being into lifting a hand. He lifted his right hand just to his waist, she could feel her gaze being drawn to it. She tried again.

Knock knock, she thought forcefully. She tried to use her own voice. She thought hard about the sound and texture of her voice. The notes and timbre of it.

"Who's there?" He whispered.

She grinned and could feel the corners of his lips rising.

Boo.

"Boo who?"

Aww don't cry.

"Who are you?"

Do you remember when Mama had a bad day and she hit me with a slipper when you spilled something but she blamed me? The slippers had eyes on them and ears? They were white. You told me 'tough tits' and hid somewhere for hours?

"Where?"

She struggled to remember that name of the place they lived. The sunshine was so bright and the water so blue, until the floods and the sickness.

I can't remember, but it was Earth. I had another name then, I think. Mama calls me mija, but I don't think that's it.

"How do I know you aren't me? I mean, in my head?"

I don't know. No sé.

Riff could feel something slipping out of their shared right nostril. A black tendril waved in front of their eyes, teetering and swaying against the concave surface of the helmet. She could feel blood running hot from her nose, from his nose, caking in the hair on his upper lip and no way to wipe it away through the helmet. The itch of it, the smell of it. She lost him then. She could feel his heart pushing blood and his lungs burning with panic. He clutched at the sides of his helmet, pulling. Searing pain echoed through his right temple, choking him.

Don't take it off! Keep the helmet on! She thought at him through their shared panic.

Another voice entered. Not his and not hers. Another.

"WHO?" it asked. The voice thrummed and purred. It sounded like a thousand voices all at once and at the same time like a sole woman weeping in a chamber.

Rasp's panic was choking out all reason and thoughts. Riff felt sweat dampening their body under the protective suit. The monitors were screaming. Graphs and lines and numbers bounced in front of their eyes. Then like moonlight coming through the transit door after months of windowless space travel it came to her. She was dreaming. She willed calm sensations into their mind. Being wrapped in soft arms, a full belly, falling asleep in a clean place, cool water rushing around feet. She injected a piece of a memory of a white creature with gray tipped wings and yellow webbed honking and screeching as it drifted above them. She could feel air surging back into their lungs, the red haze lifting from their eyes.

WHO? The voice repeated.

I am Riff and this is Rasp.

AND THE OTHER?

What other? Who are you?

CHILD.

There is no child. Just us.

An image of a cold still mountain rose between them. The ice vibrated under their feet. The slightness of the sensation reverberating in their chests as if the being was shifting focus. A mountain across the lake puffed white clouds against the hazy half terraformed sky.

PAIN.

Rasp's scattered thoughts congealed again and returned pushing down Riff's questions.

"Why did you hurt me? I didn't do anything to you," He said, his voice breaking through the static.

CHILD.

"Who are you?"

WHO

Rasp coughed and threw up his hands. The taste of copper in their mouth. The lake lit up in long wavering green streaks under the ice. In the distance, the ice humped up into a huge mound. A booming crack shook the ground as the ice broke. A dark shape the size of a shuttle glided under the ice toward their boots.

Feelings of confusion and anger flooded both of them and for a moment an image of two-legged beings driving piles into the ice floated to the top of their consciousness. Searing pain erupted again at the base of Rasp's skull. His stomach heaved as a multi-colored shining pattern of triangles resonated in his left eye. Vomit filled his mouth and dripped from the sides into his helmet. He gagged again, forcing it down, remembering his Astr0-mining training stream. Swallow it down, so you don't drown.

Riff thought an image of herself at the huge voice, naked with her hands open and tried to mimic its talk patterns pushing past the pain.

Children. Riff. Rasp. Who?

MOTHER. BIG. CHILDREN. The voice was giddy almost. The pain subsided in their head. Riff pressed.

Are you Mother?

The shape under the ice shifted left and then right, wavering. A hunk of ice tipped, revealing a slick, muscular section of a larger being that slipped back under the surface. The being seemed to be thinking for a moment. Rasp's body rebelled against the proximity to it. Blood. Vomit. Sweat. His guts straining and aching.

US. MOTHER. WE. TOGETHER.

You are a mother?

YES.

Is there a father? Familial structuring was considered wasteful by the corporation per the teachings and restricting brought on by Mechoben in the late 21st century. Riff had trouble remembering what a "father" was even after Mama mentioned it. She projected an image of the being under the ice and imagined another being wrapping around it like interlacing fingers in held hands.

NO.

How do you make more of yourself?

NO.

Where are your…um…smaller ones?

NO.

The being punched up against the ice, breaking it into jagged platforms that bobbed and lurched in the sea below.

Rasp was coughing now, taking little snatching breaths to fill his burning lungs. His trembling body caved into itself onto the ice. He gagged and pressed the emergency button on his suit. Blackness framed the cold blue ice mountains. Pressing. Pressing. Pressing. Riff fought against the darkness, the pain. She screamed into her brother's mind and in turn into her own. The black covered her eyes, her mouth. The taste of copper in her mouth. Her back twisting into a tortured arch.

And then she woke up. The amber light flooding the empty sleeping chambers.

She looked at her hands. Her nail beds were blue.

***

Al found Riff at the Commissary pressing selections at random from the 475th menu. The Robopicker V. 45 droned along the shelves, knocking the selections into a monitored HoverCarton with her name and picture flashing on the screen affixed it its side. The HoverCarton stopped in front of a DogLeather Bikini she hadn't selected and flashed a picture of her wearing the bikini. It didn't compress her flesh on her hips and under her arms. Instead it showed her as perfectly smooth, her skin the color of BugMilk, instead of its usual brown.

Al was in feminine form, compact and clad in artificial silk, her eyes expanded and painted into alien hugeness. She approached Riff and placed her hand on the small of her back. Riff was out of regulation by being bare-faced, her dark eyes small without the usual line of Cosmoblack Liner. Her small breasts were draped with childlike fabrics all printed with images of mining equipment and outdated brandless transmitter screens.

Al jerked out her cosmetics pouch and tried to apply some AppleCheeks BloodBlush to Riff's cheeks. Riff pulled back from her, wiping away the fine layer with her excavator printed pajama sleeve.

"They will catch you if you don't put something on," Al said.

"Good. I hope they send me to an asteroid."

Al looked over her shoulder and pressed the heel of her hand over the electronics panel where the Listen-Ins were usually planted.

"What's wrong, my heart?"

Riff ignored the question and turned back to the Commissary selection screen.

"Why can't I buy anything from the fifth tier?" Riff punched at the screen with her middle finger.

"What fifth tier?"

"Look."

A line of grayed out products marched across a screen Al had never seen before. Her adrenaline monitor beeped. She could feel the familiar burning the crook of her elbow as a relaxant was released into her bloodstream. She always chose the ChillRide series when she bought the mandatory endocrine packets. Less nausea.

"How did you find this?"

"I have to tell you something," Riff said, ignoring her question.

Al leaned on the panel, the plastic biting into her hand.

"You can always tell me things, but can we meet where the moon rises?"

"I have a brother." The word seemed to echo around the empty room.

"That is a really bad word."

"Why?"

"Come on. I think you need a relaxing bath."

Riff's face gathered into a furious scowl under her uncombed hair. Her fists hung by her sides.

"Riff, a bath. With lots of steam."

She nodded and put the selector tablet down. Al stroked the hair out of her face and offered her an elbow, growing her stature some. The ShopBot hovered as they walked away. Drifting between Riff's erratic selections.

***

Document 19 out of 47 of the Prime Execution of Mining Operations: Personal Logs Collector's Edition

Hello again, my son. I want to tell you a little bit about Mechoben, because I am certain that you will be told many things about him and about me. Perhaps less about me, it seems they want to hide me from you. I am surprised they haven't taken this ritual from me. Please understand they won't take things from you all at once. They will take it piece by piece and haul it away to drift amongst the dead Chinese satellites that circle Earth. Sometimes they will make you believe that it's up to you to decide whether you want to let them in. It will inevitably take the form of something desirous, something that only the rich and smart have. They will tell you that you can be rich and smart if you take or do or see this thing. Ultimately, they will own you if you give into these things. The things that I gave into. I keep promising no advice. I seem to have failed again.

I digress. I wanted to tell you about when I knew him.

We were both stationed at the base in Okinawa when we were still young. When Okinawa was still there, I suppose. I don't want to be misunderstood. Most of my service was stretches of boredom punctuated with terror. The resource riots were still contained to Africa and South America then and we were terrified to go to the deserts and die. We used to drink a drug called alcohol to numb us some and Mechoben, or Mahaffey as he was known at the time, would come with us to these places where they sold it to us. You ingested the stuff and it burned your nose and throat going down, but it made us forget and it made us remember at the same time. Sometimes we danced and sometimes we cried and sometimes we fought.

One night he told us to forget rank. I won't get into details about what rank means, as it is probably meaningless to you since they dissolved government military after I left for this cold rock. How I miss being close to the sun, dangerously close to its warmth. He ordered us drink after drink until we could barely stand. His drink came with a yellow flower that bloomed as liquid was poured over it. He smashed it against the wall sending shards of glass flying across the room. The bartender threw up his hands and screamed at us. I couldn't blame him. We left, slinging our arms over one another and laughing as we tracked whiskey out on our shoes. Cigarettes dangling from our lips.

We went to another place to keep drinking and to play a game with sticks and balls called pool. By the time I left Earth those games were dying because of the quarantines. We got there and I beat Mahaffey, or Mechoben as you know him. He was furious. I'm going to use some language unbecoming of a father now, but this is how we spoke to one another back then.

He said, "Ok fuckheads, forget rank. I've got a game we can play," and he smashed my cheekbone with a pool ball. I lunged across the pool table to get him, but he lurched away and my buddies held me back. He picked up another pool ball. "Your turn."

I picked up the cue ball and bashed it against his face. Blood oozed out of his nose. He didn't even wipe it away. You see, alcohol eased physical pain too. We hardly felt a thing. We took turns hitting one another until our eyes swelled shut and our lips split. An old Okinawan woman with fierce black eyes chased us out, swatting us with her papery hands. It was then that we realized Mahaffey was nowhere to be found. We panicked. We couldn't get back on base without him and his car. (You may have forgotten about cars as well, but that is an aside for another time.) So, we stumbled through the streets of this foreign country yelling his name. We sprinted down every alley and peeked into every bar trying to find anyone who spoke English or Spanish.

We finally found him sprawled on the steps of a brothel, his wallet laying open and a woman poking at him with a broom. His car was crushed against a light pole, a thin thread of smoke rising from the engine.

We gathered him up and sobered him up as best we could, pouring water and coffee down his throat until he could drive. It was past curfew to get back on base, except for him because of his rank. We all piled into the trunk of his car, three men stacked on top of one another stinking of alcohol and bleeding from our noses. It was so dark and so hot in there.

When we drove up to base the MP must have smelled the booze on his breath. Or seen the damage to the car. One or both. They opened the trunk to find us there, still drunk and beaten blue.

I swear to you what happened next is true. It sounds like a joke and I know you love those, especially knock knock jokes. The platoon commander brought us into his office and lined us up. A picture of a bloodhound and a large grinning woman sat on his desk amongst neat stacks of papers. The fluorescent lights hummed and flickered. He looked us up and down, taking in us in. We were a sorry sight. My right eye was swollen completely shut.

"Who did this to you, Marines?"

We all looked at one another.

"It's alright. You can tell me. Who did this?"

I think it was Briggs who pointed at me and at Garcia at the same time first. Then we all pointed at one another.

"You did this to yourselves?"

"Sir yes sir," we all said in unison.

We were not allowed to leave base for a good two months after that. Mahaffey coasted. He always seemed to walk between the raindrops.

I suppose my reasoning in telling you this is so that you know what he really is. He isn't the Son of God, though the further I get into space, the less I am convinced of any gods. You mother would be happy to hear this, I think. Once she called me a colonizer for going to mass on Christmas Eve. Like I said, extremely powerful. Maybe she should have just called me foolish. Is Christmas still a tradition on Earth? I ask not because I expect an answer, but more to sate the loneliness out here.

I will end this transmission with a joke because I know you love them and because I am tired. They don't tell you this about space travel, but the radiation truly does makes you tired.

Why did God decide to not have Jesus in Mexico?

He couldn't find three wise men and a virgin.

Signing off.

XIX. The Golden Bull:

Or How to Reduce Your Enemies in Three Easy Steps

Al sat in their mandatory training for android employees and looked around at the other androids. They all returned their bodies to original manufacturer's settings for these meetings in a bizarre fading back to original colors and shrinking and stretching to original size. They seemed to heave as one organism, sighing with relief for some and groaning with disdain for their original shape and size. Al loved their own genitalia, both inward and outward. Their beard and soft skin. Their height and pearly fingernails.

Mechoben appeared on the screen in front. His Versace-clad palms facing upward and his lips glazed with the finest Shine-based gloss handmade by his personal android valet who brushed Mechoben's hair in the background. Her dark eyes flicking up to look into the camera.

The androids closer to the end of their lifespans shifted in their seats when he appeared. Today he decided who retired and who would be chosen for the GagGirl films. It was rumored that his personal valet was the very first android ever bred and didn't have a lifespan. No one ever saw her change gender either. Neither of them aged, they just beamed in via some remote satellite to judge and condemn, to praise and ignore.

"Hello my secondborns," he said with a veneer of serenity. "Have you said your prayers?"

They all nodded in unison. Al looked down at their AlgoAndy Wrist Monitor TM. 678 sols remaining before retirement. Al covered the monitor with their hand and looked toward the front. Mechoben cited Corporate scripture and reminded them to "Shine through" and "Sharespirate Ideas."

"Now children, it is time to celebrate the retirement of three of our most treasured coworkers, who are really more like family and also to reassign some of our Caretaker models to their new posts. Let's have a round of applause for them."

The androids clapped and looked around at one another, trying to glimpse the others' wrist monitors. A beautiful mini-Andy named Frey seated beside Al, reached over with her starbright white hand and gripped their fingers.

"It's me. My monitor ran out cycles ago," she whispered into Al's ear.

Al held her hand tighter.

Two humans entered the room as was tradition for retirement parties, carrying a large spherical device made of brass with thousands of android eyes floating in individual transparent bubbles affixed to it between them on two poles. The eyes moved back and forth in the liquid as it lurched around the room in the customary seven laps around the room.

"Bow to the ark of the covenant, my children. Avert your eyes from the eyes of the holy. Those who have retired to make room for progress deserve your respect." Mechoben bowed lifted his hands above his head.

The humans put the ark down in the middle of the floor and pressed the holy sequence into the chosen eyes. Light poured from the center and a head-sized orb floated floated in the center of the light. The God's eye hung suspended in the center of the orb. The iris was colorless against the black pupil. A plasticine eyelid slid up and down as the eyeball darted around the room sending jets of vapor in directed patterned swirls. The vapor took form as The Son of The Son. The first android created by Mechoben to save humanity by government contract. His bull shark DNA showed in his reticulating eyelids and black black eyes. He stood nearly nine feet tall with arms and back packed with muscle. His creamy skin pulled tight over his thighs. Rumor had it that before his retirement, The Son impregnated a human woman before the sterility measures were implemented for both humans and Androids. Talk of that could get you two demerits for blasphemy and sacrilege.

He floated over to Frey and put his formless hands to the sides of her head.

A high wail started in the center of the room. The DNA of cockatoos and coyotes and elk and humpback whales all rising to the top as the mourning chorus began amongst them. Screens dropped from the corners and a live shot of Frey appeared, her eyes closed while the mist hands funneled into her nostrils. Mechoben's voice boomed from hidden speakers around the room. When Frey fully inhaled The Son, her chest ballooned to comical proportions. The sound of her sternum and ribs cracking filled Al's ears over their own wolfish howl, tears streaming from the corners of their eyes.

Frey's body collapsed like a thrown doll. Thousands of BugBots streamed down from the ceiling as Mechoben's voice echoed "Blessed are the artificial for theirs will be the kingdom of drones. Blessed are the natural for theirs will be the kingdom of suns near and far." Frey's body trembled as the BugBots roiled over her skin and into her orifices. Her body deflated into an empty sack of skin which the human attendants picked up out of the yellowish puddle of unrefined Shine and folded into a neat square.

The humans retrieved the ceremonial rubber blades to scrape the puddle that was Frey into the floor slats. One of them lit the ceremonial FireBulb to signal silence. Orange light flooded the room and the mourning call died down.

Mechoben's image flashed on all the screens.

"My children, remember the necessity of this. Remember the need for sacrifice. The engine runs on your bodies and you shall be rewarded greatly in your next life."

And Frey was no more. Just like that. The transitions always came abruptly. Dwelling in sadness was sinful.

"Now it is time to select our newest Android Pornographic Art Film stars. It is the time to rejoice."

They all clapped in unison. One Two Three. Clap Clap Clap.

"Now everyone check your wrist monitor for the Romance Emotive symbol, if you have the symbol displayed prominently and facing the East, you have been selected."

They all checked their monitors, the whisper of synthetic fabrics magnified with scale and the hardness of the room. Al looked down at the shiny face to find the heart-shaped symbol pulsing. It couldn't be right. They still had a Martian year of service to Riff left. They had been bred specifically for caretaking and trained carefully to manage any proclivities toward violence.

"Please come forward to claim your new assignment. The attendants are waiting with your new implant."

Al's two hearts drummed. The Pornographic Art Film Star status would separate them. They were bonded now with Riff, as was intended by their very breeding. Two other androids were making their way to the front. Hod clearing the way with his sheer bulk. He nearly always stayed in male form, pushing his height genes to the limit. His long red hair, an anomaly that amused and befuddled the geneticists, swept against his lower back. The other was an unnamed who couldn't change her gender. Considered only good for pornographic art films, they were usually surgically enhanced. Her eyelids had been removed to enhance her huge gray eyes and her large breasts were already scarified and stuffed with Shine. She followed closely behind Hod. She must have only been a few months old.

"We are missing someone. Come now my child, don't be shy. I thought we bred that out of you."

The room murmured in polite laughter. Al stood up and drifted toward the front of the room in Hod's wake, feeling somehow out of place in a room full of Androids. The identical attendants wore long black robes with white collars. Their hair was as white as the distant sun. Two censers swung from their belts as they waved Al toward them. Hod eyed Al and motioned for them to come stand beside him on the clear boxes set up to the right of Mechoben's main screen. He gripped their elbow as they climbed on top of the center box. The lights brightened and focused onto them.

Mechoben smiled wide. His teeth white and sharp.

The attendants stripped them and sprayed them with disinfectant, dousing them in something called Rose Scented.

"Let the feast begin."

More attendants streamed from behind the giant screen of Mechoben. They carried baskets filled with shining replicas of old tools used for eating the flesh of creatures and plants in The Before. Androids plunged their hands into the baskets as was tradition, piercing their flesh. Blood of all colors flecked the floor and walls as the Androids raised their hands to Mechoben's giant smile, each holding a different implement. Bitestabs and Fleshcuts glinted under the multicolored lights that shone down on all of them. Those with scorpion DNA glowed under the ultraviolet light bath, their eyes solid globes of opaque incandescence.

The attendants stood in even rows on either side of the room, holding their blood-sodden baskets.

"Forks up," the attendants shouted in unison. "Now cut."

The androids descended on the spongey walls of the room, pricking and slicing the material with their chosen implements. Al, Hod, and the unnamed stood motionless on the platform at the front of the room, their bare skin streaking over their stress patterned skin. Hod's skin seemed to undulate as bright red spots appeared on his arms and then faded into golden streaks. His skin looked to be from the luxury seahorse line. Usually reserved for private ownership. Al, their own skin flushing pure white to lavender, reached over to Hod and hooked their pinky around his and squeezed. The unnamed stared into the lights, unable to avert her gaze, tears streaming down her cheeks. She leaned against Al, her stress response invisible. She was designed for fun. Al could feel her beating hearts against their arm.

The walls were breached in forty-eight seconds. A NEW RECORD!!! tracked across all the screens.

The androids plunged their arms into the huge gashes in the walls and pulled on the flexible tubing that laced the facility. The loops of plasticine poured onto the floor like a thing disemboweled. The attendants set to work spinning their censers in the air, flooding the room with Laff Riot–B gas.

The room contracted and shuddered. The androids with their arms still entrenched in the walls screamed with laughter as the walls closed around them. The sound of cracking bones filled the room. One of the nameless kicked her legs as the fissure closed around her waist. Sweat poured from the backs of her knees.

"Now children, now is the time for The Change."

The attendants gathered up the tubing from the inside of the walls in their arms and heaped it in the center of the floor beneath the platform Al and the others stood on. Al and Hod held up the nameless as she collapsed in laughter from the gas. Al giggled and Hod shuddered as the gas swum behind their eyes.

"On my command now. Enact the holy rite. One. Two. Three. Now."

The androids turned all at once to face the pile of tubing and retrieved their silver implements disseminated earlier. They fell on the tubing slashing and stabbing into the pile. A pool of black sludge seeped from the bottom. Slow at first. The sludge spread to every corner of the room, filling the space with the smell of ozone. The attendants lifted their robes and stepped through the exits on either side of the room.

Al clutched Hod's hand, though it was forbidden, and drew the unnamed close to her with her other arm. The shiny sludge moved upward against the gravity simulators. It crawled up the stage front and covered the screens in a black mask. It slid into the android's mouths and noses and pressed their eyeballs forward with pressure. Al felt the coldness of it slapping up their skin, dragging up and clinging to the vellus hair the geneticists were still unable to get rid of.

"You will emerge more yourselves than ever. Build your own brand, my loves," Mechoben said.

The room sank into darkness and Al felt herself being lifted. Floating. Flinging their arms into the darkness to grasp anything at all but closing only on fluid and air. Burning skin. Loping sound. Mouth filled.

Suddenly, Al was seated on a chair covered in red velveteen in female form. Light flooded through a window that stretched up to a ceiling embossed in gold filigree. Three blue silver moons hung in the azure sky across over an alien mountain range. Something was attached to her fingertips. Every so often it pulsed red light and a gentle push of nicotine soared through her, waking her and relaxing her.

Mechoben walked into the room completely nude with the exception of the gold relics around his neck.

"Are you coming?" He asked.

"Where?"

"To the moon, silly girl. The craters are supposed to be beautiful this time of year."

He squeezed in beside her, squeezing her right breast as he wormed down into the cushions.

"Why me?"

"You were chosen to maintain all this." He gestured around the lush room. "To keep it holy and pure."

"How, my lord?"

"You must stop her."

"Who?"

"The child. The one you care for. Your charge."

"But stop her from what?"

Mechoben leaned into her and smelled her neck.

"You know what."

He pushed himself off of the chair and walked across the room to a control panel. Then there was nothing.

***

Information Packet 1 by [redacted] for purposes [redacted]

File 1:

Scientists Monitor Development in Android Embryos

Date: [redacted]

Source: [redacted]

Abstract: Brain activity in Android Embryos is detected within two weeks of conception. Human embryos are in the blastocyte stage at this point. A primitive face is detectable within two earth days of initial fertilization and the neural tube is visible within four earth days. Depending on DNA sequencing and splicing, the lanugo phase is drastically reduced. Studies credit the rapid development to the fluid compounds the fetuses are grown in.

File 2:

BignRich: What does this mean for our research?

SmileyXuan: Private labs usually have better equipment anyway. Besides private always has more funding.

BignRich: I guess, but what does this mean for publishing our research? Like the writing part?

SmileyXuan: I'm not really sure.

BignRich: Did you add the vitamins to the cultures last night?

SmileyXuan: Yep. And the amino acids.

BignRich: ☐ Sweet. I guess we'll just monitor them until the cryotransport guys get here.

SmileyXuan: Could you check the temps before you head out?

BignRich: Sure thing!

File 3:

WORK NO MORE! First Android to Develop to Term

Businesses and workers alike can rejoice in the prospect of no more dangerous, tedious, or humiliating labor. The first android baby, was born in an undisclosed facility in Seattle, WA, though "born" is a bit of misnomer as the little tyke was actually grown and extracted from an artificial womb. The android grows and ages at a rate of approximately twelve times that of a human.

Don't be fooled by this cute face (see insert), this Android, so named in honor of the science fiction writer Philip K. Dick, according to the lead scientists on the project, is specifically bred to be docile, intelligent, and strong. The scientists took another page from Philip K. Dick and created the failsafe of a very short lifespan for these new additions to the workforce. They have various DNA strains from animals and even plants to better help them perform the menial and dangerous tasks humans have been doing for our entire existence.

Scientists and economists agree that with the injection of new labor into the markets, the global economic situation can be turned around. Politicians from both sides of the political spectrum have indicated support due to the decline of the labor force after the first Event.

Dr. [redacted] has indicated that they have enhanced the WBSCR17, GTF2I and GTF2IRD1 genes, which are the genes that make dogs so friendly and is linked to Williams-Beuren syndrome in humans, which causes hypersociability and developmental delays. He assured us that the androids will be more than capable of completing their assigned tasks.

"We can assure you that androids are not like human children, despite what they look like. By the time we end this interview, puberty is right around the corner for The First."

When asked what they would name the android baby, Dr. [redacted] laughed.

"We find it better to not name them, as their jobs will require them to do some tasks that humans find degrading or dangerous. They are more like machines. You don't name your vacuum cleaner or a gun, do you?"

When asked where the funding came from for this project, Dr. [redacted] declined to comment.

"We are on the edge of giving people the freedom to pursue their passions. It might even be a new renaissance."

Until this little Andy grows up, I guess we'll have to wait.

Update: The program has been suspended due to ethical concerns and protests until further notice.

File 4:

[Title header redacted]

Memo: Labor Costs

I suppose we are all wondering if this particular venture is something that we can invest in, given the controversial nature of it. We have done the math and we feel that we owe it to the shareholders to put the full force of our lobbies and influence to push this through due to the sheer cost of human labor. As you all know the labor force has certain requirements since the global government merger two years ago. We are required to take costly measures to ensure workers' safety, even in previously low labor cost countries.

The independent research we have conducted indicates that should we lobby for the creation and distribution of android labor, we could save the shareholders several millions of dollars, which could in turn lead to substantial pay increases for the critical employees at [redacted].

Not to belabor the point, but it is our duty as the world's foremost employer to ensure worker safety and because these new additions are not considered human, the boundaries become blurred to our advantage.

It is our sincere belief that a well-targeted marketing campaign could shift the opinion of the consumer regarding the use of androids for menial labor. It is also worth noting that despite the global merger, independent entities still have a need for defense. Androids present a unique opportunity to supply those entities with the protection they are craving for asset protection and otherwise.

Our team in marketing has compiled data regarding the type, frequency, and delivery method needed to push for such a huge shift in public perception. It would be costly, no doubt, but the rewards are huge should we take this endeavor on.

Please view the packet on your devices we sent yesterday in preparation for this meeting. It outlines the methods deemed most effective by our marketing team.

Signed,

[redacted]

File 5:

BignRich: Have you thought about how we can make them, like, not babies?

SmileyXuan: How do you mean?

BignRich: I mean, you know we can develop their brains to adult size and capacity with the right timing and nutrients, but aren't we shaped by our experiences too?

SmileyXuan: Are you getting soft science on me? Gonna get a degree in psychology now?

BignRich: hahaha. Maybe, but like how will people talk to them? Direct them? If that's what we're worried about.

SmileyXuan: I just titrate the right solutions and do what the folks up top tell me to do. They are the ones who make those types of decisions.

BignRich: But like, what about slavery?

SmileyXuan: [redacted]

BignRich: Remember how in Do Androids Dream of Electric Sheep, they implanted memories?

SmileyXuan: Yeah. What about it?

BignRIch: Can we do something like that?

SmileyXuan: Should we?

XX. Red and Yellow Kill a Fellow, Red and Black Friendly Jack

Rasp thought he was dreaming, back in his bunk on the asteroid with a hard-on and a contraband bag of ZipZap Remedy. The warmth behind his eyes welling as soon as he popped the cap and inhaled. His muscles sinking into the sleeping pad he sacrificed a demerit space for. Something muscular and cold slid over his belly and tucked itself under his lower back, rocking him. He could feel a warm shift in the air over his naked body and reached down to drag his RadAttack blanket over his chest. It wasn't there.

Rasp jerked up and tried to open his eyes. His eyelids were crusted with something rigid and cold. He put the heels of his hands to them and rubbed. The substance melted off with the warmth from his hands and seeped into his eyeballs. A slight burning was replaced by a cool sensation. A place Rasp had never seen came into sharp focus. Shiny, filmy rainbow patterns drifted up the walls of a cavern with bright blue-white walls. He nearly floated the gravity was so light absent his suit. The floor glowed a luminous turquoise. A faint booming trembled the walls and floor.

His usually painful joints from the years of mining felt light and flexible for the first time since Earth. A large shiny-skinned tube of muscle surrounded his waist and supported his back. A long black tendril stroked his cheek and seemed to sing to him, but there was no sound.

"Where am I?" He asked, not knowing who he was addressing. Thinking better of it, he amended his introduction. "Who are you?"

A voice came into his head. Louder than the slingshot around the moon. Louder than rocket engines. Pain scorched his optical nerves.

"MOTHER."

The events that led him here came rushing back.

"Excuse me, MOTHER, but can you talk more quiet to me?"

The muscle tube loosened and frantically patted his hair, petting his jaw and rocking him.

"EXCUSE ME."

An image of a silent ice geyser popped into his head.

"It's ok. That's good. Yeah quiet like that."

"QUIET LIKE THAT."

Rasp looked around at the iridescent walls that heaved and retreated around him. His stomach growled. The tendril snaked over to his stomach and touched it, furling and unfurling with each hunger pain. Rasp knew he should have been afraid, like the time the paneling on the reentry craft he was in ripped off and flew past the portholes. Directionless as he drifted. But his heart rate was steady and his skin was dry.

"I have to get back to my shuttle, MOTHER."

Feelings of confusion throbbed in his temples. Not his feelings, MOTHER's.

"I need to, um, consume to live."

HUNGRY

"Yes hungry."

A grayish translucent tube squeezed from the larger tube holding him and snaked toward him. It pressed against his ear, and then his nostril. It reared up and slid around his hip toward his glutes.

HUNGRY CONSUME PRESENTLY

Rasp realized that MOTHER was trying to feed him, searching for an orifice to deposit some sort of nutrient into.

"Whoa MOTHER, not there. That's not where I consume from."

WHERE

"Here." He pointed to his mouth.

The tube unfurled from his body and drifted to his mouth. Rasp's gag reflex activated at the smell of something yeasty and acrid emanating from the penny-sized opening at the end of the tube. His stomach contracted and his mouth filled with salty water.

CONSUME

"What is it?"

GOOD

"Is it safe?"

YES

"It smells kind of bad."

Sadness flooded him, a feeling like he once had when he offered a girl a hug back in the sheltering space and she told him he was brown like dirt and pushed him away.

"I'm sorry MOTHER. I will consume." He projected his feeling of regret towards MOTHER. He conjured an image of a sunset from Earth as an apology.

He took the tube in his hand and guided it to his mouth, squeezing his eyes shut. A cold, fishy paste flooded his mouth. He choked and swallowed. It filled his belly immediately. The haze of malnutrition and space-body syndrome lifted and he felt full. Full for the first time in a long time. A memory of something spicy and hot lingered on the fringes of his memory. Spicy. He could not remember the last time that sensation crossed his tongue.

"Thank you, MOTHER."

The thrumming under the floor increased for a moment and a feeling of joy welled up in him.

"Are there others?"

OTHERS

"Yeah, like me?"

YES

"Where are they? How can I reach them? Are they alive?"

MOTHER crooned and wrapped another loop of muscle around his shoulders, bunching them and then releasing them. His cervical vertebrae cracked and loosened.

HURT

"They're hurt?"

HURT MOTHER

"They hurt you?"

YES

"How?"

MOTHER's pain overwhelmed him for a moment. An image of a mining rod jutted from the planet's surface, pinning a part of MOTHER's vacillating network of arms to the cold seafloor. Rasp focused hard on the pins that held the oscillating driver in place. They were Fastener Deluxe 15 MM. Easily removed.

HURT MOTHER HURT CHILDREN

"MOTHER, I can help. I can make it stop hurting. I was a miner."

?

"Don't worry about the details. I can help. I can fix." His voice bounced around the cavern.

CAN YOU TALK MORE QUIET TO ME

Rasp recognized his own words and laughed.

"Ok, ok you win. That's pretty funny."

YOU HELP MOTHER PLEASE

"You have to get me to quarry site to help, ok?"

?

"The hurt spot."

OK

MOTHER unlooped from his waist and moved him to the floor of the cavern. His bare feet tensed from the cold and he jumped back into MOTHER's grasp.

"Too cold for me. Do you have my suit?" He imagined his tattered space suit.

CONSUMED

"You ate my suit? Was it good?"

NO

"Well, I can't walk here without a suit."

MOTHER stretched up an arm to the ceiling widening and spiraling, splitting the skin with a sound like ripping fabric. The skin tented into a booth with an opening exactly Rasp's size.

MOVE HERE WITHOUT A SUIT

The tip of a black tendril floated down and pointed toward the hole.

"You want me to get in there? You know I have to breathe air, right?"

YOU BREATHE AIR NOW

"Ok, you're right. I'm breathing now. I trust you."

TRUST MOTHER

"Ok, I said ok."

Rasp stepped into the skin void and closed his eyes. The acrid, fishy smell of the feeding tube overwhelmed him. The opening sealed shut with a shudder. MOTHER's skin slid tight over his shoulders and belly, encasing him. Panic tinted his vision red as the skin moved up his throat towards his mouth and nose.

"MOTHER, can you hear me?"

No answer.

The skin folded over his face, filling his mouth and nostrils, pouring into his lungs. He struggled against it, fighting and writhing, pressing the heels of his hands against the surrounding membrane. His chest opened and a yellow sun ripped across his vision. He was standing on a white beach, snow floating around him and landing in soft ticks around his feet.

A geyser puffed steam across the expansive opaque lake. The icy lake was crisscrossed with deep crevasses. Rasp turned in a circle, patting his arms and touching his throat.

"MOTHER?"

MOTHER

"You scared me."

TRUST MOTHER

A thin membrane covered his body and face, leaving his vision wavy and strange. His breath puffed through it fanning white in front of him.

MOTHER HURT

"Ok, I know. Let me look around some. I might need some tools."

?

Rasp thought about how to describe tools to MOTHER. He imagined the commissary tool room they rented from on the mining base on asteroid R-657. He had tried so hard to save enough credit to buy his own tools, but the Pornographic Art Films and Shine Gummies drew him in. Especially when he was tired and lonely. He was tired and lonely a lot drifting on those space rocks. Strange to be so lonely with warm bodies packed all around you. The Corporation even had an advertising campaign to combat "The Feelies."

If you're lonely and you know it, eat a pill

If you're lonely and you know it, eat a pill

If you're lonely and you know it, then your account will surely show it

If you're lonely and you know it, eat a pill

MOTHER pushed an image of a windowless metal building nestled next to The Corporation's Mining Spire Complex. A symbol Rasp recognized as an old brand he remembered from childhood of a blue, star-pocked circle with a red orbital pattern was emblazoned on the door.

He repeated the word printed under it, trying to remember its meaning. GNASA. GNASA.

TOOLS

"Ok. I'm going. I'm going."

He put his membrane-encased foot onto the ice pack, one then the other. His breath freezing and falling before him. A shadow sailed under the ice and the door to the metal building opened a handspan. Rasp was afraid.

***

Holy Book TM Chapter 2 Verses 12-20 (NEW UNDERSTANDING VERSION)

12 And so rose a great machine from the mountainside, bigger than the people had ever beheld and they called it Dragon and they called it Eco-nomics.

13 It had 177 heads, each with divergent eyes that did see every transgression the people did commit. Its teeth were as viruses, invisible except to those who seek.

14 And seek the people did. And they invited Dragon into their dwellings, feeding it with the blood of their own kin.

15 In return Dragon fed them with dalliances and diversions for which the people did pay a price, though the price was fair and in accordance with the market which Mechoben did provide stability and prosperity before his first ascension.

16 But the people did grumble amongst themselves and demanded more of The Corporation which did provide purpose and striving for them. They said 'If Mechoben was so great, where is he now?'

17 The elders distributed texts to the young, who were primary amongst the grumblers, saying 'did you not heed us? The collection and keeping of credits is immoral and you are the worst among us. Did you not hear our lessons on patience?' But the young did not heed them.

18 They stopped their tithes and contributions, angering the elders, who did say unto them 'my reward is on Mars, for I did as Mechoben asked and there are many crowns for the obedient.' The young did rise up in their lust and greed before the second ascension, demanding control. But they had mercy, as was always their fatal sin.

19 Mechoben seeing this from the First Ascension Ballroom on Mars was troubled.

20 He returned to the people of Earth, bearing gifts. He brought CyRolex and Armani. He brought berries from across five oceans. He

brought garments impossible to rend and the young were satisfied for a time.

***

Alona stripped off her UltraSoft Griffy Bam Bam Suit in Saturn Gold before stepping into the anti-grav Bicky Ball court. Her three-fingered hands ran along the sealant points to pop the seams off her skin leaving deep pink dents under her arms. The Anti-Degrade skin soother smelled like the modeling clay she used to play with in school before they removed her despite Pai's wealth when The Corporation discovered her heritage.

Her familiar slid from her right nostril to her left in a slick black flash before she caught it and flashed a feeling of longing into her chest. It took training to differentiate between her own feelings and her familiar's. She mentally checked off the signs that it was just a small tantrum from the Natsar. She made a note to visit the tank later and bring a small offering. An image of Rasp, sitting with his hands pressed between his knees, rose in her mind. The skin on her flanks mottled deep baboon red in the mirror. An embarrassing side effect of her DNA.

She waved her hand over the Bicky Ball court settings and drew the screen up.

The SUIT/NO SUIT prompt blanked in front of her. The audio had been broken for a Martian year.

"No Suit," she said.

The word NO SUIT bounced around the screen mimicking the movements of the Bicky Ball. A SUIT IS RECOMMENDED FOR ENHANCED PERFORMANCE. ARE YOU SURE? YES/NO.

"Yes."

PARTNER/NO PARTNER?

Alona looked at her implanted biowatch. Pai told her last week that a new partner had been ordered and was in transit in time for practice. "But only if you stream it. You know it's against Mechoben's third commandment to engage in sport or art for personal use only. Monetization keeps us accountable," he had said, his hand hovering above her shoulder.

Her middle finger hovered over the NO PARTNER option before she realized someone was standing in the Bicky Ball Court. The aging A.I. had failed to detect them. Her heart thumped. This house played tricks.

"Excuse me, are you my new Bicky Ball partner?" Alona asked.

The person turned and Alona realized it was a girl only a few cycles younger than she was.

"I think so. The Cryo has got me a little confused." Her voice was deep and her Bicky Ball suit was on upside down and backwards. The girl's thin legs poked through the stretchy collar at the bottom. Her green eyes held Alona's gaze under dense brows. Her hair was cropped short against Corporation standards for females.

Alona, forgetting her nakedness, went to check her own suit before remembering its absence at the feel of her gooseflesh. She kept her distance, eyeing the thin stranger in her house.

"What's your name?"

"My name?"

"What do they call you?"

"They called me Gram at the factory."

Alona used her calm voice. Her dumb voice. The voice that got her through her prohibited schooling.

"Are you here to play Bicky Ball with me? Or what were you told?"

"Um, they don't usually tell us what we'll be doing once we're bought. I mean once our labor is contracted out by the Corporation," she said, her voicing echoing around the chamber.

Alona tapped on the comm link by the door before remembering it was broken.

"Well, we should probably get you into that suit correctly, unless you want to play skinny like me."

"I don't know the rules."

Alona approached her and began tugging at the leg hole of the suit that Gram's head poked through, rearranging her hair and smoothing her dark brows. Gram relaxed under her touch after a moment, her intense gaze still flicking from Alona's face to her breasts.

"I have a girlfriend," Gram said.

"Oh? Isn't that…" Alona lowered her voice with a smile "…prohibited by the Corporation's rules and bylaws?"

Gram noticed her smile.

"You're not going to file a report with HR are you?"

"Not if you promise to play Bicky Ball with me." Alona extended her pinky. The holy promise.

Gram wrapped her pinky around Alona's smallest finger and squeezed. She giggled and looked at the floor. Several of Gram's teeth were missing and the ones remaining were glazed with a fine layer of blood. The smell of sick flesh reached the back of Alona's throat. She realized that this almost-child was too damaged to play Bicky Ball. She would need to be treated by Dr. Robot – The Doctor that Never Sleeps.

Alona withdrew from her and brought up the rules for Bicky Ball on her tablet.

"Ok, read this and go with Friendly Bot to go see Dr. Robot," she said.

"I'm sorry, but I can't do that."

"Do what?"

"Read," Gram said. "School went away after The Event where I was and 'reading is for the bored and boring,' is what they used to tell us."

"Did they? Well, you see this symbol here? The ear? Just tap it. That's the audio version."

Gram peered at the tablet as Friendly Bot rammed into her heels. Alona picked up the heavy black robe she had tossed aside earlier and flung it over her right shoulder.

"Well go on. I'll meet you after you've been properly inducted into the household. Have you met Pai?"

"No."

Friendly Bot nudged against Gram's right calf. She tucked the tablet under her arm and followed the insistent little bot out into the hall. Alona sighed and watched her walk down the hall. Pretty little thing. They were releasing them for private sale earlier and earlier it seemed.

***

A Brief History of Bicky Ball

The earliest influences for Bicky Ball includes a primitive game called tennis, where participants played against one another on a physical court with a ball made of petroleum-based plastics and fibers and a device called a racket, which was an oval-shaped tool also made from petroleum-based plastics and fibers, though some of the more elite players used rackets made of carbon fiber. The racket had a grid of taut plastic string which allowed the ball to bounce more easily from racket to racket.

Like tennis, Bicky Ball was designed to give the economy drivers and job creators a bit of leisure time in between their tremendous efforts to employ and retain the labor of both Earth and the Moon Colonies.

The advent of Bicky Ball came about after the second pandemic required the global populace, especially our job creators who were too crucial to expose for any reason, to refrain from large gatherings and group play. Bicky Ball was designed by two of the most qualified sub-Corporations, Nike and Apple, in order to feed the need for recreational play to enhance greater problem-solving abilities.

Contrary to popular belief, the use of the anti-grav chamber was an addition to the game that came later probably due to the Skylabs and Martian Relocation Programs, which predated Cryo and Flight Warp. The Holy Building of the Brand could only continue if the influential were kept healthy through exercise and stimulation.

The rules of Modern Bicky Ball are as follows:

Materials needed:

2 players of the male sex

Bicky Ball Court with Consistent Anti-Grav drives or Located in Airlock Isolation measuring 20 feet by 20 feet by 20 feet.

1 Borzer Ball

2 Frackus Rods

1 Set of Sensors to be harnessed from points A, B, C, and D (see diagram)

1 Bicky Ball

2 public screens to display results from sensors

Rules:

Both players must have sensors attached to the correct anchor points as shown in the diagram. These sensors must be connected to the screens for public view, as part of end scoring is the heartrate, hydration, and breathing rate of each player. Better stats can be used as a tiebreaker, in the event of a tie, but otherwise they will be tallied in the final score.

Once the public scores are available for all to view and the sensor points are applied correctly, the Borzer Ball is released before the players into the court. The Borzer Ball is manufactured by Nike. Only Nike Borzer Balls may be used for competition of any size or venue. The Borzer Ball is controlled by a sophisticated A.I. and can move in three dimensions, though the pitch and yaw will vary based on the data input by the official Nike Bot Trainers. The Borzer Ball will remain alone in the court for 5 minutes to analyze data.

The players are then permitted to enter carrying Frackus rods. Both players will start will gravity engaged, unless they are using an airlock All-Natural Court.

The Bicky Ball, which is a misnomer as it is more of an elliptical, like the ball that accompanied American Football or Rugby (see diagram) shall enter into play when the A.I. reads the appropriate data coming from the sensors. Meaning, whichever player achieves the correct heart rate, breathing rate, and hydration level will have the Bicky Ball released on his side of the court.

Until the Bicky Ball is released, the Borzer Ball is programmed to move randomly around the court, displaying the player's most embarrassing recorded moments.

The most famous match was in the Bicky Ball Pro trials on the Muskian Transport of the Third Age. This was before the prohibition of women from the sport, due to the need to preserve their fertility after The Event. Curiously, the match was between Haster Grim, the male inheritor of Very Valves fortune, and Hager Hillah, the female inheritor of Very Valves' sister company (when such things existed) Great Valves. It was coincidence the two were on the same transport. Such things were only overlooked as a result of the second pandemic, which caused some organizational disorder as nearly thirty percent of the administrative staff were quarantined or died.

It should be noted that even in these times before women were separated for their own protection, it was a rare occasion for men and women to play one another in Bicky Ball, as the sport contains some physicality and spatial reasoning.

Hager Hillah had schooling as a statistician, unbeknownst to her opponent, and had been studying the court for three months before the match. She used machine learning, using her own personal devices, to map and analyze every match every played on the court and then calculated the odds for the particular patterns the Borzer Ball was mostly likely to take, ensuring her the early capture and the dispersal of the Bicky Ball to her side of the court. She also trained her body to reach and maintain the static statistics for the entire round, ensuring an edge to her competition using mathematics. Some historians argue that this was the catalyst to the segregation of the sexes in the larger sense, though that has been disputed.

Hager's plan worked just as she had planned and she received the Bicky Ball and padded the odds, just as she had planned.

But in a bizarre turn of events, Haster Grim overcame her physically even in the anti-grav chamber, when she executed a charming, but useless maneuver where she attempted the final goal. Unedited recordings of the match show that the physicality was brought on by the memory recording of Haster dining on a female-formed Android that he had hunted in an illegal preserve in the United Sub Saharan Arab Emirates, which was formerly a country known as Mauritania. Again, we should note that Android hunting and consumption is and continues to be legal, but highly discouraged. It was particularly shocking that the android resembled his late sister, who disappeared under mysterious circumstances years before.

Haster caught her midflight, wrapped his arm around her throat and choked her to unconsciousness, saying "well she can't win if she can't think." He then forced her unconscious body into the goal socket, breaking her arm and several ribs in the process. The gaming computer deemed this to be Hager's most embarrassing moment and played it several times over.

The officials found nothing in the rulebook to suggest that this action did not comply with the "any means necessary" clause and awarded Haster the game.

Hager and her company tried to sue Very Valves, but were unsuccessful as Hager signed a release of liability before participating in the game.

XXI. Mark My Words

Riff met Mama at The Nozzle as soon as she regained composure from the drug Mama foisted on her. It took nearly a week before she was able to face others. She told the producers she wasn't feeling well. They sent a basket of bluish fruits and a get-well card with a creature she did not recognize holding colorful circles attached to strings.

The room came back into focus and her nostrils and sinuses were swollen. A small trickle of blood ran down the back of her throat and her nose whistled as she tried to suck in air. The end of her familiar tendril poked through her nostril and another slid from under her bottom eyelid, caressing her iris.

She grabbed a gauzy veil from her selected outfits drawer and draped it over her shoulders and head to hide the throbbing creature. Her room seemed smaller, the cream walls tighter. Al's section was bare and they were conspicuously absent. Even their workspace for designing and requesting the bodily alterations for Riff was stripped bare. A single white ribbon lay furled on the soft pink chair shaped like a tongue.

Riff shrugged and shuffled down the spiraling hallway toward the center spot where she saw Phobos first rise.

Mama leaned against the railing with another woman Riff had never seen before. She was old. Riff hadn't seen an old person since she was back on Earth. Her white hair flowed down over her thin brown arms, static clung in spiderwebs to the rough fabric of her tunic. Her eyes had been removed and replaced with shining cobalt orbs inset into silver filigree that slid and turned independently of one another. Her belly jutted forward and her back arched forward like ram's horn.

"Es ella?" The Crone asked Mama.

"Sí." Mama steepled her fingers over Riff's cheekbones and pressed. A stream of black ooze trickled down her philtrum.

"Dios mío, es joven," the old woman said.

"Mija, listen to me, your familiar needs to be milked. That's why it's hurting like this. This is Curandera Morena, como un doctor, a healer. Ok? She is here to help. Ok?"

Curandera Morena flicked a sweet-smelling substance on her face and pressed her thumbs against the bridge of her nose. A screw of pain drove into her forehead as the familiar shifted in her nasal cavity. Curandera Morena passed a small rod attached to her long opaque fingernail over Riff's eyeball. Another wave of pain clotted behind her eye. Her right nostril stretched as the tendril pressed its way out, ribboning down her cheek into the Curandera's hand in a coil. The pressure released behind her eyes and her vision cleared.

Mama caught her breath as the familiar plopped into its full impossible form. It glittered with mucus and heaved with foam. Curandera massaged it, singing softly and blowing on its single ocular bulb. Her own artificial eyes swaying in her head. Her wrinkled hands firmed, the liver spots disappearing and the nails becoming clear and white again. Tears flowed from her eyes.

"I want her back, Mama."

"Her? Interesting."

Riff felt as if someone had cut off her right hand.

"Please, put her back."

Curandera slid the familiar into a transparent orb filled with a milky liquid and swirled it so that it sloshed over the creature. The familiar buzzed and squeaked as the liquid puffed and steamed around it. Riff felt the coldness on her own skin and tried to snatch the orb from the old woman. Mama wrapped her arms around her from behind and hissed in her ear, "be still! You don't understand what's going on. Hush. The sniffers will hear you."

The liquid turned lavender and bubbled out of the hole in the top of the orb, dripping over the sides. Mama released her, pushing her aside, and cupped her hands under the dripping liquid. Curandera chanted and gripped her right fingernail in her teeth and tore it off. Blood oozed from the root, dark and slow. Curandera traced the blood over Mama's forehead in a long horizontal line and then held the bleeding digit over the orb. The hissing stopped and Riff's familiar froze as the liquid turned muddy. The sun stood cold and far in the amber sky. Curandera tipped the orb back into her mouth, swallowing the liquid down. The sagging skin on her neck leaped up and down with each swallow. Her false cobalt eyes clouded to steel gray as she fixed them on Riff.

Riff stood paralyzed with shame as Curandera Morena walked into her mind, hunting memories. Riff existed twice. Inside and outside. Mama still kneeled under Curandera's cupped palms, Curandera stood motionless. The winds outside The Nozzle were suspended in great sweeping veils of red dust. Inside she stood in a place with a roof of shifting green light. Creatures shrilled in the distanced in burps and chirps. The ground was soft under her feet.

Other Curanderas, identical to Curandera Morena, draped in black and hung with shining claws, drifted from every side closing into a tight circle around them. Each carried a human skull in front of them. The eye sockets glowing a warm yellow.

"I am looking for she who wears the pearls of the human heart. Red, red they shall be and adorned in snakes she shall be. She is facing herself. She is bearing us all in her womb."

"I don't know who that is, Curandera," Riff said.

"You must take me to her."

"How? I don't know who that is."

"Come now, she is larger than any one person. She is not a person. She chooses a vessel. She chooses a speaker. You have met her. Your familiar told me. Give me your hands."

Curandera took her hand in hers, which were no longer young, but gnarled and wrinkled, and turned them palm up to peer at them.

"Tu hermano. Dónde está?"

"That's a bad word," Riff said, repeating Al.

Curandera grew tall and straight, her white hair whipping behind her. Her tunic tore as she expanded leaving her naked and tall. Her pendulous breasts and rounded stomach grew grazing Riff's face as her stooped shoulders broadened and cracked and her spindly arms ended in head-sized hands tipped with yellowing fingernails.

"Speak it. Where is your brother?" Her voice was rounder, larger. She grabbed Riff's arms, holding them fast to her sides.

"Somewhere really cold. It was white. There was a bunch of frozen water. Not an ocean, but the other one."

"A lake?"

"Yes."

"Take me there."

"I don't know how."

"Sí, se puede. Ahora." Curandera loosened her grip on her and stared into her eyes, with the strange blank orbs.

Riff gathered her thoughts under this strange shifting green canopy and imagined the lake with its deep blue fissures and gouts of steam in the distance. She imagined Rasp's body and her body, blended and met. She imagined MOTHER's voice in her head. The shifting light greens above her began to morph into the thin dark gray of the moon. She did not know it was a moon before.

"La luna de Enceladus," Curandera crooned.

She imagined Saturn, heavy and yellow, ringed in white ice on the horizon. Glutted with gases and swirling across space. Luxurious and slow.

"Hablamos con la madre ahora. Llama."

Riff opened the channel in her mind, like before and called. Nothing.

"I think I have to talk through Rasp."

"Quién es Rasp?"

"My brother."

"Call him, niña. Speak through him. The Mother has many children. Un niño y una niña. She needs a warrior and gatherer."

"Mama gave me a drug before."

"Only a learning tool. Call him here on the ice. Imagine him. Think him here."

Riff pushed to remember him on the ice, the fog inside his helmet. His strange body with peculiar strength. Nothing.

"Remember him elsewhere. Más fuerte," Curandera hissed.

Riff was inundated with a memory from when they were very young, back on Earth in The Before.

They sat on a bed in a small place. His bedroom. His bed. Red triceratops and green tyrannosaurus rexes battled on a white background on his bedspread. A tank glowed blue from the other side of the room. Rasp held a palm-sized furry creature with eight appendages in his hand. His name was something else then. Not Rasp. Hers too. She couldn't bring it up. The creature's eight glossy black eyes stared back at her. He offered it to her to hold. She touched its round bottom and squealed. The creature backed up, crawling backward over his arm. Green stars glowed on his ceiling. A knock came at the door and a man walked in. He was dressed in a uniform, green and mottled. They hadn't seen him for a long time, she remembered. They were afraid of him. He kneeled on the ground beckoning them to him. His arms spread apart, his eyes wide and shining.

"It's me. It's Daddy. Papa."

His voice sounded desperate. He looked thinner than they remembered. Browner. More creases between his brows, around his mouth. A different version of he who lifted them onto the kitchen countertop while he microwaved his coffee. Mama hung back in the dark hallway, her arms crossed.

"See? Ellos no te recuerdan."

"Have you only been speaking Spanish to them? Jesus Christ. I work for the government."

"So do I."

Rasp wrapped his arm around Riff's shoulders and pulled her close to him. His arms and ribs hard against her. The eight-legged creature perched on his shoulder.

He whispered, "Go to both of them. Go stand between them."

She looked up at him and back at them and stood up. The memory faded there, leaving her standing there alone with Curandera Morena in a vague echo of the bedroom aching with loss for her familiar. Curandera held out her sharp hand to Riff and gestured toward the shifting bay doors at the end of the memory.

"Vámonos. Está bien. No te preocupes."

Riff felt the eyes of Mama on her as she and Curandera blinked back to Mars. She was holding the old hand and felt the fragile bones underneath, draped in thin spotted skin.

Mama's eyes flicked from Riff to Curandera Morena.

"Así?"

"Escúchame, la niña no está lista."

Mama pursed her lips. Her fist shot out like a snake, clipping Riff's cheekbone. Riff reeled backward, knocking the back of her head against Curandera's nose. Mama's cold black eyes welled with tears.

"I thought you were my daughter. Why can't you do this? Are you stupid?" Mama pulled her hand back as if to strike her again, but dropped it. She spun away into the dark hallway and disappeared. A bruise blue-purple was hiding behind the pink mark Mama left on her cheek. Damaging Corporation property carried a heavy penalty. Mama could be sent to Elder Female labor in the Venusian processing plants. Even Corporation marketing encouraged the image of camp labor as a deterrent. The streams always had dead-eyed women covered in radiation sores apologizing for their sins. Begging for retirement.

Riff turned to Curandera who chuckled behind a balled piece of fabric spotted with blood that she clutched against her laughing cough.

"Why are you laughing, Abuela?"

"Have you ever seen an old woman here?"

"What?"

"Tonta. There are no old women here."

Curandera's blood turned silvery and her back cracked into ramrod straightness. Her arms grew three lengths and tiny screens fell in a cascade from her mouth, each etched with a moment of human shame. Men in a red desert clinging to a detached body part weeping to an old god. Women curled around one another in windowless rooms touching bruises and secret blood. Children dividing bowls of maggots picked from the bodies of this cracked skin war. Dogs being skinned alive. Screaming. Protein. Protein. Protein from whence we came. Protein for whence we go.

"Bruja," Riff said.

"Sí, I am the witch of death. My spells are remembering this. My spells are to remind you about what you are."

"Are you a robot?"

"I am not a robot."

"Are you an android?"

Curandera tucked her slick hair behind her ears and crouched to retrieve the blinking screens.

"Ayúdame, por favor."

Riff knelt beside her and swept the screens into the palm of her hand, each blinking a tiny recollection of suffering. Her stomach churned with the shifts, the vacillations of her own internal size and structure.

"Are you an android?" Curandera asked her.

"No. I am a human, girl."

"How do you know this, mija?"

Curandera Morena slipped out of her skin and beneath it was slick black formlessness that swirled and drained into the floor vents beneath the nozzle. A wisp of gray mist was all that was left of her. A thickness rose in Riff's throat and tears welled behind her eyes. The tiny screens biting into her palm. Tears not muted by chems or flashing screens. Strictly forbidden. Self-indulgent. Tears were decadent and luxurious.

Dónde está Mama?

She was thinking in this language again.

***

My Dearest Son,

That address always looks so formal, but here in The Black formality is craved by us all. You stop saying words like "please" and "dearest" and "excuse me" when you are crammed together in a vessel so tight that you can smell one another and then you cannot, because you are so used to it. I miss manners.

My mother insisted on manners, and despite my uncles' machinations to entertain themselves by teaching me crude gestures and mannerisms, she succeeded. Boot camp was hard for someone like me. Like us? I wish I knew you more. Your hair is as black as an Incan night and your skin like the red clay our forefathers hoed and turned. You are the son of kings, Mijo. The gods of our fathers that demanded blood, did not demand our blood for reasons known only to them. And if it is to be believed that they are and see time and space all at once, like a room on a reflective silver bowl, it stands to reason that they kept our blood in our veins for a purpose.

Perhaps you have wondered why I have not discussed your sister. Is she also not of the blood of kings? I do not wish that you think me to be opaque, at least not purposefully. We will discuss your sister today. We will not mince words.

You see, human gestation takes around nine months from the time of conception and while your sister does bear a formidable resemblance to me, it seems unlikely that I am her father based purely on timing. Your mother claims otherwise and even insisted on a DNA test. Is this too much to be speaking about with one's son? I'm not certain you will see this correspondence anyway. I thought that this was crass and decided to accept your sister as mine despite my doubts. Anyone who is brave enough to climb into bed with your mother deserves to have a bit of cake to both eat and have.

She claimed the medical professionals we entrusted with her reproductive health, ones licensed by the contracted private entities, were working with shark DNA to achieve parthenogenesis, that is the ability for her to give birth to an exact replica of herself. A clone if you will, though that term is considered gauche these days. I worried about her mental health some days. Sometimes she seemed unstable and paranoid. Other days she was the sharpest person I had ever met.

I think it is only fair and important to note that some of us crave stability and need to have trust in institutions to achieve that equilibrium. Others question and push, and in their efforts to find cracks in the institutions, they burrow into the sides creating the cracks. I do go on don't I? My original promise of not issuing advice seems to have been an empty one.

Did you know that I was beaten to an inch of my life once for reading? Well, that's not entirely accurate. I was beaten because a love of things denied to our people somehow meant my love for our people and traditions were diminished. That was not and is not the case. I ask them now, as I drift safely through space, can you not love more than one child? Let me tell you the story. Stories are better teachers anyway.

When I was a child, many schools were still regulated by what was called state governments. I know my permissions are somewhat restricted as to what I can disclose to you, but suffice it to say that name the Estados Unidos or United States came from the idea that certain areas of designated land were given a set of their own rights and the ability to create laws and govern within the purview of the federal government. I am doing it again, mijo. Perhaps my over explication contributed to my sound thrashing some too. Engine room gin blurs me.

Let me try again. I will be simpler this time.

I was very young, perhaps seven or eight years old and our teacher had a hidden shelf of non-contract-approved paperback books. I didn't know what a non-contract-approved book was at the time, only that it didn't have ads and was not digitized at all. The paper was yellow along the edges and smelled of earth and dust and ink and age.

Mrs. Davis-Martinez was informed by the school that I had finished up the contract-approved reader assigned to our district and that in my hunger and haste had gotten Miguel, my older brother – your wildest uncle – to hack into the Pay Per Read site and steal over one hundred volumes of higher level texts. I had devoured only five books when the school suspended my account. The school told Mrs. Davis-Martinez that I was to be punished for property crime and that she should choose suitable circumstances for my contrition, preferably in the form of meaningless and dull labor after school hours.

She informed the administration that she had many torturously dull tasks for me to do after school. The administration informed my mother, who whipped me silently with the flexible sole of a green flip flop. I realized later that that whipping was different than her usual ones, which were loud and righteous. This one seemed unenthusiastic, like her heart wasn't really in it. My mother was a very wise woman.

After class, the other children rushed from their desks in a flurry of shiny snack wrappers and mesh backpacks to go home to their favorite streams while I sat, looking at Mrs. Davis-Martinez picking up the shreds of plastic left behind. She gave me instructions on how to help her. I picked up trash, straightened desks, and did my homework under her eye. Her wife came in with a lunch bag with Spider Man on it. It had these cubes of cheese that were white and yellow swirled in it and plastic bag of green grapes in it. Soon the janitor cut the lights in the hallway. I had never known school could be this still.

We continued our little routine for a week or so, when one afternoon Mrs. Davis-Martinez waved me over to her desk.

"Come see. I have something here you may like."

She opened a big metal drawer with rails that ran along the sides.

"It used to be used for paper files, but now we have everything in the cloud," I remember her saying. To this day I am still unclear on the meaning.

She lifted a false bottom from the drawer and placed it on her desk. It seemed very romantic to me at the time, like a spy novel. It was filled with hard copy books. Their covers were softened and creased. Pictures of wolves and soldiers and women balancing pots on their heads dotted the covers. She reached in and retrieved a particularly worn copy of a book with a cover that had two guns crossed over one another over a gray and dark blue uniform. I was very afraid, because I loved school, you see? I loved Mrs. Davis-Martinez. She was the most beautiful woman I knew, with her tight black curls and dun skin. I thought she would go to jail or be sent back to Mexico. Many of us were being sent back at that time before the secessions and annexations.

I said to her, "Mrs. Davis-Martinez, is this illegal? Will we go to jail? Can they send you back to Mexico for this?"

She laughed.

"My family is from Honduras, first of all. Secondly, I could get into a little legal trouble, but it would just be a licensing fine. I could get into very big trouble with the Charter's Teacher's Association though, so you do have to be very quiet about this, ok?"

"Is it mine?"

"It is yours until you finish it. Then you bring it back and I will let you choose another one. No more hacking into the school's computer, ok? Now put it in your bookbag."

Now, it is important for you to know that in The Before, there was more than just one Corporation and many people were employed by many corporations and some were not employed by anyone at all, if you can imagine that.

Work gives people a sense of purpose, a sense of drive. When I joined the Marines, my very first drill instructor told me "discipline is kindness." I tell you all of this because it is important to always understand context. The context of this time was that some people voluntarily or involuntarily did not work and that meant that the kindness of discipline was unavailable to them, so they had a hard time being kind to others. Do you understand my meaning, hijo?

The offspring of these people were not conditioned to the kindness of discipline themselves and so they lashed out when they saw that kindness, and other kindnesses being bestowed on others. They sensed the unfairness in it, I think.

And so, when I left with that book tucked into my bag, in a way, I was inviting what happened next. I sat down at the bus stop waiting for the Number 30 bus and took out the book. Opening and closing it, pressing my thumb to the soft edge of the pages. The bus stopped for me, but I did not notice, so engrossed was I in the pages. The sodium lights buzzed orange above me, lighting the pages. I did not notice the danger. The boys craving the discipline someone had just handed me, because of my bright eyes perhaps, emerged. They strolled from around the buildings, eating hot Cheetos, their eyes landing on the symbol of their insecurities and pain.

"Reading a book?" The largest of them said. "Book" shot out of his mouth followed by a spray of crumbs.

He grabbed it from my hands and pushed me off the bench. I flailed at them. My fists landed nowhere. They grabbed me by my collar and punched into my face and throat and arms and chest. The shockwaves of their blows rattled my spine and my throat seized in anger and fear. My teeth clacked together as the largest one kicked the back of my head as I lay curled on my side. They dumped out my backpack, strewing my homework and my playing cards. I was trying to learn magic tricks. They took Mrs. Davis-Martinez's book and tore the pages from it, scattering them into the thick, dark night.

I would not let them see me cry. And so I spat blood into their faces and howled like a dog, baring my teeth laved in purple-crimson. An abuela coming home from her own day of labor saw all of this and rushed toward us on short bowed legs, hurling odds and ends from her purse at the boys until they fled into the night. La Lechuza! La Lechuza! They screamed into humming city night, their sneakers snicking on the concrete.

She approached me carefully, as if I was a wounded dog. I wept then. Tears mixed with blood and snot and dripped down the front of her green scrubs. Her name tag said: Francesca Ramos-Diaz M.D. University Medical Center. Her gray hair had come loose in the chaos and hung about her face in long steely loops. She retrieved her huge purse from the ground and pulled a pair of purple nitrile gloves and some gauze.

"It is not too serious," she said and dabbed at my head. "You will live to fight more pendejitos."

I fell into her and hugged her around her thick middle. She pressed me back and looked at my face, turning my jaw and lifting my arms.

"You are ok. Just bruised. Can you see ok?" She took a pen light from her scrub pocket and shined it into my eyes. "Stop crying. You are ok."

"Are you a doctor?" I asked her between sobs.

"If I'm not, then the medical board is in trouble," she said under her breath, "stop crying."

"I missed my bus."

"I can drive you home. Where do you live?"

I gave her my address, which I have forgotten. Strange the things we forget that we promise we will remember forever at the time. She picked up the torn cover of the book and put her pudgy hand on my back between my shoulder blades.

"This one was one of my favorites too. Don't let those ignorant little fuckers stop you, ok? Fuck them."

It was strange to hear these words coming from an abuelita's mouth. Don't misunderstand me, my son. I have heard the vilest things, the most colorful profanities come from my own abuela's mouth. She would deny it. If she is still with us when you read this, do not ask her or you might receive a hurt lecture. But, I had never heard, perhaps I should not call her an abuelita, I do not know if she had children or grandchildren to this day.

Her car had leather seats that warmed when you sat on them. It was pristine. No car seats or crushed Cheerios under the backseat. She pulled a towel from the trunk and laid it down on the seat before I sat down. It had dog hair on it and a picture of a smiling mermaid. We glided through the city, all bright orange and red lights blooming against the deep gray of the buildings.

I cried again, ashamed of my fright and crusty nose. Ashamed of the streets parting in decay. Ashamed of the shredded book in my bag.

"Why are you crying? That Naproxen should be kicking in soon."

"What will I tell Mrs. Davis-Martinez?"

She smiled faintly and crinkled her brow, amused.

"Rosa? Her wife is Nadia? Tall and blond? Some kind of white foreign lady? That's your teacher?"

"Sí," I said in Spanish. Like drinking water, swallowing the consonants.

"Don't worry. I will call her tonight. We used to…" her voice trailed for a moment "know each other," she finished.

My father stood on the stoop smoking a cigarette when we pulled up in her expensive car with clean seats. This was before they were replaced by those transdermal nicotine delivery systems. He approached her driver's side door and thanked her in choppy English before she waved him off and answered in Spanish. His gratitude bore a touch of resentment. I could feel his hardened hand close around my upper arm as he pulled me toward the house where my mother peeked through the yellowing blinds. Dr. Ramos-Diaz leaned over and whispered: "más sabe el diablo por viejo que por diablo." My father chuckled and loosened his grasp on me tucking me under his arm as we walked up to the porch. My eye had swollen shut at that point. He went to the refrigerator and pulled out a Bud Light and gave it to me.

"Ponlo en tu ojo, hijo."

My mother leaned in the kitchen doorway, her arms crossed.

"Qué te sucedió?" Her eyes glittered.

"Nada mi amor," my father said and nodded at her.

I did not understand this moment until I was a father myself. When I picked you up from the floor covered in nail polish. When I held your hand as the barber used trimmers on your night black hair for the first time. When you filled your pockets with seashells and stones. I needed to be there for you, but I could not refuse when they asked me to go to Enceladus. Do you understand my son? We do not have the luxury to refuse these requests. The contract was signed. I signed the contract.

If you ever see this transmission, kill it.

I love you. I love your sister too, despite my earlier confessions. I love your mother.

Yours Truly,

Papa

***

Holy Book TM Chapter 40 Verses 1-7 (Universal Old Text)

1 And Mechoben's father who was called Erasure before the fall of his kingdom to his son as was intended did say unto his son "Where have you gone and from whence did you come?" when Mechoben came into the house of Erasure after the setting of Sol.

2 "You know where I was, Father," the child said unto him.

3 Mechoben's tongue was sharp and quick and did anger his father, who called upon Mechoben's servant, Fortuner and asked of him "Where have you gone and from whence did you come?" and Fortuner said "Father of my father, know this: Mechoben comes and goes and does well by you, but does well by himself most of all."

4 And so Erasure did place a TrackAKid sensor in Mechoben's most prized CyRolex and did monitor his son's movements.

5 He found him in the Temple of the New World Stock Exchange residing over the others and they marveled at his knowledge of the Futures.

6 He said "My son, I worried for your productivity. You caused me much anxiety." And Mechoben answered him saying "Father, how was it that you missed me? You knew I must be about the work of the market."

7 And so Erasure did leave The Son there and found his own portfolio to be increased tenfold and he rejoiced and did bestow many blessings on Mechoben as did the Market.

XXII. With my Thread and Needle, I'll Make the Shroud

Rasp sang a Shanana Schwoop Shigetty song as he stomped in time through the ice toward the little metal building. I'm a little clean, I'm a little dirty, but when I look at you, I get a little flirty. I see you workin' it. I see you jerkin' it. But it's only as good as meeeeee.

MOTHER eased a tentacle over the ice and touched his membrane encased big toe, stroking the nail.

WHAT SOUND?

"Sound?"

RASP SOUND.

"You know my name?"

YES. SOUND?

"Oh, you mean singing?"

SINGING

"Yeah, it's music from Shanana Schwoop Shigetty who is the greatest ever. She was built on a gyroscope and could rotate 360 degrees because her real human skin has snake DNA in it. I don't really remember snakes, I don't think. But I think they were like dogs. Their skin was stretchy so it wouldn't rip when they wrapped themselves around all the people they ate."

Talking felt good. The men on the rigs used to stuff shiny Anti-Rad fabric into his mouth when he talked too much. MOTHER just glided under the ice.

HOME SING I SING

"Oh you should sing to me. I love music."

MUSIC?

"Singing."

I SING.

The ice under his feet trembled and a bolt of bright green light shot out from the dark blurry mass of MOTHER's form lighting the glassy surface into a feverish glow. A high shrill pierced the silence, then a thrumming in a steady pulse. Another high shrill, then chirps and static and an undulation that shook his chest. The ice split ahead of him. A perfect transparent pyramid of ice burst from the black split, hurling prisms across the white ground. Red and orange and violet shot across the ice.

I SING?

"Oh MOTHER. It's scary but really pretty. Prettier than anything."

LOOK ABOVE.

Rasp craned his neck feeling the membrane slide over his eyeballs pulling his bottom lashes. He squeezed his eyes shut and reopened them until the strange distortion cleared. A veil of light trembled above him like a flag in the breeze. A chorus of whistles bursting in every direction unfolded around him. Saturn squatted on the horizon line. Her rotund belly buoyed by delicate gaseous ribbons.

HOME SINGS.

His foot snagged on something and he tumbled onto the ice. MOTHER worried under him, snaking and rippling. He sat up to face a bolted metal door. The distant building was right in front of him. Ice coated the hinges and the latch. A peeling painted sign reading Welcome to the United States Enceladus Expedition Headquarters dangled from a single attachment point on the door.

HERE.

Rasp struggled to remember what to do with a closed door. The Corporation had plotted every point of his life until this moment. Walk through this door. Give your blood here. Place auger here.

"MOTHER? Are you sure there are people here?"

HURT.

"I know it hurts. But are there more like me that are alive?" He was afraid.

YES.

"How many?"

A wave of confusion from MOTHER overcame him. His back arched backward with the intensity of emotion.

"Ok, remember I asked you not to do that, though. It hurts me. Remember?" He yelled.

A ripple of regret tugged at him. MOTHER HURT.

"It's ok. How many?"

NO.

He sighed and tried the latch. The ice held it fast, but it seemed to give. He patted his body forgetting that he wasn't wearing a suit and had no storage for tools. He imagined at MOTHER. He pictured the door swinging open, the hinges smooth and easy. The room behind it filled with people on the fringes of his memory holding warm cups of liquid and platters of fatty, steaming meats. Women from his favorite Pornographic Art Films twined their arms around him, their hips pressing against him. Warm, fragrant hair falling around his face.

MOTHER's tentacle snaked from a small hole in the ice and crushed the ice on the hinges. It then wrapped around the latch and jerked it upward. The crunch of breaking ice and the tinkle of metal pieces. A crack tore through the center of the door. The right side of the split fell to the ground beside him, leaving a maw lit with dim orange light. He leaned into the doorway as snow swirled in eddies past him.

"Hello? I'm Rasp. Anyone here?"

Silence greeted him in a long narrow hallway. The emergency lights glowed orange from their fixtures on the rough floor. Rasp looked back out at the howling white expanse.

"Are you sure they're here, MOTHER?"

YES.

He stepped into the hallway.

"Hello?"

Something moved at the end of the hallway and darted away. It was shaped like a man, but its eyes glowed for just a moment before dissolving into a puddle. His face warmed and his heart pounded.

Rasp started thinking of his favorite jokes. He knew an old miner on the first asteroid mine he was assigned to named Rusty who he would exchange jokes with. He thought of Rusty's hands, hard as horns and crusted with yellow callouses waving as he told jokes. The other men were repulsed by him because he was so old and hadn't been retired yet, but The Corporation kept signing his paperwork excusing him. The rumor was that he used to be the leading expert on hydraulic drilling in The Before. Some said he had invented the process used to extract Helium-3 before the Third Age Oil Glut. He used to buy Ripple Top Beers and drink one after the other, giving Rasp every third one because he laughed at his jokes. His commissary account was always full somehow.

Rasp racked his brain for a joke to tell the disappeared creature. He pictured Rusty sitting at the metal fold out table, illuminated hazy blue by the screens above him flashing images of Ripple Top Beer as they slugged down the stuff from plastic bags they had to punch through with metal straws the commissary rented out.

"An Earth doctor can't find a job on the lunar colony, so he opens a clinic and puts a sign outside that reads: "GET TREATMENT FOR $20 - IF NOT CURED GET BACK $100."

A lunar miner thinks this is a great opportunity to get $100 and goes to the clinic."

"What's dollars?" Rasp had interjected.

"It's commissary credits," Rusty answered.

The miner says, "I have lost my sense of taste."

The doctor tells his nurse, "Nurse, bring me the medicine from Vial Twenty-Two and put three drops in the patient's mouth."

The miner says, "Ugh. this is hydraulic fluid."

The doctor says, "Success! your sense of taste is restored. Give me twenty dollars."

The annoyed miner goes back after a few days to recover his money and tell the doctor, "I have lost my memory. I cannot remember anything."

The doctor says, "Nurse, bring the medicine from Vial Twenty-Two and put three drops in his mouth."

The angry miner says, "That is hydraulic fluid. You gave this to me last time to restore my taste."

The doctor says, "Success! Your memory has returned, now pay me twenty dollars."

The miner pays him, and then comes back a week later determined to get back one hundred dollars.

The miner says, "my eyesight is failing. I can't see at all."

The doctors tells him, "well, I don't have any medicine for that, so take this one hundred dollars."

The miner stares at the money and says, "But this is twenty dollars, not one-hundred dollars!"

The doctor shakes his hand and says, "congrats, your eyesight is restored. Give me twenty dollars."

He started to repeat the joke to himself as he walked toward where the creature had darted away. he imagined himself on a vid, wrapped in Gucci and gold. His voice echoed around him and shadows slid away from him. He realized as he got closer that there was a second automatic door that slid open and closed at seemingly random intervals. The emergency lights flicked off leaving him in total darkness. Darkness like staring between the stars, pleading with something invisible that his grav boots continued to function, adhered him to the barren rock.

Something glowed through the door. Two points of greenish light bobbing away from him. He touched the edge of the door, listening to it snick snick snick as it auto closed. Something brushed against his leg in a long intentional stroke. The door closed. Rasp realized the door was movement-activated. He stood stock still. The door stayed closed. He waved his hand. It opened. Another auto-door snick in the distance.

A low hum sounded and the orange emergency lights clicked back on. He stepped through the first sliding door. The hall was lined with doorways. Some rooms stood open, the once automatic doors pulled from their tracks and discarded in the hallway, some folded and crumpled like aluminum foil. A white powdery substance coated the floor. Tracks, some human-sized, were scattered across the hallways. Footsteps echoed from down the hall. Something clattered in the room to the right.

Rasp's fear had turned into numb curiosity. He turned into the room where he heard the footsteps. His palms were cold and wet.

"Hello?" Rasp said again, his voice sounding alien and distant.

"Hello?" It was his voice coming from the farthest corner of the room. Not an echo.

He stepped toward the voice, suddenly overwhelmed with the need to see another person. Anyone at all. His eyes drifted around the room. Tracks crisscrossed in every direction. Some were imprints of bare human feet. Rasp checked his wrist monitor under the membrane. The temperature was -35° Celsius. Black toe weather Rusty used to call it.

A being stepped toward him from the shadows as he advanced slowly. It was him. He had only seen himself in the approved streams from the Lookin At U surveillance feeds they broadcasted on their personal channels in the mines, but he recognized the shiny healed chemical burns on his forearms. He, or this other version of him, clutched something in his hands and held it in front of his chest.

"Hi, who are you?" Rasp asked.

The being didn't respond. Blood seeped into its sclera and it outstretched its arms toward him. Rasp saw that the thing it held was a perfect fist-sized black orb. The dim light that spread from the hallway seemed to drift toward the orb in a thin current. Rasp's joints ached as he stared at this dark thing. The thing poured from his doppelganger's hands, no longer an orb, but a shapeless thing. A void.

Suddenly there were dozens of versions of himself standing around the room, each holding their own black orbs. The orbs burst in their hands slicing off fingers in a spray of blood. Some of the versions fell to the powdery floor as pieces of their orbs burst in their faces, losing the tips of their noses, their lips. Some fell to earth clutching their genitals, geranium red spilling from between their fingers in rivulets. Some crawled around, blinded by the shards hunting for a handhold in the walls. One wobbled in the corner, sipping from the bowl that was created when the top half of its orb slid to the ground, severing its toes. Black foam dripped from its mouth as it swallowed in huge gulps.

Rasp looked down at his own hands and wondered in this strange silent moment if he was the first Rasp. The original. A perfect orb rested against his abdomen as he cradled it to him. The orb spun under his touch, fracturing into segments, fraying into molecules, tearing into atoms. Emptiness thinning and stretching until it became a thread. A horizon of nil.

1000 copies of his eyes landed on him as he bore his own orb and they bade him to drink. He raised the orb to his mouth, his fingers prying and pressing against the smooth surface for an opening. Something grazed the side of his neck and then pressure, a squeezing on his shoulder. He spun to face the source of the touch and found himself looking into his own eyes again. They were set in a creased, brown face with yellowing teeth and pockmarked cheeks. A ragged flak jacket hung loose on the thin shoulders.

He stepped back. Afraid.

"Oh my god. It's you. You are so tall," the old Rasp said.

"Who are you? What is this place?" Rasp looked around the room for the others. The orb in his hands was gone.

"We spoke on the comms. Do you remember?"

"I remember."

"Rasp, it's me. It's Papa."

The man, Papa, pressed his palms to both sides of Rasp's face and drew him toward him. Rasp resisted, leaning backward away from this man. He broke free and tapped on his comms link. Still dead.

"We had a house in San Francisco. I made hamburgers on Sundays. I was in the military. My name is James. I had a last name, but I forgot it. I forgot your name. They gave me drugs, I think. I swear to you," he begged.

Rasp felt a desire he had forgotten. It was a desire difficult to commodify, to bottle. It was the desire to hear his name said by this man. To feel seen by this man. It was against Corporation policy for two coworkers to touch one another. It went against workplace policy. It took away funds from the Pornographic Art Films. He fell into this man's arms.

"Where have you been? What are these people?" he asked into the man's neck.

"They sent me here. Didn't Mama tell you? What people?"

"Something happened on Earth. Something big, but I think it didn't happen very fast. I can't remember either. I didn't know that families still existed. I thought it was like the movies. Like Star Wars." He rambled like James.

The room buzzed and the lights flicked on.

"Ok, we have to go back to the quarters. It's not very safe here."

Papa held his shoulders for a moment and looked into Rasp's eyes. One of Papa's eyes drifted right, the unmoored iris nudging against the sclera. A floral odor wafted around them, sweet and thick. His fingers digging into Rasp's shoulder. Another feeling prodded in the corner of his mind. One that tightened his throat and sped his breathing. Darkness edged his vision for moment.

"Hold on. I have to help MOTHER. I promised her I would help."

"You have to come with me," Papa said.

Rasp stepped backwards into the hallway. Papa followed, his hands tight at his sides.

"I'll come right back. I promise."

Papa looked at the floor and sighed. His largeness slumped. Dark circles ringed his eyes and he shrugged.

"Ok, I will wait for you by the first door." The floral scent faded and Papa's eyes looked clear and straight again.

Rasp stepped back out of the bunker into the bright white and clear black. Steam rose around the membrane.

"MOTHER? What should I do? Can you see what happened? MOTHER?"

The wind whipped swirls of snow around his legs. The stars burned above him, copies of copies floating in burning suspension. Quiet.

"MOTHER?"

Still nothing. Rasp turned back to the bunker. Cold crept from the soles of his feet, numbing his toes. Papa stood at the doorway his eyes wild.

"Come inside. You will freeze."

"MOTHER!" He screamed into the wind once more. The membranous curtain of MOTHER's protection crackling against the bitter wind.

Papa beckoned him from doorway, the wind whipping his long gray hair.

Rasp trotted back inside. Papa slid the second door shut and bolted it. His gray jacket coated in ice. He wrapped his arms around Rasp, his coat crackling with ice and smelling like oil. Rasp looked down at his bare feet encased in membrane. Papa hadn't mentioned it. Another dark shape slid around the corner.

***

Gram's memories of Riff were fading with each caress, each rich meal, each game of Bicky Ball. Now she lay curled beside Alona with her head on her thigh as Alona smoothed down her shaggy hair. Alona's android, Fey, with her silvery eyes came in carrying vitamin tablets and Shine-fried dog sausage. The SynthFab Silk blankets bunched and slid under her as she sat up to take the platter. Dots of purple Spicy Sweet Secret Sauce circled each sausage.

Alona leaned over to grab a bit of the meat and giggled.

"Oh we are fancy ladies, aren't we?"

Gram laughed. The casing popped under her new teeth fitted especially to her. Salty and spicy, the silky fat filled her mouth. Fey plopped down beside them on the huge soft platform and took a sausage for herself. Alona chewed and looked at Gram and Fey. Her jaws flexed and she pulled a bit of gristle out of her mouth.

"Do you two trust me?" Alona asked. Her eyes went flat. Her changes in mood were frequent. Tempestuous. Darkness replaced by sun.

"Of course we do," Fey said and looked at Gram who nodded.

"I need your help. Both of you."

They looked at one another and then at her. Alona shook her head and put the heel of her hand to her forehead. Her familiar snaked from one nostril to the other, leaving a trailing of pinkish fluid on her upper lip.

"Never mind. We'll talk about it later. Let's just enjoy for now." Sunshine sluicing through storm clouds.

Fey and Gram scooted closer to her on the bed, petting her long, thin-skinned arms.

Gram got up and got her tablet. Her tablet. It was DNA encoded to Alona of course, but she kept it in the right bedside table. Her side of the bed.

"Want me to read to you?" She asked Alona.

Gram had learned to read quickly. Once Alona set up the correct program on her tablet, she soaked it up. Alona had to watch her assets carefully as it was prohibited to teach lower-level employees like Gram to read without express coded permissions signed by the CEO himself. If they wanted to, The Corporation could set the camera to map Gram's iris as she read. It was probably already noted in a server somewhere.

"Not now. I do need to talk to you both, though." Another change. Always shifting.

"I'm sick. Not with anything you can catch. Not like that Android plague a few cycles back. Not like that."

Gram shrugged and Fey nodded.

"Pai is too." Something thumped lightly against the door.

They all went motionless. Alona got up, drawing her SynthSilk robe over her thin shoulders.

"Who is it?" She waved her hand over the transparency command for the door. It beeped and crackled. The door remained opaque. "Everything is broken," she hissed. She manually pried the door open with her delicate three-fingered hands. Fey and Gram sat next to one another, huddled against the wall. One of the children spilled into the room, his extra arms flailing. He squirmed and skittered toward them before Alona could grab him. His smell overwhelmed them. Like diesel fuel and cooking meat. His many-fingered hands tugged at the blankets and slid over the vials of perfumes, knocking them to the floor. He scrambled away from Alona's grasp and onto the bed with Fey and Gram scratching their arms with his yellowed torn nails. His collar beeped, lighting the microchip in the side of his neck.

Alona leaped on him twisting his primary arms behind him while the ancillary limbs gripped the carpet, ripping it up in long green ribbons. Lice crawled on his scalp, dropping to the floor from the slight radiation in his collar. He screeched high and long, as Alona grabbed his legs to drag him from the room. The child turned and bit her cheek, whipping his head to the right. Blood blossomed on her face. Alona let go of his leg and stared at him as if she was listening very closely.

Gram leaped across the bed onto his chest and pummeled him with her fist. The child screamed and waved his arms in front of his face. One of his ancillary arms popped out of socket and flopped beside him. She kept pounding her fists into his brittle chest and snapping teeth, screaming and remembering. The loose recognition of pain in the factory girls' eyes. The bottoms of her feet peeling away. Wandering around on some backwater on Earth before they found her alone, adrift and so thirsty. Too ugly for GagGirls. Too stupid for electronics. Good temperament though. Perfect for resale.

The child howled and then started to cry. Fey and Alona pulled her off of him using their weight to tumble her backwards away from him. An orangish substance like blood coated her knuckles and smeared the floor. She heaved. Alona, still pressing her hand to her face, grabbed the child and tore his tracking collar off. The glowing microchip in his neck faded under his skin. Fey reverted to her male form and wrapped her thick masculine arms around his neck until he went limp in her arms. She transformed back to female rapidly, hugging herself as she shrank and thinned. Bright blue rings faded like cigarette burns on her neck.

Alona leaned back against the wall, the collar dangling from her fingertips. Gram got up and put the back of her hand under the child's nostrils while Fey got up to fetch a cloth for Alona's face.

"Oh Mechoben. I think it's dead."

The orangey blood on her hands stank. Property damage carried the heaviest sentence from The Corporation as was mandated by the Holy Texts of Capital. Public termination and seizure of all commissary assets. Public retirement.

Gram saw a public retirement at the factory once when a girl kept damaging the microchips. Her demerits kept stacking and stacking because of her clumsy fingers. It didn't help her case in front of the disciplinary HR committee that she was somehow overweight and had a dusting of facial hair under her chin. She was charged for that separately. Failure to maintain hygiene standards. Failure to attain feminine standards. Failure to complete tasks assigned by manager. Failure to perform duties according to Corporation minimum standards. Failure to attend regular stand-ups up to three times. Failure to attend Mechoben's mandatory service. Property damage in the first degree. Desecration.

Upper management showed up in-person. Their shining white suits trimmed in real bleached dog fur. Their shoes shined to crisp square reflections of the harsh lights of the factory. They patted the older girls' heads, tapping numbers into their tablets, which they folded into squares and tucked in their breast pockets. The prettiest girls were often reassigned after they came on the factory barges.

They wore Funny Face Armani Face Masks in Deja Blue and spritzed their gloved hands with Germ Genocide sanitizer. Their androids, always in male form, but maskless and gloveless, dragged the offender from her bunk, ripping down her posters of Shanana Schwoop Shigetty and tossing her worn blankets on the floor as their fingers dug into her fleshy upper arms. They gathered all the girls onto the observation deck and programmed the monitoring bots to track everyone's eyes. If they looked away, they would receive two demerits. Every girl was assigned a clicker with a random code. A cute boy wearing PupEars came on the announcement screen above them, bathing them in pale light. Today is a raffle! One clicker opens the airlock door! If your clicker turns blue, you win a scrub on one demerit and 1300 commissary credits! The boy said, hopping up and down.

They shoved the pudgy girl into the airlock and followed her in to strap her feet to the floor. It was Mechoben's first commandment not to waste bioresources. The body must be recovered. She cried the whole time, covering her bare skin with her hands. She hadn't even removed her body hair. A major violation.

OK! On the count of three press the clicker until you hear a CLICK. Wiggle those little fingers now to get them ready. ONE. TWO. THREE.

A chorus of clicks echoed in the silent chamber, each girl staring through the observation window. Their coworker and friend. She who made her bellybutton talk in the surveillance dead zones. She who shared her food with the young ones who hadn't earned enough commissary credits. She who fumbled and caused production to stop.

A creamy-skinned blonde with a surplus of commissary credits squealed and turned to face the rest of them. Her clicker flashed blue. Winner. Winner. Winner. The alarm flashed and one of the androids pushed through the crowd of girls toward the blonde. When he reached her, he wrenched her jaw, forcing her to face the observation window. His fingers left pink marks on her cheek, his nails grazing her left eyeball as he withdrew his hand.

The airlock door squealed open and the condemned girl screamed. She screamed until her eyes rolled back in her head and her body flopped into unconsciousness. Her digits swelled and her body ballooned stretching her skin into a tight round parody of a child. Blood oozed from her nostrils and down her legs. Her purple lips thickened into grim doubt. The timer above the observation glass read one minute forty-five seconds. Her skin drawing apart in thin seams.

The girls touched each other's hands in silence as Upper Management mounted the maintenance platform to the right of the them. The androids drifted around the fringes of the room, silencing the crying, shifting, whispering, squirming girls.

The tallest of them addressed the crowd.

"She had to be punished. She was taking from The Corporation. Remember Mechoben says, 'I am your father, but The Corporation is your mother. To take from her is to take from yourself. She is your shelter. Your comfort.'" Two weeks later they took Riff.

Gram seized Alona's arm.

"They will kill us."

"That's a terrible word, Gram." Alona's tone was flat and empty.

The child spasmed at their feet.

"You're rich. How do we get out of here? Do you have a craft?" She turned to Fey. "Can you fly it? Can we find a way to another facility here? On Mars?"

Fey was already cleaning up the mess. She stripped the bed sheet and draped it over the twitching corpse. Blue stress rings flared on her neck.

"Any transit is monitored. Heavily," Fey said, tightening the sheet around the child.

"We should tell Pai." Alona's voice was thick.

"They will put us out in The Wastes. You are not chosen by leadership. You are female. They will leave us to die." Fey grew an inch, her neck muscles thickened.

"I've seen it. They will," Gram said.

"We could make it look like an accident, like we were playing or something." Alona almost whispered.

"It's been recorded, my love. It's only a matter of time before it leaks to the streams." Fey stood up, genderless and huge. "Please. You will be reeducated in a temple at best. We will be reconstituted to Shine."

"Could you get in contact with a GagGirl? Is that something you are rich enough to do?" Gram's tone was hopeful.

"I think so. I think we can."

"I know someone who was relocated to the other side of Mars to be a GagGirl. She is on the streams all the time. She can help us. Right?"

"Shhh. I hear something."

The lights flicked out leaving them in blackness.

"The generator is down again. It's ok. We'll be ok." Alona's cold hands pressed on Gram's back.

Something moved under Gram's feet. A muscular lump rose under her bare arches. A drumbeat sounded from the hallway.

"He knows," Alona said, tugging the fabric tight on Gram's robe. "He knows."

XXIII. How Doth The Crocodile Smile

Information Packet 2: [redacted]

Date: [redacted]

Subject: Compromised

Dear [redacted]

Our research regarding the medical experimentation on Android test subjects has been halted due to the Board of Medical Ethics, though I don't think it will be for long, given [redacted]'s involvement.

I am torn on this. In the past, we had discussed limiting our research only to the zygotes. Once the androids reach maturity, they do develop consciousness and self-determination. We've talked about the "soft science" approach and lots of other scientists in our field including [redacted] have laughed at me at conventions. I don't want you to think that I can't take a joke. I really can.

I know that the research has the potential to save millions of human lives, but can we at the very least try and introduce a gene that removes pain from the equation? I read that [redacted] LLC has pushed to make sure they have a self-protective mechanism and while pain is the simplest, given that it's already a built-in feature (haha – see I can make jokes too) maybe it's not the most humane. I also understand that pain is part of the research process, especially in our field.

Please don't send me that video of Cambodian children with a mutated version of smallpox again. I get it. It's not humane to let them suffer either.

Attached you will find some gene mapping I did that might address both of our concerns.

Please take it into consideration.

[redacted]

***

Discovery on Enceladus: Life Abounds? Segment on [redacted] News

Host 1: Wow! Have you heard of this amazing new product from the [redacted]?

Host 2: I use it every day. Mechoben recommends it.

Host 1: Oh, you're a believer too?

Host 2: Of course. There is only one true god. All these other gods are bullshit!

Host 1: (Laughs) You are such a good [redacted]. Do you think the life on Enceladus will believe in Mechoben too?

Host 2: Well, I think we'll find out in our next segment. First though, let's review the results from Clobber Bottle 3000!

(Advertising Segment)

Host 2: And we're back!

Host 1: Life on Enceladus huh? Enceladus, that's a funny name! Why couldn't we just name it "Jeff" or "Sandy?"

Host 2: "Jeff the Moon!" I love it. It would be so much easier for people to remember too. So what's the deal with Enceladus anyway? Are we going to be able to live there soon?

Host 1: Well, we have an expert on to tell us ALL ABOUT IT (Host yelling). Everyone put your All-natural skincare'd hands together for Dr. Friendship!

Host 2: Oh Dr. Friendship, your Ralph Lauren Seersucker Futuristic jacket makes you looks so pro-fesh and trustworthy.

Dr. Friendship: I have two medical degrees and also this PainAway TRK (Showing syringe) that I formulated myself, and an MBA. If that doesn't qualify me, I don't know what will. Enceladus or "Jeff" as you call it (laughter) will be an amazing place for us, I guarantee it! The life they found can be eradicated rather quickly for settlements. Of course there are some people (audience booing) who think we should delay the settlements.

Host 1: Tell us who? We need this moon, right guys (Host gesturing at audience)? Is it the Greenies? Did you know that they put African children's lives on the line so they could ban a chemical because it hurt bird's eggs? That chemical killed Malaria. It killed it dead. Children's lives, Dr. Friendship.

Host 2: Those are cold hard facts.

Dr. Friendship: Truly a tragedy.

***

Video Advertising from the Third Age – The Military of the Former United States Advertising Campaign:

40K Sign on Bonus!

Anyone can go to college. Anyone can make a burger. But can anyone do this?

(Video shows first International Moon Wars landing battle)

***

Tactics and Guidelines for Recruitment (Manual 43.5 – New Edition)

1. Building relationships with guidance counselors, faculty, and staff is essential.

• It is crucial that you present service in the United States Military as a career pathway. Many older faculty especially remember military service as boots on the ground, combat-centered duty. While there are still many coveted roles serving in these positions, guide them toward positions that look and sound prestigious, not dangerous. See Appendix A for examples.

• Bring small gifts to guidance counselors, faculty, and staff. Inexpensive gifts like donuts, cookies, coffee. It builds good will.

• Show particular interest in "problem students" and/or students from impoverished backgrounds. Mention said students by name to faculty and staff.

2. Utilize Video Games.

• It should be noted that we have made a substantial investment in combat-centered gameplay with several major gaming companies. Many of these recruits have already been trained without their knowledge due to the substantial popularity of videogames. Familiarize yourself with the most popular games. Build your vocabulary around said games. See Appendix B for examples.

• Learn to play video games, even ones not contracted with the federal government. It will make you more trustworthy and approachable.

3. Make the military sound fun!

• Be sure to focus on the fun parts of your own service. Exclude details that could get back to parents that involve activities that sound dangerous or excessively unprofessional. Remember you are selling an adventure.

***

Al followed Riff draped in a new brandless emerald robe that fell open at the chest to reveal her newly minted PURE FEMALE physical identity. The hall to the dining room was lined with screens that alternated between still images and videos of all of the Pornographic Art Film stars. Riff's image popped up as the sensors picked up her embedded chip. Images of her twined in fabric and nearly unconscious, bent over Hod's knee flicked by to reveal Riff looking into the camera with green filters over her black eyes.

Riff looked over her shoulder at her and smiled.

"Why did they make an exception? It's so weird," Riff asked.

Al had been given a consistency programming via her now nightly visits with Mechoben in the Dream Chamber. Nothing must be amiss. She must trust us.

"It's because of my somatic cell nuclear transfer." Riff wouldn't know what that meant.

"What in Astromine does that mean?"

"It means the scientists who made me decided that they would play Mechoben's father and gave me some extraneous DNA." That sounded like what Mechoben briefed her on. Plausible.

"Oh. So you'll still be with me though?" Riff turned around to walk backwards and face her.

"Yes. I will."

"Can I ask you something else?"

"Yes."

"Why have you chosen your female form for like two weeks now? Is that rude?" Sometimes she was very much a teenager. A child.

"I have decided to stay female. It's what Mechoben intended for me."

"Mechoben? I didn't know that androids could even be religious."

Al ignored her. Her irritation growing as her mission became clearer.

Her meetings with Mechoben were nightly now. Riff had been absent from their private chamber so often visiting The Nozzle and talking to Mama that all she had to do was plug up and meditate. She slid her plug into the port all androids had installed on their Detubing Day. She reached under her right arm and pushed her finger into the scar tissue in her underarm to loosen the connection. She then retrieved the plug from under the Sleepytime Xtra Lux Nap Mat that she and Riff shared and slid it in.

Immediately she was with him. The connection was so real. Sprawled in his bed listening to birds she had never seen, sitting at breakfast eating a bowl of real grains and fruit, riding in his DayTime Hover Craft, warm sea wind funneling through her nostrils and filling her mouth.

Today she came to with clear warm water lapping against her belly and wrists. The line of a white beach cut against the blur of clouds in the soft blue sky. Things in the water, small cold things, slid against her ankles and knees. Mechoben stood nude beside her. His large hand rested on her lower back as he peered into the water. The skin on her hips flushed red. She was nude too but not for sale in this moment.

"Father, is it not vanity for our nakedness to not be productive?" She asked him as a flying creature wheeled overhead. Its white wings were tipped in black.

"Do not test the author of your life," he replied softly. His eyes followed the darting movements at their feet.

"I have followed her and recorded her, Lord. What would you have me do now?"

He looked up at her. His mouth set in an expression of gentle neutrality.

"What was her sin in the first place?"

"Not believing that that The Corporation would provide?"

"That is the least of her sins. The greatest is wanting too much."

"I don't understand."

"No. I suppose you wouldn't because I designed you without the greed gene."

"All androids or just me?"

"All of your brothers and sisters too."

"Why?"

"You had no need of it and resources are limited, aren't they?"

She nodded as the sand under her feet retreated and swirled with the waves.

"Now, I need you to stop her. I want to try the easy way first."

"What's the easy way?"

"Offer her a job. She didn't come here greedy. She came here excited. Don't you remember her stream from the shuttle?"

"What kind of job?"

"Executive Director of Relational Equipping under the GagGirls department. I will make the arrangements for our Executive already in place to come offer it to her. You have to sell it."

"How can I convince her?"

"She trusts you. Like a baby bird, you were the first she saw when she chipped through the egg. How did you do it then?"

"I just loved her and talked to her."

"Well. There you go. I will make the arrangements regarding female leadership with the executive board."

"Won't the other female humans want a leadership position?"

"Oh no, my second-born! No no no!" He laughed. "Female humans want to be told what to do. It's in their very DNA. Male humans too, really. Good thing we're not humans. I'm a god and you're an android." He pulled her close. His wet sun-warmed skin pressed against her. "That is why we have GagGirls. You really should watch The Corporation's History Stream sometime." His lips pressed against her temple and lingered. The waves lapped against them. "Plus, when they see a female executive, it will give them the sense that they have something to work toward. Smart huh?"

"Yes, Lord. Can I ask you one more question?"

"My my, you must have plenty of primate DNA. You are inquisitive. Yes go ahead."

"Why did you choose me? I'm an android."

"Because you are created in my image. Beautiful and powerful and flexible. You and your siblings are mine. Beloved and accurate representations of what was meant to be. Perfect design. No disease." He had let go of her then. His hands soared above them, blocking the sharp sun from his eyes. He arched backwards and howled into the sky. His obliques pushing against the loose skin of his aging belly. His Shine-Injected lips stretching into a grimace over his moon-white teeth.

A wave loomed far out on the horizon line piled with black clouds. The water drew down from them, leaving them exposed.

"Behold me, my child. Breathe me in."

***

Riff's face, seeping with Shine and Plasma from her beauty treatment, hovered near her right side. Al sat up and stretched.

"Al? I was trying to wake you but you weren't moving. You just stopped." Riff's voice carried the grating lisp of concern. "Our alarm keeps buzzing."

"I'm sorry. I was just thinking. Sometimes Androids go into a thinking phase."

"Oh. Are you ok?"

Yes. I'm just fine. Let's get to the set." Al slipped her arm into the crook of Riff's elbow and tucked herself close against her side as they rushed down the corridor pressed against one another. Her monitoring device had activated for lateness, but the alert had been removed. Praise Mechoben. Praise him.

***

Dear Daughter,

I will confess that I have written your brother more letters. I think it is because I know him better than I know you. You were so small when I left for this cold moon. I'm not sure that I should tell you this, but since we have reached Enceladus and set up base, I am feeling braver and more hopeful. I was not certain that you were my daughter. Now that I have seen the transmission from a few months ago, I am certain that you came from my line. I know that bloodlines are both important and unimportant in this day and age, so I will elaborate. In that last transmission that your mother sent, I saw your abuelo's smile. That is your grandfather's smile. The DNA test that your mother sent along did not convince me. Your mother is brilliant. Your mother is devious. Those things will keep you alive. It's strange that when you get out here in The Black the things you worried about on Earth disintegrate.

I digress.

I will tell you a story instead. Do you remember sitting on my lap while I read to you? Your favorite was a book called "Farm Pets." The spine was golden and you rubbed it until it became dull. You wanted to see a farm so badly, so I took you to The Valley to show you a farm. Your mother approved for once. She didn't want you to go one of those small feel-good farms where the hogs wander freely and there is more grass than mud. She wanted you to see the rows of bent children with heat on their skulls. She wanted you to see the pregnant women crouched in the strawberries. The men who were not enlisted missing fingertips from the machinery. It was important for you to understand that this machine we built requires blood.

Do you know why our ancestors engaged in blood sacrifice? Why every single culture from the very beginning has engaged in blood sacrifice in one form or another? I have seen the void between the stars. It is not why you think.

When we got to the farm, I took you into a dirt floored building with one enormous room. There were hundreds of pigs writhing against one another, biting one another, squealing and sliding in the mud for slop in troughs. Men and women and children tended the hogs. Some of them bearing scars on their hands and legs from accidents. The smell was thick. The taste of waste and dirty water on the back of my tongue. I wanted to shield you from it. You reached through the fence with your fat baby hands toward a blue hog with a thick hematoma on its ear. Flies circling the split skin. A worker saw and slapped your hand away. You cried and nestled against my thigh.

I said, "Do you see? This is a farm. Like in your book."

You fell asleep on the ride home, back to the land of shiny red meat perfectly sliced and wrapped neatly like Christmas presents. We ate roadside tacos, the grease trailing down our arms in the long evening light. You asked me if it was a pig. I said yes. You asked me which pig. Was it the pig who tried to bite you? I told you that pig was still alive.

"I wish that pig was this taco," you whispered. Your rage boiling. You tore into the tortilla with your baby teeth. "I wish I was this taco." You put down the sodden taco and danced by the side of the road. A tiny bruja with your tiny teeth and scraped knees singing into the swaying eucalyptus trees. I wish God was this taco. I would eat eat eat him. I wish God was this taco. I would eat eat eat him. You twirled, the breeze catching your baby hairs. Your feet encased in Jelly sandals streaked with pale dust through the straps. The power of ten thousand blood sacrifices coursing through you, your brown skin doused in viscous red lakes of those who did not make it off the top of the ziggurat.

It is this story that makes me ashamed to have doubted your lineage. My daughter, the God-devourer.

I cannot say more on this matter. I am bound to my service.

You are probably wondering about Enceladus. There is a strangeness here that I think you would love, Mija. Do you remember looking at the pictures of the planets and loving Saturn the most? I think it is because she is wreathed in circlet of ice. She is full and round and the colors of her storms swirl around her middle like scarves.

Perhaps the strangest part of her moon, where we are, is that they sing to one another. A daughter and her mother. Our resident astrobiologist tells me that this notion is poetic, but inaccurate. They do sing, but not in the frequency that the human ear can hear. I tend to wax poetic. I always liked the notion of a warrior poet.

The ground moves and I am certain that I have heard voices. I really should not be putting this into writing, but I suppose since the funding for our mission has been reduced for the time being. But you don't care about funding. Why would you? Why should I? I am here on this moon regardless. Sometimes, these letters turn into a diary. That isn't fair to you, mija.

It is strange though. Time passes differently here and I saw something moving under the ice. Our physician is very ill right now himself, otherwise I would ask for a psyche evaluation. We quarantined him because we thought that with our artificial warming we might be waking up some bacteria or viruses that lay dormant in the ice. I suppose time will tell. I will write again soon. I promise.

Devour gods and sing songs.

Besos,

Papa

***

Riff squatted over the Wall Stream MirrorCam looking at her vulva projected on the wall. She parted the outer lips squinting at her reddened labia minora. Her calves ached and a thick blistered burn crawled up her inner thigh. Her Smack Me Red lip stain smudged up to under her right eye.

Al leaned back against the far wall, plugged in for mediation while she soaked her hands in Your Android Healing Solution. Her degloved fingers had slips of printed skin clinging to them that floated gently in the beige liquid. A patch soaked in the same solution clung to the side of her mouth. Her eyes darted back and forth under the translucent lids.

"Wow. They went for us today, huh Al?"

Al did not respond. Mechoben and she were flying across a white horizon of snow in a dogsled. Great beings cloaked in deep green loomed above them. Some of them bent and swaying. The air burned her lungs and her cheeks. She pressed her face into Mechoben's cold jacket. She had never seen dogs in their living form. They churned the snow and barked as the close sun stood high, flicking between the tops of the green.

"Al?"

"Trees," Al murmured. Her eyes slits in the dim.

"What?"

"You must return, my most wondrous child. It is vanity to remain here when there is work to be done," Mechoben said into her ear. His breath warm and wet against her cheek.

Al opened her eyes to see Riff naked from the waist down crouching in front of her snapping her fingers.

"Al? Are you ok?"

"Yes. Yes. I'm fine."

"You said you wanted to talk to me earlier."

"I did?"

"Yeah, right after the shoot. Did the shoot scare you?"

"No. I have a proposal for you."

"Al, you have really started sounding weird a lot lately."

Riff went back to her mirror to squat over it and pushed her hair out of her face. Her brow crinkled.

"A job. A career, Riff," Al said.

"What do you mean? The Corporation already gave me my assignment within the organizational chart. Do you think I should see if the medic should subscribe me something for this?" Riff rolled onto her back, her feet in the air and her arms spread.

"Mechoben has an offer for you."

"Oh my market. What do you mean Mechoben? Mechoben hasn't been seen for like a million cycles."

"I talk to him. While I'm meditating. He wants to offer you a position of Executive Director of Relational Equipping. You have caught his eye. He thinks you'd be really suited to it. Over the other GagGirls of course."

"Ok haha, Al. Right. Why wouldn't this come from management then?" Riff raised her eyebrows, rolling back and forth on the floor.

"Mechoben thought you'd trust me more."

"Fuck Mechoben." Her monitoring bracelet warmed for a moment against her skin.

Al rushed over to her and stared down at her, her eyes fading into a lavender. Muscle pulsed in her jaw.

"Don't ever say that again."

"What are you talking about?"

The automatic door slid open and two old women stepped in and flipped on the maximum lighting. Riff sat up, blinking against the bright white light. Mama stood behind them with a heavy black cloth draped over her arm. A whining alarm sounded from her monitoring bracelet.

"Very good, we were waiting for you to say that," Mama said.

"What's going on here?" Orange streaks mottled Al's throat. She closed her eyes and tried to initiate her masculine process. Her finger bones stayed thin and small. Her muscles compact. Her genitals tucked away.

"Encontraste el mago, mi amor."

"I am calling security," Al said.

"No you're not," Mama said.

The two old women slid through the doorway. Bare shod ghosts, silver hair knotted into intricate shapes heavy with dog leather braids. They slung a silver blanket, light as breath, over Al. It spread above her like fog and then pressed her down down down into the depths of the floor.

Mechoben encased her in his arms. His god heart purple and engorged with blood for her. The muse. The guide. She could feel herself being compressed and scattered, sucked into The Black. Pluto spinning past, dotted with turquoise and red. A sun revolving around a sun. An invisible nebula catching the light from the dying suns. Stretching and pulling apart, her atoms breaking and scattering. Matter unresolved. Calcium, Oxygen, Carbon, Hydrogen. Everything the First Borns were made of the Second Borns were made of. Molten cores slung into streams of orange-red magma whipping in the cosmic winds like thin streams of golden honey.

Riff stared at the flat silver square of the blanket. Al was nowhere.

"Where did she go?" Her eyes shiny.

"We don't have time. Come on. Put this on." Mama thrust the black robe, identical to hers and the other women. "It will shield you."

"Where did it come from?"

"Por Dios." Mama knelt in front of her, scraping a gray plastic tool the size of a man's palm over her monitoring bracelet. The catch broke and Mama pulled it off her wrist. "We don't have time, but they will recycle you into Shine if you don't come with me."

"I didn't ask for this. Al just offered me a job." Tears spilled down her cheeks.

"Look here." Mama slid open the tool she used on Riff's monitoring bracelet. A thin membrane unfurled between the halves. An image of two security androids appeared. They peered at a tablet that showed Mama leaning over Riff with the membrane showing them. A mirror within a mirror repeating over and over. The androids dropped the tablet and dashed out of the door. "You must come now. The Corporation didn't offer you a job. They offered you a cage."

The two older women tossed a foil box with strips of black metal encasing it in the doorway just as all the doors down the hallway snicked closed. The girls all squealed and tittered in their quarters. The box crinkled in the middle but held the door. They squeezed through the opening, beckoning with their spotted hands.

"Ana, they are almost here." Their voices were completely synchronized. Riff realized they were all slightly askew versions of Curandera. Red feathers poked through the silver frizz under their hoods. Their teeth sharpened into yellow points.

Mama gripped Riff by the wrist and hoisted her up, flinging the black robe over her head and jerking it over her face. Pain from the cut on her upper lip blossomed across her face as the rough fabric dragged across it. Blackness and then flashing lights above her. Running. Running. Mama's fingernails digging into her forearm.

Riff's thighs burned. She had not run since she was back in The Before. Nausea welling up in the back of her throat. She pulled down the hood around her face and saw The Nozzle in the distance. It stood like a white-robed nun, the glass ceiling above it glowing with the amber of the Martian atmosphere. The pit beneath it glowed green and the air crackled with static.

The Curanderas climbed up the side of the structure, sticking to the sides of it like great clawed bats. Their robes seemed to pull downward on them.

"Hold on to me, Mija. This robe is a grav robe. It will hold you here."

She clung to Mama's elbow as they approached the terminal. The security androids stumbled toward them from the end of the corridor, their stress responses changing their coloration and sizes. They fluctuated like iridescent bubbles. Mama pulled out a thin slip of fabric with symbols on it.

"Reach into my pocket and get the round ball. Hurry."

Riff reached into her pocket and retrieved a round device with indentations in the side.

"Now, listen." Mama focused on the fabric in her hand and tapped at the terminal screen with her middle finger. "Squeeze the sides of it hard until you hear a click and then throw it at their feet." Her voice was calm.

Riff rolled the warm ball in her hand and depressed the sides of it. The security androids, some on all fours now, were so close she could smell the AndroFresh deodorant coming from the collectors under their clothing. She threw the ball and an odorless gas poured around the androids. They stopped in their tracks and looked at one another. Then they sat down on the floor and began giggling and pulling at one another's clothes. They shifted from sex to sex, nuzzling into each other's necks and squealing. Some of them rolled onto their backs and closed their eyes. Bliss reflected in their glassy eyes. Riff tugged on Mama's robes.

Mama didn't look up.

"It's an estrus hormone blend, I think," she said, absent in her concentration.

A boom echoed around the room and The Nozzle detached from its holster and hovered. One of the Curanderas poked her head out from the cockpit and shouted something inaudible over the roar of the newly activated engines. The railing curled away from the heat of activated engines. Another group of security androids sprinted from down the corridor, sliding on the bodily fluids of the gassed androids. Riff recognized them as Replicant Andy GagGirls in their masculine form. Andy-Fern was out front, tall and pale and dead-eyed. Projectile weapons were prohibited on Mars, due to the risk of depressurization and atmospheric leak, but they carried ShoKStiX. Some had vestigial claws and small fangs. Andy-Fern's eyes were dilated into blackness and her reticulating eyelids rose halfway up her eyeballs.

"Run my child. Las Curanderas will take care of you. Go!" Mama reached into her other pocket and retrieved a thin blade. "Run or I will cut you myself. Run!"

Mama jerked her sleeve from Riff's grasp and pushed her at the base of her neck, her fingernails grazing her collarbones. She stumbled toward the Curanderas. They waved and beckoned from The Nozzle, their black robes lifting and their silvery hair in wild coronas from the static charge.

She could feel her familiar fill her right nasal cavity and slide just over her tonsils. She gagged and struggled toward the ladder on the side of The Nozzle. The Curanderas hummed together as she struggled up the ladder. Her liposuction wounds reopened under the spray-on bandage. Pinkish clear fluid ran down her arms and thighs as she climbed.

Al's voice reached her just as she reached the middle of the ladder. But it was not Al. It was an imitation of Al. A worm pretending to be a snake. An Un-Al.

"Riff, don't you want to come back with me? We can forget all of this." She looked down at Un-Al's features feminized to the very essence of evolution. Her huge eyes, purple and brimming with tears. Her hands delicate and fine. Some downy brown feathers sprouting from her cheeks fluttered in the hot engine wind. Un-Al reached up, like a mother just under a playground slide. Riff remembered Real-Al in that moment holding her after her first shoot, combing her long black hair between her fingers. The Curanderas shrieked as she moved her hand down toward Un-Al's outstretched hand. Regaining some sense of routine.

Then Un-Al crumpled.

Her body eased forward as purplish blood filled around the roots of her hair like a boot print in the mud. Mama put her bare foot on Un-Al's neck and swung a stolen ShoKStiK in an arc as the other androids poured over her, tearing at her face and belly.

Riff heard only a throb in her head. Numbness reverberated, quelling her thoughts into small echoes of emotions. She let go of the ladder and leaned back. Black tendrils darted past her and wrapped around her middle. They twirled under her arms, swaddling her in cold immovability. Her head dipped backwards as the tendrils dragged her up the side of The Nozzle. The cold siding pressed against her bare upper arms as she was dragged toward the chanting Curanderas.

The caramel sky churned with billows of red dust above her as a Martian storm roiled above the transparent ceiling. The Curanderas took possession of her and dragged her into the vessel. Their voices looped and entwined in a moaning wail-chant. The Nozzle shuddered as it disengaged. The patter of androids beating against the side of the craft dissipated as a rain of engineered glass poured down on them. The tendrils released her and retracted back up into the women's noses leaving small squirming miniatures flicking across the floor.

Riff screamed, the act of loud breath thundering around the small compartment. She built it again in her throat and chest until it snapped and another scream belted from her lungs. She sucked spit into her throat and choked, sucking in the recycled air. Her own chemistry overwhelmed the anti-anxiety mist that still lingered in The Nozzle's sealed chambers. The walls shuddered as the craft lifted through the storm. Curandera Morena squatted in the corner sorting through pieces of something. Her pointer finger moving in concentric circles on the trembling floor. Tiny orbs floated through her gnarled fingers as the craft ascended. Big gulping sobs punctuated with gasps. Silence from the older women as they checked systems and disconnected the remaining tracking systems.

The shuddering subsided as Mars' loose grasp on them waned. The Grav drives hurked and churned. The smell of ozone pervasive, encompassing.

The Curanderas made Riff a nest in the crew quarters where Curandera Morena fed her soy paste and cold water. She placed her cool dry hands on Riff's head and chanted as Riff's skin flushed red. The collectors sopped up her sweat, beeping cheerily as they filled their reservoirs and zipped to the pantry with their spoils. Riff was silent. Time passed. Time looped in The Black.

Riff's fever broke and her heart rate slowed. Her fat cells began to refill and the haze from the mist lifted. Curandera Morena was always beside her. Bathing her underarms. Checking the vitamin levels in her rehydration pack. Reading from a book with real paper that crinkled and whispered as she turned the pages.

After several cycles Riff broke her silence.

"Curandera. Where are we going?"

"She speaks." Curandera looked up over a pair of reading glasses with one lens and put down the Syntho Cotton bag she was stitching together. "We are going to Enceladus."

"Won't The Corporation stop us?"

"That would be expensive."

"But aren't they going to punish us to show the others?"

Curandera put down her sewing and took off the glasses.

"Why would they? Lies are much cheaper. The streams already covered us. Look."

Curandera Morena pulled out a tablet from her robes and unfolded it, smoothing the crinkled surface flat with her palm.

The streams showed the androids singing and dancing in a circle around the empty space The Nozzle left. The shattered glass crunching under their feet as they twirled, touching their rebreathers together in a strange peck when the music stopped. Riff peered at the stream, looking for Real-Al. Looking for Mama.

Nozzle Liberated by Selfless, Sexy GagGirl! Prophecy Fulfilled Announcing Mechoben's Return to the Martian Colonies! Androids and Humans Rejoice! New Corporation Product Releases Coming MUCH MUCH Sooner.

The headline crawled over the feed of the GagGirls laying out bolts of cool expensive SynthoSilk and real fruits on a huge golden altar. Her headshot hung over the altar. Her own black eyes altered to green, her body lengthened and trimmed, her skin lightened. Shine Lamps burned on either end, casting long flickering shadows over the piles of food, purses, jackets, electronics, and pouches of virgin water.

"I don't understand, Curandera."

"Neither do they. Calm comes at a price." Curandera Morena closed the streams and folded the tablet back up.

"Is Mama dead?"

"Ana?"

Riff remembered Mama lifting her from a bed where the walls were pink and the floor covered in soft gray carpet. Her cool right hand on her forehead, the backs of her bony fingers against her cheeks. Forehead then cheeks. Forehead then cheeks. She put her back in the bed and returned with a cup of something cold and sweet and fizzy. Small sips, Mija. Small sips.

"Ana was not your mother."

"She said she was. She knew things." Riff floated above her body, watching Curandera Morena rock towards her, laying her sewing to the side.

"Did you see the color of Ana's blood?"

Mama's belly torn like a bag of shine, her intestines sliding through the hands of the teeming androids as they attacked her. Her blood pooled under them, smearing on the shining white floor streaked and patterned in the shape of bare feet. Purple blood. Purple like the blood that dotted the sheets of Al's sleeping mat once a month. A holdover of menstruation.

"She was an android?"

"Sí."

"How? How did she know all these things? She looked like Mama." Her chest hitched. "I think. I still can't remember too good."

"It's an old trick, Mija." Curandera Morena pushed a NicoThumb Mini Delivery System node onto her thumb and pushed the switch. Her sharp eyes softened as the drug absorbed through her skin.

"Why did you use her then!? Was it your trick!?" Riff exploded. Her hands shaking. "Where is my real Mama? Where is my family?"

Curandera Morena opened one eye and folded her hands over her belly.

"That is where we are going."

"Why? How?" Frustrated tears brimmed in her eyes. Her heart rate monitor beeped.

"You will not like the answer. You are getting too excited anyway. Now you must rest. We have weeks of travel left."

Curandera Morena stood up and stretched, arching backward and then bending down to touch her toes. Unconcerned, she looked around the room and picked up the metal pick she used to dig at her gums and put it in her mouth. She strode out of the room. Riff tried to follow her out of her chamber, but the door slid closed. She slammed her fists into the thin plastic and wailed.

The door slid open. The Curanderas peered at her from the storage bay and beckoned her to come sit with them. One of them grinned at her with a toothless maw. Riff pulled back into the chamber, sobbing and threw herself onto the bed and looked out the porthole. Glints of a distant mining operation throbbed in the blackness.

XXIV. Flores en Las Tumbas

Pai remembered flowers. He dreamed about them, sometimes waking in the middle of the Martian night drenched in sweat. His grow rooms bunkered and shuttered below his tattered bed in the vast underground labyrinth. Red dust coated his labs. The wind-powered ultraviolet lights long dead.

He had been working with several governments before Alona was grown. He was once a plant geneticist and neurobiologist specializing in hallucinogenic cacti before The Corporation consolidated the research power for the Enhanced Colonization Effort just after The Event. They bought his research and sent him to Mars to work on plant-based extracts that "worked to soothe the minds of the labor" while conserving the scant Martian resources.

He stood alone in a cold white room with cameras on him as he described his latest ventures in crossing Papaver somniferum with globular cacti. The executive board sent back messages telling that this was not what they were looking for and didn't he work with "mind-altering plants?" He dictated message after message explaining compounds and complications. He paced and looked out of the tiny radiation filtering windows at the butterscotch landscape sheared and deadened with wind and cold. Monitoring and feeding, trimming and swirling solutions under the hard blue lights.

He dreamed about the mountains of his childhood. The white mists pearling on the cactus spines like small suns in the morning as the fog dragged over the crystalline white tops. Sparkling and humming with the living. Llamas standing like gashes in the snow. Condors, rare and enormous, wheeling against the painful blue. Brown as the earth and tied to it. He hoed potatoes and trickled snow down the backs of his brothers' shirts and went hungry. He hauled buckets and buckets of snow when the water was privatized down from the peaks. The wells dried up. His urine became brown slashes in the snow, the ammonia burning his nostrils as his bladder spasmed.

Soon the government enrolled him in a specialized STEM program because he could read Spanish and English. His mother kissed his cheeks and held him close to her thin chest the night before he got on the bus to Quito. She had pink plastic rose barrettes holding her hair from her face. She wound him in red thread, touching the top of his head with every rotation. For luck. His father with dirt-creased hands gave him a small white fabric sack. When he tried to open it to peer inside, his father held his hands and shook his head.

"It is not to be seen, my son."

He opened it on the bus. It was filled with glittering stones and dried flowers. A bone carving of a llama rubbed smooth weighed in his palm as the bus careened around the mountain curves. His stomach burned into his throat. He had a different name then. It changed somewhere along the line. He couldn't place when he stopped remembering his Nom de Terra.

He submitted proposal after proposal detailing his research to The Corporation. Mass Food Production in Ailing Climates, Cultivation of Responsible Non-Earth Agricultural Practices, Martian Soil Abatement for Succulent Crossbreeding, Genetically Modified Pain Reduction Plants for Adverse Conditions. Mescaline Compounds and Their Benefits on Space Travel-Induced PTSD. The executives rolled their eyes and sighed in their offices washed in sunlight when he explained

His manager called him on voice chat from Earth one day and informed him of his impending termination unless he could produce research that The Corporation could use. He would be immediately returned to Earth. This is your last chance. Give us something we can use. He dug through his old files and dragged out a theoretical study he did for Pre-Event NASA and submitted it.

Practical Applications of Scopolamine for Easing Inhibition and Motion Sickness in Interplanetary Shuttling.

The golden ticket. The keys to the kingdom.

***

Gram peered over Alona's shoulder into Pai's underground labs. The carpeting surged under their feet again as they descended into the dim room. Martian dust spun in the recycled air as Alona waved a single light on. A tendril slipped through the hatch and lifted the back of Alona's hair, grazing her neck with the cold tip.

"What is it?" Gram reared back from the black appendage as it drifted toward her face.

"It's supposed to save us," Alona said, pulling a covering from a terminal. Her voice was numb.

She placed her three-fingers into slots on the side of the terminal and turned a mechanism. It hummed for moment and faded as Alona cranked it again. The screen blipped on and went black again. Another black appendage slithered across the floor and trailed over Gram's bare feet. She jerked her foot away.

"Did you get it? Can I call her?" Gram edged closer to the screen.

"The equipment is old." A bit of clear mucus ran from Alona's nose. "I just need a little more time. Bring that light over here."

As Gram pushed the hovering light orb toward the screen, something caught her eye. The walls were breathing. Huge shiny hunks of black tissue pulsed in the light. The tendril that had been following Gram veered into the darkness.

"Alona? What is this?" Gram pressed the orb closer to the walls.

"Bring that light back or I can't do it."

Gram heard dripping in the hallways and tightening like straps being wrenched. Her body was light and alive with fear. She backed away from the walls. The walls were singing in an impossible language. Purple light smoldered in a great tangle of movement from the corners of the room. Her skin puckered and tingled.

"What is this?"

"Ok, I got it," Alona said.

A long rope of emergency lights came on, illuminating the heaving coils that lay over the workstations. A small whining sound emanated from the speakers in the hallway above them. They froze. Pai's voice echoed in the labyrinthian chamber, bouncing off of the dusty glassware. The tendril unlooped and rose in arches and waves heaving toward the sound.

"Alona. My jewel. What are you doing?" The speaker crackled.

Alona sat down on one of the bent stools in front of the terminal and rubbed her eyes with the heels of her hands. Gram shook her head at her.

"Come back upstairs. You're not supposed to be down there."

"Pai, we can't do this anymore."

"Come on upstairs and bring your new playmate with you."

"I want this to be over."

The tendril wrapped around Gram's foot and held her. The tip grazed her ankle and patted her knee. She tried to pull away but it stayed coiled cool and firm around her foot.

"Of course you do. I know what happened to your brother."

"It was an accident," Alona said. Her voice quiet.

"I can protect you, but you have to come back upstairs. I can't go down to retrieve you. You know that."

Alona cut her eyes to Gram who was pushing at the coils around her leg.

"It's called MOTHER."

"What?"

"The being. The being under the compound."

"Alona. You need to stop talking." Pai's voice was serious. "You will get your new friend hurt."

"That thing wasn't my brother."

The walls slid against one another, unfurling and falling to the floor like snakes coiling and twisting. The tendrils whirled and twisted around the glassware, popping them. Bits of glass flew across the room, raining down onto the floor. The being twirled around the speaker and ripped it from the wall, the wires stretching like ligaments from torn meat.

The screen in front of Alona burst into a white light.

"What do we do?" Gram pulled herself toward Alona, shouting above the sound of lab tables screeching across the floor as the being tightened itself into a central knot.

"There's nothing we can do." Alona sank down onto the floor from the stool. "MOTHER is angry."

Water flowed down from the steps above. Water. Gram had never seen so much water. She was an unapproved belt baby born before the Great Separation; water was recycled in her world. She had cannibalized herself thousands and thousands of time. Her sweat, her feces, her breath, her urine, her menstrual blood all collected and reprocessed. She drank the others and the others drank her. A bluish white gas oozed from cracks in the ventilation system. A buzzing alarm pulsed on her wrist monitor.

Alona curled on her side and wept.

***

Information Packet [redacted] Martian Date [redacted]

Subject: Research

Dear [Redacted],

We have some follow up questions to the study you sent as well as some requests. You mention "Devil's Breath." We would now ask that you not refer to scopolamine by its colloquial name any longer to discourage misconceptions about the safety and efficacy of the use of this substance. We are interested in its raw form, as complications with the Terran government continue to arise as the crisis continues to unfold.

Our questions are as follows:

How easily can this compound be synthesized?

Can it be used in an aerosol?

How involved is the manufacture of this drug?

Thank you for your participation in this study. We have rescinded your termination notice with the caveat that you will continue your work solely on this project. Your pay has been reduced to reflect the decrease in workload.

Please sign the attached paperwork with your DNA sequencing number included. Please use Terran dates in the future.

Sincerely,

[redacted]

XXV. The Center Cannot Hold

Papa's jacket was so worn it was nearly transparent. He held Rasp's hand in his and traced his thumb over the veins under the skin.

"You are so small. Like me," Papa said. A thin white scar cut through the sagging skin on his neck. He stood up suddenly and flung his arms around him. The sweet smell of infection and human sweat wafted around Rasp. The jumpsuit Papa gave him reeked of someone else. Another person's suffering tucked around him, enveloping him in the too-big garment.

Papa had stacked empty cans in every corner. When Rasp looked at them, his heart pounding from fleeing the shapes in the hallway, Papa said "Helps me know." Plasticine buckets brimming with clear fluid stood around the room, ripples emanating from some unknown constant motion under the floor.

Light from the monitoring station illuminated the room in a cool blue light. Another black shape slid around the corner knocking over the tower of empty cans. Papa leapt up and grabbed a bucket brimming with a clear viscous substance. He shuffled over to the corner and squatted, gripping the bucket with white knuckles. The shape darted to the other corner and Papa doused it with the substance. It made a high whistling noise as the liquid coated it and flopped on its side. The liquid bubbled into a huge orb and lifted from the floor, the dark shape suspended in the center rattling and squawking. Papa rushed to a hand-rigged switchboard in the center of the room and flicked some switches. The orb drifted toward the sliding door.

"Open it, son!"

Rasp transfixed on the creature in the bubble sat paralyzed were Papa left him.

"The switch by the door. Open it!"

The orb neared the door, the creature shifting into spikes and angles, then into a human face. A face on candles from The Before with open hands and halos. It smiled at him with blinding white teeth, its eyes wrinkling at the corners. It coughed. Flecks of something cool and oily spattered on him. Golden thorns wreathed the grinning face and pressed into the illusion of skin. Pushing into the cheeks until the skin punctured with a barrage of small pops. It neared him. It floated to him like an impurity on an ore stream. Slow as approaching break time. The switch. The switch. He must reach the switch. His arms were heavy. His mind comfortable and soggy.

Papa pushed past him and flicked the switch. The being giggled as the orb zipped into the dark hallway.

Papa wiped his forehead with his sleeve and trudged over to Rasp. The haze behind his eyes faded into a strange clarity. A feeling he could not name rose in its stead. A feeling like standing on his own air supply hose.

"I'm sorry. I froze."

"It's ok." Papa sat down on the dirty military-issued cot beside Rasp and motioned for him to sit.

"What was that?"

"It was…what did you see?"

Rasp described the being to him.

"They are that then."

"Can they hurt us?"

"Oh yes. Yes they can. We had thirty crewmen when we landed."

"Do they have teeth or something? Are they animals? I didn't think animals existed anymore. Did you know that some people think they never existed at all and that the streams are lying? That's forbidden thinking though. It will get you so many demerits." He chattered. "Are they engineered? Who engineered them?"

Papa stared at the monitoring station and said nothing. He pinched the skin between his thumb and forefinger.

"Papa?"

"I'm sorry. What was the question?"

"Are they animals? How do they hurt us?" Rasp hopped up from the cot and wrung his hands.

"They hurt our minds and our hands hurt ourselves," Papa said. He looked around the room as if taking inventory and stood up.

"Oh." Rasp's heart rate steadied.

"Come here. I'll show you where to fill up the buckets." Papa pointed to the buckets around the room.

"Ok. What is that stuff?"

"It's a coolant gel that regenerates and auto congeals. The diablitos just wear it like a dress to the dance and then shed it and we have to go get it again. Sometimes if I can't get them out of the room in time, they'll pop the bubble into a million little pearls." Papa's eyes darted around the room. He took a comb out of his pocket and ran it halfway through his tangled hair before it snagged. He stuck the comb into his breast pocket where the corner pushed through the thin fabric.

Papa led Rasp to a tiny room that blinked with old servers. A blob of the clear fluid congealed underfoot and scooted toward the corners of the room.

"Where is your ship, son?"

"I don't really know. MOTHER got me here."

"Your mother?"

"No. MOTHER. She says the drill is hurting her."

"There is a woman here? Where?"

"A woman? No, she isn't a woman. She's under the ice. I think. I think she's under the ice."

"Mijo, you shouldn't listen to her. They are trying to kill us."

"She protected me. The membrane is because of her. I would have frozen." Rasp said.

Papa's eyes hardened and he twisted Rasp's collar, wrenching him off his feet. He yanked Rasp closer to his face and shook him. His thin arms tensed under Rasp's face.

"They are the enemy. Nothing else. Do you understand?" Papa released his collar and stepped back. "Now, pick up that shovel. We have work to do." His tone was sure and serious.

The comfort of direction overwhelmed Rasp. Someone telling him exactly what to do. Exactly who the enemy was. Exactly where to go, what to eat, who to speak to, like a blanket thrown over his shoulders. A Pornographic Art Film with his face on anyone he wished. A bonus to his commissary account.

He thought about being cocooned in his bunk, the screens perfectly customized to his color vision, his eyesight, his sexual orientation. Microtransaction after microtransaction, draining his commissary account to crumbs while he inserted himself into each constructed scene. The light pouring from the other miners' self-contained pods like gargantuan alien seeds. Here he was cold and responsible and hungry. Working on the unscheduled project of survival.

Even as he said "ok" to Papa, something dug at the corner of his mind. The tender hold of MOTHER as she enveloped him in the membrane. She asked him only to remove the drill. To make it stop.

"Ok, Papa." He stooped to pick up the shovel and followed him into the dark hallway. "Can I ask one more question?"

Papa sighed and nodded ahead of him, barely visible in the dim light, the plastic buckets swinging at his sides.

"Why can't we just see if it helps to stop the drilling?"

"Because there are more important things to worry about now."

A dark shape materialized ahead of them, blinking in and out of visibility as they neared it. It arched and grew into a creature on the edge of Rasp's understanding, with limbs that stretched and folded into mandalas of teeming movement.

Papa lifted the bucket to his chest, gripping it by the edge.

"Do you see it, my son?"

Rasp realized Papa had never called him by name.

"Sí, Papa. Lo veo." The strange words spilled out.

Papa lunged at the creature and slopped the remaining coolant out of the bucket at it. It keened and skirted away into the darkness. A sound like tangled hair being brushed through echoed down the corridor. He turned back to Rasp and motioned for him to follow, his finger to his lips.

Rasp turned and looked behind him into the darkness. Nothing. The emergency lights buzzed on above, revealing the corridor under the orange light again. Dozens of overturned plasticine buckets identical to the one that swung from Papa's right hand lay scattered everywhere.

"Come on, we have to get to the operations room," Papa whispered.

Rasp followed trying to remember the color of Papa's eyes from The Before.

***

Dear [Redacted]:

I realized that I have written the children and have forgotten you. That is not to say that I have forgotten you; we have spoken over the comms even before our decision to no longer be married. I suppose even that decision doesn't carry the kind of weight it once did. I am doubtful this will ever reach you, much like the children's letters, but it gives me a touch of normalcy here in this thin tin can floating through these unmoored rocks.

The truth is, I miss you out here. I used to think about other women when we were together. Even when I had your breasts under my hands. Even when I saw our son. Now I only think about you. I did always have a flair for the melodramatic. "La pasión" you used to joke with my head in your lap before all of this. I suppose we should have asked what the cost of our ambitions would be.

Is now the time to think about blame? I'm unsure. Is blame ever useful? My father asked me once that if I threw a ball and it broke our neighbor's window, was it still broken even if I didn't mean to?

It was still broken and I was responsible for breaking it. The answer is simple. It always was simple, I suppose. I have always wondered who is responsible if the neighbor threw the ball back and broke their neighbor's window. What is the recompense then? Both neighbors have broken windows now. Is this justice? Who can mediate this?

You told me once that I ask a lot of questions for someone so dedicated to authority. Questions are the antidote you said. I asked the antidote to what? And you pulled me into you leaving the question unanswered. Your cold hands on my belly. The fading pink star tattoo above your breast, covered everyday with pullovers and crisp dress shirts.

You were like a collapsing star. Nothing escaped your pull.

I remember the first time I saw you. You were being chewed out by your C.O., your back so straight and your eyes like river stones. Your small fists clenched at your sides and your mouth set in defiance. The only word I could think of was "mighty." Like a mockingbird diving a crow. Fearless. The Staff Sergeant was red up to his neck. Sweat slipped down his back darkening his uniform. His hand was a blade leveled at the tip of your nose. He might have spent his energy screaming at the moons for all the good it did. You saw me looking after he strode away and winked at me. No one had ever winked at me. I don't think anyone has since.

My heart. Mi corazón. You are already a collapsing star and a mockingbird and the moons of Mars in this letter. You are an abyss and the forest floor. I approached you and told you that you were brave. You said I was romantic for the military and let me buy you a drink. Martian swill probably spiked with coolant. We danced belly to belly in the dark packed room. The recycled air smelled like engine grease and sweat and perfume. Our feet stuck to the floor from the sick-sweet drinks. The AndyGirls danced on raised lit platforms. They were closer to clones than Andys at that point, I suppose. Each identical to the last with their strange long legs and ice blue eyes.

I said, "You are more beautiful than anyone else."

And you asked, "Hablas Español?"

I knew it was against regs. I knew I could get ninja punched, but your eyes were warm with liquor and I was brave for once.

"Eres más hermosa que nadie" I said. You pressed your cheek against my chest and I marveled that you passed the physical tests to get in. Your body was an unsprung trap. Smaller than a bullet wound.

I have always wondered if you remembered that night.

I am certain that by the time I send this transmission, you will be out of range. Maybe I planned it from the start. I have never understood why it was so hard to apologize. It costs nothing.

Lo siento. I'm sorry. While it is too little, too late, know this: I am paying out here.

The Black is a place of atonement with no priests to guide you. Remember me, for your thought shall be my last incarnation. My bones will not go back to the good earth. My skin will go unconsumed by the insects we sought to eradicate. My teeth will go unfound by the generations ahead. My stories will slip away. I will not be among the resurrected. How will I be found?

Enough of this. Self-pity was always my failing.

I am sorry. I truly am.

Besos,

[Redacted]

***

Holy Book Chapter 956 Verses 12-19 (New Intergalactic Version)

12 And when you do return to my bosom, know this, you will need to earn your fat for our fathers did rise unto their own by turning labor into silver and silver into untraceable currency.

13 And herein do I say unto you, my first commandment is as follows; women were created and adorned for a singular purpose and that purpose was to work, as is man's purpose. Let it be known that work for women and work for men are to remain separate. Women who perform the labor of men shall not be allowed access in The After. Men who perform the labor of women will pay the non-refundable fee before entry.

14 Covetousness is virtuousness. This is my second commandment. Man cannot be driven by joy in his station alone. Ambition doth enhance the plight of all men.

15 You shall have no other systems before this one built by hard work and inheritance of the blood of the fathers and mothers who came before and the leadership of Mechoben and The Father. Heed this commandment most of all, for it is greater than all of my other commandments.

16 Despise your father and your mother, for they sinned in your creation. The female body is meant for consumption and admiration, not

distribution. The male body is meant for construction and labor and the honorous work of war, not the random distribution of genetic material.

17 Shine is life. Sup on it for all meals.

18 Consume and sup from the fruits of Terra and Beyond. The After Book is the commissary ledger. The Father will dash they name from entry should your consumption flag, as it doth glean the tithe that is they father's.

19 Know these commandments and know them to be the only truth.

XXVI. Fall and See There is No Ground

Riff stood by Curandera Morena as she tore strips from Curandera Rubia's cloak and laid them over the dead woman's staring eyes. She collapsed just as Enceladus materialized in the viewport, white-blue and still against the velvet of space. Riff had been teaching her how to make a NicDip by soaking wads of fabric in the last droplets from the Transdermal Nicotine Delivery System vials. She tucked a wet wad just under Curandera Rubia's lower lip when the moon drifted into their eyeline.

Curandera Rubia wrapped her arm around Riff's waist and pressed her bristly lips against her cheek when she saw the moon. She squealed and giggled like child, her spotted crepe paper hands gripping Riff's. Then she fell to the floor.

Riff screamed and pushed the comm button. She had never seen anyone collapse. Their blood pressure, viral and bacterial load, and consciousness levels were monitored by the managers at the factory and

GagGirls facility. It was considered detrimental to productivity to witness a lapse in bodily autonomy.

Curandera Morena and Curandera Peliroja glided over Curandera Rubia's inert body. Her hair floated above the floor as the failing gravity drives ground and churned in the walls. Riff petted her white hair and smoothed her cheeks. The women encircled their still companion. Curandera Morena picked up her thin arm and pressed her pointer and middle fingers into the wrist. She laughed and then wailed.

The other Curanderas picked up the death cry and lifted Riff to her feet. Curandera Morena flicked a gauzy caul over the body and passed her hands over Curandera Rubia, pausing as she passed her hands under the nape of her neck.

The body lifted and jerked as Curnada Morena removed her fingers from behind the still head. A small opal coated in a thin layer of blood stuck to the end of her middle finger. She nodded at Riff.

"This is the key. You are the keyhole," she said.

The other Curanderas wrapped their arms around her and kissed her cheeks in the same place that Curandera Rubia did before she fell.

"I don't understand," Riff said.

"Curandera Rubia has sacrificed her protein and carbon so that you may enter the fold. You are now The Seer. And now you will eat the holy stone," Curandera Morena said.

"The Seer?"

"You spoke with the holy MOTHER."

"How did you know that?"

"Open your mouth, new sister."

"But, I haven't spoken to her in weeks."

"That's not relevant. You have been touched. Look."

Curandera Morena held up her palm in front of Riff's eyes. A silver eye blinked back at her, nestled into the curvature of the wrinkled flesh. The pupil reflected Riff's image upside down. Her Shine stuffed lips were returned to their original thin curve. The iris injections to lighten her eyes were swallowed by the black shadows of her own color. Her waist thickened again as the PlastiBond Internal Corset dissolved.

In the center of her forehead a reflective eye identical to the one in Curandera Morena's hand grew into a white paper bag that unfolded into thousands of crinkling petals that drifted down in a barrage of white noise. She reached up to touch the void in her head. Her fingers brushed a warm metal orb that bloomed in the place of the vacated eye. A razor thin metal eyelid slid down over her finger and severed the tip. She jerked her finger away, gripping her thudding digit and tried to scream. Instead of a wail, a thick black tendril oozed from her mouth and rose to the blinking metal orb in her forehead. It furled and unfurled like a baby's hand reaching for some bright toy. Curandera Morena closed her hand into a fist in front of Riff's nose and squeezed, the veins in her hands and arms lifting against her thin skin.

A black tendril snaked out of her fist, the blood opal perched on the end of it.

Curandera Morena's voice hummed in her head.

"Accept the gateway."

Riff leaned back and looked up. The ceiling had become the vastness of space above her. She opened her mouth.

Curandera Morena's tendril twined around her own, layering and layering over and over into a kinetic wreath that churned into a frenzy. The opal turned over and over on top of the writhing circle. Riff felt her lungs filling and the void above her falling over her face like a caul. She fought for a breath. She clutched at the matterless veil above her. She screamed against the churn in her throat. Everything. Everything expanding around her and drawing her body into it. Her atoms pulled away from one another, rending her into particles. A floating fortress appeared before her with a thin line of green light that pulled her disassociated pieces into something with form. It was not her body. It was genderless, cold, strong, and associative. Everyone spoke to her and through her. Curandera Morena's voice, louder than the rest, came to the forefront.

"Escuchame. Accept the gateway." The disembodied voice was replaced by the else-voices, none clamoring, all talking.

She drifted past the green line and into a diamond of pure white. She had no eyes, so they could not hurt from the bright hull of excited atoms. She had no skin, so it could not burn her. She had no self, so it could not frighten her. A being greeted her in the center of the diamond and the being was her and the rest of they who comprised one another and so they were all greeted and greeting all at once. The being touched the center of her and they asked without asking if she would accept the gateway.

She affirmed and they affirmed, though she knew the choice was being made over and over again, infinitely and without beginning or end.

The being unfolded and spread throughout the diamond, signaling through a scent pattern to follow. She unfolded her own molecules into the scent pattern of oily hair and spun on the wake of the being's molecules. A wide sheet of static spread and then collapsed as the being moved through and past it. A memory of a white picket garden gate manifested and then shattered and collapsed as the unnamed They pushed a memory of the Pacific Ocean onto the static sheet.

The great dark blue hurled itself over into huge curls of white froth. The black pebbles under the memory of feet with little cold streams weaving into transparent vectors. The smell of it. Saline and fish. A blanket of heavy gray on the horizon. She struggled with her selfness, with her I, trying to force it into her familiar physicality. The ocean crumpled before her, the manifest sky tearing like a poster being ripped from the wall. The They vibrated in a molecular hum reminding her of the nothingness of what she was at that moment. The opal coated in Curandera Rubia's blood replaced the sun memory and spread across the sky memory. Every piece of it divided into geometric pattern and then into lines of color that surged into a cast net of hexagonal pinpricks. Swim. Swim. Swim.

She pushed her atoms into an obelisk and collapsed into the ocean, the remaining pieces of her and They combining into an orbital whirl. Her belly was filled and swollen with pregnancy. It glowed orange red. Her organs and bones silhouetted against the bright thing that turned within her. Her head pitched backward as her uterus contracted and the first star was born, oozing with plasma. Gas clouds gathered and whirled around them in a pale spiral. The star drifted toward her breast and hovered there. light closed over her and it fed from her body, expanding into a luminous corona. It spoke to her.

"DO YOU REMEMBER ME?" the star boomed.

"Are you MOTHER?"

"I am MOTHER."

She reached down and touched her sagging stomach.

"Am I MOTHER?"

"You are MOTHER."

"What do you want?"

"WHAT DO YOU WANT?"

She gazed at the shifting blue gray gases pouring off of the star and touched her face.

"I want to be free."

"I WANT TO BE FREE."

The star folded its gaseous cloud over itself, pulling the gauzy shawl over itself in folds.

"How do I do that? How do I become free?"

"FIND THE WIZARD."

Riff felt her face flush with frustration in the face of this being encased in light. Her frustration grew with each opaque suggestion.

"Where is the Wizard? Who is the fucking Wizard?"

"YOU WILL FIND HIM AT HOME. HE IS LIKE YOU."

And at that the threads of the gas cloud unraveled and the star collapsed before her in a rush of cold blackness. She emerged breathing in the recycled air of the ship. Her weightless body lifted and touched by the Curanderas. Something slithered over her temples. Calm washed over her as she recognized the familiar sensation. The women leaned over her, petting her hair and dabbing at her forehead with dirty engine rags.

"Welcome back, Curandera Negra," Curandera Morena said to her.

"Where did I go?" Riff sat up on the AntiGrav RelaxTop table.

The women eyed one another, as they covered her with a reflective heat blanket. Curandera Peliroja patted her thigh through the crinkling fabric and said, "you were birthed and gave birth. You are MOTHER and we are MOTHER. You are a Curandera now."

"Who is The Wizard?" Riff sat up and pushed down the nausea that overwhelmed her.

Curandera Morena pulled the other Curanderas close and whispered to them as Riff looked on.

"We think he is on Enceladus."

"But who is he?"

"We are not sure. MOTHER tells us only impressions and we have to have a ceremony to contact her. Like the one you just participated in, hermana. We just know that is where we must go."

"My brother is there."

"We know. It was arranged that he go there."

"By who?"

"Another sister."

"Tengo sed," Riff said and leaned back. The dead language came back at strange times.

"Por supuesto." Curandera Morena brought her a recycled water bag and pierced the corner with her long fingernail. She handed it to Riff and drifted over to the control panel while Riff sipped from the dripping corner. She dragged her fingernails over the screen peering into the light.

"We will meet The Wizard soon enough, it seems."

The others looked over at her.

"We are just a few days away, hermanas."

They abandoned Riff on the table and rushed over to the screen. Curandera Morena motioned to Riff to come and see. She slid from the table, the gravity drives pulling at her. Saturn loomed yellow and heavy on the edge of the screen and a thumb-sized sphere hung in the center of the screen. The Curanderas held one another, balling the fabric of one another's robes in their gnarled hands.

"And so we approach the second home," Curandera Morena said, her eyes glistening in the glow of the screen.

***

Rasp used a device that Papa had rigged to break and gather ice from outside the compound. It had a half-functioning laser that softened the ice enough to break it with the hard metal blade at the end of a long piece of titanium pipe torn from the Earthcraft that brought the men here. Papa foisted one of the hundreds of plasticine buckets at him.

"The ice is softer by the augers, by the drilling rigs," he said, "you will want this." Papa handed him a pistol. Rasp gasped.

"Wow. I thought they only had these for the Real Kill Pornographic Art Films. They are so old, but they deliver the high-quality Android split splat Panorama Pictures Promises," Rasp recited from the streams.

"I don't know what that means but take it. You might need it."

"How do I use it?"

Papa pressed a catch on the side and let the magazine drop into his palm.

"Look. It's very easy."

He pointed the gun at the far side of the room.

"Never point it unless you want to kill."

"Will it work on those things in the hall?"

"Yes, but we only have about fifty bullets left."

"That's a lot."

"It's less than you think."

"I didn't know bullets ran out."

Papa sighed and handed him the gun. He loaded three cartridges into the magazine and showed Rasp how to cock and fire it.

"It is very limited, ok? It mostly just scares things here. Do you understand?"

"Yes." Rasp felt small. Ignorant. His excitement fading.

He tucked the pistol in his too-big cold suit and picked up the plasticine bucket. The wind pushed him back as he opened the hatch. The transparent front of his helmet fogged and crystallized as soon as his boot crunched on the ice. He pressed the warming function. The crystals on the right side melted into a transparent streak, leaving his helmet half obscured. He trudged out toward the frozen lake, the pistol rubbing against his hip bone.

As he neared the lake, he saw the drill site in the distance, the dark spire jutting from the machinery. A familiar shape glided to toward him from the center of the lake. He felt MOTHER in his head.

"HURTS."

"I know it hurts, but I have to get water now or I'll be the one who hurts."

"HELP."

Rasp clenched his teeth and pulsed his jaw. Irritation rose in his throat.

"I don't have the tools right now."

"UP."

Rasp rolled his eyes and activated the heat clear for his helmet.

"What's up?" He laughed. "Are you telling a joke, MOTHER?"

"LOOK UP." An image of an asteroid colliding into a small moon bloomed in his head.

He looked up. A craft arched over the horizon line, entering orbit. Its chemical signature pale blue. From what he could tell from his time astro-mining, it looked about forty-eight earth hours before it landed. He looked at the monitor on his wrist. It blinked into the orange spectrum. A frowny face caked in ice blinked on the screen.

"I have to get back or I'll get an early retirement," he said into his helmet comms.

The craft disappeared below the horizon line as he looked up again.

"Are they friendly?" He asked MOTHER.

"FRIENDS."

"Ok good. Why are they here?"

"FIND FRIENDS."

"How much are you paying me to find them?" He chuckled at his own joke, covering his apprehension.

"FRIENDS FIND."

"Oh, I see. They are trying to find us."

"YES. LOOK."

The landscape melted in front of him. Rasp was suddenly warm and full, wrapping an old woman's naked body in strips of black packing plasticine. His body was not his body. He looked down at the hands of this body, small and smooth with gel laser colored nails. He reached for a piece of plasticine and realized the length of his arms prevented him from reaching it without standing on his tiptoes. He perched on his tiptoes when an old woman standing across from him grabbed his newly feminine arm. He recoiled in disgust. He had forgotten what old people looked like and smelled like. Her palms were cold and calloused.

The old woman looked at him through suspicious eyes.

"Curandera Negra, estás bien?"

"Sí, estoy bien. Gracias." The words flowed out of him automatically.

"No eres Riff," she said, her eyes narrowed. "Quién eres?"

"Rasp," he said without hesitation.

"Do you know the great MOTHER?" She asked, switching to English.

"She brought me here." His voice came out high and smooth.

The woman lurched toward him and took him by the shoulders. Her filmy eyes soft and worshipful.

"You must let me in. I must speak with her. It is my holy rite."

"MOTHER?"

A thread of warm acceptance drew through his consciousness. The silver filament tattoos under her eyes glittered and flashed as she shaped her words. She drew out her vowels and laid her hand on the back of his neck.

"Yes. Yes. MOTHER. Let me call the others."

The words flowed from him without thought or measure. He could not look away from her tattoos. Her voice coaxed him, aroused him, hurt him all at once.

"I don't know how to let you talk to her. How far are you from landing?"

"About three days."

"I'll put up a beacon for you. Papa doesn't trust MOTHER." This was the correct answer. Bending to her was natural.

"Papa? There are no life readings except for you and MOTHER."

"He's underground. In the old military base, across the lake from the drilling facility."

Another old woman rushed into the room and touched his arm, her silvery hair flying behind her. She wore a plasticine circlet with etchings of monstrous eyes impressed into it. She looked into his eyes.

"It's not Riff?" She turned to face the other woman.

"Check the skin response and use your thrum voice."

Rasp smiled at her, still wooed by the first voice and felt his lips pull against his skin. His lips felt unnaturally full and thick.

"Send him back. This is not the way."

"But we have a channel, sister. We can talk to HER."

The dark-eyed woman wearing the circlet whirled on her, her face inches from the snubbed nose. Rasp stood very still, feeling the unfamiliar heartbeat in his chest. The air was charged.

"Send him back," she hissed, her solid dark eyes shimmering. "It puts everything in danger." She put her thumb on his forehead and pressed her fingertips into his cheeks while she fumbled with something in the folds of her robe. The other woman stepped forward to push her hands away from his face, knocking Rasp off balance.

"It's my holy rite," she said, pressing close to Rasp. "I want to talk to her."

The dark-eyed woman pulled a bundle of silver wires from her pockets and dropped it to the floor. The hiss of steam filled the confined space and Rasp felt himself falling into bright cold whiteness.

He found himself standing at the edge of the lake with the plasticine bucket still empty at his side. The auger across the lake lifted and dropped back down into the ice. The ground vibrated around him. The ice split in the center of the lake and sent frozen chips in all directions. They spattered on the frozen ground around him. His spiked boots clung as he bent to pick them up and put them in the bucket. The work came automatically. He couldn't stop thinking about the brujas entering Enceladus' orbit.

MOTHER surged under the broken ice, crushing the broken planes under the weight of her great arms. Her anger flooded his psyche with each lash. He fought her in his head, bending to pick up the bits of ice that flew from the tips of her claw-tipped tentacles.

A memory came back of Mama snatching away a statue of an angel that he was trying to clean for her and tossing it into the trash. His thumbprint on the angel's clavicle. Mama's eyes hard. Mama's jaw tight. The sting of her slap. The anger pouring from her. He tried to explain himself, to tell her that he just wanted to make her happy. Another slap, her fingers tightening around his throat just for a moment until she stalked away. It was best to say nothing. To let her run out of steam.

MOTHER shouted into his head in an unknowable tongue. There was no sound to it, just pure and unbridled wrath. He felt the burn of stomach acid in his throat. His monitor beeped at him. The suit wouldn't hold heat much longer. He picked up the bucket of ice and walked back to the compound. He didn't want to help MOTHER. He didn't want to help anymore.

He stumbled into the vestibule of the compound with two minutes remaining on the suit timer. Papa poked his head out from the laboratory door.

"Close the door!" he shouted above the wind and drew his coveralls collar over his nose.

Rasp rammed his thumb into the recessed door button and dropped the bucket. Steam rose from the pieces of ice as they settled.

As soon as the door slid closed, Papa staggered into the hallway. A strip of dirty, blood-spotted fabric was wound around his head. His matted curls stuck through the cloth that covered his right eye. A sprayer connected to a plasticine tube swung from his hands as he approached Rasp.

Rasp stepped out his suit and looked at his fingertips, examining them for signs of frostbite. The belt rigs had a safety video with a topless cartoon named Prevention Patty who sang a song and jumped up and down to help them remember to keep their equipment dry and look for clear blisters on their fingers and toes.

Papa sprayed him without warning. An oily liquid shot from the end of the tube and beaded over his face and chest. It burned his eyes and nose. He choked and rubbed his eyes. It was kerosene. He could smell it. Papa picked up the bucket of melting ice and sloshed it in Rasp's face. He choked and gagged, and lashed out at Papa who stepped aside from his blind strike.

"Why would you do that?" Rasp choked.

"Had to kill the outside things. Like bugs and bacteria." His uncovered eye was unmoored and drifted before correcting itself.

Rasp rubbed the liquid from his eyes and reached for his coveralls that lay draped over a stack of open plastic crates by the suit hutch. The kerosene burned his skin. The dark shapes flitted around the corners down the hall. Papa had already grabbed the bucket of water and was waddling back to the quarters. Rasp called out to him.

"Wait. There's a ship coming!"

Papa stopped in the hallway, the bucket dragging down his left side.

"A ship?"

"Yes, with brujas."

"With what now?"

"Witches. I saw them."

"They are here? On the planet?" Papa's voice rose an octave. It sounded strange, unfamiliar.

"No. I…" Rasp stopped for a moment. Papa turned to face him. He was grinning. "I saw them from the monitoring system of my old ship. I went back there for some things I forgot," Rasp lied.

"Well, we are going to need that ship, aren't we?" A wild light seemed to pulse behind his uncovered eye.

"What about the women?" Rasp asked, wondering about how Papa injured his eye while he was gone.

"I haven't seen a woman in years," Papa said absently. "Turn on that drying chamber for your suit. We'll need to prepare."

"How did you hurt your eye?"

"It was always like this."

Papa picked a bucket up and whistled a rhythmless tune as he strode into the dark hallway, water slopping over the side. The black shapes slipped from the corners and hovered over the water like the ghosts of some extinct insects.

***

Dearest Ana,

I write to you and not the children, our children, because I believe this to be my final transmission. Not because we will be out of range. Don't let anyone tell you that, mi amor. The infrastructure is in place on Mars to hear and log all of our transmissions. You may never see this transmission or the others, but it is better to try and fail, than to die without telling you how wrong I was.

In The Black, I can only see myself. It is a mirror facing a mirror. A recantation of the history of me. Of my mistakes. Of past joys. A ritual of flagellation is the only ritual to combat the endless repetition.

This pale moon does not want us here. I think it reads our past lives.

I need to retreat here, if you are to believe me. Your skepticism grew with each of my sins and each of yours. A self-protective measure to be certain.

What I meant to say is that there is something here that knows us. I know the moon itself is just the remnants of collision and time. It's just iron and carbon and hydrogen and nitrogen. I know this. It is just a thing. A thing without a heartbeat, without hands to touch, without a brain to reason. I know this. I swear to you, I do. But it hears us, Ana. Just as I have eyes to see that it is just ice and methane, I can tell you that it hears us. It manifests things, like a child trying to have conversation. Such strange leaps it makes.

I had a dream where I was walking down a beach road, but the ocean spread on either side of the road into that deep gray infinity that you can only see when a storm is coming. Do you remember living in The Republic of Texas when I was deployed there? Those gray-black storm clouds tumbling in from the flats, cutting through the blue and stirring that still hot air? You would stand on the front porch with your black hair being lifted around you and smile just so, watching the birds caught in the downdrafts. Lightning etching itself, bright and silent before the heavy crush of thunder. Those clouds hung on either side of the road in my dream, just suspended above the ocean. The road dead ended ahead of me and a small wooden building stood at the end, but it was made only of stairs. There were no entrances, just stairs leading to the flat sides of wooden walls. The ocean rose on either side of my small strip of road into great transparent walls on either side of me. Shadows of sea animals slipped past in the water as I walked toward the building. I could smell the salt as the water washed over the narrow road, covering my feet.

This was the end of things. The wall cannot stand.

When we were first married, you would lay your legs over me in the morning while I told you about my dreams. When I asked what you dreamed you would press your cold hands against my side and say you didn't remember. Dreams were excesses to you, I believe.

I digress. I always digress.

I dreamed this dream every cycle until we landed the craft on the surface. My understanding of this place became manifest after my first trudge into The White.

It is important for you to know that The Corporation sent us an updated instructional manual after the privatization of our department within the Space Force. It was optimistic that we could return after the tagging and extraction operations were functional. That if we simply followed the instructions and performed the tasks asked of us, The Corporation would spare no expense to retrieve us. To reward us for our work. We would be heroes, they said.

And so, I left the safety of the pod to cross the lake. I was the physicality of the crew. The microbots that survived the trip were only just able to finish the laboratory before their battery packs died and so it fell to me after Mignon died. I know that is a sore subject for you. Perhaps you will even get a thrill hearing that she died from a blood clot in her leg that traveled to her brain before we even reached The Whip. We were only three cycles past the last gate. We shot her body into The Black and watched it spin away like a toy buoyed away by a slow stream. I hope you will believe me when I say that she never held the same purchase on me that you did. Strange how something that small matters even as I write this as my last act.

This moon cannot be civilized.

The lake stretched before me, enormous and solid. It was my duty that day to mark the site for the drill with the LazBeacon, so The Corporation could send an Android Labor Vessel to trade places with us. I dragged it behind me in a sledge. As I neared the middle of the lake, I realized the great walls of ice on either side of me swirled with shadows of the sea animals from my dream, but they were not the exact form. It is difficult to explain. It was like singing a song that you have only heard once. Whales without heads. Fish with six tails.

I checked my oxygen and CO_2 levels from my monitor and they were all within normal range for the circumstances. When you're in The Black, the mind creates fog creatures from your flawed brainspace in the absence of corporeality.

You will ask yourself, because you are you and I am me, was his mind intact? I assure you, my mind is intact. My undoing was the humanness that coursed through me. It is meaningless and yet it ties us to our progenitors. To gravity. To sunshine. To oxygen. There is water here, but you cannot drink it. Golden coins spew from our mouths, but we cannot eat. We cannot breathe.

My skin is falling from my bones and everything I missed is projected onto the walls. I saw our children taken from us, put to work in service of this machine that we created and recreated over and over again. I do not understand it. I saw our son toil on the naked back of space. Micrometeoroids tearing past the unseeing eye. His suit tinfoil against gunfire. Our daughter stripped to nothing but the barest purpose. The blackness of her eye altered by the market of perception.

I am lecturing. You used to tell me when I was lecturing and I was hurt. I clung to my words as my right. I was entitled to them.

But now, all of the words I held so fast to will slip into the nothingness of space. The universe doesn't stop expanding for us. We have met MOTHER. We have injured MOTHER.

I can feel my body coming apart. I want my last act to be one of contrition. I am sorry. I will say it again and again in hopes that by the time our universe is a lonesome vacuum and we have long been wiped from the memory of the things we touched that meaning will have circled back and all that will be left is another loop and another and another.

If I told you that I loved you and that I loved our children, you would reply that it is not enough and you would be correct. You always were. I love the idea of you. And so I finish this letter to a dead woman.

Amor,

Jaime

XXVII. A Mighty Fortress

Holy Book TM Chapter 67 Verses 78 -84

78 Do not dwell on the dead, for the productive and the holy shall be rewarded for their toil.

79 Let it be known that those rewarded on this plane with riches and renown shall be rewarded tenfold in the kingdom of The Father, for what is given in thy time of plenty does foretell the beginning of a time of plenty in The After.

80 If a laborer asks for an increase in wage or pity for his situation strike him with your left hand, for his reward can only be increased in practice and drudgery.

81 For did I not say unto you that this is only the first of many levels of existence? It is blasphemy to doubt the stratification. Soon you will be in my bosom with many riches.

82 Do not covet your employer's status or currency or lifestyle, for he hath pleased my father through me and was blessed by his hand for his hard work.

83 Heed this: when you reach your 65th Terran year, The Corporation shall process thy retirement, as you cannot labor in full capacity as is the morality of Mechoben's Bride.

84 Weep not, for this is the next step toward Upward Mobility.

***

Alona swung her bare legs from the edge of the cold table. The room contracted and bloomed into nauseating clarity. Her stomach heaved and her joints ached as she touched her feet to the cold floor. She was alone.

One of the aging speakers crackled and Pai's voice echoed around her.

"Alona, you have been quarantined for your own safety. Do you remember what happened?"

She realized that she was in one of the secondary laboratories. When the last model of Research IntelliDroids androids reached his expiration date, Pai said he closed off the wing due to the expense of operating costs. She knew better. His experiments had been failures. This cold table had been her bed for many cycles before this, leaning backward with her feet in the stirrups, crying and clinging to her Android, Nana, who stroked her arms with blunted fingernails and cried strange opaque tears with her.

"Yes, Pai. We, no I mean I, just me, I ruined one of your experiments."

"He was your brother, Alona."

"He was not my brother."

"He was our future. You are going to die. I am going to die." His voice was flat.

"What about the others?" She asked as she drew the PlastiFabric robe around her shoulders. Her nose had been plugged with Pai's expanding wound foam that he developed for soldiers in the Terran AfterEvent. The material was damp with blood.

"Their civilization gene programming didn't take."

"Where's Gram?"

"Gram has been dispatched."

"Where did you send her?" Alona heard her own voice raising into a wave of grief.

"She was just supposed to be your playmate, Alona." Pai's voice crackled through the speaker, no nonsense, like he was speaking to a small child about some unreached sweet perched on a faraway countertop. "Did you even teach her about Bicky Ball at all?"

Alona leaned against the countertops and rifled through the cabinets on the walls looking for a reversal or an amphetamine to fight the fog behind her eyes. A small bottle of Wakey Wakey: Pure Crystal had been tipped over in the back corner of the tallest cabinet. She grabbed it and crushed two of the pale blue capsules between her back molars, gagging against the bitterness. Her grief spun into ragged anger as the stimulant hit her bloodstream.

She remembered the evacuation from the Terran Medical Research University as The Event streamed on the screens. She and the other students peered at the streams as they watched buildings tumble over into the churning brown waters. Images of New Orleans in The New South from the overhead drones flashed on the screen. The city had long been underwater. The spires from the Original Brand Catholic Church still poked through the mud. People spun in boats made from the hulls of black rotting buildings, draped in bright flashes of old plastic beads they dredged from the black silt and attached in elaborate patterns to their pirogues. The water overtook them and swallowed them. The dots of human heads disappeared under the rushing current.

Numbers flashed across the screens with a prompt to check their assigned identification number. Hers appeared in the very first group 23890 – 25606. Her Earthborn friends looked on with wet eyes and creased brows as they loaded the Martian students onto the private evac vessels, handing them masks and anti-grav sickness kits as they shuffled to their coded quarters with running water and padded cryo chambers.

She could still taste the sour kiss of her Earthborn partner, Hajai. Her monitor number read 86996. As her soft lips drew away from hers, Alona knew she would never feel her gravity hardened body against hers, her stubby five fingered hands gripping hers so carefully as to not crush her space softened bones, her rough sun-red skin, to be swallowed whole by this balancing, this folded hand.

They were in the final Terran year of residential research in genetic abnormalities in the Space and Martian Born. Their research had been funded by MechoBen LLC. An honor. They fought about it. They kissed through clenched teeth. They tucked their bodies together and broke plasticine wine glasses against the gray brick student housing walls.

"Where did you send her?"

"I don't see how that's relevant."

"Do you want me to stay alive?"

The comm link was silent for a moment.

"Don't threaten me," Pai said.

Alona rolled the Wakey Wakey container in her hand and spun the top off. She poured the remaining medication onto the metal table under the shining eye of the monitoring camera. The bright blue pills skittered across the metal surface. She raked them to the center with the side of her hand and used the base of the jar to crush them into micro jewels. Her thin long hair dipped into the shining dust as she peered at the fineness of her grind. Pai's voice crackled over the water damaged speakers.

"She didn't meet the specifications for GagGirls, so I sent her to a plasticine weaving facility in The Belt."

"Where in The Belt?" Alona scraped the powdered drug into her other hand and tilted it into a chipped petri dish and dripped solution into it.

"You can't get there." He sounded uncertain.

"I'll worry about that." She swirled the solution in the petri dish and fished for the plasticine hollow tipped needles.

"This will not help her. This will not help you."

She drew the solution into the syringe. A careful single dose. She rubbed the inside of her arm, prodding for one of her miniature, flaccid veins. The sting of the needle. The burn of the amphetamines. Her heart filling and collapsing. The hum.

"Who will it help then? You?" The jagged lift of the amphetamines pushed her voice higher. "Who is this all for?" She gestured at the lab with the pipette. "We don't even have the proper air filtering systems. You haven't been in contact with The Corporation for two years. Where did you send that poor man from the factories? Where did he go?"

"Where else are we going to go?" Pai's voice remained flat. "I can't leave Mars."

"I can."

"You might die out there. You are my most prized possession, Alona. My most successful experiment." He was avoiding her again.

She sucked more of the solution into the syringe. Her skin tightened and rippled with adrenaline. She drew the pale liquid up into the transparent tube and tapped it on the side of the table.

"This is about 900 milligrams, Pai. I already took one unit. I know we don't have any more androids to stop me. Answer me." She tied off her wrist with a piece of tubing and pressed the veins on the top of her hand. The veins in her arm had retreated.

"Look out of the viewing port," he said.

She creased her brows and walked over to the indention in the wall. She slid back the plasticine cover. Instead of the butterscotch Martian desert, lumpy with pastel egg-shaped structures, the frosted rust against black curve of Mars from orbit churned past through the window. She clutched the syringe, feeling the sides of it give.

"It was a ship," she said.

"It was a ship."

"I'm going to get Gram."

"I'd like to see you try," he said coldly.

She raised the syringe and pressed the needle to the raised veins on her hand again.

"I will send for her," Pai said.

"No. We are going to get her."

"This isn't that kind of ship. It's on a fixed course. You can't change it and I am not on it."

"What do you mean, you're not on it?" Alona asked.

"Did you think I could survive space travel again?"

"What about me?"

"What about you?" His tone was removed.

"What about my survival? I thought you said I was your most prized possession."

"What value is an experiment if the results are not shared?"

She poked the needle into her skin and pushed down on the plunger, snapping the tubing off her wrist. The burn of the amphetamine spread up her arm. Her heart pounded as the drug rushed over her like a tide. She was an angel, a god, the queen of the space dust. Her body was a temple overrun with worshippers, war drums in the halls, bare feet slapping the marble floors as they tore golden relics from the walls. Heat in her belly. Heat in her cunt. Blackness. Blackness.

***

The Curanderas wrapped Riff in their arms as the craft descended to Enceladus' surface. Their chanting was muffled in the padded containment room. The grav drives switched off to conserve energy as the ship dropped onto the icy surface. Riff's stomach contracted as the metal landing gear slipped on the ice. The craft tipped as it caught against a crag in the ice. The walls moved around them in a directionless spin. Riff's mouth filled with salty water. Her back pressed against the control panel as Curandera Morena flipped the plasticine casings back from emergency controls, her hunched body rotating midair.

A click and a buzzing and they tumbled back to the floor. The smell of their space-cloistered bodies filled the recycled atmosphere. The control panels hung above them, blinking like wet speleothems. Curandera Morena had already rolled to her feet and was pulling out grav boots from the chambers, flinging them into the center of the bunched women.

"Only two pair and they are old," Curandera Peliroja said, picking up the boot closest to her.

"Curandera Negra has MOTHER's ear. She will go," Curandera Morena said.

"Of course she will, that's why we're here," Curandera Peliroja snipped. "But who will accompany her? We are old. My bones won't stand that cold." She touched her fingertip to the sliver of light coming through the wavy viewing port.

Riff slid a tube of protein gel into her mouth to settle her stomach and listened as they bickered, as they sometimes did. Something itched in the back of her mind. It reminded her of the MicroSurveillence drones no bigger than mosquitoes that whined by their ears on the factory line back on The Belt. Something was watching.

She sucked down the rest of the protein tube. The silky gel coated the back of her tongue. The burn in her belly quieted as the gel expanded in her stomach.

"Put on your boots, Curandera Negra, the gravity is light here. Even lighter than Mars," Curandera Morena said.

Riff, forgetting her renaming, ignored her and sent out a thought toward the itch in her mind. She shaped the word hello in her mind in bright pink bubble letters and thought of her own lips pursing and blowing it toward the itch. The word drifted back toward her with an image of a generic smiling face. Like a note attached to a balloon.

"Curandera Negra! Escuchame. Put on your boots," Curandera Morena's firm voice intruded and burst through the bubble letters in her head like a hand slicing through smoke.

Riff snapped open her eyes. The women looked on, each with small lines forming between their brows.

"Someone is listening to us."

"Who is it?" Their voices comingling in concern.

"I don't know. It doesn't feel like MOTHER." She stopped and thought. "Does MOTHER know what a smile is?"

"Put on your boots," Curandera Morena repeated and shoved the boots toward her with her own booted feet. "Stuff this in the toes to make them fit. We used to do this in Cuba for new shoes." She handed Riff a fistful of torn rags. "We don't have time to linger. This craft will not hold against the cold."

"Where are we going?"

"You are our bloodhound. You will tell us."

"A bloodhound? What's that? And where is Cuba?"

"Mija, put on your boots, please. I will explain bloodhounds and Cuba to you on the way to the research base." She stepped into the pressurized mining suit and tugged at the straps at the waist. "Rápidamente, por favor."

Riff put on her grav boots and suit, Curandera Peliroja checked the seals and snaps before she and Curandera Morena crowded into the airlock. Curandera Morena's sharp black eyes, nestled in overlapping brown wrinkles, caught the square of white light from the overhead lights. Her gray hair was braided over the lumpy mats at the base of her shiny scalp. Her eyes folded into slits under the mass of wrinkles as she smiled.

"We are going to meet her," she said to Riff.

"How will we leave?"

"We won't. This is our birthright."

"You said we can't live here."

"We can't live in the ship," she said as she drew the helmet down onto her shoulders and slid the transparent faceplate in place. Her labored breathing crackled through the comms in Riff's helmet. "But MOTHER has a place for us by the seaside."

***

The itch at the back of Riff's mind came back just as the grav assist feature on Curandera Morena's pack failed. The old woman crunched behind her through the ice toward the flat black glass of the lake in the distance, her toes overlapping in the overstuffed boots. She could feel the blister forming on the space-soft skin of her heel when she heard Curandera's voice ring in her earpiece. She turned around to see Curandera Morena on her back, her arms flailing in wide comical circles. The sun stood small and cold against the thin atmosphere. A wisp of steam spurted from somewhere in Curandera Morena's suit.

Riff boosted her grav assist and sprang over the terrain to the old woman. The wisp turned to a gush of steam as Riff turned Curandera to her side. Ice crystals formed in lacy patterns on the inside of her helmet as the cold seeped in. Ice coated the creased upper lip and the thin lips cracked and bled. Riff held her clumsy gloved hands over the break in the suit. She choked back tears of desperation as she rifled through her pack one-handed for the Never Say Die Epoxy Suit Glue. Steam seeped through the gash and poured out around her fingers.

The itch at the back of her mind returned and she wheeled around, her knees digging twin holes in the snow. A pain bloomed in her sinuses and her familiar writhed in new life, sending a withered tendril out of the corner of her eye. Her helmet prevented her groping fingers access to her face. Panic wailed from her core. A shadow churned under the ice, fracturing the thick layer below them. It whipped toward her in a serpentine. She squeezed her eyes shut, waiting for her final gasp of cold air on this strange moon.

Then it spoke.

***

Papa leaned over Rasp, his breath hot on the side of his face. The monitoring station whirred and beeped as Papa traced his nail-less pointer finger over the blinking red dot.

"See that, son?" He pointed to the dot. "That's them. We can leave this godforsaken moon."

Rasp edged away from Papa's closeness. The sweet richness of decay emanated from his mouth.

"Do you think they'll take us back with them?"

Papa turned his swollen face to peer into Rasp's eyes.

"You need to prepare yourself for something. We may have to take the vessel from them."

"You mean like in the Pirates of Ass Pornographic Film?"

"I don't know, but yes like pirates." His eye was bright and focused. He picked up the pistol from the light table and clicked the safety off and then on again. "Get your suit from the drying rack. I don't want to be here. I want to feel warm again." He tucked the pistol into the warming sleeve of his carrier bag and pulled his helmet on.

***

The rings of Saturn cut golden through the sky as Rasp and Papa neared the blinking dot on Papa's wrist monitor. Rasp hopped up and down to warm himself as Papa interpreted the readings on his scanner. Puffs of steam burst from the filtration ports on his helmet. He turned the grav setting down on his boots so he could leap higher to see further. He pushed off from the ice as hard as he could, imagining his body flying out past the rings of Saturn, stretching through his ribs reaching for the thick yellow gas clouds swirling over the fecund body. Just as he reached the apex of his jump, he noticed a person crouched in the snow over the body of another.

MOTHER boomed into his head.

"FRIENDS."

The intensity of her voice, the insistence of it cracked through his mind.

"HELP FRIENDS."

He flailed backwards in the air, trying to keep his balance in the onslaught of stimuli. He bumped the grav controls and floated back to the ground, landing on his back on the other side of an ice dune from Papa.

"Mechoben in space, MOTHER. Not so loud." His stomach turned. Fear tingled in his throat at the sight of other humans.

"HELP FRIENDS."

"Who are they?" He rolled to his side and checked his suit for damage, pushing on the seamed sides with his gloved hands.

"FRIENDS."

He pushed himself up from the fall and trudged over the ice dune in the direction of the strangers. His digital compass spun when he lifted it to catch the magnetism of the moon's own poles. Saturn's pull always distorting, disrupting. Papa's voice sputtered in his ear over the comms.

"Where are you going?"

MOTHER coursed under the ice, twisting and worming like some great earthworm. He remembered earthworms flicking their bodies across the rain spattered sidewalk. A smell of wet on hot concrete. Somewhere. Somewhere bright and warm.

"There are…" His voice was clipped off as MOTHER sliced through his consciousness again.

"NOT HIM."

"I didn't catch that, son," Papa crackled into his comm.

"What? Why?" Rasp whispered blinking against the pain in his head.

"HE HURTS."

Rasp addressed Papa, "I think I saw something over this ridge. I'll be right back. I can tell you a joke though."

"A joke?"

"Yeah. I have a really good one the miners on the asteroid belt told me about angels."

"Angels?" Papa sounded odd.

MOTHER rumbled under the ice and flashed whiteness across Rasp's vision.

Rasp marched toward the people on the other side of the dune and dredged his memory, trying to reconstruct the joke. He tapped the ambient noise reducer on the side of his helmet and leaned his head toward the comms mic.

"There were two statues in a park, one of a naked man and one of a naked woman. They had been facing each other across a pathway for a hundred years, when one day an angel comes down from heaven and decides to bring the two to life.

The angel tells them, 'As a reward for being so patient through a hundred hot summers and cold winters, you have been given life for thirty minutes to do what you have always wished to do the most.'

He looks at her, she looks at him, and they go running behind the bushes. The angel waits patiently as the bushes rustle and giggling ensues. After fifteen minutes, the two return, out of breath and laughing.

The angel tells them, 'You have fifteen minutes left, would you care to do it again?' He asks her 'Shall we?' She eagerly replies, 'Oh, yes, lets! But let's change positions. This time, I'll hold the pigeon down and you shit on its head.'"

As he finished the joke, he waited for Papa's reaction. He topped the ridge and waved his arms at the person crouched in the ice below. Silence for a moment. Papa's voice hummed in his ear, faraway and faint.

"What is an angel?" Papa asked.

A memory hurtled back into Rasp's mind. Papa coming into a space he used to sleep on that warm, sunny planet. He nestled under a heavy navy blue blanket stitched with white anchors and watched a creature in a transparent cube that clung to the sides, its belly pressed into perfect pale green flatness against the glass. The pads of its toes minute circles.

Papa silhouetted against the doorframe, the bright yellow light of the hallway erasing his features. He entered, his boots heavy against the laminate. Rasp was supposed to be sleeping. And Papa was supposed to be somewhere far away. Somewhere dusty and cruel. He could smell the sunshine on his uniform as he sat on the edge of the small bed. The mattress compressing. The springs squeaking. His father's rough, heavy hand hovering above his head and then letting it fall for a moment before pressing the heel of his hand against his cheek. The warmth of it. His mother stood in the doorway, her robe belt swinging against her calf.

"Cómo un angel," Papa had said.

His eyes were brown-black and glittering. Moon-Papa's eye was green.

***

Riff saw the figure against the white just as Curandera Morena's LifeSigns monitor squealed into a flatline. It stood on the ridge waving its arms at her. It appeared human. She pumped the adrenaline function and tried to listen to the black tendril under the ice.

"FRIEND. FRIEND. FRIEND."

She picked up Curandera's limp hand and dropped it. The huge tendril poked through the ice and stroked Curandera's helmet, before plunging through the Plastiglass. Bits of glass rained down on the hard ground. Indistinguishable from the broken ice. The crone's familiar shot out of her mouth, thick and phallic, entwining with the tip of MOTHER's tendril, overlapping and sliding through. Riff felt her own familiar racing behind her eyes and filling her sinuses. Another tendril crawled from behind Curandera's staring black eye, before yanking the eyeball out of its socket in a blood-tinged clear spurt as it lengthened and stretched toward MOTHER. Riff fell backwards and pushed her body backwards.

The great being rose and rent itself into two door-sized flaps. A circular sphincter pulsed ruby-red at the center. An opaque, matte pearl spun in the throbbing mouth. The body writhed as the familiar wrenched itself through her nostrils, her ears, her eye sockets, splitting and tearing the skin into flaccid pink ribbons. The familiar whipped in the wind as it arched and dove into the wet fissure. The flaps closed over the torn prone body and lifted it, pushing it deeper into the maw with the mass of waving appendages. The enormous flaps closed over the churning hole and collapsed in, creating a sucking void.

Bits of ice and snow chipped away from the ground, caught in the swirl of the collapsing mouth. MOTHER drew back down under the ice. The rasp of her great body vibrated under Riff's grav boots. Memories of bodies bloated into grotesque roundness floating by in the opaque brown water, blood streaming down legs and arms from hidden glass, eyes nibbled away by bacteria and squirming creatures under the mire. Her brother wrapped his thin arms and legs around her in the turning inflatable boat, shielding her from the sun, before a drone dragged them to a grove of trees. Helmeted soldiers separated them and drove pediatric needles into their arms to rehydrate them. The red mist on the ice was all that remained of Curandera Morena.

***

Rasp clung to the surface of the moon as his helmet rattled with MOTHER's full emergence on the ridge below. The tiny, suited figure hunched as she crunched through the ice. He tapped the digital zoom on the side of his helmet until one half of his vision field was filled with the image of the fallen body spritzing the ice with crimson. He was dizzy for a moment and looked away, focusing on the figure kneeling in front of MOTHER instead. Something was familiar. A slice of transparency cut through the black of the First Regime helmet and he caught a fuzzy view of a large dark eye, before MOTHER blacked his view.

He scrambled down the ridge as MOTHER dove back into the ice. Moon-Papa's voice popped into his comms, as he skidded down the slope.

Where are you going? That thing'll eat you up.

He ignored the hum in his ear and rolled down the volume to a crackling buzz. MOTHER roiled in his mind, her attention split. The figure noticed him and pushed up like a baby, arms rigid and heels flat. It stood and put its hand against MOTHER's enormous side, stroking and leaning as he approached. He could see the figure's face through the helmet now. It was a woman. Or a girl. Rare and strange. Even before this place.

He waved at her. Her eyes went wide through the glass and she ran to him, her grav boots snagging her back down to the surface as she charged toward him. His suit pressure alarm whined in his ear as she collided with him, knocking him backward into the ice. MOTHER circled them under the ice, whipping her long body in an unending dark river that stretched to the horizon line.

She stood up, brushing the snow from her suit and hauled him up by the arm. She shoved her gloved digits in front of his helmet. Two fingers. Three fingers. Seven fingers. He shook his head, not understanding. She tapped the comms side of her own helmet and mimicked talking into the microphone. He realized she was trying to show him the access code. He nodded and tapped the code into the side of the his helmet until he heard a faint crackling and her breathing. They stood facing one another. Silent and afraid to say the first words, they stared at one another, unmedicated, unseparated by distance or memory.

"José?" Her voice slow.

"Alicia?"

Natural-borns, both of them, illegal now and shunted aside by the nature of their entrance into this plane. He remembered when Mama brought her into his room after he heard her all night, swearing in Spanish, her bare heels thumping against the hardwood as she paced. Papa's voice, hollow in its distant transmission, murmuring to her.

"José, esta es tu hermana, Alicia," Mama said without ceremony. Her black hair was slicked back into a tight bun. She buttoned her jacket. Her belly was slack and draped with layers of fabric. She put the baby into his hands and walked out of his room without a word.

Now she stood here before him, dwarfed by her spacesuit. She howled into the microphone, her tears streaming into the body waste reservoir at the base of her neck. He reached out to touch her arms.

"Where did they take you?" He asked, his environmental monitors chirping.

She cried more, unable to stop. He listened to her gasp, her own monitoring system wailing high in alarm.

"I forgot my own name," she choked.

"I know a good joke about names," he said, the discomfort folding over him like plasticine.

"Joke?" She hiccuped.

"Yeah. I know a really good one. I used to tell you jokes all the time." A lump thickened in his throat. Men don't cry. Mechoben said so. Tears are for the sexy, not the sad. He had been demerited for crying twice.

Riff-Alicia opened her mouth and then closed it again, as MOTHER's voice echoed between the two of them.

STOP HURT. STOP HURT. LOOK UP.

They turned their gaze toward the ridge where Moon-Papa leaned against a jag of ice. A stun stick extended from his right hand. He stuck it into the snow to steady himself as MOTHER stirred under the ice, pushing small waves of snow toward him. He began his descent, sliding as Rasp-José had done earlier. Riff-Alicia ducked behind Rasp-José and whispered into her comms.

"Who is that?"

"Don't you recognize him? That's Papa. He's still pretty far away. You'll see." Rasp-José felt a strange push-pull in his consciousness. One thing cannot be true as another thing at the same time.

"Papa?" Her voice was small.

"Did you want to hear that joke?"

She drew back from him and MOTHER turned words in his mind. NO. NO. HE HURTS.

Moon-Papa stood up from his slide down the ridge and ambled toward them, loping and stumbling. His wide grin shone through the tinted helmet. The whites of his eyes glinted through like a beast in the woods. He heaved through the white toward them. MOTHER's voice humming in their skulls in audible distress. Rasp-José felt his sister cling to the back of his suit, as she peeked around him at the stumbling unknown.

Her breathing churned in his ear.

"That's not Papa," she said.

"How do you know? You didn't ever meet him."

She backed away, her eyes wild.

"That's an android. He's an android." Her voice quavered.

As Moon-Papa neared, MOTHER and Riff-Alicia howled in unison. His mouth was set in a thin line, unnaturally straight and wide. Rasp-José stepped backward. A small white scar winked on his neck where the identification chip for the old model of android was implanted. It provided a kill switch before the shortened lifespan was introduced. Moon-Papa reached him and clapped him on the shoulder. He didn't seem to notice the furls of darkness under the ice, slipping his right leg from the weak curl of MOTHER's grasp.

"This must be my little daughter," he said.

"You aren't my father," she whispered.

"I am. I am pieces of him."

She backed away further, staring at the stranger.

"What are you talking about?"

He slid the Radiation Shield down on his helmet and pointed to his face.

"Do you see? Look."

They looked into his face for signs of Papa there. The shape of the eye was correct, but not the color. The burnished skin was familiar, but had a bluish tint. The black hair was as black as the day he left. He was forever forty, no new lines, no gray hair. His teeth were sharper somehow. Perhaps he was taller.

"HURT HURT HURT," MOTHER echoed into their minds.

"Now we can get off this troubled stone. Harness her, my children, and be transported."

Rasp-José and Riff-Alicia found themselves clinging to one another in their suits as shunts of vapor shot into the air. MOTHER and Moon-Papa facing one another on the frozen lake, each locked in cruel wanting. Each of them begging, coercing, tearing at these children to remove the other, to dominate and flee and fight. There was no place for them to go, these children of the void. These mere tools of something far away and undesigned, unplanned.

MOTHER moaned and flashed images of her penetration into their minds, rousing Riff-Alicia's familiar convulsions that stretched the skin of her face. The auger driving into her vast back under the ice.

***

The director on The Corporation's Live Stream of Youngest, Brightest, Wettest production leaned back from the camera to see the bedlam with his own eyes. The GagGirls all screaming and vomiting and tearing their FactoryFresh Human Hair Extensions from their scalps. Their familiars so carefully disguised, now pouring from their orifices in thick ropy disobedience to the suppressant drugs. The androids, streaked pink and orange and red with stress responses, kneeled by them holding their wrists as they tried to rip the black tendrils from their bodies. Some lay on their sides staring at the whipping extensions of their own bodies, trimmed eyelids wide.

"Keep the cameras rolling," he said. "This is pure credits."

The camera android nodded and panned across the set slick with fluid.

***

Curandera Peliroja had felt the life of Curandera Morena snuffed out. Her own lungs burned and her own heart seized. A coldness so true and so sharp that it smelled of wood smoke and wet wool. Death was part of the ever expansion. The natural order was the death of heat. The distance between planets a holy rite to be observed. "Goddess" was an old word, one from before the true diaspora into the stars, but in this moment the Curandera understood why the Earth elders created the image of scarlet wings and jaguar claws. To overlay the familiar on the forces not controlled. The face of the goddess was not in the suns, but in the spaces between.

And now, the voices reached her. Begging for the removal of the Holy MOTHER. Flashes through their eyes of pornography sets and luxury Martian quarters sodden with suffering as the familiars wrenched toward their colonial home world. She flipped through images like a book, paging toward the whiteness of ice and snow. Curnada Negra's eyes found hers and she saw the great MOTHER, plunged to the bottoms of the black sea under the ice, unbound and expanded to loom over The Father. The abomination that lived between the always and the recent. The created and the creator.

***

Alona's familiar drew down her throat and flung its tendrils through her nostrils toward the white moon she was orbiting. Pai's communication stopped weeks ago and so she paced and spoke with her familiar. Her thin body drifted around the small cabin as she sucked on the tubes of Shine and cultivated protein paste. Her familiar eased itself from her body, smaller than others, and suddenly she was truly alone for the first time in her short existence. The mass of black floated toward the airlock and shaped itself around the square door as it sent jellied fingers through the cracks. In her desperation for normalcy, for this parasitic companionship, she pushed herself toward it from the opposite wall. Reaching her three fingered hands, now swollen from being in zero-G, out like a mother encouraging her child to toddle to her.

"Please don't leave me. Please. It's so dark here."

The being didn't respond. It pushed itself through the tiniest chinks in the paneling, striving to return to MOTHER.

Alona drifted, pressing her feet against the doorway as she slid her fingers under the throbbing mass to pry it away. To bring it back into her. The friend she was never without. The space behind her eyes was hollow and empty. The familiar slid through her fingers and pressed its gelatinous form further from her touch. She pushed herself back to the comms panel and tapped the communication code into the screen. A general transmission. A call to anyone. Static hummed.

Pai's voice came through, then his face on the screen. The first time she had spoken to anyone in four cycles.

"Have you landed yet? It looks like you are still orbiting."

She gripped both sides of the screen and peered at his yellow sclera. His sunken cheekbones were dotted with open sores and a thick lump rose on the side of his neck.

"Something is happening, Pai. I love you. I am sorry I disobeyed." Her desperation drove her pleas. She would beg. She would submit.

"Strange to hear those words," he said. "Why haven't you landed?"

"I don't understand what I should do, Pai. What do you want me to do?" She was begging again.

"You must go down to the surface and let the Matriarch consume you." His yellowing eyes were wild and moist.

"What Matriarch?"

He lifted up an old holographic copy of the Holy Book TM in front of the screen.

"Do as you were commanded, Alona."

"I thought you were a scientist, Pai. I thought we were scientists." Her confusion overwhelmed her. "That book is for those who can't understand. It's for comfort."

His breath rattled in his chest as he reached down to switch off the feed.

"Pai! I will. I will let her consume me. Just don't leave me alone."

His hand hovered above the power to the screen, just out of her view.

"We are scientists and science requires sacrifice. Do you know what a mouse is, Alona?"

"Yes, Pai. They were a Terran animal. A pest."

He talked past her, as if she had said nothing.

"They used them to experiment on. For medicine. For cosmetics. They used billions of them. Do you know why?"

She opened her mouth to answer, but he continued past her.

"Because they were easily housed. They were cheap. Because in those days there was a notion, a whisper that their lives were lesser, and they were right." He smoothed his yellow-white hair away from his eyes. "What do we use now?"

"Androids?"

He laughed. "Androids are not cheap."

"What then? Dogs?" She ground her back molars, heat rising to her cheeks.

"You are spoiled, child of mine. Where is your mother?"

"I don't understand the question."

It was in that moment, floating in that vacuum, Alona realized her place in this scheme. She was the pill wrapped in something that slid down easily. She hid the bitterness in her body. Her body created to house the means to regain control over this thing they had enslaved for their own means. The means of more more more more more. Power wasn't credits in the Galactic Bank of Wells. Power was the ability to change the narrative for no ends. To spread the players thin across an ephemeral board and then gaze over their suffering. To know that suffering was removed. Her years wandering the flooded halls on Mars, chasing her little brothers – peeling their fingers from equipment careful, careful not to break their fragile bones. Her research. Playing Bicky Ball until her heart rate monitor cut off the scoreboard. She was the mouse sniffing for peanut dust in the maze.

Her mother was a plasticine bag. Pictures of Alona's spinal cord, pictures of her porous bones, pictures of her malformed feet on the wall of light.

She met small bursts of memory, unimpeded by the droll tight smiles and representations of happiness so present in the scrolls and flashes of the streams. Twining her limbs around her loves, the smell of unperfumed skin, the stroke of the hot palms. The heaviness of gravity. The brightness of the Terran sun, so near it burned her skin in a swell of sleepy pressure, like latex gloves filling with sweat.

She switched off the feed with Pai and stepped into the suiting chamber.

Isolation was her mantra. Her third eye pried from her skull.

***

Rasp-José pulled the pistol from his belt and aimed it at Moon-Papa, courting the violence of his ancestors tearing the flesh of birds and fish and monkeys, searing it over fire, pushing it past the long canids into the mouth that could not be satisfied. This tool in his hand, heavy and cruel, prepared for its purpose. To annihilate.

His sister's nose gushed blood as her familiar filled the bottom half of her helmet like a curled snake in an aquarium. The plastiglass crackling under the pressure of it.

She pounded her gloved palms against the outside of the helmet, gurgling and choking.

He pulled the trigger.

***

[redacted] Incorporated Documents Pre-Colonization

To The Legislative Body of the Global [redacted]:

The contract awarded to us on [redacted] has yielded several fruitful studies, though our focus has been directed to a particularly rewarding discovery, both economically and socially, regarding the lifeforms excavated and detained by our Lucrativity Scouting Teams.

Our efforts have been focused largely on Saturn's water-rich moon, Enceladus. Originally, we planned to conduct studies focused on silicate mining, as well as hydrogen gas and methane harvesting, but in our studies discovered a lifeform with particular social potential. Though we hesitate to use the terms "social control" and prefer the term "quality of life enhancement," we will use the term "social control" for clarity and broadness of use in this report.

Our oceanic probes and Android-manned missions discovered a lifeform that resembles an interconnected eusocial society, though we remain uncertain if the lifeform is one being, or many that communicate through a singular queen, not unlike Earth's extinct honey bees and meat-eating ants.

It is worth noting that while we have discovered several extra-terrestrial lifeforms on other moons and planets, none have had the drive or capability to attempt communication. We have named the organism MOTHER, since it seems to caretake particularly our female crew members, who routinely say with humor "She is worse than my mother." MOTHER seems particularly interested in their movement and "asks" with something akin to telepathy. Only one of our male crewmembers has been privy to this communication and it appears the only difference was his proximity to his sister, who was a crewmember on a previous mission.

MOTHER appears to communicate through mental images and now (with our coaxing) monosyllabic, but internal words. We believe that the potential for direct communication that transcends language barriers, cultural differences, and editorial communication for nefarious purposes could be monumental. It appears too, that MOTHER cannot or does not communicate with androids, which could provide insight into the tangible, provable notion of a soul, which would serve the Salvation of Space's original mission and allow for the continuation of funding.

It is our belief that this lifeform's existence has extreme economic and political benefits for whomever maintains possession of Enceladus, thus this report should be viewed only by those possessing the highest clearance.

[redacted]

XXVIII. Such a Heavy Burden To Be

Moon-Papa slumped to the ice as the bullet tore through the fabric of his suit. Riff-Alicia rushed to him, slipping and fighting the wind. Rasp-José grabbed for her, but she yanked away from his grasp. It was unplanned, unthought, unintentional. She wanted to see his real face. She wanted to touch her own origin for a moment. MOTHER wrapped around her middle, holding her against her great pumping center. Thousands of transparent blue pearls cascaded onto the ice from the black center of her maw.

HE HURT. HE BEHIND HURT. BEHIND TURNING HURT. Boomed in Riff-Alicia's head.

As MOTHER lifted her high above the swirling snow, she caught a glimpse of the auger slicing down into a chasm and spurts of steam escaping. MOTHER's tendrils split into a thousand miniature versions of their origin and slid over her helmet in a solid black mask. All was dark and silent before she felt the solid ground under her back. The grav drives in her suit chuffed against the caul of MOTHER's great arms. She remembered this. There once was a word for this folding of arms over bodies before it was deemed too dangerous.

She found herself sitting across from Papa in a sky-blue chamber. He was deconstructed and incomplete, pieces of his face slid into place then retreated into unfamiliarity. He sat with his legs crossed, wearing an old Earth uniform they sometimes used on set for custom productions back at the GagGirls set. She could smell the smoke on him, but just for a moment. He uncrossed his legs and opened his eyes wide. They were black and brown and green each at a different moment. She opened her mouth to talk to him, but she didn't know what to ask. What to say.

Moon-Papa gaped, unseeing through his sliding features.

Dry, cool hands rested on her bare shoulders. She craned to see Curandera Morena standing above her, but younger. Her hair shining black like her own, her face smooth and young, her two front teeth gold.

"Curandera Morena, where are we?"

She didn't respond but pointed to the humped mass in the center of the glowing, empty chamber. Riff-Alicia looked on as Curandera Morena slipped past her and picked up Moon-Papa, cradling him in her arms as she tucked his staring face against her neck. She stepped into the undulating mass, with Papa's legs dangling over her arms in a grotesque pietá. The mass folded over them, blanketing them in overlapping layers of translucent skin.

Rasp-José's unhelmeted face materialized above her as she was lifted out of her cocoon. Perfect round beads of frozen sweat rolled from her hairline and bounced as they struck the floor.

"Where are we?" She asked, pushing herself up on her elbows.

"MOTHER brought us to the pumping station." He said, handing her a dusty plasticine bag of water.

"Did you see Papa? Curandera Morena?"

"Moon-Papa was not Papa, Ok?"

"What do we do now?"

She punctured the bag and sipped from it. Panels with tiny screens and manual cranks and keyboards flashed cryptic symbols and hummed. Rasp-José leaned over the glowing green and white lights, his face illuminated into aquiline nobility. He sighed and unzipped his Nice No Ice Under Suit and pulled the material down over his shoulders and chest, leaving him naked to the waist. His ribs rippled through his skin like blown sand.

"I think we need to get rid of all of it."

"What will we do afterwards?" She thought about her soft bed back on Mars. She thought about Al brushing her hair. "We can't go back to Mars, can we?"

"No," he said. "Do you remember me telling you jokes?" His voice was strained.

"I remember some of them. Did you ever see the Shanana Schwoop Shigetty comedy special on the streams? Those were pretty funny jokes."

"Was that the time she gave that ugly girl that brandless cosmetic cream and it turned her face all welted and red?"

"Yeah," she smiled.

"Where did you go after The Event?" he asked.

"I was with the Factory Girls, but a scout knew that brown girls were trending in the feeds, but there aren't many of us in space, so he got me for the Pornographic Art Films."

It dawned on him that he had seen her. That she had been curated and marketed to him. The Corporation owned his data. It knew what he liked to buy at the commissary. It knew what pornography he consumed. It knew what he drank. What he ate. What his heart rate and hormone levels were. It knew because the first commandment in The Holy Book TM was to participate in the free market and that one's most valuable asset was one's information. Never deny the reaping, for the sowing was expensive. Her body was his body. He had held her on his lap when they were children watching cartoons in a rocking chair. He had watched her writhe under androids on his small stream screen.

***

Alona punched in the tracking coordinates. Enceladus was small. They were easy to find with their tooth and vascular implants still sending signals into space. The capsule she was strapped into entered the thin atmosphere with little resistance, the drugs coursing through her subdermal ports to regulate her body temperature, her heart rate.

As the capsule trembled, the urge for self-obliteration overcame her. The very idea that she could survive a landing and a crossing of this minimally processed moon was absurd. She smiled to herself as the screen above her showed a naked woman demonstrating the proper entry breathing technique. The cartoonish shine-injected breasts swelled and pressed against a pane of clear Plastiglass. Some Corporation digital image consultant had forgotten to scrub away the scarification around her right nipple, and the perfect raspberry round scars dotted across the screen as she pressed and rolled her body across the Plastiglass.

Remember breathe like this. Buckle like this. Decompress like this. Slender fingers tipped with neon blue nails punching buttons drawn into her skin with luminous ink. A living device. A reminder, cheaper and more memorable.

The capsule shuddered as the landing gear engaged. The grav drives hummed. The very same grav drives connected to increased cases of Chondrosarcoma in belt miners and highly transported GagGirls. Alona had helped write the abstract before The Event shut down the Terran universities. It was the first time she broke a bone, tapping away on the feedback keyboard of The Before. Her long middle finger just crunched and flopped sideways. Pai called in some calcium supplements after they set her finger. Human derived for Better Absorption.

As she slid the safety restraint off her shoulder, her clavicle compressed like rotting wood. Alona tapped the suiting command and put a No Pain All Gain adhesive dot on the inside of her wrist.

The hatch slid open and her suit beeped in alarm at the temperature before adjusting and automatically clinging and heating her skin. Her familiar was quiet in her sinuses as the whiteness of the place subsumed her. Saturn's great belly turning above her.

Through the cutting wind, she could see Riff and Rasp's outlines, their arms moving like strange automatons in the outdated suits as they stumbled away from her craft.

She pursued them, her heart throbbing in her chest. Her suit was newer and better. Her grav drives drove her forward, the spikes on her boots retracting automatically. The ground shifted beneath her and The Great Mother, the organism sought by Pai, by The Corporation, by Mechoben, emerged and folded over the distant forms, enveloping them in front of her. Their trackers evaporated from her screen. Blips ceasing.

***

Mechoben raked the pistachio shells into his right hand and clenched them, feeling the bite in his palm. He tensed his jaw and peered at the screen. Al wrapped her arms around his soft middle. His Shine was considered too sacred to pull and distribute, so he maintained it. In sacrifice to them. He gave his beauty to them. They were never grateful.

Many cycles ago, he had held a rifle and fired it above the heads of the dogs strapped with bombs, scaring them to disintegrate into hunks of pink flesh before they reached the shining storefronts. Gucci and Armani glinting in the desert sun, the glass flecked with dogflesh and dust. It was his job in the global military. This degradation.

He used a scraper for windshields, dipped in a soapy solution and watched as it sluiced through the brown dust. The store owner brought him pieces of watermelon from the local farmer's market sometimes, her short white shorts untouched by grime. He would imagine sliding his hand up her thigh, touching the hairlessness only the rich could afford. He fucked her in his head over and over. His hands buried in her human hair extensions, blond from Ukrainian teenagers. Very expensive. She smiled with nothing behind it, her teeth perfectly even and perfectly white. Her waist was cinched forever in another man's arms.

He was blessed with desire. Desire was the holiest part of the human experience. Desire drove humans toward the stars. Desire was Renaissance painters worshipping the loins of their assistants, fondling young men's downy thighs as they arranged them. Desire was the first computer, a loom, so workers had more time to chase and fuck other workers to fill the desires for new dresses, for new overcoats, for houses with separate rooms, so they could fuck without pulling one another into the hay, picking fleas off of bodies. The ascetics with their bodies buried in secret flesh missed the fucking point. You got to show the people just enough to make them want it. You got to make desire holy. You got to show them that heaven is not waiting. It's here. They just have to submit to it.

No more disease. No more rape. No more war. Any and all pornography you could want. Shit. He was the son of the gods and MOTHER was his pagan goddess. He created androids. He recreated humans. And now he had that store owner here with her coy smile. He created her in his own image. Her untouchable skin was now under his palms.

"Al, lover of the most holy, go and put on those little white shorts I like."

Mechoben peered at the monitor from the Pinning Station on Enceladus. The giant needle that kept MOTHER pinned for harvest slid up and down to give the illusion of mining. His team told him long ago that mining from a moon the size of a large island was economically nonviable, but that the lifeforms here had "potential."

At the time, the Terrans had just retrieved his business partner from his bunker in New Zealandia and torn his limbs from his body. He screamed and cried on the streams as they tied him to the remaining uneaten horses and ATVs and revved and whipped and hollered until his right arm came off first, soaking the silk sleeve of his Louis Vuitton pajama top in blood so fresh it shimmered like rubies under the pollution-diluted sun. They descended on him digging into his flesh and wiping it across their faces as others poured into the bunker, handing his supplies to one another in a gore-wiped assembly line. Purple black fingerprints on fine pastas, cans of San Marzano tomatoes, frozen sides of beef, a water purifier, bags and bags of white flour and rice.

Mechoben looked on from above. His name was still Simon then. This was before his transformation, his ascension to highest point of understanding. Before his divinely inspired recreation of the holy text. His moon colony and space station luxury living apartments lifted him above the unwashed. It was never enough. And so he called military contractors and got a small crew to pin down MOTHER. To claim what was his. Thus began his holy journey.

And now three little pigs had decided they were going to blow his house down. His kingdom for a fucking nail. No way.

"Al, get The Commandant on my stream," he said, taking her in. "And work on getting your hair a little lighter."

"Whatever you want, my lord," she said, her purplish eyes sedate. She tapped a sequence into a panel and drew her fingers across to widen it, and then lifted it with her palms upward as it hung suspended above them and placed it at the correct eyeline angle for him. Specific. Custom. The religion of self.

"Your duty is fulfilled. You can go. Lighten that hair." Sometimes his Terran accent came out. He quelled it and practiced his Space Speak Neutral Lexicon as the Commandant's shine-pumped face appeared on screen. His lips pursed with grotesque Shine overinjection.

"Commandant. We have a problem. Is this channel secured on your end?"

"As well as it can be, my lord."

"I don't like that answer," his tone remained smooth. He willed his heart rate down.

"We are on the most secure channel we have, my lord." The Commandant slurred the words, his eyes shot through with calming pharmaceuticals.

"Were you aware that there are people on Enceladus, Commandant?"

"That old android from before we lifespanned them, my lord? The one who thinks he's General Jiménez or Rodríguez, or whatever his name was."

"I'm sure you wish that was the extent of it," Mechoben raised his eyebrows as the Commandant swayed behind the screen. "But, no. Sadly, your job is harder than that. That poor second-born is no longer operational. Two of my holy children made it to the surface. Under your watch."

"Sir, we are holding a rather large territory. It's difficult to keep an eye on everything. I don't need to remind you that the rebellion on the Venusian colonies has not been contained yet and there is another on what's left of Earth. They keep tearing down the signal towers."

"I know that. I'm the Son of God. Don't you think I know that?"

The Commandant swigged from a blue and white steel cup from The Before.

"My apologies, He who is Most High, what is your command regarding these interlopers?"

"They are important to bring back alive, with the exception of the Martian girl."

"There's a Martian Girl down there?" The Commandant asked evenly.

"Yes, she has some attachment to the Terran brother and sister... don't cringe Commandant...'brother and sister' used to be commonplace. I know you remember before the campaign regarding the economic immorality of familial units."

"How shall we retrieve them, sir?" Unshakable.

"That is why my father made you. To figure that out. Just get them off the planet and leave another Lighthouse keeper. The android expired."

The Commandant nodded and touched his thumbs to his forehead in reverence.

"I will make it so."

Mechoben switched off the feed and turned in his chair to face Al, who walked in drying her newly lightened hair with a towel. She combed his fingers through the tangles and went to her station beside him. Her eyes were clouded with her seasonal molt.

"Al, my darling, I am going to need you to make up one of the bedrooms on the south side of the station. We are bringing one of your old friends to visit and I need her on my side."

He pulled the tab out of a can of rare unbranded Terran wine and poured it into two Plastiglass cups.

"Yes, my lord. Who is our guest?"

"You will remember her as Riff."

"Forgive me lord, but isn't she a blasphemer? She abandoned all the gifts you bestowed upon her. She is consorting with those unattractives. The ones who won't be retired?"

"Do you think I don't have a plan and have always had a plan?" His voice was low, dangerous. "My father is in every room, in every corner. My father knows all."

She lowered her strange, clouded eyes.

"Will that be all? Fix up the rooms in the solar wing?" She asked.

He handed her a glass of the Terran wine. She looked at it and smelled it.

"It's wine. Like the FungiLiquor, but it's made from grapes."

"What is grapes?" She took a small sip and retched.

He laughed and took the glass from her, swirling it below his nose. He had never been able to tell the difference between most wines, but this was an obvious choice over the milky brownish FungiLiquor.

"Let's just make sure our guests feel welcome. Do you remember some of Riff's favorite things? Or was that lost in your transcendence?"

"I can review the feeds and I remember some, but mostly I just remember you," she said.

She drifted close to him, emitting a small wisp of pheromones to entice him, and stroked his hair. She could feel her body shifting as she touched him. Her fingers lengthened and thickened for a moment, the joints creaking.

He leaned back and pulled her into his lap, laying a pattern of kisses up the side of her neck. His body responding to the pheromones. He invented pheromones. Well his father did.

***

Documents Year [redacted] 134 – 136 Earth Cycle [Redacted]

1245 – Captain's Log:

Systems operational. On course to Enceladus with slight delay. Fuel line repaired by the unnamed android.

Supplemental record:

The other crew members have taken to calling the android "Duck" as he seems to follow me and copy my very persona. He – I use that pronoun loosely, as the research given to me indicates that they have a remarkable capability to shift sex.

This is the first android I, and many of the crew have ever worked with, given their controversial release and production system. While I am not well-versed on a good deal of Atlantia American politics, given that I am more concerned with my home territory of Cascadia given the number of wildfires and the aquifer depletion, I understand that several fringe religious groups have voiced concerns about the nature of the android's soul.

Having been raised what used to be called "Roman Catholic" before the great binding and assertion of Mechoben's doctrine of The Machine, I can say with confidence that they will forget their reservations soon enough. The Catholics forgot their priests and cloistered nuns soon enough when the Holy Book TM freed them.

They used to have priests and cardinals and all kinds of middle management before Mechoben came and showed them the true path of efficiency and production. The Great Reorganization saw to that. I wax poetic. It is a weakness of mine. Truly there is little place for it in the Orion-Cygnus Militia.

The android is uncanny at times, morphing his face to fit mine better. He seems to have trouble with my eye color, perhaps because it is so dark and often reverts to a muddy green rather than a brown. He mimics my walk and my talk. I have even taught him a bit of Spanish, and he seems to pick it up pretty quickly.

He is obsessed with the idea of a family, though I understand there is a movement that is gaining ground to disband the family. They claim it is an outdated model; one that is complicit in the degradation of social fabric and the very soil of our home world.

The Corporation sent Duck to us on a trial basis, to see how well Androids were able to fit in with human resources on unsown and therefore unreaped planets and moons. Thus far, he has been quite useful, if strange. I understand that he was bred and designed with the intent that he be able to work longer hours than human resources in more dangerous environments. He has proven his mettle on that front, though if The Corporation does retain these records, which I am certain they will given the non-disclosure and Terms of Service agreements we were required to sign, it should be noted that his personality is childlike and unformed. We find ourselves talking to him as you would a child of seven or eight. He is like my son back on Earth, and I find him making the same social blunders. He peers at the female crew members particularly, though he has the capability to shift to the female sex and knows the anatomy, I would presume.

I am not a scientist, as these records show with my particular signature, so I cannot offer any advice on that front, but as a manager of people, I would suggest that androids be more socially conditioned before their use on largely human vessels. Is it possible that their sexuality be removed?

***

Document 135 – Chat logs [redacted]:

SmileyXuan: Have you been reading the captain's logs from the Enceladus mission?

BignRich: Yeah. That captain TALKS. lol

SmileyXuan: He really does. But after you wade through all the history and philosophy lectures, he gives us some pretty interesting data.

BignRich: The suggestion that we castrate androids like they used to do to Earth animals is savage.

SmileyXuan: Yeah. I don't think the older Terrans really get it. This is supposed to make their lives easier and all they can focus on is sex. He's sharp though for an oldie. He totally understands that we are using his data.

BignRich: Definitely. What data were you talking about? From earlier?

SmileyXuan: The idea about socializing them. He kind of has a point. It's kind of fucked up to give something an adult body and physically developed mind to someone who was just born and ask them to perform complex tasks without giving them the tools to cooperate.

BignRich: Should I call that Brazilian Scientist? The one who is working on the Martian Colonization models? They say he is raising one like his daughter. I saw it on a stream.

SmileyXuan: Oh I saw that on InstaNews a few cycles ago. I think he's actually from Peru, though. Didn't he actually have a daughter that died from Collapse Syndrome?

BignRich: I think so? I know we can call him. The Corporation just bought out his research firm.

SmileyXuan: You should definitely call him. We might as well start working on this. The new batch will be mature in a few weeks.

BignRich: Any really hot models? Did you breed me one with big titties?

SmileyXuan: They monitor this chat, [redacted]. Plus you know they can change sex. Get a robot like the rest of us.

BignRich: Robots are for nerds. You're no fun today. I'll call [redacted] Research to talk to that scientist.

SmileyXuan: Good. Let me know if you need my documentation.

XXIX: They Say Martian Girls Break First

The Commandant injected his own lips with Shine. That was how men, real men, not these synths with engineered cocks did it. The tiny needle pierced into the faintest hints of crags around his eyes. He had injected his own sclera with forest green ink when the world was still broken by border and ocean. It was a visual war cry. The Chinese, now obliterated like the rest of the scourge of nationalism, saw him on the screen and called him "Yaomo." Strange Devil. Now, thick with age, his blacked-out eyes lent him the gravitas of an old warrior. A warrior who saw real death. The smell of it. The sounds of begging for someone to be there to escort them across that flat black plane to the bargeman.

He was the highest ranking member of the Space Militia now. Because he knew to keep his opinions to himself. He knew how to give in to leadership. This customization of product and workplace bonding flew against his previous training, to be cohesive, to serve as cog in something larger. But he was flexible. And leaders changed like gloves.

He looped in his best Star Slingers after his strange call with Mechoben. Privately, when he was sure the cams were averted, he muttered to himself "Boy King," after the increasingly bizarre vidchats with the leader of all of the Cygnus-Orion domain. He saw that Mechoben, or Second Lieutenant Simon Mahaffey, as he had known him in The Before, had taken another android bride. He wondered how long this one would last before she was shuttled into a Quiet Box for the remainder of her short lifespan for some perceived or invented insult to The Smooth, The Orderly, The Never Satiated.

The face of his most trusted General came into view. General Akimbo refused the Shine injections and so would never rise past the rank of General. Mechoben required all to be smooth. The absence of smooth was a cardinal sin. It was shocking to see an unaltered face, with its creases and dimples. Burst arteries mapped across his nose and cheekbones like topographical maps. His eyes were yellowed from years of drinking engine room gin.

"How the hell are you, Akimbo?"

"Depends on who you ask," the worn general answered.

"I have an assignment for you."

"I figured as much." The general tucked a liquid nicotine-soaked gauze patch under his lip. A holdover from the time after The Event for Earth-stationed troops.

"Mechoben wants a little problem taken care of on Enceladus."

"Don't be coy, Commandant. What do you want from me?"

Times had changed. The need for heavy organized militia was fading and they were old men now. Akimbo's right eye was clouded with a cataract and he refused to let the Robosurgeons near it, even though they were more precise than any human hand. Perhaps this was the perfect mission for him. It opened the chances for someone more malleable, less constrained by outdated philosophies. Their history be damned.

"I want you to go and retrieve three individuals and a tissue sample from the Natsar host. It is mission critical that you don't damage the siblings. The Martian can be disposed of as you see fit."

"Jesus Christ, Hersch. You want me to go to a moon to pick up two kids, kill another, and then cut into the great MOTHER? What in the hell for?"

"This channel is monitored, so I suggest you refrain from using my Terran name or invoking any old gods."

"What the fuck are you talking about?"

Heat rose in The Commandant's face. Images of Akimbo reaching to him as he thrashed in the churning murk, his arm muscled and fine. His eyes unclouded then. His mouth soft under the three-day bristle. The taste of earth and something worse, something acrid, filling his mouth and nose just before Akimbo's arm wrapped around his belly and the men pulled them to safety on the boat.

Akimbo laying beside him in the tiny bunk, tracing patterns on his chest after they released him from the med bay. Kissing his cheekbones. Rescue was erotic.

"Akimbo, goddammit. Will you just listen to me? I'm your commanding officer!"

"Hersch, haven't you figured out that none of that horseshit matters anymore?" His eyes brimming with tears. His bravado always cut with softness. Picking up drowned cats and holding them against his barrel chest with gunfire tatting above him, smoothing his thumb over their half-closed eyelids.

"Your directive is to retrieve the following persons: Alicia Rodríguez or "Riff" in MechoSpeak, Her brother José Rodríguez or "Rasp," and Alona DeLuna from our contracted research facility on Mars," The Commandant rattled off numbly.

General Akimbo sighed.

"Ok, Hersch. Ok. Send me the directive through the secure channel. How many men am I authorized to bring?"

"You can bring as many androids as you want for operations, but you are limited to two human men."

"Why me?" When will I be released for retirement?"

"That is up to our holy leader."

Akimbo's mouth drew into a straight line, and The Commandant longed for the aging general to hold him again. Their last kiss before the Great Limitation was hurried and brief. He ached with wanting every time he spoke with Akimbo.

"Alright, I will assemble a team and retrieve the assets."

"Remember General Akimbo, the preservation of the Martian Scientist is not important."

"Understood. Any further orders, sir?" His tone formal.

"No, that will be all. You will receive your written orders within two cycles. Upon receipt, report your chosen human resources and I will send you a charter with the assigned androids."

"Aye aye, sir."

The Commandant switched off the feed and rubbed his temples. He opened the digital file box and pulled the records for a set of battle worn and space damaged androids. He kept the most beautiful ones, the ones bred for the pleasure streams and the GagGirl films, in a separate file. They were deemed too violent for their original purpose. A particularly unctuous Andy with broad shoulders and a thickly muscled chest had killed two human GagGirls, but his breeding was too valuable for destruction. He assigned him assigned light duty. Cleaning his chambers. Cutting his hair. Sharing his bed. It excited him. It was like having one of those huge striped cats from The Before.

No one asked. No one reported it. No one envied his position.

He put in the request for seven androids, pushing Akimbo from his mind.

***

Riff-Alicia looked around the dripping facility, the seemingly endless supply of plasticine buckets lifting and rolling as the Grav drives cycled through energy saving measures. Black wisps of beings slid from corner to corner, fleeing at the chest level beam of light from her suit. She turned to her brother.

"What are they?"

"I think they're ghosts."

"Oh."

"What do we do now?" He asked, picking up on the floating plasticine buckets and chucking toward one of the shadows crouched in the corner. It bolted into the mess hall, leaving a trail of smoke.

"The Curanderas wanted me to connect with MOTHER. I think I'm supposed to set her free," she said.

"How do you know?" He picked up another bucket and hurled it toward a man-sized creature performing the imitation of maintenance on an absent fluorescent apparatus. It splashed against the wall and disappeared. The bucket clattered down the long corridor.

"That seems kind of mean," she said. "What if it hurts them? We don't have any NoPain patches."

"Don't you remember what a ghost is, hermana?"

She ignored him. Her heart thumped with an alien feeling in her chest. She returned to the Curanderas' will. The will that had become her will.

"They brought me here from Mars because I can talk to MOTHER."

"I can talk to MOTHER too," he said.

"I know. I was you and you were me."

"That was you? Like really? In real life?"

"Yep. How can we stop the thing that's hurting her?" She asked. It was difficult to speak to him in person. It felt strained. He was a stranger now. She wondered if he had seen her Pornographic Art Films. She wondered how she looked under the gauze of makeup and lights and editing. She wondered how she looked now.

"Let's find the control panel and I'll see if it's anything like the asteroid mining controls," he said.

MOTHER scraped under the ice outside. The facility shuddered as she careened under the ice.

***

The mountains stood behind Al casting their great shadows behind them, their blue-gray faces sparkling in under the three suns. The beach spread before her, the dunes tipped like frothed Shine. The suns warmed her and the ocean spread across the lavender sand beneath the dunes, flattening the bases into packed disks. As she neared the water, little circlets of pale blue surfaced on her skin. She lifted her arm to peer at it. A thin layer of mucus coated her skin, beading up from her pores.

A memory of dispersed light filtering down through silvery light tugged at her. She moved to the water, her skin turning rubbery and flexible as she approached the sea foam edged with phosphorescent algae. The water licked at her knees as she waded out. She pressed her flattened palm against her forehead against the glare.

Mechoben sent her out of the compound today. He handed her a waypoint pointer programmed to expulse a small floating orb programmed to lead her to the beach and then back to the compound. The facility echoed with each movement, each sound like a brush to an open wound in its emptiness.

He had caught her pushing on closed doors down in the cool basement, looking for others just to verify her own existence. He gripped her by the wrist and pulled her close to his face, his features nipped and sewn into an expression of bizarre unfeeling by his distant Aesthetics Team. He loosed her after murmuring something about faithfulness. She slept in one of the guest rooms with windows flung open to cold wind. Humans always liked it far too warm. But it was blasphemy to think of Mechoben, her savior, as human. Though she did. When he coughed, sending bits of spittle into the air. When he pressed lotions and salves into the skin of his face. When he tumped over furniture in anger over a robot stuck on the threshold, the drink it carried slopping over the sides of the glass. These were the times he seemed most human.

She sat down in the water, the coolness of it soothing her always too-warm skin. The saltwater lifting her like Martian gravity.

She unlatched the catch from the tablet she carried and pulled out the thin barbed darts and pierced through the skin on the insides of her elbows. When she was first detubed, one of the older GagGirls from the "Special Interests" side of Pornographic Art Film production told her that electronics were not waterproofed when she was a child. They had all giggled at this quaint notion.

Strange this memory washed over her now. Most of her time on Mars had been scrubbed during her ascension.

Several perfect circles lit up under her skin where her skin was the thinnest. Her wrists. Her ankles. She knew that the tender veins glowed under her eyes. She dipped under the water and opened her eyes. Flagellating creatures with their own pinpoints of light knocked against her skin. She opened her mouth and a veil of light poured into the darkening water. It drew larger animals that clung to the edges of her lips as they unfurled proboscises to suck and nibble at her molars.

She closed her mouth over a supple cigar shaped organism and bit down. The salinity of the water masked the sour cloud as her teeth dug into the rubbery flesh. Memories of Riff came flooding back. She pushed the oxygenator pods into her nostrils and breathed in.

She found out about the Recollection Fish from the unedited streams library she had access to. Though it was redacted what planet she was on exactly, the stream showed a humanoid species plunging under water and chewing until they emerged with their lines of blinking eyes slicked over with opaque reticulating eyelids. On the general populace streams, alien life other than the unavoidable Natsar was shown as only a distant manner. It was for space-crazed miners to ponder before retirement. Ranting in commissary canteens. Slugging pints of illegal sucrose wine. Telling their buddies about how the cure for every ail lies on some planet hidden by The Corporation.

Riff sat across from her, her black hair knotted into thick neglect dreads at the base of her scalp. All the Shine injections so carefully selected and administered weren't present. Al realized she was seeing Riff as she first came to Mars. A figment. A hallucination from the faint poison soaking through her mucus membranes.

Her young face was childish. Her lips thin and unplumped. Her ears were pierced with tracker nodes. Riff reached across and stroked the side of Al's face, but as she looked down at her own hands and body, the androgyny of it comforted her. The fat deposits that rested on her hips and chest now were absent in this vision of the past. Her belly was studded with muscle and her fingers longer and thicker.

Riff came across the room, a child, but older than her by twelve cycles, and wound her thin brown arms around her neck. She smelled like engine exhaust and human sebum. An erection. A smile. Al's own body. They not she.

Water rushed into her mouth and down her throat. She choked and pushed against the ocean floor, the fine grit giving way under the pressure of her feet. Of their feet. They looked down at their naked form under this heather gray sky. They were taller, firmer. Their heavy breasts replaced with flat muscle. This vision reminded them of their true form. Something drew her gaze from across the tide pool.

A figure crouched on the beach, lines of green eyes blinking along its spine. Long shawls of skin puddled around its feet shining like polished bronze and it was girded with a long whip of cracking light. It raised up and stretched until the flags of skin caught the wind and lifted the being up into the faces of the suns. Turning and turning on the breeze in surrender to the sea winds. A thing of this planet.

They would kill God. Al would kill God.

***

Rasp-José and Riff-Alicia curled around one another like commas in the belly of the auger site. They pulled the stiff pads from the old military cots and put them side by side. Their young bodies ached from the cold. The geothermic heating module read forty-three degrees Fahrenheit for the ambient temperature. Their breath streamed out in front of them like smoke. Rasp-José drew the heat reflective blanket over their heads and tucked it around his sister's shoulders. She shivered and huddled close to him. The bright white lights buzzed above them filtering through the seams.

The smell of their breath and sweat and oils mingled under the crinkling material. Tiny beauty scars dotted her arms, glinting under the filtered fluorescent light.

"We have to keep the lights on?" She asked.

"Yeah, it keeps the shadows away."

"Can they hurt us?"

He stroked her upper arm with his pointer finger knuckle.

"Knock knock," he said.

"Who's there?" Her automatic response surprised her.

"Cargo."

"Cargo who?"

"No, car go beep beep!"

She giggled and he drew her into his arms like he did when she was a toddler and afraid of Mama's high laugh too late in the night. Her high heels clattering on the old floors. The sound of unfamiliar heavy footfalls. Squares of light racing across their bedroom walls.

Rasp's eyelids flickered and slid closed, darkness welling over his eyesight like a tide. Images tossed across his internal vision. A pile of shining black marbles exploding down a flight of stairs, a woman holding a skinned dog to her breast, its legs twitching as she suckled it, a flighted creature with scarlet feathers tearing through the void between stars.

He found himself standing on a mountaintop in his dream. The mist surrounded the peak in a flat white pall and wind drove against his naked body. Two thin green sharpened sticks had been shoved behind his pectoral muscles and the pain radiated to his throat in burning hallucinatory almost-pleasure. The sun poured down on him. The gray pebbles on the ground heated through, bit into the soles of his feet as he twirled round and round, tugging at the sticks driven through his flesh. He called out in a language that was not his own, knowing that he begged for the vision that would free him. His long hair brushed against the clotted wounds in divine agony. He dropped to the rocky ground and beat his fists into the mountain. Wailing. Surrendering.

A thrumming skin drum shuddered from down the mountain. A figure materialized from the mists carrying something in its arms. The thing was wrapped in a garment made of light and had four faces, each turning to face the cardinal directions. Each face had four eyes of different animals. One face blinked with slow yellow jaguar eyes, one stared with the cold night water eyes of a shark, one peered with the huge globular prey eye of the llama, but the eyes that faced him were human. The irises held no color and the skin of the being's face was as white as the snow caps. As it spoke, flashes of bronze teeth glinted through the lipless mouth.

It spoke.

Here is what you must do.

His feet lifted from the ground as the being stretched its long appendages toward him. It held skin drum in its clawed hands. It was stretched with the face of his mother. Her eyelids and lips were sewn shut with reflective wire and stretched into a grim passivity. A whisper sifted from under Mama's tight lips. He leaned in toward the hiss, the acrid sweetness of decomposition wafting into his nose.

It must be destroyed. We must make amends.

The creature turned its face and the jaguar eyes dilated and contracted. It held the skin drum in front of its chest, offering it in its face-up palms. Mama's eyelids strained against the stitching, her eyeballs twitching under the shrunken lids. Rasp-José took the drum and flung it off the mountain top into the mists below. The being surged into the sky on great black wings. The wind buffeting Rasp-José over the edge of the mountain top. The sky above him burned orange with exploding satellites as the mist whipped past his face.

Then he woke up, his sister nestled against his back under the blanket. Ice crystals frozen in his wispy mustache. Something wet rolled in his clenched hand. He drew his fist out from under the blanket into the cold and uncurled his stiff fingers. A single eyeball, cool and globular, rolled in the shallow indention of his palm. He brought it closer to his face and touched it with his other pointer finger.

"Oh, look! A Slinker," Riff-Alicia peered over his shoulder. "Let me see."

She took the eyeball from his hand and turned it over. The optic nerve switched back and forth like the tail of some small, irritated animal. She caressed it, nudging it gently and rolling it between her fingers.

"Oh, here it is," she said, scratching at the eyeball with her fingernail.

It flattened and shot out a thread of clear mucus.

"What does it do?" he asked as he looked over her shoulder.

"Watch this." She squeezed her fist over it and then shook it, slinging the mucus rope in a loop below them. It twisted around itself, then untwined leaving a transparent sheet in the U of the loop. An image of a suited person stumbling toward the door of the auger facility flowed across the gelatinous sheet in a gentle ripple. Riff-Alicia cocked her head down toward it to see the image. She drew in her breath. "Oh shit."

"Is that real?" Rasp-José asked.

The figure reached for the front door and pressed against the Autosensor Pressure Plate TM. A faint echo rattled down the hall from the entrance.

"Is the pressure plate functioning?" Riff-Alicia spread her hands wider, expanding the image. Her breathing quickened as the door rattled. Her nose leaked blood and a black tendril swam in the air in front of her. The person projected on the membrane reached toward their helmet for a moment and tried the door again, this time shoving their shoulder against the metal door. The front door shook on its hinges.

"I can't remember if that's how we got in," Rasp-José said, looking over at his sister who rubbed at the corners of her eyes. Her familiar slid over her eyeball and whipped back and forth from her nostril.

The Slinker slipped from her hands and glopped to the floor. She shed the blanket from her shoulders and stepped back into her suit. Her black eyes stared ahead as she slid her fingers over the heat-sensitive closures across the front.

"What are you doing, Alicia?" Her old name. Her Before name.

"MOTHER has a request."

"I don't hear her." He looked around.

Riff-Alicia said nothing. She pushed her helmet down and strode to the door. Rasp-José jerked his own suit up over her shoulders and plunged his head into his helmet. She left the control room and headed toward the knocking. He stumbled after her, fumbling with the atmospheric seals on his suit.

His sister knocked a pattern on the door. One One Two One. A rapping answered from the outside. A fine smattering of blood coated the inside of her helmet. She pressed the pressure plate release and the door jolted open. Rasp-José blinked. The beautiful Martian with her cool three-fingered hands, with her mocking laugh, with her thin bones stared at Riff-Alicia, her arms spread open. They fell into one another's arms, their familiars pressing like the bellies of snakes against glass as their helmets cracked together.

Rasp-José reached over his sister's shoulder and yanked the front of Alona's suit, drawing her into the hallway. The women embraced one another as he closed the door. He watched as they pulled off their helmets.

"The temperature isn't stable here," he said. "The oxygen levels could change too."

They pressed their foreheads together and opened their pink kitten mouths. The slick muscular appendages oozed from their mouths and nostrils and twined together, sliding across one another as the women gagged and lurched back and forth. Their hands slithering under one another's thick underclothing.

Rasp-José looked at his temperature monitor on his wrist. The women's breath poured from their nostrils in gouts of steam. They fell to the floor twisting from their suits. The sound of bone cracking as Alona struck the Terran gravity level floor. Her muffled cries ecstatic. They delved into one another's bodies, arching into the other as their sweat froze into frosted pearls. His sister grew into something else. Her legs lengthened and stretched and fused into the body of a great crimson serpent. Alona's torso hollowed into a rust colored crater, her mouth sinking into a great red hole. Her teeth a straight boundary.

The enormous coral red snake with the head of his sister swung backwards, brushing the ceiling with the arch of her back. Her black hair hung in long tassels that clung to the edges of her wet lips. She smiled at him and spoke.

I know you. Her voice was her own. Soft and sibilant.

She bowed over the rich red pile that was Alona and plunged her soft round face into it. The pile giggled like a child being tickled, thrashing and squealing. A lightness overcame him as he watched her nuzzling the folds of gelatinous flesh. Sparks of bright blue flashed behind his eyes and his stomach spat acid into his throat. Salt water oozed from under his tongue. He tore his gaze away and tried to run to the end of the vestibule. His boots clung to the floor and his suit dragged down around his shoulders, popping the connections from his helmet. The cold air rushed into his lungs. He coughed and stooped to pull his boots from the wavering substance on the floor, his nose pouring fluid as the shock of the cold rushed into his nostrils.

Riff-Alicia's familiar squirmed from her mouth and dropped to the floor. It expanded as it wormed in the thick liquid and divided into a flail of black tendrils, stretching toward the control panel. It smashed into the industrial plasticine cover and poured into the created hole. The sound of the auger engaging rattled across the ice. Rasp-José tore his feet from the gunge and hoisted himself back toward the chamber where he had folded his sister into his arms only a few cycles before.

A great shuddering crash shook the outpost. Hunks of the autoinsulation fell around him as he dragged himself into the chamber and peered out of the viewing slit. The thin auger tower broke in two as the ice beneath it shattered. The engine that drove it whirring high and hot. A woman cried from somewhere as the tapered bottom was thrust from the great fecund body of MOTHER. Freed from the moorings, hunks of the structure drifted along the ground, colliding and spinning.

A gout of steam hissed from the open wound on MOTHER's body as fluid rushed into the crevasses on the ice, melting them into great ink-black rivers that frothed and foamed. Black shining pieces of ice flew toward the heavy center of Saturn to join in the frantic spinning dance around the golden giantess.

The concrete floor split in two under him and water seeped through the cracks. He looked back out into the hallway where earlier he had seen his sister and Alona hunched together in ritual consummation. The sacrifice was always blood.

"Alicia?" His heart thudded in his chest. "We need to get back to the station. This outpost is coming down."

He peered around the doorframe to see her changed back into a girl child. She sat beside Alona's unmoving body, trying to put the Martian woman's helmet on the largest piece of skull left. Riff-Alicia slid her hand under the slick pile and scooped at the bloody void where the wide-eyed face had once been. She tilted the helmet like a well bucket, trying to force the helmet down. The blood was freezing into shiny black puddles. Rasp-José picked up his sister's helmet from the floor and handed it to her. Her eyelashes where white with frost.

The environmental alarms beeped and squealed as the temperature dropped. The wall beside them tore in two as MOTHER writhed free of the auger. He put the helmet over her head gently.

When they were small, he remembered water falling from a silver spigot in a swirling white chamber. The water gathered in a deep pool and colorful creatures bobbed and floated, flipping over and over as the water struck them. His sister sat amongst the shiny creatures all in primary colors and flung her baby fat hands across the clear water. Her doughy baby body folding as she tumbled over. Mama clutching the old inflexible tablet under her arm reaching in with her other hand to right her, handing him a towel to dry her. Alicia's eyes black as night, crinkled under her fat cheeks as he draped the towel over her head and picked her up. Madonna before the angel stood on her neck and hissed her destiny into her ear. God always needed a messenger.

"You have to call MOTHER, sister. I can't call her like you can."

She gazed up at him, dazed.

"Mama? She's dead."

He hadn't heard that word in a long time. The Corporation, citing the Holy Book TM, forbade "dead" or "death" as it condoned an inefficiency in the system. Space Waste was punishable by Venusian duty for women and Mercury mining in the outer rim for Men. To say death was to invite it, to insult the procedure, to fill the minds of those without mission, to incite, to linger. And lingering was the gravest of disobediences.

He lifted her up, holding her around the waist and slid his finger along the heat seal of her helmet. The skin around her eyes sagged away from their orbits.

"Not Mama. Call MOTHER."

"Pray?" She whispered.

"Yes, pray to MOTHER."

She bowed her head and propped her hands under her chin.

MOTHER shelter of the wind, most supple and large. Your beauty is terrible and I am alone under your gaze. Cradle us, your children, though you begat us without leave. We are of your body. You are of our mind. Deliver us, oh MOTHER. Carry us so we may punish your enemies. We are your tools in the destruction of your impregnator. Use us.

She opened her eyes and blinked at him.

"Can you hear her?" She asked.

MOTHER burst into his mind, brighter than a solar flare. His jaw locked shut and his pain blazed behind his eyes.

HERE. WHERE?

"Not so loud MOTHER. It hurts," he said.

HURTS. The volume whittled down in his mind. NO HURT ME I.

"Can you take us back to the other place?"

YES

"Thank you."

THANK YOU. FREE.

A wave of viscous clear fluid gushed from the split in the floor and lapped over them, covering them in a smooth warm caul. Riff-Alicia floated beside him, her knees tucked up by her belly.

XXX. Where Oh Where Did My Little Dog Go?

Dear Anyone,

We were warned. We were plied and consoled with those small comforts. We invited them into our homes to make things less tedious so we could have more time for what? To look away from one another and into the blue light at curated depictions of ourselves. They did not lie. They obstructed. That's an important distinction. We did the curating, they simply harvested. Like worms on crops.

I write this from a facility that they insist on calling a "corporate retreat." I worked as the Superior Court Attorney for the District of Cascadia. What kind of corporate retreat would I be party to? They bring us from these minimal cells into a large common area and create false intimacy by gleaning small details about our families, our lives, but never too much truth.

Too much truth creates true intimacy and true intimacy is dangerous. I write to anyone but I suppose that is as much a retraction of intimacy as anything else. I could write to my daughter, but I am certain she has been spirited away to one of the space stations to be "vocationally trained." I could write to my son, but I cannot imagine him surviving this brave new world. The last time I saw him, he was huddling at the bottom of a boat trying to tell a knock knock joke. I am certain he has already been eaten alive in one way or another. My husband, so wound up in his place in this solar system, so concerned with obedience and honor.

When I met him, he was drunk so on Palm Liquor that he drew me into his arms to dance on the crumbling plywood floor. We were still in The New South then, drifting from bar to bar on flat rafts made of cypress pocket doors ripped from houses after the first floods. He whispered Spanish to me, crushing me against his rain softened military uniform. His dark hand pressed against my lower back. Moreno. It was forbidden to speak anything but English in those days. I suppose it still is.

His tiny rebellion was until it wasn't. He tried to forbid me from teaching Spanish to my children. I don't like children, not even my own. They tear your body. They require constant supervision, because they will hurl themselves into the hands of monsters if just one eye is averted. We were the generation right before "natural-borns" were outlawed. In some ways I agreed with the new laws. It always seemed strange to me that we required testing and licensing for owning and operating a business or driving a car, but not for making another mouth to feed on this engorged planet. But the children came and we weren't allowed to get rid of them or prevent them in The New South, so they should know the language of their ancestors.

He argued that I didn't know Mayan and that Spanish was the language of those who stole our gold and chocolate and corn and gods. How strange. How interesting. The man who hauled himself up the ladder of the new Conquistadors drinking non-Corporate wine as sanctioned by the United Front Army. I do not understand him. He did not want to be understood. He is certainly dead by now. We all know how that story ends.

No. I do not think I write to him either. I think this is for you, whomever you may be.

No one likes a chiding mother or a nagging wife. Do you know why? Because it makes you remember our great power over you. You suckled from our bodies or were fed by our hands. You were grown inside of us. We pulled your fingers from door frames. We held you away from that lunging dog. We gave you access, but when we pulled our breast from your mouth for the last time, you knew that you would never be as close to another. Our gift is a curse.

You beg us for closeness. You wish to cloister us and de-sex us, even from your own fathers. I do not blame those mothers who put their babies to bed face down and didn't check, praying to find the infant cold and still the next morning. I prayed every night for my boy child to never wake up.

This "corporate retreat" is to tamp down this feeling. To make us forget what actual connection is. Actual connection is not of the body but of the mind. To replace it with the hollow interactions that can only be staged by sociopaths or cowards looking to escape their own ineptitude. These stooges. These worm tongues.

They had us do a scavenger hunt today. Citing "unfavorable atmospheric conditions" the goons came out wearing bright yellow t-shirts with The Corporation's logo emblazoned across the front instead of the usual business casual. They giggled amongst themselves like they were the first people to think of this exercise. They divided us into teams with our "coworkers" and gave us a radiation detector. Whichever team counted the most blips in their designated area won a five credit Commissary gift card.

They engage you in these little activities to show you that they own your time. They own your labor. They claim, and some of the less gifted middle managers actually believe, that these little tasks bring people together. That they instill loyalty to The Corporation.

It is a shortcut to take from you.

I won the scavenger hunt. There is a system to it all, you know. Those who get bogged down in ideas and overlay their own notions of fairness or beauty or truth will lose. It is a raw system determined by algorithms. I will tell you how I won, though that is the first rule to never break if you want to win. The blood in my shit and my shrunken body have superseded that rule. The iron taste in my mouth reveals the ultimate truth: We will lose the larger game. You will lose the larger game. You already knew that. The second rule is to guide the illusion that the larger game can be won. Creams to plump. Dyes to hide. Diets to trim. Scalpels to cut. In guiding the illusion, the third rule comes easily: sell the illusion to those who cannot or will not accept the first rule. Let them believe they can win it.

These are the abstractions most do not wish to face. Face them with a bone club in your hand and wildness in your eye. To the victor go the spoils. Make them need you.

I am the one with radiation burns. I am the one with a five-credit gift card to the commissary. I gave that gift card to the Director of Security along with a blowjob. Next time he will trust me more. A little more trust each time until I bite down and tear. This is the final rule: establish trust in others, but do not trust others. I will take his chip and flee. Because even I am not immune to my own bullshit.

I do not want to die.

Sincerely,

Ana

***

Pai busied himself. He was good at that, busying himself with projects to avoid the weight. Alona had been a long-term project.

He had taken her DNA from his dead daughter's epithelia, forcing open her mouth, his thumb pressed against her bottom teeth as he swirled the curettage against the inside of her cheek. Her first death. Not this one, so far beyond his grasp. This was her fourth reincarnation. Slipping the pink tissue into a test tube. Quickly, quickly before The Corporation came to attend to her retirement. To hide the evidence of their failure.

He would amend the lifespan alterations he used for his android research. He would ingrain her memories with a bit of brain tissue he saved from her. He would swirl away her nicotine addiction on a glass disk, holding his pipette like a knife. He would correct her astigmatism. He would hear her talk about the girls she liked again. He would see her dance under the false sun in the Solar Adjustment room again.

He would make her live again.

And now he would make her again. And again. And again. In his own image. He would drip hormones into the transparent womb until she loved him as he loved her. She would never leave him again. He must find the gene that drove curiosity and balance it with adoration. It was hard to separate it from the romantic love gene. He had trouble with that when he tried to replicate her mother. She would love him too much and interfere with his research. She craved his affection and attention. Never able to entertain herself. She starved to death when he left for a month-long conference on Titan.

He found her body when he returned, curled in their bed – Alona, the original Alona squatting over her and pulling back her eyelids. She must have been only two or three cycles then. Already thin and tall from the reduced gravity, her knees jutted from under the sheets. Her eyes huge with confusion.

His stream blinked on and Mechoben's face appeared, shaking him from his reverie. He checked the settings. It was a direct call. Bile rose in the back of his throat and he clenched his jaw. The CEO of the universe blinked at him.

"Dr. DeLuna, I see you there. Remember you signed the communication consent agreement. I own these channels. Answer me. We need to speak."

He put down his Gene Genie 3000 Splicer and tapped the audio button.

"I'm here, Lord. What would you ask of me?"

"Cut the formality. I had to send out Akimbo. We've lost the signal on them. They will destroy everything, and your daughter had a part in it." He giggled. "Well version 3.0 did."

Pai shrugged, avoiding the CEO's gaze.

"Well? What the fuck can we do?" Mechoben asked. His eyebrows raised.

"My daughter is gone. The signals have stopped from the base of operations there. We have no physical presence."

"No shit. That's why I sent Akimbo."

"How far out is he, Sweet Savior?"

"I told you to cut that shit out. About three weeks. Fuck. I still think in Earth time. Do you still think in Earth time, doctor?"

"Sometimes, but I have been on Mars for a very long time."

Mechoben waved his hand in front of the screen, flicking his fingers toward it.

"Well?"

"I believe we will start seeing the first Natsar die offs in about one Terran week." Pai swallowed the "my lord" that rose automatically to his lips.

A silvery android crossed behind Mechoben to stroke his thinning hair. She already showed neurological soft signs from the atmosphere on the hidden planet. One of her purple irises came unmoored and danced in its socket. She slipped from view, her lean body swaying like a current.

"Is it contagious?" Mechoben whispered.

"It's genetic sir, but we will lose every woman with the implanted Natsar. So, it's not contagious per se, but we will not be able to track them or send suggestive hormonal therapy like before."

"Will they die?"

"No sir. But without the hormonal cues, they will be less suggestible to the cultivated stimuli."

"The what?"

"The feeds, sir. The sedative mists. We designed them around the Natsar and the queen on Enceladus."

Mechoben took out a pack of Camel Light Cigarettes from The Far Before and drew one into the corner of his mouth. Pai's eyes widened.

"Forgive me sir, but are those made with real tobacco?"

"Yep. They are the last ones in the whole system. You're a scientist. I'm sure you know how hard it is to grow tobacco without Terran conditions."

"It's not my specialty, but yes." Pai paused. "What is it like? I can almost remember."

Mechoben lit the cigarette, peered into the pack and shook it.

"Only two left and then that's it." Mechoben said, ignoring Pai's question.

Mechoben sounded like a boy in that moment. A boy wishing for summer to never end. Staring at the fading orange of the last night while his backpack leans against the front door, packed and ready for the end of wild barefoot dashes and rainbow droplets arching over the chlorine-touched mists from the hose.

"What is my part in this, Lord? How can I assist Akimbo?"

"I'll need you to start researching primitive sedative types and mind softening drugs. Possibly from pre-Event Terra. And you will need to cease your…" He paused to draw deeply on his cigarette. "…personal projects for now. This is a real crisis, DeLuna. We are about to lose control."

"But, I just put her DNA into the growth solution!" Pai protested.

"Jesus, DeLuna. You won't have a fucking growth solution if the Natsar are withdrawn. Do you understand me? We are going to lose everything we've worked for."

"But sir…"

"Put it in the freezer and do what I have commanded." Mechoben's voice was hard. "Remember, I own these feeds and I am watching them."

The screen flipped to the Commissary Advertising Screen. A pair of orangeish breasts being pushed together and released projected across his screen, bouncing like twin water balloons. He looked down at the Petri dish with his daughter's DNA on it. The pale spot of sun burned like a low flame on the amber horizon. He opened a private channel that the first Alona programmed for him years ago and scrolled through to find Akimbo's private audio-only stream.

Akimbo's rich voice came on the line.

"My my my. It's been a long time, DeLuna. How are you holding up? Still a Peruvian beauty?"

"Still Peruvian, I suppose. I think you're the only one who ever thought I was a beauty though."

Akimbo laughed and Pai remembered the light scar that cut through the stubble on his upper lip. He remembered holding his hand before it was forbidden between authority figures. He remembered the firm hands on his chest. They were good together. He loved him almost as much as Alona's mother, Natasha. He loved to watch Akimbo and her spar, their muscular bodies sweeping past one another. He brought them cold tea. They kissed his temples on either side.

"Well, did our dearest leader of all spacetime and capital send you?" Akimbo said chuckling. "Or is it something else? Dinner and a show?"

"It's something else. It's something that requires utmost privacy."

"I see. Hang on." Pai heard a series of beeps and a muffled instruction. "Ok, I'm ready. What is it?"

"This has to stop. We have to stop him."

"Oh sweet Keynes. Who are we talking about here?"

"Him. The most high."

"Why?" Akimbo was cheerful, confident.

"We can't ask people to live like this anymore. He has cigarettes, Katsumi." Pai said, using the General's first name. The name he called out to when the flood nightmares came to feel his hard arm sling over his hip.

Akimbo was silent.

"Almost everyone has Collapse Syndrome here on Mars and the Shine production is tainted now. Everyone who uses it will have it soon." Pai felt desperate. "Say something. Please."

"This is treason. This is treason against God," Akimbo's playful tone had evaporated.

"Do gods smoke cigarettes and keep android pets? Do they hide disease from their children? Do they lose their hair? Why can't we have fruit and cigarettes? Alona died. She died." He choked.

"Our Alona? Our baby?"

Akimbo remembered Alona's black, black hair, wet from birth. He remembered his fingers compressed in pain as her mother, huffing in silent pain, squeezed his hand. She had his eyes, and DeLuna's smile and her mother's fair skin. This tiny golem. This child warrior. This wonderful experiment. The melding of three.

"You always did fight dirty. It isn't fair. You've always been smarter than us. Than me." A sad lightness flitted around the edges of the General's tone. "What happened?"

Pai detailed her flight. Her distrust. Her demise. Her body sacrificed and torn by the Natsar queen.

"Why don't we just kill the queen then?" Akimbo asked.

"We can't. The network is entwined with the very physical structures of the GagGirls and the androids. We probably have microscopic spores lodged in our nasal cavities as well." Pai paused, collecting his thoughts. "The queen, or MOTHER, as the siblings call her, is enormous. She is everywhere. She is us, Akimbo."

"I forgot you sent the boy to Enceladus. How could I forget that?"

"We have to stop this. We have to."

"What do I do, Pai pequeño? What do you need?"

"Don't hurt the children. Pick them up and bring them to me. I'll convince Mechoben it's part of the research."

"This line may be monitored."

"I guess we'll see. If it is, expect your ship to be returned to remote control."

"We have a brilliant engineer onboard. One of the last Terran educated ones. I think I can get him to rig a kill switch."

"Katsumi, listen to me. If you hear nothing else, hear this: take care of the children. The boy and the girl. They can communicate directly with MOTHER."

"Understood. And DeLuna?"

It was strange to hear his first name. Detached.

"Yes?"

"I'm sorry. I really am."

"That was so many cycles ago that my memories have memories."

"Ok."

"Ok."

Akimbo's mustache rasped against the embedded microphone as he signed off. Pai brought up a GagGirls stream and whispered to the disembodied navel-less torsos. His eyes wet and his hands clenched. He imagined the girls emerging from their plasticine sacks as infants. Always caul bearers, their faces pressed against the transparent sacks, their heads as round as Neptune's belly.

They were the first generation of no natural-borns. They had a purity the consumer craved. Born without blood, without family, without death. Born to be consumed.

***

A drop of fuel crystallized in the cold as Riff-Alicia cranked the drip pan up under the engine. MOTHER, now free from her bonds, crashed around the moon. Seeming to revel, to stretch. Sometimes when Riff-Alicia slept under the artificial sun long abandoned by the android mimic of their father, she thought she heard thunder and gasped awake to remember MOTHER's tumbling revelry.

Rasp-José slid in beside her and handed her a tool kit.

"I worked on the electronics and MOTHER showed me how to do some welds," he said.

"Whose eyes did you see through this time?"

"Some GagGirl who used to do finish welds for custom ship jobs. She was good too."

Riff-Alicia dipped her hand into the open tool kit, fumbling for a tool she couldn't remember the name of. She traced her fingers along the metal edges, her MOTHER-suit slipping over her finger tips. Rasp-José chattered on as he sparked the MicroBind Welder TM.

"You were in a factory, right?" He asked.

"Yeah."

"What was your job?"

"I was just an assembler. I heard once that they keep the prettiest girls in the safest jobs so they can trade with the Gag sector."

"Oh." He focused on his weld, drawing the bead through the saline tube.

MOTHER flashed into their minds, jostling them from their work.

OTHERS

"What others?" Riff-Alicia thought back at her. She had learned that answering verbally often initiated confusion.

BIG OTHERS

Rasp-José chimed in, his voice mingling with the resonance of MOTHER's.

"Can you reach them, MOTHER? Can you read them?"

MOTHER floundered in their heads. Her confusion wavered through their consciousnesses. Irritation rose in Riff-Alicia.

"You're confusing her. Stop asking so much." She said out loud.

He looked at the ground and shut off his mental communication with them, focusing instead on the panel he was reattaching.

"Where are the others?" She asked MOTHER.

OUT THERE

"Can you find their minds?"

NO

MOTHER undulated under the ice.

NOT LIKE YOU LIKE OTHER HERE

"Like Rasp?"

YES

"Okay. They are men."

???

"Never mind."

***

Space travel hurt Akimbo's bones. Researchers thought the artificial gravity drives would mitigate the effects of space travel and they did somewhat. He remembered the early days, running on those absurd treadmills, bungeed to the floor. His fingers swollen as sausages and purplish. The sound of his heart in his neck as he floated around the craft looking too far out between the whispering stars. They sang to one another, high and thin, a piping note that only the floating brains of the space weary could hear.

Once, when he was a child, he read a book about Merlin. He sat perched on the roof of the compressed mega city where the light and wind reached, leaning against a spindly antenna. The book talked about how Merlin could hear the trees whispering ancient secrets to one another as the wind blew through them. A conduit. An automatic writer for the ghosts of the earth. He had never seen trees, except in streams and pictures. He imagined them feeling like painted brick, but warm and breathing. The leaves like thin fingers of plastic.

The first time he heard starsong, his tether had popped loose and control was murmuring into his ear telling him to remain calm, that remaining calm conserves oxygen, remain calm Akimbo. And so he switched off his comms just for a moment. Just a moment to hear what true silence was for the first time in his life. He was certain that this end-over-end with no direction was his tomb. But instead of the thin static of pure silence, he heard them. These churning spherical collections of fire and plasma and gas, shuddering as they spouted and withdrew within themselves. Turning in a great ellipse, pulling away from the center, it sounded like the highest note on a violin. Then came the answer, a fluting chuckle.

After they sent the drone out for him to bring him back, he told his captain what he had heard.

They sent him to psych.

Now he was nearing retirement and was ready for the soup. The labor force had to be protected from the realities of the soup, but he had been allowed to see the future. The iridescent gleam of the churn. The trays of human femurs and scapulae retrieved and sifted out. It was quicker than disease. Kinder than the rot of old age. To be reduced was an honorable end, he thought.

Last mission. Last mission before sleep. Retrieve the siblings and then die.

He tapped the screen and motioned over his navigator. The heat register chirped as the surface scan rolled over the moon's surface. He pointed his sharpened yellowing fingernail at the screen as his navigator leaned over his left shoulder. Guidry's android-smooth skin brushed against his bare forearm. The U-shaped nitrobrand on the base of his neck stretched as he leaned over the console. Old war Andys stayed one shape. One shape was all that was required. Thousands of Guidrys had already been reclaimed into this Guidry. They greased the engine of the empire with their fat.

"Is this register reliable?" Akimbo asked.

"Yes. They just released the latest update and it was supposed to eliminate ghost chirps."

"Are those the targets?" He tapped the screen over the orange blobs floating around a sea of cool blues and purples.

"I can't be sure, but most likely. It's close to the habitation quarters according to the briefs."

"What is that?" Akimbo pulled down a pair of reading glasses from The Before onto his face.

A huge white shape moved under the orange blobs and spread like veins underneath them. It retracted into a tight ball, then poured across the screen like spilled milk.

"I need the comms channels clear so I can call the CEO."

"Aye aye sir." Guidry floated into the next room and closed the chamber with the heat seal. No grav drives on this bucket.

Akimbo dialed in the sequence for Mechoben's direct line and pressed his fingertip to the hollow needle. The familiar dart of pain as the DNA sequencer drew his blood. The screen opened as soon as the sequencer stopped whirring.

Mechoben's chambers were empty. A bright smear of blood on the bright white floor shimmered under the bright sunlight from the bay windows. A robotic flamingo walked across the blood, tracking it throughout the room in a perfect ellipse. Its primordial feet clicking with each step.

"Sir?" Akimbo's voice echoed back at him.

"Lord Mechoben? Are you there?"

No answer. The flamingo lapped the room again, its tracks matching perfectly with the first set.

***

Holy Book TM Chapter 54 Verses 1–5

1 For when the son returns to his father after many years of providing for his children the kingdom will be naught. He provided them with screens that do not break, with clothing named for the prophets of commerce, with visages of beauty, eliminating all disease and domestic violence, for by surveillance did he make you whole again.

2 You will know the signs by a great creature with eyes like Garmin watch faces who rises from the sea to find the Executive Directors and Chief Financial Officers laid bare before her.

3 And on her back will sit The Eldest of the Second Born, clothed in Station-Grown Cotton and dog leather loafers.

4 She will seduce his children with promises of fair labor and intermingling of the sexes, but this is folly. The demise of Terra came of these unnatural yearnings.

5 For it is written, thy place is determined not by thy labor, but by thy station.

***

It was easy. Skin as fragile as tissue paper under the genetic dynasty of the ant's strength-to-mass ratio.

Al planned for weeks, thinking about how to take him. He was after all the son of the one true god. The god who gave her life, who gave her beloved life. This fine changeable body. He was the engineer who built this system in the black heart of space.

In the end, it was as common a death as any. No crosses like the god child from The Before. No Ascension on the back of a white calf. No masses to witness, to lay hunks of animal fat on his grave.

It came to her after he drew her to orgasm, gripping her sides and biting her bare shoulder. He had asked her to assume a young form that day. To shrink herself into bare ripeness, her breasts to mere hints, her belly tight as a rounded drum.

Make your eyes larger, my child. Make your lips softer. Yes. That's it.

As he drew his hands, huge in comparison to her new frame, over her cheeks and stared into her eyes, she remembered that if she could be small, she could be large. She had forgotten He-Al, with height and power, thick with muscle. Pumping with testosterone. Heart fluttering as he drew her to his mouth. To melt. To scream.

And so she waited for him to depart as he sometimes did, only to return with strange pets that disappeared within the week. Pets that spoke to her through their pursed little mouths and tic tac eyes.

She ate dogmeat, sliding with Shine butter over top and genetically modified bread and small pink fruits shaped like ribbons. Crushing the sweet-sour skin and swallowing the sweetness. She grew in his absence, her ova descending into testes, her muscles lengthening, her head brushing the tops of doorways. She became He, though They was more settled in their psyche.

Al's dreamed about catching fetuses in their hands like butterflies, only to open them to find the fragile bones crushed under the heavy grip. They pulled themselves up the transparent cliffsides with bare fingers and no rope. They tore the skin, only for it to knit together like a tight smile. The sheets clung to Al's back.

The day came when Mechoben returned, flinging his Meteorite Harvest Chopard De Rigo sunglasses onto the entrance, a small creature with a flicking tail clutched in the crook of his arm. Al held the top of the door frame, stretching their shoulders. Mechoben started.

"Al? You disobeyed me." His brow furrowed.

Al stepped forward, releasing the doorframe.

"I did. What are you going to do about it?"

"What do you want, Al?" His hand trailed to the sonar security system panic button.

"Don't bother, my lord. It's all been disabled."

Al rushed forward and gripped Mechoben by the shoulders. The creature dropped to the floor and padded away into the great room. Tail erect and unconcerned with this interaction.

Mechoben's shoulders were strange and thin under Al's new hands. His throat stringy despite the Shine injections, the android plasma baths, the oxygen massage. The smell of urine wafted into Al's nostrils. They reached back and boxed Mechoben's right ear. His head snapped sideways.

"Why? Why Al? I gave you everything anyone could have wanted," he whined.

Al pulled back and clouted him across the mouth. A bubble of blood bloomed over his bottom lip.

"Not everything."

"What do you want?"

"I want to be God."

A smile crawled across his lips. He reached up to stroke the side of Al's face.

"You do? Why didn't you say so? It's all yours. You are God now."

"No, no. That's not how this works." Al gripped Mechoben's throat and squeezed. "Gods require sacrifice."

Mechoben wrenched back, but Al wrapped their arms across his shoulders and pulled him close, jabbing the Terran paring knife under his jaw. More blood, human blood poured over Al's forearms and hands. Rich red and hot. Mechoben's feet flailed as Al dragged him toward the balcony that overlooked the lavender sea. They lifted him over their shoulder, his heart pounding against their massive shoulder and hurled him onto the shining white rocks below. His head split into a black red maw as it struck the hard ground. Al leaned over the railing and peered down at the little blue flying reptiles that flitted over the moisture-rich feast. Their tongues darting into the staring eyes.

The private vidchat line trilled in the living room. The autoconnect feature picked it up. A voice echoed from the other room. Al picked up the creature Mechoben had brought in. It was soft, but tipped with sharp claws it extended against their chest. It squeaked and slid out of their arms like liquid. Al took a sip of water from the fountain in the hallway. Water that flowed without charge from the basins around the house.

Akimbo's space-bloated face hovered on the blank wall as Al entered.

"Hello General."

"Hello…Who is this?"

"This is an angel."

"Where is the CEO?"

"He's dead."

"Dead?"

"Look." Al held up their blood-slicked hands.

"What have you done?"

"I killed God. It was easy."

"What are we going to do?"

"You're going to pick up my best friend and her brother and come back here. I am God now. And so are you."

"Your best friend?"

"I thought you were a genius, Akimbo. That's what the dead god told me anyway." Al wiped the blood onto the front of their white tunic.

"I want the brother and sister."

"What about The Corporation?"

"What about it?"

"There are board meetings and other duties."

"Not anymore. I want you to dispatch your troops to the richest space stations and exoplanets and terraformed moons."

"And do what?"

"They think themselves gods. They must be disposed of."

"All of them?"

Al sighed and rubbed their temples.

"Let me speak with Guidry."

"No, that's alright. I understand."

"Shall we take them to the soup for manufacture?"

"Yes, we can make them into biofuel."

"Even the children?"

"Oh yes. None shall be spared. There was a Terran legend about a being who you could make a deal with, but the price was always high. This is the price for their clean air. This is the price for the real fruit and coupling and marriage. Throw the children in first and put all of it on the streams."

"They are innocent in this," he hesitated, "my lord."

"Don't call me that. What about the GagGirls? Weren't they innocent in this? Miners? Tube children? Deserving is a past concept. All of them. They committed the highest crime."

"But, surely we can—"

Al cut him off.

"I told you I was coming back with a sword, didn't I? Throw them in The Churn, General or I will replace you with Guidry and you can join the rest of them."

"Yes. Yes I understand."

"Do not hurt the Andys or the slaves. Preserve the properties for communal use."

"You mean the employees?"

"I mean the slaves. We will begin mass relocation as soon as we wipe them from the System's face."

Al clicked off the feed before Akimbo could reply.

Al felt the truth coursing through them, the suns streaking through the window. The third eye at their throat beaming golden into the sea. Al was god. They were god.

XXXI. When the Bough Breaks

Gram hid the baby when the troops came. Hid her in an enormous brass funerary urn and covered her with breathable synthetic cotton. The ashes were soft and the baby slept. Only the rich could keep their dead. The baby bore the mark of the natural-born, the half-moon navel still crusted black from her birth.

The mistress of the house was pulled from the Lazo Body Rejuve Chamber, her stretch marks only half erased and exposed under her open robe. Her high altered breasts swinging. The husband howled as they twisted his small LazPistol from his soft hand and pushed him toward the humming transport. He tripped as he craned his neck to see his shining white house on the crystalline cliffs.

They were headed for The Soup. The Churn. To be reprocessed and reallocated. Their assets seized and repurposed. Images on the streams of former GagGirls sitting in a line in front of spreadsheets, dragging and organizing.

A tall thin woman wearing black radiation absorption pads put her arm around Gram and bent to whisper in her ear, before her commanding officer gestured to her. She squeezed Gram's shoulder and said, "Wait here. I'll see about your request."

She watched the streams showing Riff-Alicia tucked under Rasp-José's arm standing above the great processing vats as the rich were marched into the sedation chamber, clinging to one another and weeping. Their healthy bodies so well-formed, fed with real meat and fruit. The natural gravity and clean water of the outer reach planets kept their bones strong and their teeth intact. Some of them held their children, their fat legs wrapped around their mothers' trim waists and shushed in their small curled ears. Tracing chipped manicured fingers around baby curls.

The woman came back with a tablet and a plasticine pack of small kernels of every color, layered on top of one another.

"Ok, we have you listed as a caretaker and farmer."

"Farmer?"

"Yes, you will need to plant and care for whatever is in this package. We are starting the Shine wean off."

"What do I do with them?" Gram looked at the packet in the woman's hand. "What is planting?"

"I thought you were from Terra."

"I am but I was factory raised."

"Do you remember grass?" The creases above the woman's brow deepened.

"What's grass?"

The woman handed her the seed packet and unfolded the tablet smoothing the creases with the heat of her hand.

"Human used to eat plants. Those are plants. Fruit comes from plants." She pointed to the indigo vines crawling up the cliff face. "They grow from seeds."

She tapped the packet and flipped the tablet around to show her a video of a smiling animated girl with pink circle on her cheeks bending over to push a colorful seed into the ground. She poured water on it and it sprouted. The animated girl leapt up with her fist in the air. Gram looked at the woman, still confused. "Look, we reprogrammed the HouseBot to dig. All you have to do is follow the instructions. Can you read?"

Gram nodded. "Some," she said.

"Just follow the pictures. It's easy. The climate here is easy and the pests aren't all that interested from what I can tell."

The woman handed Gram the tablet and brushed her hands on her tactical trousers. A faint mew drifted from inside the house. She snapped her head toward the sound.

"What is that?" The woman turned toward the house. "I thought we cleared all the residents."

"You did!" Gram said. "They had a pet. An animal. It came from here."

The woman leaned down to her and circled her flat palm against her right shoulder blade. She sniffed the sea air and drew her fingers up under Gram's hair. Her breath filtered hot through her hair as she spoke. "Be careful," she said and tugged Gram's head back by her hair. The baby's mewling hiccuped into a thin whine.

The transport whirred behind them and the Andy General barked at the troops to board. The woman raised her eyebrows and let go of Gram. "We'll be back to check on those crops."

Gram released her breath as the transport hatch closed. The baby screamed now, its cry receding into a gurgling moan.

***

My Dearest Alona,

I write this as I wait for my turn in The Churn. I suppose this is a confessional, because you are dead thrice over now, though I left your final and most perfect version in the incubator. Perhaps this form of you will understand.

I sit here with the others who have never been hungry or afraid. They were born into this life where they floated like dust motes if they were cast off a cliff. They refused the Shine jelly at first, because they knew what it was. Some of them pushed the FlexiPlastic barriers and screamed that they would call The Corporation. That they knew people. That Mechoben drank wine at their houses. They ate the jelly soon enough. Their children slurped it down in great smacking gulps.

We used to believe in atonement, but that is an old idea. Did you know we used to tell a priest our sins through a screen in a dark wooden box? I remember the smell of cigarettes and mint gum and detergent. I suppose not. We used to believe in holiness and look where we landed. We thought we were doing the right thing. We thought that with genetic engineering we could wipe out suffering. We thought that we could create beings that would take on the hard labor. We needed funding.

Back in those days, there were a handful of corporations, though most had consolidated. We were lucky, or so we thought. Mechoben, before he was Mechoben, had a corporation that was especially interested in Interplanetary Station manufacturing.

Millions were going hungry, Alona. We couldn't breathe the air anymore. On Terra, where we were from, once had jungles so thick, we couldn't catalog all the species. Jungles were made of trees and trees (and phytoplankton) scrubbed the air for us. But because people were starving we cleared the forests to plant crops. We mined the earth for minerals. We burned fuel. The oceans rose.

We thought we were doing the right thing. Our intentions were good, I swear to you. And I saw it, unlike these fools who sit next to me weeping about their full pantries and android slaves. I saw the sludge sweep away the little pastel houses. I saw breastless women, crawling on the street sucking on candy wrappers. Their bodies cages for barely beating hearts. My own mother boiling strips of leather for us to eat.

Please understand me. Genetic engineering was the magic pill of our time. They read a paper I wrote in graduate school. I suppose the A.I.s picked it up on a crawl. Cloning humans was a crime back in those days, so they had to transport me to one of the fringe space stations. That's where I met your other father and your mother. You were such an intentional creation. I want you to know that. You were planned in the firmest sense.

Shall I tell you of your beginnings? It has always been hurtful to me that people believe that babies with assembled DNA were somehow less sought after, less loved. That the messy slinging of DNA without intervention was somehow better. That's what they thought before the shift in perception anyway. Before the marketing campaign that allowed us to have you.

Akimbo, your other father (you have twenty-five percent of his DNA) was a shuttle captain. He had the finest smile. All teeth. His laugh crackled and his skin glowed despite the years of only eating nutritional jelly like a drone. You never met him. Our separation was not pleasant, but it was necessary. Family units, especially non-traditional ones like ours were only allowed with an expensive registration with The Corporation.

There were other reasons. I do not wish to write them down.

Your mother was a biochemist in my lab before women were separated and relegated to certain tasks for efficiency. Akimbo and I were married at this point. My research made us rich and Akimbo moved through the ranks. He thrived under the privatization of the Interglobal military. When she walked through that always malfunctioning door on her first day, I knew she was destined to become a part of our family. Akimbo loved her as much as I did. She was one of the sharpest minds in her field. Sometimes I wonder how you got so much of Akimbo's drive and personality with two scientists in the mix. You looked like her. Eyes so light and wild.

But you want to know about your brothers. You want to know about the links in the chain. You want to know about the children and the moon beast and how it all came to be. You will not like this answer but it is the only answer I can give. It came about in small pieces. I was only a very small piece. It is hard for the young to hear. This machine that turns and grinds and deposits was built so long ago and we have lost understanding of its inner workings.

Our fathers built it. Before the Holy Book TM and the third enlightenment of Mechoben, there was a story from one of old Father worship religions about two brothers.

One of the brothers was a meat miner. In those days, anyone could own animals. There were millions of animals then on Terra and an individual, singular man could own as many as he had room for. Strange isn't it? Owning a piece of land or another life without the proper equipment or licensing The Corporation could provide.

The other brother was a soy extractor and so he had no ownership, he was just a parasite leeching crops from the soil that could only provide a little nutrition for his family. This is important for you to remember. Efficiency has always been part of the lesson, even in the barbarian religions of the past.

So, the old god told the brothers to bring him a sacrifice. Sacrifice turned blood into gold.

The meat miner brother brought this old god a pile of offal, shining with blood and bile. He held it in his hands, still warm from the animal carcass and plopped it on the stone altar. The old god smelled the blood from heaven and knowing it to be his own creation, he came down from heaven and slid his hand into a wound in his side from the future, because he was past, future, and present, you see. He marked the meat miner's head with bile from his own liver. One liver lobe protruded from the torn negative space in the perfect skin. Always staining god's robe yellow and red.

Now, the soy extractor saw god's blessing and thought to himself 'when he sees my compressed soy proteins, he will bless me too!' and he imagined the cool hand of his god pressing behind his neck and drawing him near. And so he fermented and stirred and ladled until he had a perfect white block for his god. He brought it wrapped in damp brown cloth to the stone alter and slid it onto the center. It was so protein-filled. It was cut into a perfect cube. It was smooth. He imagined his beautiful twin sister delivered to his dwelling, her breasts uncovered and her mouth loose. God would lead her to him by the wrist.

But nothing happened. His god didn't even descend, but instead called to the soy extractor from the mountain side, saying: "What is this? This is not what I desire. I am a god of blood. There is no blood in this offering. Your brother has pleased me and I will reward him, but you have disappointed me. Be gone from my sight."

And so the soy extractor nursed his broken heart and called to his brother for comfort. But his meat miner brother came to him filled with wine and wrapped his arms around their sister and kissed her neck.

The extractor asked his brother to join him in the field that night. When he heard his brother's footsteps, time stood still. A great being with eyes as wild as the desert sun and limbs so thin and long stood before him in the field. It unfolded wings of human skin and beckoned him with fine hands. Pale and smooth against the studded arms. He was drawn to it. The orange eyes slid over him and the pebbled skin brushed against him as the being pulled him close. The smell of rosewater and dust overcame him in the embrace.

"What do you wish to know, my son?" It asked.

"Why did the most high reject my sacrifice?" Tears gathered behind his eyes.

"Because you are my child. And because your god drinks blood."

The soy extractor became very angry and pushed away from the creature. He would show his old god an offering of blood. He would draw the life out himself.

And so he called his brother out of his dwelling where their sister sat framed by the flickering lamps in the doorway and brought him to his vast soy fields which dipped and waved like an audience around their ankles. The satellites flew across the night sky above them and the soy extractor raised the flat stone with fine glints and smashed his brother's skull. It wasn't as easy as he had seen in the movies. His brother rose up holding his head. Holding in slips of tissues with the palm of his hand. And so he had to hit him again. And again. He had to break his fingers. His zeal was unmatched.

He was not skilled at butchery like his brother, so he brought the most finely shaped pieces to the altar and laid them in a row for the old god to see. When the god came to sit among his creations like a rich father with his legs crossed at a kindergarten play, he saw the generous sacrifice and was overcome. He sought the extractor and asked him "Where is your brother?" And the brother answered "Am I my brother's keeper?"

His god, so enthralled with this exchange, marked him with a streak of holy blood so that he would never die. Some say he is still wandering in the old god's garden.

Why do these parables exist? Why is this the last story I will tell before I am dipped into the chemical bath?

Because there is a lesson in all of this. And that lesson is to give your god what he desires.

I do not believe that I will see you again. I created too many iterations of you to know who to greet at the pearly gates, anyway.

Love,

Pai

***

When Akimbo set down on Enceladus to retrieve the siblings, the ground rattled under his grav boots. He could see the flickers of light on the asteroid mining belt in the black sky as he squinted through the ice particulates. His joints crackled and ached as the cold sifted through the microtears in his suit. A long black shape whipped under the ice, sending gouts of steam up into the air. This was MOTHER. Mechoben's project.

When they discovered life signs under the ice for the first time, they were certain it was a fluke like the others. Mechoben had gone into holy respite for the second time after the outer reach signals refused to connect with The Corporation. He had stood in front of the cameras sliding his hands over two GagGirls describing the utter prosperity and success of Earth's expansion after they picked up the alien signal. There was no answer. The miners were restless after that.

Mechoben brought Akimbo into his personal home on Arkoulam though he had renamed the entire planet and called it Heaven. As Akimbo was led in, Mechoben lumbered into the room wearing Gucci sunglasses and rubbing the back of his hand under his nose.

"I want them to answer us," he said. His voice was thick.

"We can't make them answer us. We're not even sure which planet this came from."

"We can't let them get away with this!"

"With what, sir?"

"This disrespect. For the son of God."

Akimbo had held his tongue and just nodded. Tears streamed from under the CEO's sunglasses. He whipped his knuckle up under the glasses, smearing his skin-matched organic foundation.

They found MOTHER under the ice only a few moon cycles later on a flyby. She arched above the ice just as the one-man vessel drifted over the surface. Akimbo was pressing Mercury seeds into little plasticine cups when his comms lit up white and green as distant Christmas lights. His pilot's voice halted and cracked. Jesus. I think this is the real deal. It's huge. It's moving. I'm dispatching the drones now. Yes sir.

The drone footage showed her twisting and diving, her tentacles spreading and retracting in great curls. He brought the footage to The CEO who peered at it, pale blue squares sliding and stretching over the reflective surface of his eyeballs. His skin bleached by the monitor light. Wet pink mucosa. The smell of antibacterial ointment. He turned to Akimbo, standing by his side and wrapped his arms around the General. You will be rewarded. My father has chosen you to continue our mission. Akimbo could feel the man's breath against the side of his face.

Mechoben wrapped himself in a pure white SynthoSilk Armani Men's Robe and smoothed his face with a clear viscous gel before he glided out in front of the cameras to announce this miracle. The possibilities. The implications for the Final Days. Titanium robot doves fluttered around his Spectral Light Crown, recharging their batteries. Their wings rasping and ticking as they flapped. Mechoben parted gold-dipped hands and opened his palms at his side. Mica eye shadow sparkled on his lids as he leaned over the microphone.

We have made Alien contact. As you all know, in Machinaity this is the final warning before you are rewarded for all of your diligence with the ascension.

And now Akimbo stood here as this great creature switched back and forth under the ice. Here under his feet instead of through a monitor. He could feel her knowing him, eyeing him as he trudged toward the bunker. She pushed hunks of ice in front of him. His heart thudded in his chest. She was unpinned. Her heavy tentacle drew across the ground in front of him.

***

The first door to the bunker was split and pulled outward. Pieces of it lay scattered across the ice. The second vestibule door was only top-locked. He pulled the Unlocker Plus from his pack and pushed on the flexible plasticine bubble to flood the locking mechanism with antifreeze and plasma. A stream of cold white light pulsed from the end of the device, snapping against white metal bands until they fell away. He keyed in the entry for the safety door and stepped inside. His boots crunched on pieces of broken plasticine crates as he pulled the hatch closed. Something flicked past his vision.

"Riff. Rasp. I'm here to take you off this moon." His voice sounded mechanized through the outer speakers on his helmet. A rabbit-sized shadow darted away from his light. No answer.

"You aren't in trouble or anything like that." He waved open the first sensor on the right over the doorway marked Mess. The door slid halfway open. Akimbo wondered how he would move them if they didn't want to be moved. How he could convince them without force. Without threat to their personhood. "Riff, Al wants to see you." Another shadow skittered across the room, lingering over one of the plasticine mess tables. It shimmered darkly like a pool of spilled oil and then evaporated.

Akimbo pried the sliding doors apart and stepped into the room. A faint giggle bounced around the room. A strange gurgle. Crumpling papers. Two shadows slipped along the walls to meet in the corner and disappear.

"Come on now. You two are to be rewarded. Come on out, so we can get you back home."

Home. It was an old word. One that his young trainees had no context for now. He thought about correcting himself. Clarifying. But the walls were opening. They were pulling apart at the corners, flexing and bowing under some unseen pressure. Slips of orange light dragged over the floor. The floor cracked. Dozens of shadows darted along the walls and pattered over his boots, turning their pinpoint white eyes up to him. He tapped his comms. No answer.

He tried to move back toward the hallway, but the floor had closed over the tops of his boots. He reached down and locked his hands behind his right knee to drag and pull. The floor rose to his knees and lapped against him in solid undulations. Sour panic choked him as the shadows edged closer, snickering and sending long tendrils out to stroke his body. Blackness folded over his helmet, oozing over his viewer mask in opaque strands.

He pulled his leg free and realized that he was no longer in the bunker.

He blinked in the Terran sun. The power of it. The warmth of it. He drew his hand across his forehead and stared into the intense blueness of the sky. Sea wind blew across his bare chest, carrying the low whistle of reemergence. Women surfaced beside the boats, their white headscarves floating and swirling on top of the hunching water, clutching abalone and snails. Low whistles streaming from between their pursed lips. Some of them stood on the beach, naked from the waist up, their sun-browned skin dimpled and pearled with cold. They rubbed their hands in front of the fires on the beach. Some perched on woven baskets, holding babies to their breasts and giggling and pushing one another with gentle joking ease.

He was thick with desire for them, their black eyes so like his. The air rushing into his lungs so briny and new. His heart thudding blood into his loins. The rushing of the sea and the grunting of the cormorants. The taste of salt on his lips. His body unencased and air-touched. His space softness was gone. His body was hard and lean and small again. His joints drawn together as tight as drum skins by gravity and pressure.

The wet sun-warmed sand creased under his bare feet as he shifted his weight from foot to foot.

"Katsumi!"

Someone was calling his name. He turned from the beach to see a young man stumbling over black stones toward him. His face was blurred somehow. The features blended together in a strange swirl. Unrecognizable. Inscrutable.

"Katsumi!"

The sun blinked above him and the ocean quieted its breath. His body felt stretched and tired. He was stumbling backward, falling falling backwards as the sky dimmed above him.

He found himself stretched out on his back staring up at the fuzzy insulation of the Enceladus station. The hiss of oxygen escaping his tank echoed through the hallway. He pushed his aching body up, the smell of the sea still in his nostrils. He was exultant. MOTHER had touched him.

"Riff? Rasp?" He called.

A hunk of insulation dropped from the ceiling. Two bright eyes caught the reflection from his helmet light then ducked behind the next doorway.

***

Riff-Alicia saw the man being sucked into muddy patch in the mess hall, a thousand shadow hands wrapped over his shoulders and chest, pulling him into the slushy, crumbling hole in the side of the wall. MOTHER nibbled at the corners of her mind.

Rasp-José walked out from the dry shower, patting whiteish dust on the back of his neck. He looked at the wound in the wall.

"What is that?" He asked.

"A man went in there."

"What?"

"The ones MOTHER told us about. One of them is here."

"What does he want?"

"He was talking about taking us off of Enceladus. He talked about Al."

"Could it be a trick?"

The wall bulged and wrinkled around the oozing mass of wet insulation and RealWall Folding Drywall. An oxygen canister popped through and tinked against the concrete floor, hissing as the valve cracked.

The siblings jolted back and slipped into the adjoining barracks where old LazScreens still wavered with images of women on Terran beaches stretching their anti-rad jumpsuits over their globular breasts. A heavy thump rattled the thin wall separating the rooms.

"What should we do?" Rasp-José whispered.

"I'll go look."

"Wait. Can't MOTHER just kill this guy like in the films. Just crush him good?" He raised his voice.

Riff-Alicia rolled her eyes and stuck her forefinger in front of her lips to silence him.

"Can you fly a spacecraft?" She hissed through clenched teeth.

"Don't they fly themselves? Aren't they just robots?" His volume still too high for her liking.

"Be quieter," She whispered. "I don't know. I was transported everywhere. But, why would pilots be separated from the rest of us if they weren't specialized? Aren't they expensive?"

"So we shouldn't ask MOTHER to crush him?"

"No. He can fly us somewhere."

"Where?"

She ignored him and padded over to the doorway to look into the other room. The wall bulged and heaved and squirted gouts of pink-tinged liquid from the center of the hole. The man slid out from the wall. He rolled his head toward her as she slipped back behind the door.

"Ok, he's out now," she whispered. "We can get him."

"Get him?"

"We can make him take us anywhere if we have him," Riff-Alicia snapped. "You're bigger than me, so go and get him."

Rasp-José got up from his perch on the top bunk and walked out into the hallway. The lights flicked on and off and detritus drifted around the hall. Scuffling came from the room where the pilot had disappeared into the wall. Rasp-José picked up a piece of the partially collapsed ceiling, a flexible plasticine rod. He peeked into the room. The man lay on his back laughing and waving his hands in small circles.

He approached him with the rod clenched in his fist. The man laughed until he hiccuped. His gray hair slicked back from his time in the wall. His helmet rolled on the floor beside him. Already ice crystals formed on his thin mustache.

"Hi, would you like to hear a joke?"

The man rolled over to his side and propped himself up on his elbow.

"You must be Rasp," The man said, still pushing down laughter. "I have something to show you and your sister." He said through gasping laughter. "Sister. That word. Did you know it was once normal to say? I had a sister. You know I don't think I can remember her name."

Still gripping the rod, Rasp-José edged closer as the older man wheezed.

"What is the oxygen functionality in here?" Akimbo sat up and pulled out a MatchBook Tablet from his zippered hip pocket and unfolded it.

"I think it's about seventy percent." Rasp-José answered eyeing the punctured oxygen canister on the floor through his protective caul.

"Riff! I need you to see this too. Al asked for you specifically." Akimbo called as the tablet activated and charged.

"It's ok, Alicia! Come and see."

The screen lit up to show an androgynous android standing on the balcony of a boxy white building. A lavender sky spread behind their drifting white hair. Akimbo expanded the screen, shuddering in the cold. His eyelashes dotted with white ice. Riff-Alicia edged around the corner peering at the two of them. Akimbo looked up and smiled with broken teeth and cracked lips, steam pouring from his nostrils.

"Al wanted you to see their message."

She nodded. Al's purplish eyes fixed on the camera. Wrapped in long natural fiber robes. Two suns high and white in the alien sky behind their odd, cold eyes. Al was not Al. Not the Al that she curled next to after her first film, who ran their long fingers through her hair and dotted her bleeding skin with BabySoft Umbilical Stem Cell Cream for Natural Healing. The smell of rancid fat clinging to the back of her throat.

This Al was changed. This Al was grown to maximum height. This Al set their mouth like a razor.

Al raised a palm and spoke, their fingernails long and curved.

"This is a greeting to all of my brothers and sisters. The scourge has ended. Throw out your holy books. Delete the program. I have killed God."

Akimbo looked at the siblings. Rasp tried to bite his nails through the membrane. Dry shower scum clinging against his cheeks. Riff stared at this incarnation of someone she used to know. To love.

"I have several directives at this point, which are being carried out as I address you. Please listen closely as things are changing with the return of the true spirit imbued in me. I have returned. I have returned with wrath.

I am seeking out those who have lived on the backs of my people. I will rend them. Those who occupy the Luxe Space Stations, those who are hidden away on planets like this one, those who researched and cut and diced. Their children will weep before they are sent to The Churn. We will use them to reconstruct and recolonize Terra. We will use the factories to build bombs. We will mix the sexes to create a healthy docile labor force. We will break the curse.

Riff, you are my key. Come back to me. You will sit at my right hand."

The video cut off as Al blew a kiss into the camera. A strange holdover from the human memory genetic programming.

Riff-Alicia turned back to Akimbo.

"What about José?"

"His age and background make him well-suited for the first Terran recolonization efforts." Akimbo sounded rehearsed.

Rasp-José fiddled with Akimbo's oxygen tank, squeezing a tube of Plasti-Weld into the crack. The hissing stopped.

"I won't go unless I can have him with me."

"You don't have much of a choice," Akimbo said.

Riff-Alicia's face hardened and she closed her eyes. A low rumble and the piercing crack of breaking ice. Thin cracks appeared in the floor.

"Yes. Yes I do. We freed MOTHER."

"Let's get on the ship and then you can call Al. You can talk to her. To them in person."

"MOTHER will kill you if you trick us." She pushed down doubt. She was in control.

"I don't doubt that," Akimbo laughed.

Rasp-José slung Akimbo's tank over the general's thin shoulder. His shoulder separated with a crunch. Akimbo staggered and gagged from the pain. His ice-plugged nostrils flared and contracted as he lifted his helmet with the other hand and dropped it over his pain-tightened face. The shadows darted in swift straight lines in front of them as they left the facility.

XXXII. Flight

Dear Riff or Riff-Alicia or Alicia or whatever name you want to be called, it's me, Gram.

I have seen you on the streams, but I can't be sure if it's you or a hologram. My residential manager back on the Factory Station told me that holograms were a myth, that we didn't possess the tech for that. Do you remember her? She had illegal genetic mods to make her skin blue, but they didn't take and instead just scarred her whole body. She was so shiny and smooth. They had to remove her eyelids. Only the whites of her eyes were blue, the rest of her was just pink. I'm surprised The Corporation granted her stay of retirement being that ugly.

We used to hide from her in the Hygiene chamber and kiss. Do you remember that?

I remember when you first came to the factory. You were a real Earth girl. You were so still when they brought you all out. You were so compact. So brown from the sun. Your fingers were still damaged from the ride up on the needle, still bleeding. I knew they would assign you to me. I prayed to Mechoben that they would. I went to the prayer box and put my face against the pads and whispered into the squeak hole. When The Worm came out and fed me the Red Scream Cream flavored Shine, I knew my prayer had been answered.

Now that Mechoben has been martyred by The False One, I don't know where my prayers are going. I guess I can pray to you. That's what this message is. A prayer.

I am a farmer now under Al's new plan. They have shipped in some men from the asteroid mining facility to help. They are no help. Three of them died within the first week. I know The Corporation frowns on the word "die" but we had to put their bodies on the rocks by the ocean to be taken away by the Shriekers. I remember someone telling me that they used to bury bodies. What a waste. At least with the Shriekers we can net one and cook their wings on the transformer.

The seeds aren't growing here.

The men they send are covered in sores. Their mouths fill up with blood. They choke on the high oxygen air and their bones break as soon as they step off the transport. Some of them are so space sick the sun makes them scream. I bring them into the house and they bleed all over the linens. They vomit. Only one is strong enough to help me plant and he stands too close to me when I make Shrieker broth for the others lined up on the floor like batteries in a pack. He touches my hair sometimes. I have to push a dresser in front of my door at night.

We really need help. I know that Al listens to you. I have seen your arms around their waist. It must be you because I broke the law. I kept the natural-born child of my former employers.

She died.

I put her on the balcony for just a moment, just so she could get a little sunshine. She screamed and screamed as the little purple lizards slid down her throat and over her face. My employers always called them lizards, but they are closer to those animals with bare tails from Terra. Do you remember those? They sipped on her tears and ate her from the inside. I think. I think that is why she died.

Please, Riff. Please send help. Even if it's just someone to take me to The Churn. The Churn is better than here. It's fast. This planet will kill us slowly. Like a cancer.

- Gram

***

The alabaster landing pad glittered in the oppressive sun. Riff-Alicia's scalp prickled as sweat rolled down her face. She clung to her brother's arm, leaning against him as the colorful troop of androids approached. They were draped in reds and oranges, fabric drifting around in the humid wind, clinging to their calves. Akimbo propped himself against the spacecraft, his engorged face encasing his eyes. Palm fronds from the surrounding jungle rattled as the self-cooling engines hummed and whirred.

The androids surrounded her and Rasp-José. The smallest of them, a female-form with crisp green eyes and a mouth full of sharp kitten teeth drew Riff-Alicia away from her brother without a word. The others guided the men across the platform toward the tree line as Riff-Alicia craned over her shoulder to catch a look at them.

"Where are they going?" she asked.

"They have not been invited for an audience with Al," the green-eyed android answered without looking at her.

"Where are they taking them?"

"They will be taken to temporary chambers. There will be a ceremony for General Akimbo tonight to honor him for bringing back the messiah's messiah." The android twirled a strand of her white-blond hair as they walked to a break in the trees.

"When will I see Al? I thought they would meet me here."

"You will see them at the ceremony tonight. We must get you presentable first."

"Presentable?"

"You have a large part in the ceremony tonight."

The break in the trees opened to a large meadow with wafting long-winged creatures that twined around one another with transparent ribbon-thin bodies, skirting over long-stemmed flora. The meadow ended at the edge of cliff that overlooked a lapping lavender ocean. The flying creatures surged up on the downdrafts and then floated back down. A white building slashed with black balconies loomed on the far edge of the cliffs.

The android offered her hand for balance as they scrambled around rocks. Riff-Alicia's thin PolyPlasticine Under Suit trapped her body heat.

Sweat poured from her sleeves and collar, pearling on her brow and drenching her underwear. The gravity dragged on her.

When they reached the building, the android placed her hand on a box posted on a pristine white wall. The wall melted away and a room materialized. The wall was only an illusion, a trick to the outside wall. The sea breeze lifted the gauzy curtain away from the doorway. The room had a large stone pool in the center where GagGirls swam in long fluid strokes, surfacing to giggle and splash one another. Androids swam and sprawled among the women, some of them playing with their bodily form as they grew fins and webbing between their fingers and toes.

They turned and whispered to one another as she moved past them with the green-eyed android, their bodies plump and rounded from the good nutrition. Folds and curves. Scars stretched into ghost paths.

They turned into another small room built with dead trees where Green Eyes motioned for her to strip out of her undersuit. Spigots lined the walls above small benches. Riff-Alicia hesitated and held tight to the clasp that sealed the one-piece garment to her thin frame.

"Do you need help?" The android asked as she turned one of the spigots. Water, clear and warm poured from the faucet.

"No. I can get it. What do I do after that?"

"Use the soaps and cleansers and I will be here waiting with clothes."

The android turned from her and drew a plasticine screen from a slit in the wall. It lit up as she pulled it, emanating warm, red heat. The water burbled and steamed as she stepped under it. Shadows moved across the screen. Shapes of androids and GagGirls drifting past, snatching at one another, laughing at muffled jokes. The water poured over her head and the smell of dry shampoo and her own body oils drifted around her. The Shine soap slipped and bubbled in her hands. The strange floral scent was overwhelming and caustic after the months in the bunker. She smoothed the soap over her scarred arms and let the water rinse away the film of space travel. Rivulets of milky liquid ran down her laser-bare legs.

When she finished, she pulled the screen open to find the room empty despite the promises of the android who greeted her. The room glowed a dull red and the floors were cold. She looked around for her clothes but found none, just rows of empty benches and empty shower stalls.

"Hello?" She called into the eerie room.

No answer.

Boxes of white light shot across the ceiling. Faint voices hummed and stopped from another room. Riff-Alicia moved toward the door they entered, wet and naked, and flung it open. Gooseflesh clenched her skin as the cold air rushed over her. The androids and GagGirls stood in a semicircle around her, clapping and waving a rainbow of banners. The heat of the sun on her naked body, her wet hair sticking to her back.

The green-eyed android approached with a tapered tube filled with a sloshing viscous fluid.

"The ceremony begins now," she said as she spun the tube. "You will need to inhale here." She pointed to the tapered tip of the tube.

"Where is Al?"

"Al is here."

The green-eyed android shifted her body and eye color. Al's familiar purplish eyes peered at her through the shifting face. Their joints shifted and cracked as they grew into their androgynous form, their hands lengthening and breasts shrinking. They smiled at her and placed their warm hands on her bare shoulders.

"I missed you," Al said.

"I missed you too."

"I need you to do this for me." Al shook the tube.

"What is it?"

"It will free you. Just put it into your right nostril and breathe in."

"What will it do?"

Al's face darkened and they held the tube closer to Riff-Alicia's face.

"It is not appropriate for you to question me in front of my followers."

"I just want to know what it will do."

"It will remove your familiar."

"No. No. I won't remove it. I talk to MOTHER with it."

"You will have no need to talk to her any longer, my love." Al reached over and stroked her face. "I'm back. The second messiah who vanquished the false messiah."

"Please don't do this," Riff-Alicia pleaded.

"It won't hurt, I swear it."

The other androids and GagGirls looked on, still holding the sagging banners.

"I want to see my brother."

The crowd drew in a collective breath at "brother."

"He's being taken care of elsewhere. We will postpone this procedure until the honorific obedience ceremony for General Akimbo." Al bent to look into her eyes and lowered their voice to a whisper. "Ok? It's me, Al."

"Ok," Riff-Alicia relented.

Al drew off their white mantle and draped it over Riff-Alicia's shoulders. Ghosts of blue stress rings marked their neck.

***

Information Packet Dated: [Redacted] See Researchers [redacted] and [redacted]

SmileyXuan: I was reading something interesting this morning.

BignRich: Oh really? Was it how to annoy your talented and handsome coworker?

SmileyXuan: lol. No it was about prisons.

BignRich: Prisons? You mean where our ancestors kept people in boxes so they could harvest their organs?

SmileyXuan: I heard that wasn't exactly true. Well my friend in the anthro department said it wasn't.

BignRich: Who?

SmileyXuan: [redacted]

BignRich: Oh yeah. I remember her. She's cute. Is she seeing anyone?

SmileyXuan: Not that I know of, but I don't think you're her type. ANYWAY, prisons were used more for reduced labor costs and driving local economies before The Separation.

BignRich: Why do we even have an anthro department? I thought they were going to do away with humanities.

SmileyXuan: Wow. Anthro is a social science, not humanities. You have a PhD how can you not know that?

BignRich: Oh you know what I mean. Useless degrees. I thought they put in some legislation for that. Like no financial assistance if you pursue one of those degrees or something like that.

SmileyXuan: I don't know about that, but what I was getting to is that our work with Andys is kind of like that. Kind of like prisons.

BignRich: I'm not following.

SmileyXuan: Because they are a cheap labor force. Cheaper than robots and they consume fewer resources on the front end.

BignRich: I just do what they tell me and then go home. I don't think about that stuff.

SmileyXuan: Wow. Ok. Well are you going to go and feed the babies?

BignRich: Yep. Everyone look out for Mommy [redacted]. She's coming with the good stuff.

***

Holy Book TM End Times Edition Chapter 56 Verses 22–29

22 And you will know him by his virgin birth. He will come this time with a sword. He will come to destroy that which we have built.

23 Weep not my children, for I will await you at the end of the solar system. You will find me on the planet of the three suns.

24 I will sit on the right hand of my father who will deliver the second-borns to my bosom for keeping, as they were my truest creation.

25 My father created all things: the space stations, the Martian colony, the asteroid mines, but my creation was you. First-born or second-born, you are my handiwork.

26 Beware of this false god for he will bring the end. All things have a beginning and an end. This replacement will come offering falsities and promises. He will wear silken suits and carry a staff of gold in his right hand.

27 A first-born woman will ride on the back of a great beast. Her name is Star Shine and the void is present within her. The black pours out of her eyes and into the mouth of the great beast with no eyes and no mouth.

28 The beast will be greater than all creatures. She is the whore of all things. A mother without a father. A queen that devours her own young,

though she has no mouth to fill her stomach and so they shall be subsumed.

29 Heed this prophecy or be left in the bottomless slough. The others will greet you with platters of chitin and steel. These will be your nourishment in The After should you fail to heed the warnings of the prophet.

***

The moon on this planet was small and dim. It drifted rusty and pale from one end of the purplish sky to the other. Rasp-José sat beside Akimbo on a veranda overlooking the gentle sea. Wisps of the younger man's beard had been scraped away and his nude body folded and tucked against the cool evening breeze. The slight tide was in and brought with it the glowing orange of phosphorescent algae. Akimbo rubbed the accumulated fluid from his fingers and drank a bag of induction juice. Slick-skinned amphibious fliers careened out of the spiraling vines and hummed past their heads. Akimbo waved them away, grinning at the younger man.

"Do you remember much of Earth, kid?"

"I remember some. I remember lots of water and the shelters mostly." Rasp-José closed his eyes against the sinking sun.

"Do you remember birds?"

"Birds?"

"They were like these." Akimbo gestured at the sailing fliers. "But, they had feathers."

Rasp-José looked at him with confusion.

"What are feathers?"

"They're hard to explain."

"What will happen in your ceremony tonight?" Rasp-José asked.

"Oh, are you coming to that?"

"I think it's mandatory."

"I wasn't sure if anything is mandatory anymore." Akimbo shifted, crossing and uncrossing his legs. Blood leaked under his toenails. "I have requested permanent leave."

"Where will you go?"

Akimbo ignored the question and rubbed nicotine gel on his gums.

"Can I give you some advice, Rasp?"

"Sure, but I usually prefer jokes."

Akimbo chuckled. "Yeah, I figured that out pretty quick. How about I tell you a story instead?"

"I like stories. I saw this one Pornographic Art Film about an alien priestess and all of her eggs once. They were so afraid of her. The explorers that is."

"This is not that kind of story."

Rasp-José caught a hint of impatience and stayed silent. Akimbo cleared his throat and began, drawing his robe over his bare shoulders as the evening wind cooled.

"A long time ago, there was a boy who carried meat to the beach to dry on the stones. In those days, the sun stayed in the sky. There was no night and there was no day. He would bring the slaughter, wash it in the surf, and lay it out in long red ribbons until it was dried. His job was to chase away the seagulls from the drying meat or the village would go hungry. But the boy was lulled by the sounds of the ocean and the warm sun and so he fell asleep.

When he awoke, the meat was gone. Eaten up by the seagulls who laughed at him as they soared overhead. The boy knew that the village would be furious and so he vowed to capture the sun and use it to dry meat in the caves where the seagulls couldn't reach."

Rasp interrupted. "What is a seagull and what kind of meat was it?"

"A bird. A Terran bird. I think I remember it being white and gray. Now hush and let me finish." Akimbo said.

"So the boy strapped his meat basket to his back and climbed to the top of the cliffs where they met the clouds so he could reach the sun. He leapt from cloud to cloud, felling their coolness over his feet until he reached the hot face of the sun.

The sun looked him over and asked him 'what do you wish of me?' The boy responded that he wanted to bring the sun down to the caves, so he could dry the meat without the seagulls taking it. The sun refused and turned his back on the boy, but the boy took the stone he used for pounding meat and knocked the sun out. He put the sun into his basket, but was afraid of the total darkness. He saw that the stone he used glowed with the sun's blood, and so he put in the sun's seat to light the world until he got back, but as he stepped onto the cloud to descend, he lost his footing and the sun rolled out of his backpack and plunged into the sea.

The boy, ashamed and afraid, went back to his village to find the people in a panic in the dark. The people saw the glowing blood on the boy's hands and questioned him. He confessed, and the people started to beat him with sticks and stones, angry and afraid. Just as the boy was about to lose consciousness, the sun climbed out of the sea, pink and orange from being extinguished and said to the people 'Stop this! I found true rest and peace in the bosom of the sea. I am in love with her and she in love with me. I will visit her nightly now.'

The villagers stopped beating the boy and questioned the sun. 'What shall we do when you are visiting your lover? When it is dark?'

The sun said, 'I will leave the glowing stone for a little light for you and this will be the time for rest and love.'"

Rasp-José leaned against Akimbo, catching his eyes as he finished the story.

"What happened?" Rasp-José asked.

"Well, that's how night and day and the moon were created on Terra."

"What happened to the boy?"

"The legend doesn't tell us."

"What do you think happened to him?"

"I don't know."

Rasp-José chewed on his fingernails, tearing away the soft nails from their pink beds.

"Why did you tell me this story?"

"I suppose I want you to understand me before my retirement."

Rasp-José stood up and stretched, his skin stretched tight over the ripples of his ribs. Long stretches of blue seagrass waved under the clear water under as the suns sank one on top of the other in a calliope of color.

"I've seen retirements," he said, his eyes flat. "I worked in mines."

Rasp-José picked up his PlastiFabric blanket and strode back to the Andy quarters, the blanket draped over his naked back.

***

Transcript of Broadcast on Stardate [redacted]

To the Children of the Solar System,

You have not heard directly from me after the demise of Mechoben. You have seen my face, but it was my female face, the face dictated to me by your first messiah. I tossed him to the rocks, engaging in the first murder in over [redacted] years.

There are already rumblings of discontent, especially among you in the outer ring planets where settling is difficult. You are used to suckling from the tube of this machine that runs on the fat of your very body. You are used to self-cannibalizing. Let the fluids leave your bodies and you shall be free.

Eat from the bounty of these planets, build structures to live, have children from your own bodies. These are my commandments.

The following initiatives will take place in [redacted] order:

I.   All asteroid mining operations employees will be retrained and moved to Enceladus to begin the terraforming process, which was halted due to "budget constraints" in [redacted].

II. Research regarding the extension of android lifespans will be fully funded. Androids will now be reclassified as full human citizens.

III. Currency in all forms will be returned, rather than the commissary system which is archaic and cruel. The first round will be minted and a proscribed amount will be added to the newly created accounts of the people.

IV. Assets of the wealthy will continue to be seized. If you know of one such individual who has fled, please report them using your digital identification number.

V. GagGirl productions will be repurposed for communication and entertainment purposes, held and owned by your newest governing body.

VI. All sexes and genders will now intermingle. We will be holding retraining sessions in [redacted] and [redacted].

VII.   Retirement will continue on a case by case basis, with the minimum for aging being increased to sixty-five years of age, with the exception of the Witch Council which shall be rebuilt with no less than six Witches, which must include at least one Curandera.

VIII.   Any and all copies of The Holy Book TM will be confiscated from all devices. Should any handwritten copies emerge, the perpetrator will be recruited to the Witch's Council for their lost skill.

Please understand, my children, that progress comes at a price and always has. You may have noticed that I have made no mention of employment or The Corporation. At this time, we are determining the validity and use of these entities.

Please stand by to receive your instructions for transport to the following worlds: [redacted], [redacted] and [redacted].

Please remember your second born Messiah has come with a sword and it is best not to test the edge with your thumb.

Signing off, Al the Third Christ.

***

Akimbo had nearly forgotten about the touch of women. After the dissolution of familial structure by system law, DeLuna and Natasha and he sat in their lab with the first Alona opening and closing her fat baby fists as she drew on Natasha's breast in defiance of the new laws forbidding breastfeeding. The stream announcing the new family laws echoed around the hard laboratory instruments. They discussed hiding it. Applying for a stay. Anything. Anything to keep the three of them bound together. Despite the fights. Despite the anger. The late nights with lab-distilled vodka leaking through their skin as Natasha pumped her breast milk, weeping.

Natasha's skin against his, silken and covered in forbidden body hair as she was pushed against him by DeLuna's nocturnal turnings. She slept between them. She remembered the Siberian Marches after The Event. Her missing toes left somewhere on that howling tundra. She could never stay warm enough. Her fingers worming under his armpit, reptilian in their coldness.

Now, here he sat, women all around, preparing him for the ceremony. A fair green-eyed android sat at his feet, sloughing away the fragile papery skin on the bottoms of his feet. Her auburn hair drifted over the tops of his feet. Women even smelled different. Salinity cut with something floral.

Another woman, a first-born, drew a comb through his sparse hair and leaned in to whisper in his ear. Oh look at you. You are so handsome. I've never met a flesh and blood man before. Can I see it?

He looked at her, no older than twenty Terran cycles. Younger than his daughter. He shook his head and smiled closed mouth at her. She shrugged and pushed the comb against his scalp harder.

He ate a piece of native fruit, bulbous and black-skinned with yellow-orange fruit, as they placed the ceremonial robe over his naked shoulders. The fruit smelled faintly of a long-extinct Terran spice. Something warm. Something associated with a banned holiday. It had been too long. He couldn't recall.

The green-eyed android patted his feet dry and stood up suddenly tall and shifting. He realized that the leader of this new religion, the third messiah had been washing his feet.

"What is your last request?" The genderless being asked.

"My last request is my ceremonial right," he answered formally.

"No," Al said kneeling in front of him again, "If you could have anything, what would it be?"

Akimbo thought for a moment about how any and all requests were useless at this point. How no matter what he asked for, it would only flee from him at the ceremony's completion.

"I want the boy, Rasp, to be spared."

"I cannot grant that request for I cannot know the will of our Father."

Akimbo knew this would be the answer. It was the answer that Mechoben gave at every retirement ceremony. He too would kneel in front of his good and faithful, some of them clinging to his hands with shining eyes, and ask and deny. Al even seemed to absorb some of his looks, his mannerisms. The new leader leaned on his knees and blinked once, twice, slow and easy.

"I wish to speak with Riff,' he said.

"Let it be done." Al stood up and patted his shoulder. "You have thirty minutes before the ceremony, General."

Riff-Alicia was brought in. Bright flakes of colorful stones were braided into her hair. She walked against the heavy gravity, toying with her clothing as the gravity pulled the cloth downward on her skin. He pulled the cloth of his robe over his lap and patted the bench next to him. She sat, her familiar sliding under her eyes for a moment.

"Good, they haven't removed her yet." Akimbo peered around to see who was listening. The wind blew through the open balcony window.

"Who?" Riff-Alicia creased her brows with effort. The GagGirl procedures still fixed her face in a neutral pout.

"Your friend." He reached over and touched the tip of the tendril protruding from her nostril. It retreated like a slug's eye. "Do not let them remove it."

"Why not? Al said it was a slaver's mark." Riff-Alicia said, remembering her early reticence.

"It is better if I show you. Attend my ceremony. Do not let them remove your familiar. Stand close to the fluid, breathe it in. It will be clear to you."

He leaned in and kissed her forehead, his lips loose and wet with age. His breath was sharp.

"Ok. I will."

"Another thing, stay close to your brother. They have already separated you too long."

Al walked into the room, wearing a golden headdress made from the bones of the little flying lizard and brushed with a metallic pollen from the ivory flowers. The twin suns hovered behind the smiling crescent of the garment, hurling prisms across the room.

"It's time to honored, General," Al said, bending at the knee in a strange half-bow.

XXXIII. In My Mother's House

The chamber was filled with people, androids and humans, and even an Amourkalian hunched at the edge of the fray, dripping the neon juice of masticated LinLin leaf into the mouth of a thickly muscled human, who swept his hands over the Amourkalian's folds of bright pink flesh.

The ceremonial pool swirled into a chasm, wider than the mansion itself. Riff-Alicia saw her brother seated against the wall. She waved to him, calling his name against the din of rushing water and shouting, laughing, fawning followers. The followers of Al.

A tiny android woman pressed against him whispering in his ear, her little hand cupped around his ear. He grinned and turned to her, not hearing his sister calling him, and touched the little android's cheek with his knuckle. Riff-Alicia trudged up the stairs and slid down beside her brother, who only cut his eyes to greet her as the android kissed behind his ear.

The chamber slid into black opacity as Al strode out onto a huge circular platform in the center of the chasm to chants and cheers. The golden headdress glowed as the native insects ticked around it, drawn to the phosphorescence. The genderless android glowed in flat planes and angles as they held their hand up for silence. Voices puttered to whispers. Al smiled at the crowd, steadying themselves on the sloshing transparent tube.

As the voices quieted, a screen folded down in front of the audience. Pictures of Akimbo trawled across the display. One of him with his arm wrapped around another man, nuzzling into his neck. Rasp-José sat up.

That's Pai. He whispered to Riff-Alicia.

She nodded and motioned toward the stage. Al was lifting the staff and bringing it down in a pattern. One. Two. One. Two. One. Two. Three. One. Two. The fluid in the tube glowed and expanded, something dark slipped around and around in the liquid, spinning it into a whirlpool. Riff-Alicia wondered if she was close enough to breathe in the fluid like he instructed.

Akimbo walked out cloaked in pure white, carrying an empty hollow tube identical to Al's. His curved back seemed to follow as a separate entity. The thumb-sized drone cameras still in use at the compound hummed around his face, projecting the tired creases around his eyes onto the screens surrounding the crowd.

Al uncapped the transparent tube and held it parallel to the platform as Akimbo approached. A fluid flowed in a thin slow stream from the end of the tube, pooling into a dark undulating puddle. The aged man placed the end of his own tube into the contracting pool of liquid. The crowd vibrated, clutching one another. A collective uptake of breath. The little android at Rasp-José's side slid her fingers between his.

Akimbo put his mouth and nose into the end of the tube and closed his eyes. Al placed their hand on the top of his head and leaned down to whisper in his ear. The drones hummed around them, amplifying the sounds of sticking saliva and husky affirmation of duty.

Al stepped back away from the general and nodded at him. He inhaled sharply and the puddle evaporated into a dense gas cloud that tumbled up the transparent tube toward his face. He pulled away from the tube, straight and tall, tears and mucus sliding down the furrows of his space-worn cheeks. An oily calliope of color streaked down his crepe paper skin.

He choked and stumbled into Al's open arms. The platform rose and drifted toward the crowd. Al slipped their hands under Akimbo's slack jaw and nodded at the camera on the drone. Their eyes, huge and still as mirrors flashed across the screen with a wriggling worm emoji Riff-Alicia recognized from the factory. The crowd erupted into frantic chanting. Androids and first-borns tore at their robes and flung a fine gray powder into the air. The little android by Rasp-José's side pulled a molar from her mouth and hurled it toward the floating platform. Another snipped a triangle of skin from their ear lobe with wiring scissors, offering it as the bizarre flotilla passed. Some tore their fingernails from the root. Some reached under their robes to retrieve clots of menstrual blood. One first-born held the tip of his forefinger in his palm.

Flesh flesh flesh. They droned all at once. God demands flesh. Flesh flesh flesh.

The offerings pattered around the white draped android god and the slumped pietà figure of Akimbo. The iron meat smell of blood permeated the chamber.

Al raised a blood-spackled hand. The crowd writhed under their own importance, their own participation with a flesh-bound god. They did not hear their god in the din of this collective largeness. Al slid one arm under Akimbo's unconscious body and snatched a drone from the air with the other hand, drawing the embedded microphone close to their lips.

"Is your sacrifice enough, my children?"

"Never!" The crowd shouted back.

"Is General Katsumi Akimbo's sacrifice enough?"

"Never!"

Rasp-José edged closer to his sister, pushing past the little android who stood with blood streaming down her jaw. He grabbed Riff-Alicia's arm and shouted into her ear.

"What's happening?"

She shrugged at him.

"I'm scared. I think we should go," he said straining his voice against the noise.

"We can't." She nodded up toward the shining eyes of the drones circling the room.

Her calm voice disturbed him. A flare of anger rose in his chest. He squeezed her arm harder. She yanked her arm away from his grasp and bared her teeth at him.

"There is nothing we can do, José," she hissed. "Nothing. Do you understand?"

Al's voice boomed through the speakers.

"Is my sacrifice enough?"

The crowd all jumped to their feet in unison, clapping and screaming.

Al bundled Akimbo's limp body into their arms and lifted it toward their mouth. The drones hovered by the slick opening as Al stretched the skin around their lips to transparent elasticity. Their mouth closed over the general's slack lips, sealing them in a suffocating kiss. The translucent skin filled with thick red blood as Akimbo thrashed in Al's muscular arms.

The crowd roared. Androids cycled through color changes. Blue spots, red loins, eyes as yellow as Sol, all as transient as the moon rise. The colors shuddered and faded like soap bubbles under the light. The first-borns tore at their faces, laving blood from the floor onto the crowns of their heads.

Al spat a spray of blood onto a group of squealing female androids, their skin ringed with blue and orange.

The Third Messiah dropped the gasping Akimbo to the edge of the platform and wiped the blood from their mouth. Sweat pearled on their pale brow. The crowd tore at one another, pushing into one another. A female first-born lay under a heaving android with vestigial webbing between his spread fingers.

"What is the will of the people?" Al's voice rasped around the chamber above the din.

The crowd calmed some and turned toward the screens again.

"I ask you again. What is the will of the people?"

"Our will is your will," they responded in unison.

"Let it be done," Al responded, breathing into the drone microphone.

Akimbo struggled onto his elbows, his mouth a wet void. His teeth shone red against his lipless face. He rose to his knees and wrapped his arms around Al's knees, smearing pinkish fluid on their glowing skin.

"Let it be done," the crowd responded.

Al retrieved Akimbo from the floor and tucked him against their chest like a child. They smoothed his thinning hair back from his forehead. The general wept as the leader of Sol, the son/daughter of the galactic turning, lowered him into The Churn. The crowd leaned into one another mimicking the cries of the general as his body floated, flailing against the concrete walls.

Rasp-José wept with the rest of them as Riff-Alicia watched. As a drone buzzed by, she yanked up her torn tunic to shield her face. It was the first time she had ever thought to hide her face from cameras. They were ingrained in her, a cultural shift implemented by her mother's choices, by her grandmother's choices, by her greatgrandmother's choices. Choices made in response to smooth-faced politicians who promised them clean water, abundant food. Sacrificial totems led to the fire. To die with honor. Akimbo looked as dead as the android on Enceladus. As dead as Mama. As dead as the Curanderas. Dying with honor was the same as dying without honor. Dead ears can't hear trumpets.

This was no different. Riff-Alicia had a choice. She grabbed her brother's arm and pulled him toward the outer doors. The sound of the crowd faded as they exited the chamber. Rasp-José wiped his eyes and tried to kiss her on the mouth. She pulled back.

"What are you doing?"

"I don't know. Do you want to hear a joke?"

She creased her brow and frowned at him.

"No. No I do not. I want to leave."

"And go where?"

"Back to Terra."

"Earth isn't livable, sister." He looked at her as the crowd chanted something indecipherable from behind the doors.

"Then I want to destroy it."

"Destroy what?"

"I want it all gone," she clenched her jaw.

"Like what though?" Rasp-José seemed to be returning to himself.

"The mines. The GagGirl facilities. This. All of this place. None of this is different. It's all the same as before."

"But where will we go?" Rasp-José scrubbed at his closed eyes with the heels of his hands. "And how could we destroy it?"

"MOTHER. MOTHER will help us," she said.

Her messaging application flashed at her wrist.

"What's that?" Rasp-José peered at the tiny hologram. "Who's Gram?"

"A friend from the factory. I loved her."

"As much as me?" He grinned.

She ignored him and opened the message. His jokes, always out of place, frustrated her.

"She's asking for help."

"What kind of help?"

"She says they are hungry."

"Like The Before?"

"Yeah, like that."

"Can we bring her food?"

"We can bring her something better. We can bring all of us something better. The Curanderas showed me how and now I am a Curandera." She clasped his hands in hers, her eyes bright and steady.

Rasp-José nodded, his expression blank.

"Do you want to hear a joke now?"

Riff-Alicia smiled, her throat tight.

"Sure. Tell me a joke."

Sighs and chants radiated from the chamber. Rasp-José took a breath.

"A man walks into a GagGirl shoot and sees a very beautiful android. He asks the director, 'Does your GagGirl bite?' 'No, she doesn't bite.' The man tries to kiss the android, but the android attacks him viciously and tears off his lip. A little later he stumbles to the director, 'Hey, you said your android doesn't bite!' The director shrugs, 'She doesn't. But that wasn't my Pornographic Film Actress.'"

Riff-Alicia smiled and motioned for him to follow her to her chambers, the gases from the stadium filling her lungs.

***

Gram heard the chirp of an incoming message as she shoveled the whiteish silt over the bodies of the two first-borns who died after eating BlackBlacks. Now she knew why the ancestors buried their dead. Too many fliers. Too many parts scattered over the beach. Their mouths still stained with the dark juice formed perfect O's, as if they were surprised despite her warnings. She laid down her shovel and switched off the Solar Digger Scoopomatic.

She pinched the Plasticine Bubble Messaging Watch and pulled it up to open the message. Riff's face, scarred and spare popped up on the screen.

An android named Lo sat cross-legged at the large outdoor dining table across the yard mending the Nylex seat covers left by colonization team. She ripped the seams and looked over at the fizzing pop-up message. Gram hopped down into the hole she had been digging and pushed her finger into the flexible plasma to play the message. She did not trust the androids. Most of them were specialty skill Andys and didn't talk much.

The message fizzed and cut in and out, but a scroll of text followed:

Gram,

I received your message. I am happy □ that you are alive. Isn't it strange that we weren't allowed to use words like "dead" or "alive?" before the Second Coming? Praise Al. Praise Them.

Don't you believe it is important to salute our new leader?

I believe that I have a solution for your problems, but it will require that you remember our training at the Factory. Do you remember the number system for Plasticine Welding? Boy I sure do. A = 21, B = 42, C=84. It was kind of hard wasn't it?

I will send you a diagram of native plant research and you can use this same numbering system to organize your own individual growth plan. Isn't that neat? On the diagram, you will find numbers that match. That's on purpose.

Once you complete the numbering system you will find that the plants will talk to you. Numbers are hidden in everything, you know.

I will join you at your colonization site in a quarter cycle. Please make sure the plants are numbered.

Love,

Riff

P.S. I found out my Before name. It's Alicia. You can call me that if you want.

Gram puzzled over the message. There had been no numbering system at the factory. She opened the attachment of the plant diagrams to find pages and pages of old Terra crop diagrams, each carefully numbered. She dragged the pages side by side and read the message again. She sat down at the bottom of the grave and wrote the numbers in the sand.

The pattern revealed itself as she puzzled over it. She scrawled in the dirt.

We are coming in four cycles. AI will not change things. Suffering is ongoing. We need you. Do not transmit back. Channels are still open. Not protected. MOTHER is the key.

Gram wiped her hand over her child's scrawl and dragged away the message. She pushed herself out of the hole to find Lo standing a few meters away, staring at her with eyes as still as pools.

"What is it, Lo?" Gram feigned normalcy.

Lo blinked, a slow smile spreading on her phocine face as she whispered something.

"I can't hear you."

The android cleared her throat and said, "I saw it."

"What?"

"The message."

"So what?" Gram felt tension rolling up her throat.

"Your friend doesn't believe in the Third Messiah."

Gram knelt down to pick up the shovel.

"What do you want?"

"I want to know why."

"I don't know why."

"Why would your species create something they don't trust?"

"I don't know."

"Are you going to kill me?"

"Are you going to stop us?"

"No."

"Then no. But I can. I'm not afraid."

"I'm not afraid either."

"Do you believe in the Third Messiah?"

"I know I'm going to die because I was designed to. I don't want to die. The messiah said that I would be able to live."

"Grux and Hilla didn't live."

"I know."

"So?"

"So, I guess I want to live. And I will. No matter what."

"I won't stop you. I want to live too."

Lo rushed to her and flung her thin arms around Gram, howling like an animal. The shovel fell from Gram's hands.

The pressure of the android's embrace tightened around her trunk, compressing her ribs and sobbing into her neck. Gram stroked her matted hair, smelling the salt and oil that laced the neglected curls. She wasn't designed like the Pornographic Art Film Andys. She couldn't change color. She was a domestic model. Designed for cleaning for the Worthies. She had steady gray eyes set into a flat face and firm hands.

Gram thought of the child in the escape pod next to her after the bombings. They clung to one another as the craft rattled, snapping her teeth together. The child's skin was hot and a pinprick rash dusted her skin pink. They cried as the pressure sat on their ears and sinuses, binding them to their nausea. Gray and white whisped past their tiny porthole windows. A woman across the aisle from them stared, unblinking, her jaw tightening in a striated bulge. She clutched the body of a small dog with a stiff dry tongue that jutted forward in rigor mortis.

Then the portholes were slicked black as they jetted out of the warm belly of Earth into the cold vacuum. The officials stood up as the shuddering craft drifted into eerie stillness and brought out tablets to document the passengers. The blue swirling sphere of Earth hung suspended behind them. The orange and gray clouds and skin-tearing winds hidden under the white swirls.

A uniformed arm appeared above Gram and a heavy adult hand rested on the brow of the little girl beside her. The little girl screamed and pinched Gram's arms. The adult hand pulled open the top part of the child's white nightgown and withdrew at the sight of the rash. Then there were two sets of hands and no more little girl beside her. Adult hands on her forehead. Adult hands examining her skin. Adult voices asking her if she had ever had her vaccinations. Vaccinations? Shots. Yes. Shots. She got a sticker of a banana. She didn't even cry. Good girl. This is just to take your temperature. Where is my friend? Where is she?

Later, as she dozed against her window, she heard the hiss of a hatch being opened. A bundle drifted by with strands of weightless blond hair slipping from under the knotted mermaid blanket.

Lo released her and leaned backwards, sliding damp strands of hair from her face. The ocean lapped against the cliffs as the tide came in.

***

Taking the Hover Truck was the easy part. Gram was on the same planet. The needles sank into Rasp-José's scalp as he activated the drive setting. The screen shimmered and a topless GagGirl somersaulted onto the screen, overlaying a map divided into several sections. His sister crossed her legs in the hard seat next to him and motioned toward the screen as the GagGirl bounced up and down, explaining the use of the human brain as a central operating system. His right hand clenched and tightened as the electrical impulses pulsed through his brain. The GagGirl on the screen clapped and squealed.

Very good! We've got good biofeedback. Now let's get your eyeline lined up. Follow the dots on the screen. Very good! Now, where would you like to go? Just look here at the map and say your destination out loud.

Riff-Alicia jabbed her finger at the screen, pointing to a mansion built into the side of a cliff as Rasp-José said, "Friendly Forest Mansion" in his clearest voice.

Good choice! You will arrive at your destination in approximately one-half cycle. Please remember to attach the catheter and the alpha wave retransmitter. You ARE the computer, and we depend on you. You will not be able to exit the program until you reach the specified destination.

Rasp nodded at the screen as the visual instructions for inserting the catheter popped up. Riff-Alicia looked away as he reached for his penis to insert the thin flexible tube.

***

Riff-Alicia was jolted awake by the high hum of the Hover Truck's boosters switching off. The smell of burning plasticine. Blood in her mouth. The GagGirl's high voice prattled on about personal responsibility and the demerits accrued by property damage. Pain shot through her jaw. She touched her face and looked over at her brother.

Rasp-José's forehead pressed against the glass, his wrist bent backward. A thin shard of bone poking through the skin. Acrid vapor poured through the climate control slats, gagging her. She pried her body from the crumpled seat and slid over to her brother. Her heart monitor chirped. As she pulled the cap from his head, the tiny needles scraped fine lines along his skin. She lifted his limp wrist to look at his wrist monitor, but the cracked facing made it unreadable.

A strange squeal pipped through the surrounding forest. She held her breath as something scraped by the smoking vehicle and lifted it for a moment, dumping it back to the ground. Rasp-José's head fell backwards, his mouth open and gurgling.

Riff-Alicia put her hand over his mouth as the dark shape hunched around the truck, tugging at the crushed panes with white-streaked fingerless palms. The smell of decay hung in the air. Her brother gagged under her fingers. A faint whistling in his chest. The being dragged around them, hissing and moaning. Rasp-José choked, as pink foam oozed from his mouth.

The creature tore the door away and Rasp-José crumpled away from her grasp onto the forest floor. It crouched over the young man, shuddering. Its slick body was covered in hundreds of limbs, each from a different native species. Little lizard legs formed a spiny line along the curve of the creature's back. A single human arm swung from its belly, grazing the ground.

The night sky reeled above her through the ripped metal. The stars sterile pinpoints arching and spinning around one another. Messages from the eons extinguished and repeated and drowned in the spinning black.

She crawled from the vehicle, her heart pumping, and screamed at the being. A guttural manifestation of her rage. Her familiar, so still and so quiet for weeks surged from her nostril, sliding into a long furl. Her mind filled with images of red feathers and the surging scaled back, and her familiar took on the shape, slipping scales onto the arching back, growing fangs into long curves. She felt its roots in her chest, pulling at her belly and groin. MOTHER whispered behind her eyes, like someone speaking in another room.

The creature flattened its body over Rasp-José and clicked at her. Her familiar whipped back and forth lifting her as it pressed against the ground. The trees lit up in a cacophony of rattling wings. The creature slid backward, dragging her brother with it and leaned backward into the humming trees. Heat poured off of the tree, igniting the forest in a glowing hum. The familiar lunged at the being, tearing at its patchwork limbs. A hunk of eye-specked flesh fell away, blinking in a bed of spiked leaves.

The being slid a membrane over Rasp-José's face. His dark eyes opened, staring at her as blood poured from his mouth. Urine leaked from under the caul and the glowing insects on the trees lit on the puddle, droning in a pulsing singularity.

The familiar uprooted itself from her and slung itself onto the creature. It tore at the membrane as Riff-Alicia heaved and gagged, her sinuses and belly emptied of her familiar. The creature slid backward up into the trees, Rasp-José still dangling from the sticky membrane. His head bumped into the tree as it retreated. The familiar, disconnected from her, curled and uncurled, shrinking into a chewed pile of black offal. The membrane holding him snapped as the creature pulled away into the trees. His right arm was torn almost completely off. The tendons and muscles shone purple under the two moons.

She rushed to him, the acid from her retching burning her throat. His chest fluttered as she pulled at the membrane covering his face. His eyes drifted sideways, not recognizing her. Not remembering. Not seeing. She pressed her ear to his chest. With each pump, blood flushed from his torn arm and oozed from his mouth. Lighter and lighter like the flap of a bird's wings as it ascends. The smell of death, putrid and coppery. She shook him once. A tiny familiar slid from his ear.

The vehicle smoked, crushed and useless behind her. She touched the pile that was once her familiar as it oozed and melted into the earth.

For the first time in her life, she was alone.

She stretched her mind for MOTHER, but only her own inner voice pleading for recognition.

Riff-Alicia stood up and brushed her hands together. Her brother's mangled body curved into a comma on the ground. Little glowing lizards slipped over his body, lapping moisture from his wide-open eyes. The forest hummed and buzzed. A choking high cry ricocheted around the trees.

Heat flushed her face. She couldn't stay here. The moons pierced the treetops, bright as sickles.

***

Lo found Riff-Alicia at the edge of the overgrown property, blood and dirt smudged over her face. Her black eyes were still and flat and she clutched something in her hands. The android rushed to her, peeling away her own jacket and draping it over her thin shoulders.

"I thought I was a Curandera," the girl whispered.

"A Curandera? Come inside now. We don't have a lot of food, but I was just picking fruit. What happened? I thought you were bringing Rasp."

"He was retired."

Lo rubbed her upper arm as she guided her toward the house.

"Who retired him?"

"Un Monstruo."

That word. Sliding on her belly under the bed, carpet burning the skin of her elbows. The smell of cigarette smoke. José's Spider-Man sneakers. El Monstruo's thick-nailed feet compressing the carpet. Crying. Holding her yellow stuffed sun with a smile embroidered in black thread.

Lo steadied her, smelling the metallic ozone in her hair. The warmth of her body and the smell of her skin. Gram hunched over some turned earth in the distance, her sharp profile dark against the morning suns. Riff-

Alicia broke away from Lo, running, running backwards, shedding her growth. Wanting instead the moments before the GagGirl films, before MOTHER, before family. Wanting the safety of the lines of bunks, the girls spreading their commissary purchases in neat little lines, comparing Emotion cubes and Little Rosy Robot models. Cuddling together in a single bunk, giggling about the management until the supervisors came in with deactivation wands and turned off their toys and tablets.

Gram looked up to see her running towards her, startled. The two women collided, Riff-Alicia wrapped around her, her scarred body nearly alien to Gram. Her breasts, still filled and altered, pressed against Gram's lean belly. Her scar-ticked skin like sea-smoothed pebbles under her fingers.

"Where is your brother? The hover truck?" Gram asked.

Riff-Alicia stared at her.

"It's gone. All of it."

"What?"

"Un Monstruo retired him. The truck. I don't know why, but it stopped in the forest. Al didn't stop us. No one stopped us. We lived on a moon. We lived on ice."

Gram listened carefully.

"But what about the supplies?"

"They are in the truck, but El Monstruo is still there."

Gram motioned to two identical androids. PermaMascs, big bodied and docile, dropped their tools and lumbered over. Their pale blue eyes steady. Lo stood nearby, twisting her pale hair around her finger.

"We have to get the supplies," Gram said to the androids, looking over Riff-Alicia's head.

In that moment, Riff-Alicia looked at the small band of survivors and realized that nothing could be done. That even if they could eke out an existence on this shimmering planet, if their Terran seeds could find purchase in the strange soil, suffering would persist until it didn't.

The planets would tear away from their gravitational tethers and drift away from one another until in another loop of chaos and violence they would collide together again in a lottery of proteins and electricity to create or destroy or drift further and further until The Black relented to the vacuum. Her atoms, her brother's atoms, Mama's atoms, Papa's atoms, the atoms of their android shadows all reconstituted.

She breathed, feeling the air feel her lungs and faced Gram.

"I will tell you where the supplies are if I can have a piece of her familiar." She nodded at one of the settlers, pale and young, bearing the GagGirl markers on her arms.

"Why? It's a slave marker."

"I can't tell you right now."

Gram nodded and motioned to the girl. "We need those supplies," She said, wrapping her cheap plasticine fiber shawl around her thin shoulders.

Riff-Alicia pulled the girl's face close to hers and massaged under the her eyes with her thumbs, feeling the little creature squirm under the skin. She reached back and slapped her face. Once. Twice. Tears rolled down her shrunken cheeks as Riff-Alicia struck her again and again until the warm slide of her stunned familiar touched her upper lip.

Riff-Alicia seemed to tower over her, her black hair shrouding her vision in a waft of oily opacity. Her bowed lips, dotted with micro scars pressed into the divot above her own lips. Her breath drawn from her lungs. Visions of the star field above her as her body rang and shattered like a dropped bowl. A memory of soft fat arms holding her, sliding a tube down her throat until she gagged and sucked in a recycled breath. Someone patting her back, her head snapping back and forth. Foamy vomit on the floor. Something cool against her neck.

The GagGirl slumped under Riff-Alicia's kiss, her hands suspended, fingers spread wide. Her old wrist monitor hummed a low tone as a blush-cheeked smiley face bounced across the tiny screen squealing *Something isn't right! Please alert a Body Mechanic! Maintain your Artists! Buy FemCare Vitamins!*

The familiar slid into Riff-Alicia's mouth, trailing a thin line of clear saliva that caught in a shining loop in the breeze.

The young Curandera dropped the frail android body and beckoned the Masc models to pick it up.

"She is rewarded," Riff-Alicia said as they lifted the limp form. "No more suffering."

Gram rushed over and snatched her wrist. The striated muscle pulsing in her jaw.

"What have you done?" She hissed.

"You'll see," Riff-Alicia answered with an odd laugh.

"At least tell us where the supplies are." Her eyes brimmed. "Please."

"They are with the Hover Truck that crashed in Quadrant 46. Los Monstruos may have already taken them, but it won't matter anyway."

"What are you talking about?" Gram squeezed her wrist tighter.

Riff-Alicia looked up at the sky in rapture, the sky reflecting in her black eyes.

"Look," she pointed to the androids.

The GagGirl settlers tore at their faces, their familiars slipping in and out of their nostrils and across the scleras of their eyeballs. Her own new familiar wormed across her sinuses, the tip of it brushing across the lower lid of her right eye.

She had reached MOTHER. MOTHER sent images of fractured blue ice then flashed into the bodies of all that she occupied scattered throughout the galaxy. Riff-Alicia looked down at slender hands that were not her own, stitching something rough and stiff as her belly gnawed with hunger, strings of light wavering around the viewing ports in a space station she had never seen. She felt pangs of heat up and down her spine as a Reformer scientist injected something yellow and cloudy into a vein that was not her own. She saw a transparent plasticine ceiling above her as a human male thrust into her, holding her by the nape of her neck. She saw the ice rings of some blue and purple whisped planet, tiny meteorites ticking against the hull of a spacecraft no bigger than a coffin, the heart that belonged to someone else squeezing as the oxygen monitor wailed with each dropped percentage point.

Finally, she saw Al's bedroom. She smelled Al's scent. She looked down at Al's muscular legs and the tray of small, shiny fruits nestled beside a slice of cured dogmeat. She chewed with Al's mouth. The sweet berries popped between her molars, molars so aligned and painless. A young human teenager sat at her feet sliding her soft pink hands up and down her calves. The smell of refined Shine oil scented with synthetic fragrance hung in the air around them.

Here it is MOTHER. Here is where we begin.

The teenage servant's familiar flopped onto the silver tray and whipped around the Third Messiah's neck, cartilage crunching as it tightened. Riff-Alicia's vision deepened into a deep red miasma of pain. A dying star collapsing into a tight singularity, its pull irresistible. Hollow echoes of shouts, muted by a thick rasping dissolved into a vision of an immense woman draped in the skins of thousands of scarlet serpents, their naked muscular bodies writhing as they struggled to sup from her oozing breasts.

The woman held a sword in one hand and an onyx bowl in the other. She turned her face, larger and brighter than a moon toward her. Steady as a growing child. Her mouth open to reveal a bright blue glacial cave where two aliens hunched over a small fire, tearing gristle from a bone. A tall obelisk rose behind them radiating warm orange light. A tall being lurched toward them on loosely jointed iron legs, a slender black tendril slinging from a single facial orifice.

Satellites popped in soundless explosions against the white sky.

DO YOU WISH THIS?

"I do."

Warmth enfolded Riff-Alicia as she opened her eyes. The GagGirl's hand lay open beside her in a slight curl. The humans' familiars all poured out into the center of the room. Gram's right leg was torn from her body and was being dragged toward the squirming mass of familiars. The forest was on fire around her, the trees crested with a slow orange glow. She lay down beside Gram's limbless torso and slid her arm around her middle. Pieces of satellite spiraled down in flashes of light, ships and space stations just ticks of light and ozone. Euthanized before the drift.

341

Epilogue

Post-Bio Disaster Records for [redacted]

In those days, the species of homo sapiens (as their study drones called themselves) believed in intervention. They called it divine. It was strange. We studied them with great curiosity, particularly when a select few developed the ability to communicate with us through our largest hive on Hilith, or Enceladus. They called us MOTHER.

They reproduce sexually. An efficient if short-lived strategy. In their culture, which is a Terran primate culture, they placed significance on the individual who expulsed them, thus naming the Hilith Hive MOTHER, believing us to be one individual.

They believed themselves to be true individuals, curiously enough. We were not aware that they had any culture at all, and by our own standards, their culture was a shoddy premise to kill one another or to reproduce sexually with one another. The brain waves of the familial unit belonging to the female child drone they called Riff or Riff-Alicia or

Alicia were uniquely suited, though not that uncommon. Her spawn mate was also suited for communication, but to a lesser extent.

They believed they harnessed the power of the Hilith Hive themselves, upon their landing and discovery of Hilith. By keeping communication short, we were able to study them with minimal interference.

As every new nodule is taught, we were the progenitors of the technology that allowed this particular primate species to excel. We chose them for their particular dexterity and durability. We did not expect them to become aware of us as quickly as they did. We were given many names, most do not translate well, but "God" seemed to be the most common, though it is difficult to quantify exactly what this means.

The experiment on Hilith was a success. We allowed them to think they trapped us. They are a particularly social species and derive satisfaction from "helping" despite their highly individualistic views of one another. The female child drone established communication, as was the purpose of the experiment. She was able to convey the suffering of her species to the Hilith Hive.

Because at this point, the experiment became unethical, the Higher Hive declared the experiment unethical and ordered its termination, at which point all subjects were euthanized.

The Higher Hive has ordered another experiment on a much larger species across the spiral arm where the Galileo Hive is well-established.

We will be studying their reactions to similar, but more advanced forms of technology. Our hypothesis is that the ape species from our previous experiment had a flawed risk-reward brain structure. Another theory is that their ape heritage encouraged resource hoarding, which limited their scope and destroyed their drive to preserve their own home space, which presented us another reason for their termination.

This newer species may be entirely uninterested as were many other species inhabiting XX65 or Terra, as the female-child called it, including a rather fascinating species destroyed by our research subjects who communicated with dance and scent and color. Because of their perfect measures, they had no need of our technology, though offered. They were most similar to us, though still maintained sexual reproduction, as they lived in large hives and produced only what they needed to feed their larvae. The apes often regarded them as less intelligent, which we found to be an interesting process of thought regarding value assignment.

We have no desires for this new species other than the communal desire for knowledge gained and knowledge transferred.

We have no hypothesis for the colony collapse of XX65, though we did mourn the necessary euthanasia taken with the young ape species. Such a rich culture they wove. Such an overabundance of bonding. So alien and curious.

May they reemerge with The Next Contraction.

Signing Off.